"I am captivated by A. Meredith Wal
beautifully flawed characters that s
Every book she writes is an aut

—Sawyer Bennett, *New*
bestselling author of the Off series

Praise for
Lead Me Not

"Dangerously sexy. . . . Amazing. . . . I felt I was standing right next to Aubrey feeling all the emotions and turmoil she was feeling."

—*The Book Enthusiast*

"An amazingly real portrayal. . . . Aubrey and Maxx left me heart-broken [and] will be in my head for years."

—*Thirty Second Reviews*

"I really, really loved this book. A. Meredith Walters made me care so much about these characters, I was still thinking about them days after I finished the book."

—*A Nook for Books*

"Intense, heartbreaking, and emotionally charged."

—*Vilma's Book Blog*

"Beautiful. . . . The characters are well developed and the story will take you on an emotional journey to the very end."

—*Anacely's Books*

"So raw and so honest. . . . An amazing story . . . [that] I didn't want to end."

—*BCS Reviews*

ALSO BY A. MEREDITH WALTERS

Twisted Love Series

Lead Me Not

Find You in the Dark Series

Find You in the Dark

Light in the Shadows

FOLLOW ME BACK

A. MEREDITH WALTERS

GALLERY BOOKS

NEW YORK LONDON TORONTO SYDNEY NEW DELHI

Gallery Books
An Imprint of Simon & Schuster, Inc.
1230 Avenue of the Americas
New York, NY 10020

This book is a work of fiction. Any references to historical events, real people, or real places are used fictitiously. Other names, characters, places, and events are products of the author's imagination, and any resemblance to actual events or places or persons, living or dead, is entirely coincidental.

First Gallery Books trade paperback edition June 2015

For information about special discounts for bulk purchases, please contact Simon & Schuster Special Sales at 1-866-506-1949 or business@simonandschuster.com.

The Simon & Schuster Speakers Bureau can bring authors to your live event. For more information or to book an event, contact the Simon & Schuster Speakers Bureau at 1-866-248-3049 or visit our website at www.simonspeakers.com.

Manufactured in the United States of America

10 9 8 7 6 5 4 3 2 1

Library of Congress Cataloging-in-Publication Data

Walters, A. Meredith.
Follow me back / A. Meredith Walters—First Gallery Books trade paperback edition.
pages ; cm.—(Twisted love ; [2])
I. Title.
PR6123.A4695F65 2015
823'92—dc23

2014042869

ISBN 978-1-4767-7416-9
ISBN 978-1-4767-7417-6 (ebook)

For Gwyn

Remember that true love should never be conditional.

prologue

aubrey

Trust.

Faith.

Belief.

Every relationship is built on them. Without these three words, everything around you would crumble. I wasn't sure if these were things Maxx and I had ever had.

So how do you begin a future without the foundation it needs to thrive? How could I believe in a life that had only just begun when I wasn't sure I could trust the man I was building it with?

I wanted to. In my heart I had an unwavering optimism that this time it would be different. That *we* were different.

But our past was a twisted, ugly thing and it was difficult to move on from it. No matter how much we wanted to. It lay in wait. Poised and ready for the moment when we thought we had finally worked through our demons.

Then they would strike. Distrust. Suspicion. Doubt. They were the poison in our souls that threatened to undo everything. But there *was* the light. The glimmer of possibility that shone out of our dark. It was hope. And that was just as powerful.

But as much as I tried to trust, I could never truly forget. That heart, brimming with this illogical hope, wouldn't let me.

So how do we build a life on such a shaky foundation? One painful brick at a time. And just maybe we'd find our happily ever after.

Before our past burned it to the ground.

chapter one

aubrey

"Miss Duncan, you have been asked here today to discuss the allegations that have been lodged against you in regard to your behavior toward a member of the support group you had been co-facilitating. These allegations describe a personal and inappropriate relationship that is a clear violation of our ethical codes of conduct."

I looked steadily at the three people who sat at the table in front of me. I picked at the skin around my fingernails and tried not to fidget in my seat. My day of reckoning was here.

I was nervous. I'd be an idiot if I weren't. This was the possible end of all of my dreams and aspirations. Three years of hard work crumbling around me. But losing my place in the Longwood University counseling program wasn't what kept me awake at night for the past two weeks. It wasn't what had my insides twisted into knots and tears drying on my cheeks.

My state of emotional upheaval could only be attributed to one thing. One pivotal moment that had shredded my soul and threatened to unravel me.

Saying good-bye to Maxx Demelo. Choosing my sanity over his pain. Leaving him when he needed me the most. And even though our dysfunctional love had almost ruined me, I still couldn't shake the guilt.

But I wasn't defeated yet. It was time to be a grown-up and face the consequences of my disastrous choices head-on. It was my only option now that I had lost the person I had thrown everything away for.

Dr. Lowell, my academic adviser, sat beside two of her university colleagues. She was stoically looking at the paper in her hands. Her mouth was pinched and her brow was furrowed. She was upset and disappointed in me. And she had every right to be.

I had been her most promising student. I had a good GPA. I had been on the fast track to a great career as a substance abuse counselor. I had taken my future seriously.

Until the day Maxx had walked into the support group and blown my life apart. Now when she looked at me, all she saw was a screwup. It sucked.

"We have read over your written statement and it seems you aren't denying the allegations. Is that correct, Miss Duncan?" Dr. Jamison, the head of the Counseling Department, asked, pursing his lips. He looked at me over the rim of his wire-framed glasses, condemnation written all over his face. Obviously he had already made up his mind about me. And it wasn't favorable.

I sat up straight and squared my shoulders. I took a deep breath and readied myself. Because all I could do was be completely and totally truthful. I was long overdue for a healthy dose of honesty.

"That's correct, Dr. Jamison. I admit to engaging in an inappropriate relationship with a member of the substance abuse support group. As I wrote in my statement, I was aware that my actions were a violation of the code of conduct and I accept any and all disciplinary action." I was proud of the fact that my voice never wavered. I didn't cry, whimper, or plead. I would take my punishment, whatever it may be. Inside, however, I was crumbling.

Dr. Jamison looked at Professor Bradley, a slight woman with obviously dyed brown hair and a nasty habit of mixing plaids with stripes, and said something under his breath. He then turned to Dr. Lowell, who continued to keep her head down. Dr. Lowell nodded, her hands clenched on the table in front of her.

They talked quietly among themselves while I fiddled with a piece of string hanging from the hem of my skirt. I looked at the clock on the wall. It was a little after one. I had been in this chair, sitting in front of my judge and jury, for only half an hour, but it felt like forever.

I knew that my friends Renee Alston and Brooks Hamlin were waiting for me out in the hallway. Brooks would be pacing the floor, while Renee twisted her hands in her lap. I could practically feel their anxiety through the walls.

Anxiety I should have shared . . . if it weren't for the shards of a broken heart piercing my chest.

It had been fifteen days since I had last spoken to Maxx Demelo. Fifteen days since I had told him I couldn't stay and watch him destroy himself as he fell deeper and deeper into an addiction that I had tried to save him from. Fifteen days since he had almost died.

I convinced myself that I had done the right thing by walking away. Continuing to stand by his side while he slowly lost control would have destroyed me. I couldn't have watched him make the same bad choices that had taken the life of my sister, Jayme, years ago.

I should never have fallen in love with him in the first place.

"Aubrey." Dr. Lowell's voice brought me out of my suffocating guilt. I blinked and tried to refocus on my situation.

"Dr. Jamison, Professor Bradley, and I all agree that you have behaved in a manner that is both unprofessional and inappropriate. Your actions have had a negative impact, not only on your reputation within this department, but on this department's reputation in the community." I swallowed thickly but I never looked away from the narrowed eyes of my favorite teacher.

"You have put me and the rest of the department in a very precarious position. Despite your exemplary academic record, we can't be shown giving lenience to you, particularly considering the severity of the violation," Dr. Lowell stated sternly.

"We have come to the decision that you will be placed on academic suspension until it is agreed by all parties that you are to be permitted to resume your place in the program."

I blinked, hardly breathing. It had happened. It had really freaking happened.

I had potentially trashed my school career for the dream of a future with a man who had selfishly thrown it away. My chest felt tight and I felt panicky.

What was I going to do now?

How could I crawl back up from rock bottom? Was it even possible? I felt the door slamming shut on me, and even though I had prepared myself for the likelihood of it happening, I wasn't quite prepared enough.

But I wouldn't cry. I wouldn't allow myself to be reduced to a weeping mess. Aubrey Duncan was made of stronger stuff than that, even if the thought of curling into a tight, compact ball seemed incredibly appealing.

"However . . ." Dr. Lowell began, and my heart skipped a beat at the slight change in her tone. A sliver of something other than displeasure laced her words.

"Positive reinforcement is just as effective as negative consequences. And I think it's important that you be given the opportunity to earn your place back in the program. This suspension does not have to be permanent. But that will have to depend on you. You have assured us that the relationship is no longer a source for concern and that you have accepted accountability for your actions. Despite the severity of the offense, I don't think it should negate the years of hard work you have put into the program. This doesn't need to be an indefinite punishment."

Was I supposed to be relieved that my professors were giving me a second chance? Was I expected to do cartwheels because I was given the opportunity to win back their approval?

I couldn't help but feel a flash of bitter resentment toward the individuals sitting in front of me, looking down their noses in pious disapproval. How easily they cast their judgments. A large part of me was very aware that I deserved it. But there was also a defiant, rebellious side of me that wanted to scream.

I swallowed the momentary need to tell them what I really thought and nodded. It was the only response I could give without making my situation worse.

Dr. Lowell watched me for a few minutes, and I knew that she had picked up on my warring emotions. Dr. Lowell had always understood me—she had been my mentor, the woman I had looked up to. The deterioration of her goodwill was in many ways the toughest part about this.

"Your volunteer hours will be rescinded, and should you regain your place in the counseling program down the road, you will have to begin your clinical hours again, which could greatly impact your graduation next spring." Dr. Lowell glanced back down at the paper in her hands, as though looking at me had become too much for her.

"You will continue with your other coursework as normal. Your gen-ed requirements will continue as before. However, you will not be attending any of the counseling and psychology classes. Though it will be mandatory that you audit Dr. Jones's Boundaries and Ethics in Counseling class."

"I completed that class last fall, Dr. Lowell. I earned a B," I pointed out. Dr. Lowell gave me a patronizing look and continued without pausing. "We feel that a refresher is necessary. And it goes without saying that you will have absolutely no direct counseling interaction. After the suspension is lifted we can discuss how to make up for the time you have lost and what your best move forward will be."

Not being able to complete my counseling coursework was going to put me so behind I wasn't sure I'd be able to catch up. How would I ever be able to graduate on time when I would be essentially starting this year over?

"You will be required to meet with me once a week to evaluate your progress and discuss your options. All of this is mandatory if you wish to return to the counseling program. And I don't think I need to tell you that any sort of contact with Maxx Demelo will be strictly prohibited while he is considered a therapeutic client."

I wanted to laugh at the last statement, knowing *that* particular caveat would not be an issue. Dr. Lowell removed her glasses and folded them slowly, laying them down on the table. Dr. Jamison was making notes and Professor Bradley seemed to be counting down until the end of this uncomfortable hearing.

"Aubrey, I don't need to tell you again how your actions have reflected on this department within the community. It has strained relations with the community service board, which has been our partner in providing services to our campus for over fifteen years. But that doesn't change the fact that you are a smart, capable young woman . . . who happened to make a mistake that could have ended your career before it began." Dr. Lowell's mouth turned down.

"I hope you take this opportunity for what it is. A second chance to prove to us, to the department, and more importantly to yourself, that you can put aside your personal feelings and act in a manner that is both professional and appropriate."

"I will, Dr. Lowell. I promise," I let out in a rush, not able to identify exactly what the swirling emotions running wildly inside me were.

Disappointment? Definitely. Anger? Most likely. A little bit of relief that I still, after everything, was being given a glimmer of hope that I could get myself out of the mess I had created? Absolutely.

"We will send you an official letter with the panel's decision in writing. This will also define the requirements of your suspension and what will be expected of you. Do you have any questions, Miss Duncan?" Dr. Jamison asked.

"No, sir," I said, hoping I wouldn't pass out. I just wanted to get through those last few moments and get out of there.

Dr. Jamison nodded, and just like that, I was dismissed. I quickly gathered my purse and hurried out into the hallway. Brooks, as I suspected, was pacing and Renee was chewing on her thumbnail. Both looked up as I opened the door. Renee got to her feet and rushed over.

"What happened?" Renee asked, sounding almost as frantic as I felt.

I looked from her to Brooks, still in a daze. Renee gave me a little shake. "Damn it, Aubrey, what the hell happened?" my best friend and roommate demanded.

"Suspended. I was suspended," I answered, the words sounding dry and brittle in my ears.

"Shit. They kicked you out?" Brooks asked, squeezing my shoulder.

I let out a shrill laugh that sounded almost manic to my ears. "Yeah, they kicked me out. But Dr. Lowell says I can earn my spot back. You know, after I jump through a few hoops."

Brooks gave me a reassuring smile. "Well, that sounds promising. It's not like it's forever."

I shook my head. "I don't know, Brooks." I wasn't ready to hear words of encouragement from him just yet. A part of me still wondered if he'd been the one who'd ultimately told Kristie, the woman who co-facilitated the counseling group where I first met Maxx, about our relationship.

Renee looped her arm through mine and I found myself leaning on her, appreciating the sign of solidarity. "Oh come on. You've got this, girl. If there's one thing I know about my friend, it's that she's a survivor. And you can get through this." Brooks nodded in agreement.

I began to feel bolstered with a renewed sense of strength. Dr. Lowell was right: I needed to take the time to sort myself out. To prove to everyone I wasn't a total head case.

Brooks walked on my other side, a few feet away from us. His presence was surprisingly comforting, considering how strained things had been between us recently. Our friendship had taken a hit after he had found out about my relationship with Maxx. He had been understandably disapproving. And it didn't help that Brooks also happened to be my ex-boyfriend.

At the time I had been infuriated by his censure. But Brooks had been right all along: I'd been building a relationship with a man who was hell-bent on self-destruction. And that relationship had torn everything apart: school, my friendships, my self-respect. In the end, Maxx had almost died, and I had come perilously close to losing it all. Now here I was, standing in the rubble, trying to figure out how to put all of the pieces back together.

I looked over at Renee, who gave me a reassuring smile, and realized that one good thing had come out of all of this ugliness. Our friendship was stronger than ever. We had a connection that hadn't been there before.

If anyone could understand how difficult it was to move past a destructive relationship, it was Renee. Like me, she was trying to rebuild a life that had gone dangerously off track as a result of her love for the wrong man.

Brooks reached out and grabbed ahold of my arm, pulling me to a stop. "Hey, you'll be fine. You're one of the strongest people I know. And you won't let anything or *anyone* hold you back." Brooks took hold of my hand and gave it a squeeze.

"I know you're still beating yourself up. But that needs to stop. I think it's time you let all of that past shit go. Move on. It's way past time," he advised, and I knew he was right.

He had given me versions of this speech many times in the last two weeks, and I hadn't been ready to hear it. But walking away from the psychology building and experiencing one of the lowest points of my life, I think that perhaps I was finally hearing him. Finally taking it in.

I gave him a small but genuine smile and then extracted my fingers from his and tucked them into my pockets. Even though I appreciated his faith in me, I was discomfited by his expression of physical affection. We hadn't held hands since we'd dated a few years ago, and his touch, with its familiar intimacy after all this time, felt strange. Not exactly wrong, but not exactly right either.

Not when my skin still remembered the feel of hands that I missed more desperately than I should.

"Thanks, that means a lot," I said sincerely.

"If you're okay, I've got to head to my study group. I can come by later . . . if you want," Brooks suggested, sounding uncertain. His hesitance was obvious, as though not entirely sure he should even be making the offer.

I jerked my hand out of its hiding spot in my jacket pocket and took his again, feeling the need to give him some reassurance. I had to force my hand to curl around his. My fingers seemed to have a mind of their own and almost flinched at the contact.

It's just Brooks. I care about Brooks. There's nothing wrong with touching him this way.

Why did I feel like I had to convince myself? What was I trying to prove, anyway?

"Of course I want you to come over. But only if you bring the new Nicholas Sparks movie," I teased, trying for some normalcy to drown out the abnormal feelings that raged inside me. As I looked up at Brooks, his dark hair falling into his eyes, I wondered if things between us would ever be easy again. The discomfort made me edgy.

Brooks held on to my hand, his fingers lingering on mine for a moment too long. My stomach twisted, my heart recoiled, and I immediately moved away. Something that looked a lot like disappointment flickered in Brooks's eyes as I took an obvious step back.

Brooks gave me a lopsided grin that was more than a little forced. "You got it," he said, hoisting his book bag up over his shoulder, and looked at my silent roommate.

"See ya, Renee," Brooks said offhandedly as he turned to walk away.

I let out a sigh and pulled my scarf tighter around my neck to ward off the late afternoon chill. I was tired of the achy cold. I felt it from the inside out and longed to feel warm again.

But I wasn't sure that was possible.

Renee walked beside me, her chin tucked into the collar of her jacket. "It'll get better, Aubrey. I promise. This is your second chance. Your time for something *more*."

I hoped she was right. I was desperate for that something better.

I can be so much more for you. I want to be everything you could ever want.

It had only been a matter of weeks since Maxx had said those words, his intense blue eyes staring into mine, and had given me his heart. Only weeks since he had made promises he hadn't been able to keep. It was such a short amount of time for my entire life to change.

But it *had* changed. And now all I could do was accept it and move on. If only it were that simple.

My eyes were drawn to the brick wall that ran along the edge of the green. The once vibrant colors of Maxx's street art had faded, but I could still see the painting of a woman walking off a cliff. The word *Compulsion* was woven into her familiar blond hair. It was a small part of the complicated man who continued to own me. The tiny, intricate X's dotted throughout the picture seemed to scream at me. Taunting me with their presence.

Even when he was gone, Maxx was everywhere. His art. His love. His chaos.

I couldn't escape him. And I was terrified that in the darkest recesses of my heart I still didn't want to.

chapter two

aubrey

Monotony.

Routine.

Blasé consistency.

That is what my life had deteriorated to.

At one time I had wanted these blissfully mundane adjectives to define my life. I had sought out the plain and unassuming. But after losing my sister, Jayme, in my senior year of high school, I hadn't been in a position to be spontaneous or exciting. Impulsivity scared the shit out of me.

Jayme had danced on the edge and had fallen over. So I wanted my feet firmly on the ground. I needed to know what came next. That there was a B after A. That when I walked out my door every morning I knew exactly what to expect. So I became boring. And that was A-OK.

Until Maxx had stormed into my life and turned everything upside down. His intensity had scared me. He pulled me under by the force of his passion, and when I threw myself into his wild world, I found a piece of myself that had lain dormant for entirely too long. In a way, Maxx had brought me back to life. And I had loved him for resurrecting the girl who'd disappeared long ago. But when we lost control, when he hit rock bottom and I tumbled along after him, I made the decision that spontaneity and chaos simply didn't have a place in my life anymore.

But I missed it. Life on the edge of the blade had been exhilarating. Now that he was gone I found myself trying to fit back into a life that I had so obviously outgrown. To become a woman I no longer knew how to be. And no matter how much I tried to force my feet back into those shoes, they didn't seem to fit anymore. That piece of me that Maxx resurrected was there, lurking beneath the surface.

"Dude, are you still breathing?" Brooks asked, poking my arm from his spot beside me on my worn-out couch.

I focused on my friend, who was peering at me with a mixture of concern and blatant incredulity. My mouth stretched into a mildly lunatic caricature of a smile, and Brooks blinked, clearly disturbed by my psycho grin. "Just spaced out for a minute, sorry," I said a bit too brightly, reaching into the bowl of popcorn in his lap.

I felt like Brooks and Renee spent most of their time on "Aubrey watch," waiting for me to crack and lose my shit. And to be fair, it was an honest concern. I was one giant, waving red flag of impending doom.

Brooks gave a disingenuous laugh and it was obvious that he, too, was trying desperately to force himself back into a role that wasn't necessarily his anymore.

"So, are you ready for graduation?" I asked, steering the subject into what felt like "normal" territory, and immediately hoping that he wouldn't point the question back at me.

Where is your *life headed, Aubrey?* Abort! Abort! Scary life planning ahead, detour into blissful ignorance!

"I guess. I won't hear about grad school for another month or so. But I think I've got all of my ducks in a row. What about you? Have you thought about what you're going to do after you graduate next year? Are you still thinking of applying for the LPC program?" Brooks was referring to the Licensed Professional Counseling program at Longwood. Six months ago, that had been my plan, which was why I was putting in all of the volunteer hours—essential for graduation *and* it looks great on grad school applications.

I took a deep, calming breath. "I'm not so sure that's an option right now, considering everything that has happened. Hell, I doubt Dr. Lowell or anyone else in the department would be in a rush to give me a recommendation anytime soon," I said, with only the teensiest bit of bitterness.

"Eh, you don't know. Just ride out the suspension, do what you need to do and keep your nose clean. You'll be Dr. Lowell's darling again in no time."

"We'll see, I guess. But what about you? Is Longwood still your first choice? Haven't you had enough of our boring little campus?" I asked.

I had been surprised to learn that Brooks had plans to pursue his graduate degree at Longwood University. The graduate counseling program was decent, but with his grades he could go anywhere. I knew my reasons for wanting to stay had always been about putting down roots in a place that felt comfortable. But that was back before staying at the same, tiny campus hadn't meant facing the aftermath of your screwup every day.

Now change didn't seem like such a bad thing, and the idea of leaving no longer left a bad taste in my mouth. In fact, it seemed like the best option I had.

"I don't know. I like it here. I like the professors. I think there are a lot of benefits to staying." Brooks's eyes flickered over to me, barely making contact.

"Yeah, well, I think you're kind of crazy, Brooks. I'm beginning to see a lot of merit in getting the hell out of Dodge," I stated.

"Give yourself some time to get over all of this, Aubrey. And then you may feel differently," Brooks argued.

Give yourself some time to get over all of this. The words bounced around in my skull, tattooing themselves on my brain. It had been my mantra since I had left Maxx. I was convinced that time was all I needed. Even if there was a niggling of doubt that I was deluding myself.

"Sure, maybe you're right," I agreed, working to convince both of us. Even though I knew how ridiculous it was to tell someone to *give it time.* No words in the history of words were less helpful. When you were going through something horrible, the last thing you wanted to hear was one day, down the road, you'll feel better again. Not when you wanted to feel better *right now*!

My phone started to ring, and I looked down to see the number that flashed across the screen. It was a phone call I had been avoiding for the past three weeks. The phone call that could turn my sort of crappy day into a full-blown shit fest. I heard the melodramatic booming of drums in my head as I stared down at the vibrating phone.

"Ugh," I groaned, picking up my phone, my thumb hovering over the ignore button.

"Your mom again?" Brooks asked.

I nodded. He had seen me send her calls to voice mail multiple times over the past few days.

"Have you spoken to your parents since your hearing?" he asked, already knowing the answer.

"Nope."

I'd been startled by a call from my mom a few days earlier. Apparently Dr. Jamison had called them in advance of my disciplinary panel, and to say my mother had been unhappy to hear about all that had taken place was a drastic understatement. I then had to endure forty-five minutes of hearing about her disappointment. It had been the first time we'd spoken in months, which doubly pissed me off. I felt like my parents had lost the right to vocalize any opinions on my life, given that they hadn't taken the slightest interest in it since Jayme died. So having to sit silently and take the acid oozing from her mouth had almost tipped me over the edge.

As much as I tried not to let my mother get to me, it was impossible to ignore how much it hurt to hear her ugliness. She had gone straight for the jugular. She had been merciless and hateful. *Jayme would never have done something like this. You should do better for her if you can't do it for yourself.*

How quickly my mother had forgotten the truth of who my fifteen-year-old sister had been. She had turned a complete blind eye to the grief Jayme had put our entire family through. And even though I loved my sister and missed her every day, I hadn't forgotten about why she was no longer with us. But it seemed as though my parents had reframed her death in their minds and turned it into something they could live with.

The counselor side of me understood and accepted this. The daughter side, not so much. It made me resentful and angry and less than willing to revisit that particular brand of heartache by answering my mother's calls.

"Don't you think you should answer it? You know she'll just keep calling until you do. Might as well get it out of the way. Like ripping off a Band-Aid," Brooks advised, and I rolled my eyes, hating his calm rationale.

"Well, you'd better go, then. Because this won't be something I need an audience for," I said just as the phone stopped ringing. I knew she would call back in a few minutes, as had become her habit this week.

"Are you sure? I can stay if you need me to," Brooks offered. Even though I appreciated his thoughtfulness, I knew that nothing would help me deal with whatever my mother had to say.

"Nah. You go on. I'll meet up with you at the commons for dinner, okay?" I suggested just as my phone started ringing again.

Brooks looked down at my phone and then into my face, his eyes softening. "Okay. But you know how to reach me if you need to. I'm always here. Don't forget that."

"Thanks, Brooks," I said as he leaned down to kiss my forehead, his lips lingering. I ignored the implications of his less-than-innocent gesture and gave him a shaky smile, lifting my phone up to indicate that I was about to answer it.

"Good luck, kiddo," he called out as he left.

I blew a noisy breath out of my nose and put the phone to my ear.

"Hello?" I said cheerily.

"I got a letter in the mail about the outcome of your hearing. I wanted to talk to you about it," my mother said by way of greeting, getting right to the point.

"Why?" I asked, knowing my attitude would piss her off. But I wasn't in the mood to really care.

"What is wrong with you, Bre? This is serious. What in the world are you going to do now?" Her use of my sister's nickname for me made me cringe. It always did.

"Major in basket weaving?" I said dryly.

I could practically hear my mother grinding her teeth. "I think you should come home for a visit. It's clear that things have gotten out of control up there. You've lost sight of what you're doing and where you're headed."

"And what exactly am I doing here?" I countered, knowing damn well my mother had no clue what my plans were for my future. She had never once asked me about what I wanted to do with my life. Those sorts of discussions had gone off the table once my sister's casket had been lowered into the ground and the heart that had once loved both of her children had shriveled up and stopped feeling anything at all.

"Maybe that's what we should talk about. You need to come home. Just for a few days. Your dad and I would like to see you."

There was a slight quiver in my mother's voice that threw me. She sounded, for the briefest of moments, like the woman who had held me after my first breakup when I was fourteen. The woman who had cleaned my scrapes and tended my bruises. The woman who made me sausage gravy on homemade biscuits for breakfast every year on my birthday because it was my favorite.

But I couldn't let myself be deluded into thinking she had changed. That maybe, just maybe, she was trying to be the mother I needed her to be once again. I had experienced enough crippling disappointment to last me one lifetime.

"I can hear about how I'm failing Jayme's memory just as easily over the phone, Mom," I said quietly, trying to speak around the lump in my throat.

My mother didn't say anything for a while, which surprised me. I was prepared for a hateful comeback. I was on edge waiting for the next barb.

"Aubrey, we're worried about you," my mother said, her tone altering into something resembling concern. Which couldn't be genuine. My mother had stopped expressing anything other than furious displeasure a long time ago.

"This thing with that boy in the support group, being almost kicked out of the program at school—it's not like you," she continued.

"And what do you know about what I'm like anymore, Mom? It's not as though you have bothered to know anything about me in years!" I shouted, losing control of my emotions. I wasn't used to having this sort of conversation with my mother. I didn't know how to talk to her anymore.

"Stop yelling, Bre!" my mother snapped, and I was almost relieved to hear her usual irritation. *This* woman I could deal with. The concerned maternal act was one that I couldn't stomach. Not now. Not when things were already so off-kilter.

"I'm not coming home. If there's something you or Dad need

to say, then say it to me now." I sounded petulant, but I couldn't help it. Clearly my mother brought out the best in me.

"Why do you have to make things so difficult?"

"I've got to go, Mom. I have a life to screw up," I said, ending the call before we could spend any more time making each other miserable.

I threw the phone onto the couch and picked up a pillow, covering my face. I screamed as loud as possible into the plush fabric, letting it drown out the strength of my anger. After I had exhausted myself, I got to my feet feeling jittery and uneasy.

"I'm just one big, fucking mistake," I muttered, grabbing my keys and leaving the apartment, knowing that if I stayed there I'd end up throwing stuff. And as much as I loved to clean, I had had enough of sorting through my impulsive actions.

I got into my car with no clear idea of where I was headed. I just needed to drive. To find a place where I could unwind.

I shouldn't have been surprised when I ended up outside of the Quikki Mart. The dark alleyway to the side that led to Maxx's apartment was shadowed and ominous. In some strange way, I guess it made sense that I came here. This was the one place that I had been able to let go and be myself. To be loved by the only person to accept all of me. Despite the dark, complicated nature of my relationship with Maxx, his home was a place that I felt safe.

I put my car into park and was suddenly hit with a paralyzing thought.

What if . . . what if Maxx was home?

I hadn't contemplated that during my mindless drive here. And now, sitting in my car outside of his apartment, I was itching to go inside . . . but I couldn't stomach the thought of facing Maxx.

I imagined thick, blond hair and piercing blue eyes. Strong arms that so easily wrapped around me. Full lips that fit against mine perfectly. Everything about him was irresistible. Combustible. How would I ever be able to resist his magnetic pull?

Yet I impulsively got out of the car and walked down the narrow space between buildings and quickly climbed the staircase that led to the apartment door I had walked through so many times before.

The hallway smelled of stale urine and garbage. I could hear the thumping of club music from the apartment next door. I sorted through my keys until I found the one I had never given back.

I felt suddenly guilty for invading his space like this. To expect that my presence would be welcomed. How could I possibly explain showing up like this?

I'll just stay for a moment. See if he's okay. Then leave. No big deal. This is just about my closure. If I know what he's up to, it'll be easier to get over this huge bump in my road.

I didn't want to acknowledge how delusional I sounded, even to myself.

Walking into the darkness of Maxx's home was like a punch to the gut. I closed the door behind me and leaned back against the wall, trying to get my breathing under control.

Why had I come here?

Why would I do this to myself?

How could I ever make myself leave again?

I felt along the wall until I found the light switch and turned it on. Light flooded the small, cramped apartment and I put a fist to my mouth to stifle the sob that crept up my throat.

He wasn't there. And by the looks of it, he hadn't been there in a long time. Nothing had been touched in quite a while. The space felt empty, devoid of life. Like listening to the echo of the person who used to inhabit it. The wave of overwhelming disappointment almost brought me to my knees.

But honestly . . . what had I expected? What had I hoped to gain by unceremoniously walking into his apartment only weeks after telling him good-bye?

Maxx's T-shirt was strewn across the back of the tattered

couch. A Styrofoam cup sat on the coffee table. A plate with a half-eaten sandwich covered in something fuzzy sat beside it.

The air was ripe with the smell of rotten food. I slowly walked through the rooms, turning on lights as I went.

My heart tripped over in my chest as a realization hit me. If Maxx wasn't here, then *where was he*?

Maybe he was visiting his brother. Or staying with friends.

Yeah, and maybe he ran away and joined the circus.

Each scenario seemed equally unlikely. Images of Jayme as she had looked when I was called in to identify her body flashed through my mind, and I almost crumpled into a heap.

If something had happened to him, I would know, right? Landon, Maxx's younger brother, would have contacted me. I frantically thought of every reasonable explanation for his absence and tried to calm down. I couldn't allow myself to imagine the worst. I'd lose what was left of my good sense and run off trying to find him.

Because my life wasn't about Maxx anymore. It couldn't be.

And yet . . . I couldn't bring myself to leave. I walked down the hallway and pushed open the closed door in front of me. Light from the street filtered in through the window. This room didn't smell of rancid garbage or stale air. It smelled like him.

Like Maxx.

I didn't turn on the light. I walked carefully over piles of clothes until I reached the bed. I slowly sat down and let my hands fall between my knees. It was crazy that despite everything, despite all this man had put me through, his home, his space, felt so right.

Almost against my will, I picked up his pillow and buried my face in it, inhaling deeply. His scent clung to the fabric. Behind closed eyelids I saw Maxx's desperate face, blue eyes pleading, blond curls in wild disarray from my fingers. I remembered words fraught and needy.

And I want you, Aubrey. All of you. Every tiny, perfect part. I want you to belong to me, only to me, so that you'll never leave. Please don't leave.

But I *had* left.

I threw the pillow back onto the bed and abruptly got to my feet. I stomped back out to the kitchen and opened the cabinet beneath his sink. I was glad to see several bottles of generic cleaner. I grabbed the paper towels and pulled the trash can over from its spot by the wall.

I started scooping the trash off the counter and into the bin. I began to spray down the counters and scrub them clean. I found a broom and systematically swept the remains of food and garbage from the floor.

When I was done, I began to attack the piles of dirty dishes, washing and drying them, then putting them away. I wouldn't allow my mind to ask the questions about where he was and what he was doing. I couldn't let myself consider how much not knowing bothered me.

I just kept cleaning.

After half an hour the kitchen was spotless, but I wasn't finished. I moved on to the living room, gathering up dirty clothes and putting them into the hamper. Maxx didn't have a vacuum cleaner, so I made do with the broom.

I straightened the couch cushions and wiped down the coffee table, trying not to gag as I disposed of the moldy food. I wasn't entirely sure why I was doing it. Cleaning had always had a calming effect on me. It was the best way I knew to find some control in a world that had lost all sense of order.

And maybe there was a part of me that wanted to make this space clean and safe again. That maybe by scrubbing the dishes and washing his clothes, I could get rid of the remnants of the chaos that had defined both of our lives. That putting things in order would allow me to rid myself of the ghosts of this recent past. Erasing and removing the hurt and persistent longing.

And maybe if and when Maxx came home to his pretty, clean apartment, he'd be able to turn his life around.

Stop thinking about what-ifs, Aubrey! It doesn't matter! I chastised myself.

With an armful of cleaning products I went back to his bedroom. Turning on the light, I could only stand there and look around as I was assaulted by a thousand memories that threatened to gut me all over again.

The nightstand was overturned; empty bottles were strewn across the room. I could see Maxx, in my head, searching desperately for his drugs. And then when he couldn't find them, turning to the stuff that had almost killed him.

He had nearly died from a heroin overdose. I never realized he was messing with hard-core stuff. The pills had been bad enough, but shooting dope into your veins was something else entirely. How hypocritical it was of me to turn the other way when it came to him swallowing a few prescription meds but drawing the line when it came to a syringe full of smack.

The guilt flooded me with the excruciating memory of our last conversation. Of Maxx's anxious pleas for me to stay. And how I had denied him the one thing he wanted so much.

I started carefully gathering the empty prescription bottles and tossing them into the garbage bag I had brought with me. There were at least thirty littering the floor. Thirty dirty little reminders of how deep into his addiction Maxx had been.

The cold plastic bottles practically burned my fingers as I picked them up. They disgusted me. Maxx disgusted me.

I disgusted me.

I turned my attention to the clothes that lay in piles everywhere. Some I put into the hamper to be washed. Others that appeared to be clean I put back in neat, tidy piles in his drawers. I straightened the clothes, my hands digging among the socks and shirts. My fingers brushed against a cool smoothness.

Knowing what I had found, I pulled out the crumpled photograph of Maxx with his family. Looking at the innocent smile on his boyish face hurt too much to bear. I quickly shoved it back into its hiding spot, unable to deal with the sight of a family that had been torn apart and the boy who would grow up to be a man hell-bent on destroying himself.

When I was finished with the clothes, I finally made my way to the bed. The disheveled sheets looked as though Maxx had just gotten out of them. With shaking hands I started to pull up the covers and line up the pillows.

Images flashed in front of my eyes. Memories of being tangled in these sheets, Maxx wrapped around me. Whispered words of love against sweaty skin.

I've been waiting my entire life for you. Maxx's words had enfolded my heart and squeezed mercilessly. I had become addicted to those moments of sincerity and vulnerability that, to me, seemed to reveal the real man beneath the mask.

I blinked, clearing my head before another memory assaulted me.

He was on his side, his face pressed into the floor. His left arm was bare and stretched out beside him with a thin white strip of plastic tied tightly, just above the elbow . . . I laid my ear against his chest, listening to the strained beats. My tears soaked his shirt as I watched his chest stop moving and the beat of his heart fall into silence.

Then I lost it.

I fucking lost it.

I collapsed into a heap onto his bed, curling into a fetal position as I hugged his pillow tight to my chest.

When would it ever stop hurting so much?

Love was ruthless.

Love was pitiless.

Love was cruel.

Love fucking sucked.

Finally, when I had no more tears left, my body started to unclench, and I found that after the violence of my despair I could be soothed into relaxation. Because no matter the anguish Maxx had unleashed on my world, I felt the strongest sense of peace in his space, with his scent around me.

And there in the bed of the man I had loved and lost, I fell into an exhausted sleep.

chapter three

maxx

There was a five-inch crack in the plaster above my head.

If I stared at it long enough, it seemed to grow and move right before my eyes.

I blinked and it stopped. Then it would start all over again.

Right now, that fucking crack was the most interesting thing in my life.

What a depressing realization.

"It's time for group, Maxx."

I didn't bother to look toward the voice coming from the doorway. The air was stale with the smell of sweat and too much Axe cologne. My roommate, Dominic, an obese pothead, seemed to think that dousing himself in that shit replaced the necessity of a shower.

It was day eighteen at Barton House, a state-run rehab facility that had, for a brief period, seemed like the ticket to starting over.

I was now starting to rethink everything.

It had been easy to make the decision to come here. In the beginning I had been coming off the worst withdrawals of my life. I was still reeling from the fact that I had almost died and that all the people I loved had left me.

I had been alone.

Completely and totally alone.

I had not been in a good place.

So I came here thinking this was my new lease on life. This was my opportunity to show everyone that I didn't want to end up another scary statistic in a brochure about addictions.

I would beat this shit before it beat me.

But then the days started to drift into each other, and once the initial desperation had worn off, I was left with the second-guessing.

Because the physical withdrawal was long gone. The seventy-two hours in the detox unit had taken care of that.

Now I was left with all the urges that came after my body had returned to stasis. The ones that were entirely in my head. The ones that made it really hard to stay.

Because the longer I stayed here, playing the part of the recovering addict, the harder it would be to face what waited for me *out there.*

The things that I missed so damn much.

Aubrey.

Landon.

The club.

The fucking drugs.

Always, always the drugs.

"Maxx. Seriously. Come on."

I let out an overly dramatic breath, feeling more than a little irritated. I swung my legs off the bed and slowly sat up. I refused to look at Pete, the rehabilitation assistant. I ran my hands through the hair that hung in my eyes. I needed a haircut. But there was no way I was getting ahold of a pair of scissors in this place. Too tempting to slice a vein or two, I guess.

Nope, can't let the recovering addict have access to pointy things.

"Getting depressed is normal . . ." Pete started to say.

Jesus Christ, kill me now!

I wasn't entirely sure what Pete's job was at the clinic. He wasn't a counselor. He didn't lead any support groups. He just walked around trying to talk to the patients about their feelings. He was overly self-righteous, seemed to think he had the inside track on everyone's addiction. It was more than obvious he was floundering through his dead-end job. And no matter how many token buzzwords he used, he sounded like someone trying way too hard.

I stared at him, eyeballing him through narrowed slits. He wasn't much older than me, but his thinning hair and sad comb-over made him look middle-aged. He suffered from a clear case of bad genetics, poor bastard. I watched Pete swallow audibly and take a noticeable step back into the hallway. I intimidated him. For a brief second, I got a sick sense of satisfaction from that. Then I felt slightly guilty for enjoying his discomfort.

The old Maxx would have loved his reaction. I would have used his clear intimidation to my advantage. But *this* Maxx didn't do those things. And honestly, I wasn't sure what I was supposed to do. I didn't know how to be without the drugs in my system. I had to learn how to be this stranger taking up residence in my own skin. I had to develop a personality separate from the drugs. And I wasn't exactly sure how to do that when so much of who I was had been wrapped up in a scene I was forcing myself to leave behind.

"I'm not depressed. I'm bored," I told him. I got to my feet and followed Pete out into the hallway.

I had checked myself into rehab convinced I was making the right choice. Hell, it was probably the only choice I had. When I got out of the hospital, I had been coming off the aftereffects of a crash course in detox. My body had been weak and my mind even weaker. I had felt horrible, both physically and mentally. I couldn't remember a time I had ever been so low. But all I could think about was making things right again.

Because Aubrey had left me. Smashed my fucking heart and walked away without looking back. I both hated and loved her for that.

I was miserable without her, but it was also the swift kick I had needed to make some serious changes. For the first time in my life I had wanted something more than the drugs. I still wanted that rush. I was scared I always would. But more than anything else, I just wanted *her* back.

So I had been convinced that I could change. That I could be a better person. That I'd clean up my act here at Barton House, then get out and sweep Aubrey Duncan off her too-good-for-me feet.

But the initial sense of desperation to get my life in order that had gotten me through my first week here was fading fast as the reality of this depressing, hopeless place started sinking in.

The lure of my old life was poking me in the subconscious. Reminding me that it was still there, waiting for me. And the longer I stayed locked behind these walls, the more I wavered between wanting to do things right and wanting to get back to the life I used to have. The one where I didn't feel so small and helpless.

The one where I felt in control.

Because here I was most definitely *not* in control.

Every second of every day was monitored and accounted for. I couldn't take a piss without someone knowing where I was and what I was doing. And losing control, my *autonomy,* on top of everything else was proving almost too much to handle.

But when I thought back to what rock bottom had looked like, I did my best to push aside my inner grumblings and go to group. Sit through therapy and vow that I would never allow myself to be that person again.

But every day was a new battle between the old Maxx and the new one. And I never knew which one would win.

"Is your brother coming this weekend?" Pete was asking, though I barely heard him.

"Huh?" I asked as we walked down the hall toward the conservatory where the support group was held.

"Is your brother coming up for visiting hours this weekend? It would be a great opportunity to utilize family counseling. That's a huge part of the program. It could be a great step for both of you."

My hands clenched into fists, and I had to work hard to control my reaction to the innocent question.

My feelings about my little brother were all messed up. Guilt and shame and anger. It was a festering cesspool of twisted, dark stuff inside of me.

The memory of Landon's visit to the hospital, looking at me with absolute disgust while I lay in that bed, was still heavy on my mind, every day.

I had tried to talk to Landon, but he wouldn't hear me. And after a few minutes of uncomfortable silence he had turned and left.

Finally, he sees you for the worthless shit you really are. He'll hate you forever, Maxx. And you fucking deserve it, my uncle David had sneered before following my brother out of the room.

That had been the last time I had seen Landon. I had attempted to call him several times over the last few weeks but was put through to his voice mail every time. I knew it was completely intentional.

My brother was avoiding me. Not that I blamed him. I had disappointed him. Shattered the illusion he had held of his competent and capable older brother. I stopped being the guy he could count on, and I only became the failure. Knowing how he felt about me, the *real* me, was my biggest shame.

I had never intended for him to know the truth about me. He had been my responsibility since the death of our parents. I hadn't wanted him exposed in any way to the ugly reality I lived in. But now he had been. And because of that, he wanted nothing to do with me.

"No, he's not coming," I said shortly, grinding the words out like glass in my mouth. I was done talking about him.

"Why not? It would be an excellent opportunity—"

I cut Pete off with an angry grunt. "He's not coming, all right?"

Pete was clearly flustered by my response. I shrugged, unapologetic, and left him rambling about taking advantage of services or some shit. I shouldn't have snapped at Pete. He was just doing his job, whatever that may be. But I couldn't talk with him, or anyone, about Landon. I entered the conservatory and found a spot in the circle of chairs.

This support group was the same as the last one I had attended on the LU campus in a lot of ways. Same topics, same overly emotional talking points. Same mundane activities meant to make us "think." But it was the one significant difference that made sitting here day after day extremely difficult.

I love you so much, Maxx. I do. And that's why I can't watch you kill yourself. I won't.

It had been weeks since I had spoken to Aubrey, but the decimation remained. And I couldn't think about Aubrey without thinking of other things. Gash. Marco. The club. The world I had lived in that was as much of an obsession as Aubrey could ever be.

And of course that made me think about the drugs. Which wasn't surprising. I always thought about the drugs. The way they tasted on my tongue. The burn in my throat. Those horrible yet blissful moments while I waited for them to take over. The thrill as they wasted me away.

If losing Aubrey had almost destroyed me, then losing my

drugs damn near ripped me apart. Not having that part of my life anymore had taken away the person I had spent years becoming. Without the drugs, without the club, who the fuck was I?

Who was Maxx Demelo, now that he had nothing to offer anyone?

"Everyone, take a seat." Stacey, the drug addictions specialist, waved everyone to their places. I made a point not to make eye contact with those around me. Though I couldn't help but stare at the chick on the other side of the room who looked as though she wanted to crawl out of her skin. She picked at her fingernails until they bled.

She looked like how I felt. Just about ready to lose my mind.

"Hey, man." A hand touched my shoulder, and I acted instinctively. I shoved the hand away and snarled.

"Whoa! I was just saying hey. You all right?" Dominic looked at me apprehensively. I rolled my eyes but attempted a casual smile. He might smell bad, but I didn't want to make him piss himself.

It was pretty obvious Dominic wanted to be my friend. I attracted needy dudes as much as the women.

A few months ago, I would have loved his brand of schoolboy ignorance. The clueless student living off Mommy and Daddy's money and possessing zero common sense. I would have been able to sell him a quarter for the price of an ounce, and he wouldn't have questioned me.

I used to eat guys like Dominic for breakfast.

I knew he was here because his parents thought his weed habit was a problem. It was almost laughable. He really had no idea the lengths some of us would go to for our addiction. How easy it was to lose everything for the high.

"You need to learn the concept of personal boundaries before you lose a hand," I warned, though I tried to laugh to lessen the sting of my words.

He grinned and I smiled uneasily in return.

"Right. Personal boundaries. I get it," Dominic chortled. "Did you do the homework? I wrote like five pages in my journal last night after you went to bed. Did you know you talk in your sleep? It's pretty freaking funny. You talk a lot about a girl named Aubrey. Who is she? Is she your girlfriend? Whoever she is, you say her name a lot. You should tell me about her. She's obviously important to you. At least you don't snore. My roommate at school says I snore. Do I snore? It's cool, you can tell me."

My face started to burn red. What the hell? Any attempted goodwill toward my nosy roommate vanished. The sound of her name on his lips made me feel almost homicidal.

"Are you getting lunch after this? I think they're serving fajitas. I freaking *love* Mexican food. You can tell me about Aubrey if you want. That's what friends do. They talk about stuff."

I could only stare at him with a mixture of irritation and confusion. I wondered if he had more mental problems than a supposed addiction to marijuana.

"Dominic," I said quietly.

"Yeah?" he asked, leaning forward, his face eager.

"Shut up and stay the hell out of my business. I get that you're a talker. But I'm not. I'm not here to make friends. I just want to get through my time and go home. Got it?"

"Uh . . . okay . . . but I'm here if you want to talk and stuff . . . we're roommates and we shouldn't keep secrets—"

"Dominic, seriously, back the fuck off already." I rubbed the spot in the center of my forehead, feeling a headache coming on. "And stop listening to me while I sleep. It's fucking creepy."

Dominic didn't say anything else.

Stacey started passing out worksheets. I took one and handed the pile to the person on my left. I looked down and had to suppress a groan.

The ABCs of Addiction. Understanding Your Triggers.

I looked at the rest of the people around me and was instantly sorry that I had. No one looked happy to be there. Even my considerable charm was lost on this group.

Aside from the manic nail picker and Dominic-I-refuse-to-bathe, there was an older woman who clearly thought heroin chic was a legit thing. Then there was the old biker dude who was missing most of his teeth and the scrawny tweeker who twitched uncontrollably every few minutes. I looked at my fellow screwups and felt like throwing up.

They were each damaged in their own particular way. They were all here for different reasons. What really sucked was while I sneered down my nose at their wretchedness, I also saw myself in every one of them.

Suddenly it hit me that maybe that's why I hated them so much. Because deep down, they reminded me of myself. Of what I almost became. Of what I might still become.

My heart thudded in my chest. My lungs constricted painfully, and I was suddenly finding it very hard to breathe.

My eyes darted around the room, my gaze resting first on the meth-head-nail-picker. She must have sensed me looking at her. She raised her dead eyes and met mine.

I stood up so abruptly that my chair clattered to the floor. I backed up, my legs hitting the overturned chair, and I stumbled, almost falling.

"Maxx? Are you all right?" Stacey, the addictions specialist, asked. The patented counselor expression of concern was plastered on her face like a mask. Did she really give a shit that I was on the verge of freaking out?

Somehow I doubted it. This was just a job. What did she care if a bunch of smacked-out addicts got their lives together or not? If we came back over and over again, that just kept her in business.

I felt hollow knowing that the only people who had ever truly given a crap about me were the ones I had betrayed the most. The ones who had walked away.

I suddenly didn't want to be alone with only my demons for company.

If only I had a few pills, then I'd feel so much better.

My addiction's irresistible voice purred soothingly in my mind.

Just a pill or two. That's all I really need. It would be so easy to leave and find what I want . . .

No!

I didn't need pills! I wouldn't leave! I thought again about lying in the hospital bed. Sick and alone. I thought about Landon, who refused to talk to me, and Aubrey, who had left me.

I didn't want pills! I wouldn't let myself want them. But I also couldn't sit there surrounded by a roomful of people who represented the absolute worst of myself. I looked around the group, feeling the bile rise in my throat.

I practically ran from the room, my feet smacking against the linoleum as I fled. Thankfully, no one followed me. Once I was back in my room, I collapsed onto my bed. I was sweating, and the tightness in my chest was only just starting to subside.

Fucking hell. I'm pretty sure I just had a panic attack.

I needed to pull myself together. The desire to pack my things was almost overwhelming. Because that would be the easy thing to do. Run away from the hard stuff. Drown myself in the world I used to know. To lose myself in old habits. I wanted to so damn badly. But I knew that leaving would only prove to the people I cared about that I wasn't taking any of this seriously.

And I wanted to take it seriously. I needed to.

Because at the end of the day I was doing all of this for one reason only. I was doing this for Aubrey. And for Landon. For a future I wanted to have with both of them. And one that I couldn't have if I couldn't stick this out and show them that I meant business. That when I hurt them, I was sorry.

So I'd stay. I'd try. I'd force myself to wake up in the morning and not think about how much I wanted to leave.

But I made a promise to myself. That after this was over, I would get out of here and I would get Aubrey back. I would show her that she didn't need to run away from me. That I could take care of her. And take care of myself.

I felt a renewed conviction, and that felt good.

And as my heartbeat slowed and my breathing returned to normal, I began to think of other things besides all the ways I had messed up.

I started thinking of how to put the pieces back together.

The caged tiger of my addiction snarled angrily from where it lay trapped but noisy inside of me.

Aubrey.

Just her name quieted the voice in my head that wanted something altogether more damaging.

Aubrey.

The scary truth was that I couldn't do this without her.

And I was determined that I wouldn't have to.

chapter four

aubrey

"I love you so much, Aubrey," Maxx murmured, his lips tracing a path from my temple down the side of my face. I could feel the imprint of his mouth on my skin. The slight tremble as he kissed a line along my jaw.

I took a deep breath, pulling the scent of him into my lungs. My eyes were closed. I couldn't see him, but I really wanted to. I wanted to look into his blue eyes and see how much he wanted me. How much he loved me.

But I couldn't open my eyes. I was trapped in a world of darkness.

"I've missed you so much," Maxx whispered, his breath fanning across my face. His hands slipped up the front of my shirt, and I felt his confident fingers molding to my breasts. I relaxed into his familiar touch. I ached for him. Every cell, every nerve responded to only him.

I wanted to say his name. I wanted to tell him that I loved him. That I missed him. That I was miserable without him in my life.

But my mouth, like my eyes, seemed to be fused shut. I was blind. I was mute. I could only feel as Maxx rubbed my nipples, a sharp bite as he pinched them almost viciously and then rubbed again gently, worshipfully. The soft pressure an unspoken apology.

"You're mine, Aubrey. Always mine." Maxx sounded so angry. Betrayal was thick in his voice as he pulled my shirt over my head and all but ripped my bra away from my hot skin. He sucked on my chest, and I felt a sharp prick of pain as I felt his teeth dig into my flesh.

Maxx was biting me! Hard!

I tried to lift my hands and push him away, but I couldn't. Everything was dark. I couldn't yell. I couldn't move.

I could only feel as the man I loved pulled the skin from my bones with his teeth. The searing pain burned in my throat with my need to scream.

I felt Maxx's tongue as he lapped the warm blood that flowed from the wound. And he wouldn't stop. Not until he had consumed me completely.

He was devouring me. Eating me alive.

"You lied to me, Aubrey. You said you'd stay. You said you loved me. But you walked away. You left me all alone," Maxx growled, his fingers piercing into my back, burrowing their way into my skin.

He was tearing me apart.

Literally.

And I was helpless to stop him.

"You were supposed to save me, Aubrey!" His anguished wail was like ice picks inside my head.

"I love you! Why wasn't that enough?" Maxx roared just as his teeth punctured my heart.

✦

I sat upright in my bed with a gasp. I was covered in a fine sheen of sweat, and my pulse fluttered madly. My hands shook as I pushed hair from my face.

My God, that was intense.

I put my fingers to my chest, touching the smooth skin. I could still feel the sharp twist of dream Maxx's teeth. The warmth of my blood. The sound of his angry but panicked voice in my ears.

I took a deep breath and turned on my bedside lamp. Looking at the clock, I saw that it was only three in the morning.

I knew there would be no going back to sleep for me, so I got up and slid my feet into the worn pair of slippers peeking out from beneath my duvet, which had fallen onto the floor.

Insomnia and I had become close friends over the last few weeks. And when I did eventually fall asleep, it wasn't for long. My nightmares made sure of that. My subconscious was attacking me when I was at my most vulnerable. Reminding me of everything I should be ashamed of.

Strangely, I had slept a deep, dreamless sleep at Maxx's apartment. It had been the first time I had gotten a few solid hours without waking up shaking and covered in fear-soaked sweat.

I didn't want to focus too much on the implications of *that.*

I sat down on the couch and turned on the television, flipping to the channel I knew was showing reruns of *I Love Lucy*.

"Can't sleep either, huh?" I looked up as Renee walked into the room. Her red hair was pulled back in a ponytail, and there were dark circles under her eyes. It seemed I wasn't the only one who had been trying to slay their demons while they slept.

I patted the cushion beside me. "Have a seat and enjoy Lucille Ball with me," I told her, offering a wan smile. When things with Maxx had gone so horribly wrong, Renee had been there. And when the sounds of my friend's crying had pulled me out of my self-indulgent misery, I had comforted her in the only way heartbroken people can. With complete and total empathy.

We had learned how to help each other and in some small way mend the parts of us that had shattered.

Renee gave me a tired smile in return and sat down on the couch, curling her legs up underneath her. She didn't say anything, and I recognized in her the same pain that resided in my chest. Sometimes, looking at my best friend was like looking in a mirror. As much as I hated it for myself, I hated it for her more.

After watching her lose herself for months, seeing her resurrection was inspiring. Devon hadn't been one to go away quietly, and I knew that he pushed and pulled my friend, trying to make her cave and come back to him.

I heard his sobbing messages. I saw the notes and flowers he left by the front door. And although she hadn't shed a tear for Devon since the day she had gotten the protective order, I knew how hard it was for her to turn her back on the man she had loved, no matter how horrible he had been.

Renee rarely spoke about Devon anymore. The few times I had brought him up, she had been firm in her resolve to stay away from him.

"There comes a point when a person can only take so much, Aubrey. And even though my heart doesn't agree, my head knows I'm better off without him." Her words had resonated. And I was envious of how strong she was.

Because every day I waffled between firm resolve and wishful thinking, with a splash of delusional hope.

I turned my attention back to the TV, hoping Lucy's antics would erase, at least for a little while, all of the anguish neither one of us could escape. We sat in silence, watching the black-and-white television show, neither of us really paying attention to what was on the screen.

"Will it ever stop hurting?" I asked quietly after a while, rubbing the painful spot over my heart that never really went away.

There's a saying that *time heals all wounds.* Whoever had spoken those particular words hadn't had their life uprooted by Maxx Demelo. I couldn't imagine time making any of it any easier.

If anything, time only intensified the sense of emptiness in my gut where his love had once been.

Renee reached out and wrapped her arm around my shoulders. I stilled, unsure how to reciprocate the physical affection, feeling stuck in that strange place between needing the comfort and wanting to deny needing it at all. In the end, I slid closer, and the two of us sat in the lingering stillness of our silent agony.

"I sure hope so," my best friend whispered back, an unspoken understanding in her simple statement. There were no false assurances. No insincere declarations.

It was only a plain truth given from one broken heart to another.

And there was no point in saying anything else.

✦

By early evening I was a walking zombie. Functioning on four hours of sleep was proving more than a little difficult. The fact that I wasn't sleeping was making me extremely edgy.

I strode across campus with my head down. I had never been an overly social individual, but now, after everything that had happened with Maxx, I was even less inclined to raise my head and make eye contact with anyone.

I still felt as though people were looking at me. I knew that I was being paranoid and more than a little narcissistic to think people would be at all interested in my life. But I couldn't shake the horrible feeling that they all *knew.*

I was trying to walk as quickly as possible past the psychology building, when I was enveloped by a swarm of people filtering out the front door.

I instantly recognized the faces around me.

It was the campus addictions support group.

Crap.

I tucked my chin into my coat and tried to be as inconspicuous as possible. Unfortunately, playing the part of Miss Invisible was an epic fail.

"Hey, Aubrey!" I gritted my teeth and wondered how pathetic it would look to run away as fast as my legs could carry me.

"Hey, Twyla," I said, trying for a smile but accomplishing only something close to a grimace. I nodded at her friend Lisa, another member of the support group I had been co-facilitating until a few weeks ago. I wondered, not for the first time, how Kristie had explained my absence.

I soon found out.

"Sorry about your *personal issues,*" Twyla said with a touch of condescending scorn. I had never really connected to anyone besides Maxx in the group. And that wasn't the sort of rapport a counselor should ever have with a client. I was afraid of what that really said about me and my ability to perform in a therapeutic capacity.

"Personal issues?" I asked stupidly.

Twyla and Lisa exchanged a look. It was loaded with suspicion.

"Well, that's why Kristie said you weren't in group anymore. You know, 'personal issues,'" Lisa chimed in, lifting her fingers in air quotes.

I cleared my throat to delay my response.

"Well, I um . . ." I stumbled inarticulately.

Lisa and Twyla exchanged looks again. They really were the epitome of the bitchy sorority girls. With their perfect hair, glossy smiles, and impeccable manicures, they carried themselves with a confidence that came only to the effortlessly cool and attractive. But to look at them you'd never know they were as fucked up as the rest of us.

"Oh, I get it, it's not something you want to talk about. Whatever." Twyla waved her hands as if bored with the conversation. The rest of the group had already wandered off, but I couldn't help but notice the hard stare of one particular person.

Evan and his downtrodden girlfriend, April, had taken their time as they passed by, Evan attempting his patented form of intimidation through narrowed eyes and clenched teeth.

"Do you know where Maxx is?" Lisa asked, snapping my attention away from Evan and April and back firmly into awkward territory.

"What do you mean?" I asked, and I hated the way my voice trembled, no matter how hard I tried to control it.

"He hasn't been to group since before you left. You guys seemed tight, we just thought he may have said something to you." Twyla eyed me closely. Her benign words barely concealed a deeper skepticism.

Maxx hadn't been back to group.

I wasn't surprised by the news, but it added to my unease. His whereabouts were proving to be more than a little concerning. His apartment was unlived in. He hadn't been back to group. He had essentially disappeared.

Where the hell was Maxx? I squared my shoulders and gave them an insincere smile, not about to tip them off to my inner turmoil.

"I barely know Maxx. Why would I know where he is?" I lied with effort. My words sounded fake, even to me. I was a shitty liar. And I was pretty sure Twyla and Lisa weren't fooled in the slightest.

"Okay, well, if you see him, tell him we were asking about him. I owe him a cup of coffee," Lisa said, and I wanted to scratch her stupid eyes out. The irrational, jealous harpy inside reared her ugly head. I wanted to ask about this so-called owed cup of coffee. I wanted to grab handfuls of her hair and force her to tell me exactly how well she knew my ex-boyfriend.

Instead I shrugged, trying too hard to come off unconcerned.

"I don't think I'll see him," I stated. I sounded irritated and defensive and way too obvious. If I had any sense of pride and self-preservation, I'd shut up and never utter Maxx Demelo's name again.

So why did my traitorous heart thump his name wildly in my chest?

Maxx. Maxx. Maxx.

Lisa and Twyla traded a loaded look. "Okay, well, never mind, then. We must have been mistaken," Lisa replied shortly, a smile as fake as my own plastered on her face. Twyla wiggled her fingers in my direction as the two walked away.

I let out a breath and looked up at the overcast sky.

Maxx, where are you?

Damn it! I hated that I was worried so much. I wished I could shut down and turn off the way I had always been able to do before.

But I knew I wouldn't stop worrying or wondering. Maxx, even though he was absent from my life, was the most pressing thing on my mind.

What else was new?

"Aubrey, what are you doing here?" a voice asked with more than a hint of accusation.

Kristie Hinkle stopped in front of me. I hadn't seen Kristie since our horrific meeting in which I was rightfully accused of my crimes. She looked less than thrilled to see me, but her professionalism stopped her from telling me to get lost.

"I was just walking by," I explained.

"You're not supposed to be interacting with group members," she stated, as though needing to remind me of what I was and wasn't supposed to be doing.

When I had first started co-facilitating the support group, I had admired Kristie. She had been eager to help me learn the ropes. But as time wore on I found her to be judgmental and unsympathetic to human failings. Particularly mine.

"I'm not *interacting* with anyone, Kristie. I was walking home when Twyla and Lisa asked me where I've been. I didn't have a chance to really explain my *personal issues,*" I said, not able to suppress the thinly veiled sarcasm.

Kristie made a choking noise in the back of her throat that could have been a snort or a cough; I wasn't really sure. I wanted to roll my eyes but thought better of it. There was no sense in adding more fuel to an already smoldering fire. Kristie shook her head and walked down the steps of the psychology building and started to pass by me. She stopped just before walking away and looked at me over her shoulder.

"Just remember that any infractions will be reported to Dr. Lowell and the Counseling Department. I don't think either of us wants to be in that position again," Kristie said, her voice firm and gruff, though I detected a note of regret on her face before she looked away. I opened my mouth to shoot back a response, but changed my mind.

"Have a good evening," Kristie said tightly, starting to walk away.

Then, as if possessed by the devil, my mouth opened again and words poured out that were the absolute worst I could have said in that moment: "Has Maxx not been coming to group?"

Kristie's shoulders went rigid, and her dull brown eyes flashed with disapproval. Why oh why had I asked her that question? Where was my common sense when I needed it?

But I couldn't help it. I needed something . . . *anything* that would give an indication to Maxx's whereabouts.

"Aubrey, that is extremely inappropriate for you to ask." Kristie's mouth turned down in censure. But my concern for Maxx outweighed any sense of pride or self-preservation.

"I'm not trying to be inappropriate. It's just, he had an incident a few weeks ago, and I was just worried . . ." I trailed off, feeling like a complete ass.

"I'm more than aware of Maxx's *incident.* As to his current treatment, that is none of your business," Kristie said archly.

"So, he *is* in treatment?" I couldn't help but ask, latching on to that tiny shred of information that it was obvious Kristie hadn't meant to give me. Was that where he had gone? Was that the explanation for his sudden disappearance? And if he had, what did that mean for Maxx? For me? For the ultimatum I had given him?

Kristie shook her head, then turned and walked quickly toward the parking lot. Even though Kristie's opinion of me shouldn't have mattered, I felt ashamed as I slowly walked back toward my apartment. Even more, I hated the mad flutter of hope that Kristie's admission had unleashed.

But I couldn't ignore it. Old habits die hard, I supposed. Once it had taken root, the thought wouldn't leave: there was a chance Maxx was out there somewhere, doing the very thing I had wanted him to. Putting himself back together.

My steps quickened and I broke into a sprint.

My words to Maxx during that last fateful phone call weeks before flashed wildly through my frantic brain: *Get your shit together, Maxx. And do it for yourself, and for no one else. And then maybe I can learn to trust you again, trust myself to be with you.*

If Maxx was in rehab, that meant he had heard me. He had taken what I said and decided to live it.

What did that mean?

Why did it have to mean anything?

Suddenly I was running hard and fast, as though chased by the thoughts that seemed to dog my steps.

I burst through the door of my apartment, my face flushed, my breathing erratic. I needed the calm of my own space in order to sort out my spinning thoughts.

"Whoa! Where's the fire?" Brooks asked, coming from the kitchen.

I frowned. "What are you doing here?" I didn't mean to sound rude. But I couldn't deal with Brooks. Not now. Not with uneasy questions about Maxx on my mind.

Renee appeared behind him, a bag of carrot sticks and a jar of dip in her hands. She took one look at my face and knew something was up.

"Okay, well, can we rain-check on the movie, Brooks? I can tell Aubrey isn't really up to it. You look exhausted, sweetie," Renee cooed, dropping the carrots and dip on the coffee table and crossing the room to where I was standing, feeling completely overwhelmed.

Brooks peered at me in his analytical way. "What happened, Aubrey?" he asked, thankfully keeping his distance. I knew I couldn't handle any physical contact from him right now.

"Nothing, I'm fine. Just extremely tired. I'm not really in the mood for company right now, Brooks. No offense," I said, grimacing.

Brooks looked as though he wanted to argue with me, but he grabbed his car keys, and with a strained smile, walked out the door with a promise to call me later.

"Okay, the testosterone is gone, now tell me what the hell happened to make you look as though you have seen a ghost," Renee demanded, taking me by the arm and leading me to the couch.

I covered my face with my hands. "It's so freaking stupid," I groaned, feeling silly for my over-the-top reaction. "I ran into some people from the support group," I began.

"That had to have been awkward," Renee deduced, and I nodded.

"Yeah, it wasn't what you would describe as . . . *comfortable,*" I admitted, biting my bottom lip. "Then Kristie came out and pretty much chewed me a new one for 'interacting' with the group members," I said, rolling my eyes. I was happy to feel anger replacing embarrassment.

"That's ridiculous! It's not like you were hanging out with them or anything," Renee reasoned, and I threw my hands in the air in exasperation.

"I know," I said quietly.

Renee sighed. "But that's not why you look like that. What else happened?" she asked.

I ran my hands through my long blond hair, pulling slightly until I felt a sharp tug at my scalp. Somehow the bite of pain cleared my head.

"I think Maxx went to rehab," I said finally after a period of silence.

Renee didn't say anything. She dropped her eyes to her hands, which were folded in her lap.

"He hasn't been back to the support group since being in the hospital," I continued in a whisper.

"So . . ." Renee began.

"And he hasn't been home in weeks," I said in a rush, not making eye contact with my friend.

Renee frowned. "And you would know that how?"

"Because I went to his apartment," I told her quietly, my face suddenly hot.

I sounded like a stalker.

Or worse . . . an absolute idiot.

Renee cleared her throat and thankfully chose not to address my mortified confession.

"So you think that because he's not in group and hasn't been home that he's in rehab? There are other possibilities, you know, Aubrey. Possibilities that are just as likely and not so pink and rosy," Renee pointed out.

"Yeah, I know. But it was something Kristie said. Something about Maxx's *treatment* not being any of my business."

"And she's right," Renee replied gently.

"No! Don't you get it! If it's not my business, then that means he's *in* treatment! He's doing the very thing I wanted him to!" My voice rose, and frustrated tears stung my eyes.

I was getting entirely too worked up, and I knew it. Renee shook her head. "So what if he's in rehab? What would that change?"

"*Everything,*" I let out on a breath, admitting the thing that I would never be able to voice to anyone else.

Renee frowned again, two thin lines forming between her eyebrows. "How does Maxx being in rehab change anything, Aubrey?"

I twisted my fingers together over and over, not sure I could admit what lay in my heart.

"I don't know!" I agonized, covering my face with my hands. I was confused. I was angry. I was irritatingly hopeful.

I was a freaking mess.

Renee gently pulled my hands away from my face and gave them a squeeze. The naked sympathy on her face curdled my gut. I knew what she was thinking.

That I was dancing back toward that place I had only just left behind. That seeing me losing my head over the man I had sworn to have nothing to do with only proved how incapable I was of letting him go.

Was she right?

Damn it, yes, she was.

"What if I told you Devon was getting help for his anger? That he was in counseling? Would that automatically erase all of the things he did to me? Does it change the fact that together, we were dysfunctional and unhealthy?" Renee asked quietly.

"The situations are completely different," I countered sharply. Why was I being so defensive? What was I trying to convince her of? Or was I trying to convince myself that hearing the news that Maxx might be in rehab could quite possibly open that door again.

What was wrong with me?

"Are they? Because three months ago, I know what your answer would have been. You would never have let me hold on to the unrealistic possibility that the man who hurt me so badly would change. This isn't a romance novel, Aubrey. Love can't make things all better. No matter how much we want it to." Renee's face was wet and her lips quivered.

"You spent the last year watching me lose myself in a relationship that almost destroyed me. I didn't see the damage my love for Devon was inflicting. But now that I'm on the other side of it, it's easy to see those same mistakes in someone else. Aubrey, Maxx loves you. I have no doubt. But he is not someone you can depend on. At least not right now. You made the right choice when you walked away. You almost lost everything, and now your focus needs to be on you and fixing what went wrong in *your* life."

I needed her realism. Her heavy dose of common sense. It was the medicine I had to swallow no matter how bitter the taste.

"Don't think about Maxx and what he's doing. You can't. You have to think only about you," Renee said firmly.

I knew she was right. Of course she was. But I had to admit that it still hurt to hear. And it didn't dissolve the shame I felt for allowing myself, for one brief, insane moment, to fall back into the chaos only Maxx could create.

I thought about how out of control I had felt as I watched Maxx lose himself to the drugs. I had isolated myself by being so wrapped up in his dysfunction. But I had been happy to drown in him, because he was all that I wanted.

And look where it got me. I wouldn't be that girl again. I needed a decisive break. I knew, deep down, that I had been holding on to the painful hope that Maxx would come back a changed man and sweep me off my feet.

It suddenly hit me that I had been waiting for the crumbs of confirmation that Maxx was getting help. I had been inadvertently living in a delusional fairy tale with a warped happily-ever-after. But what I really needed was to let him go before I lost myself all over again. I grabbed my keys and rattled them in my hand, feeling agitated.

"I need to get out of here for a bit. Clear my head. I'll be back later," I explained, not making eye contact.

I needed to get my head together. To cleanse Maxx from my system before I suffocated.

"Do you want some company?" she asked, getting to her feet.

I shook my head.

"I'll be fine. I just have some processing to do," I told her.

Renee's lips twitched into a shadow of a smile. She was upset for me, and I wished I could tell her she needn't be. That I would be all right.

"Is that your clinical opinion?" she joked.

"Absolutely," I said softly.

I couldn't tell her I was all right. But I would be able to soon.

I would make sure of it.

chapter five

aubrey

Ever since I had gotten my driver's license, taking to the open road had been my surefire way of getting myself together. Whether it was a bad grade, a fight with a friend, or dealing with the death of my much-loved younger sister, I would get behind the wheel of my car and drive for hours. Often with no particular destination in mind.

I took the unfamiliar curves of the backcountry road with ease. I loved the feel of the cold wind whipping through my hair, my music blasting through the speakers. My mind wandering to the topics that were at any other time off-limits. My parents. Jayme.

"Come on, Aubrey! Let me come with you!" Jayme wrapped her arms around my neck and hugged me, a clear attempt at manipulation that she knew I could never refuse.

I had just gotten my license earlier in the day, and as a reward Dad had given me the keys to his car, saying that I could go take a ride around town. I was excited. This would be my first time in the car without one of my parents. I felt like such a grown-up. I was taking that first, decisive step toward adulthood. I was buzzing on it. And Jayme was just as excited about my new license as I was. We had always celebrated in each other's successes, and this was no different. Though I knew it had just as much to do with the fact that her days of riding the bus to school were now over.

I grinned at my baby sister, never able to deny her anything. I wagged my finger in her face. "If you want to ride in the car with me, there will be rules, Jay," I warned teasingly.

Jayme rolled her eyes. "Yeah, yeah, no R and B or rap, I got it," she said, beating me to the punch. Our differing music tastes was one of the few points of contention between us.

I chuckled. "Okay, well, as long as we're clear about that."

"Woo-hoo! Let's go! Maybe we can stop for ice cream!" Jayme squealed, grabbing me by the hand and pulling me out the door.

I found myself smiling at the memory. The awaiting ache of grief was ever present, but it couldn't erase the joy that I felt at remembering my sister. It felt amazing. I found that I didn't want to force myself to forget about Jayme. I wanted to remember her. And the hole in my heart began to mend . . . just a little bit.

Then I thought of Maxx. The joy disappeared, and the hole in my chest ripped open all over again. I tried to shift my thoughts to the dark side of Maxx, to the club. To the addiction that owned him. It was important to remind myself that letting him back in was dangerous.

Compulsion had been a fixture in the underground club scene since the midnineties. The stories and rumors about it had become the stuff of urban legend. The main allure was the sense of mystery—it was never in the same location twice.

And that is where Maxx had come in. When I was first introduced to the club scene months before, I hadn't realized that Maxx was the mysterious "X," whose intricate street art left randomly all over the city provided the clues to the club's location each weekend.

Find the art, and you find Compulsion. The details were

wrapped within the painting that was unlike anything I had ever seen. Maxx's alter ego had created a reputation for himself, not only with his intense artwork but as the man to see if you were looking for a particular type of diversion.

And while he was slinging drugs and defacing buildings, I had been completely oblivious that my Maxx was actually the dangerous and volatile X.

Until it was too late and my heart was so ensnared there was no turning back. But Compulsion had given me something I hadn't known I had been looking for . . . an escape.

And suddenly, I knew that's where I needed to go.

I just had to find out where the infamous club was located tonight. And it hit me that finding the picture would not only lead me to Compulsion, it could quite possibly answer the question that was eating away at my insides.

I needed to know if Maxx was still around, doing the same things I had left him for.

I needed closure, and hoped that the answers would finally allow me to move on once and for all, whatever those answers were.

I started driving around aimlessly, looking into the darkened alleyways and on the sides of buildings, trying to find the elusive X's handiwork.

After almost an hour I was close to giving up. The knot in my stomach hadn't eased, but I was forced to admit that it looked as though I wasn't going to find what I sought.

I pulled into a gas station to fill up my car. I had been driving long enough that I was dangerously low on fuel. I twisted the gas cap and lifted the nozzle off the lever.

"Here," a guy said, shoving a flyer into my hands before walking away to stick the papers in his hand under windshields.

"Uh, thanks," I said, crumpling the waste of trees in my hand. The bright colors and manic writing caught my attention before I could throw it away. I smoothed out the flyer on the hood of my car and could have laughed at the irony of this moment.

The word *Compulsion* arched over the top of a reproduction of one of Maxx's more elaborate paintings. At the bottom was an address that wasn't too far from where I was.

I had never seen the club distribute flyers before. That meant Maxx wasn't painting his pictures.

I thought about calling Renee, just to tell her what I planned on doing. I almost wanted someone to talk me off the ledge. To tell me that going to the club, the place where Maxx has indulged in the darkest parts of himself, was the dumbest thing I could do.

But instead I stuck the flyer on my dashboard and headed toward an unknowable future.

✦

I ended up at the old Longwood Residential Center, which used to be a nursing home almost thirty years ago. The sprawling, rambling buildings were derelict and falling down in places. It looked condemned, which is why this location was perfect for the club.

I was surprised by how close it was to the center of town. It was a bit more conspicuous than was usual for the underground scene. I got out of my car and was hit by a wave of déjà vu. The pounding bass could be heard in the distance. The dizzying wave of energy seemed to emanate from the building ahead of me.

Groups of people moved forward, beckoned by the siren's call of madness and illusion that Compulsion promised. I felt a momentary apprehension and thought briefly about getting back into my car and heading home. But I also felt the pull of the music. Of the knowledge that what lay inside was unlike anything I'd experience anywhere else. Though knowing how easy it would be to surrender myself didn't provide the comfort it once had. But I was powerless against it all the same.

The line wove in and out of the trees as one by one people were admitted or denied entry. The usual extremes were out in force, from the woman who seemed to be wearing plastic wrap and a bow tie, to the guy with his entire face covered in tattoos. Each person had done all they could to make it seem like they belonged. Because that's exactly what they were searching for.

Belonging.

I looked down at my woefully inferior club attire and almost laughed. Once again, here I was, waiting to be let inside and dressed like a walking, talking J.Crew catalogue.

But I joined the line anyway and waited my turn. I recognized Randy, the bouncer, and Marco, Maxx's friend taking money at the door. I only hoped one or both recognized me. Though I couldn't count on that. They encountered hundreds of people every night, and my interactions with Marco had been brief. I seriously doubted they'd remember me.

I rolled the hem of my shirt, knotting it between my fingers in my sudden bout of nervousness. Why did I think this was a good idea?

"Are you for real?" Randy barked, pulling me out of my thoughts. I blinked, a little confused by his antagonism.

"Excuse me?" I squeaked out.

Randy pointed at my gender-neutral ensemble. "You can't come in wearing that shit," he growled, the words getting lost in the growth of his beard.

"Let her in. I need to talk to her," Marco cut in, stepping in front of Randy and waving me past.

"Thanks," I mumbled, looking up at Marco. I offered a smile, which died a sad little death as I took in the irritation on his face. Was that directed at me? What had *I* done?

"Cover for me for a few minutes," he told Randy, who only nodded. Marco looked back down at me, his eyes hooded in the darkness, the metal in his lip and eyebrow gleaming in the dismal lighting. He didn't just look irritated. He looked pissed.

And more than a little scary.

He wrapped his hand around my upper arm and all but dragged me into the club. The music jarred my bones as I was pushed into a dark alcove off from the dance floor.

I tried to wiggle free of Marco's pincerlike grasp, but he wasn't letting go.

"You're hurting me!" I protested, straining to be heard over the thumping bass.

"Where is he?" Marco shouted in my face.

His question caught me off guard.

"What?" I asked.

"X, or Maxx, whatever he's calling himself. Where the fuck is he? There are people, *serious* people, who are looking for him." Marco glowered at me, as if I was the one responsible for Maxx's MIA status.

"How would I know?" I argued, though Marco's questions gave me some of the confirmation I had been looking for.

Maxx wasn't here. He hadn't been in some time.

And even though it still didn't answer the question of where he had gone, I could at least be comforted in the knowledge that he hadn't gone back to *this*.

Marco gave my arm a little shake. "Because he's been stuck up your ass for months. I knew he was pulling back because of you. I know the signs of pussy-whipped when I see it. Now, where the hell did that little fuck disappear to?"

Remembering some old-school self-defense, I stepped on Marco's foot and gave him a hearty shove in the center of his chest, causing him to fall backward and let go of my arm.

I rubbed the throbbing skin and took a few steps away from him.

"Don't ever grab me like that again! I don't know where the hell Maxx is!" I seethed, wincing as my fingers ran over obviously bruised flesh. But clearly my indignation overruled my fear of this scary-looking man.

Gazing around, I didn't experience the energetic rush that I used to have. Compulsion wasn't the mysterious and seductive world it had once been. I didn't care about the pounding beat or the promise of surrender that lay beyond me.

Instead, the place just seemed dark and terrifying. Without Maxx, without his enigmatic but constant presence, it felt cold and lonely. The people swaying to the frantic beat looked desperate and delusional. This place was a lie that they couldn't see.

It wasn't an escape. It was a trap. Because none of it was real.

This was the mask that hid an ugly reality. One that had almost killed Maxx.

One that had almost destroyed me.

Marco advanced on me and once again invaded my personal space. "Look, I'm not trying to be an asshole here. I'm just the guy trying to keep your boyfriend in one piece. Because I can tell you, if he doesn't show up soon, there are certain individuals who would like nothing better than to mess up that pretty face of his," Marco warned, and I was relieved when he didn't touch me again.

I pressed myself against the brick, wondering about the chances I had if I kneed him in the balls and ran for it.

Marco braced one hand on the wall beside my head and leaned in close. I could smell the stale cigarettes and mint gum on his breath. It made me faintly nauseous.

"I've watched his back for years. And what do I get for it? My ass in a sling. You tell him he owes me. More than he realizes," Marco said in a low voice. I felt a shiver of alarm.

Marco brushed my hair away from my neck and leaned in close. "He's put a lot on the line for you. I hope you're fucking worth it," he whispered before pushing himself away from the wall.

I stood paralyzed in the darkened corner. Coming to Compulsion had been a very bad idea.

My feet wouldn't move. I was trembling so badly that I thought I'd fall over. Finally, after I was able to walk without wobbling, I inched my way into the large, open room where the club was in full swing. The lights flashed madly, creating a strobe effect. It made me feel as though I were walking in slow motion.

My eyes scanned the crowd, but I didn't recognize anyone.

I didn't feel like dancing. I didn't feel like getting lost in the throng of moving bodies that pressed around me.

I was done with the whole damn thing.

The mystique of this world was lost on me now that I saw it for what it really was. And in some small way and in spite of my run-in with Marco, it made the entire trip out here worth it.

The tantalizing taste of closure was there, just within reach. And I finally felt strong enough to grab it.

And it was time for me to get the hell out of there.

Before I could make my way through the crowd, someone knocked into me. I lurched forward, my hands coming out in front of me as I collided with the very hard floor.

And just like the first time I had come to Compulsion, I feared that I was two seconds away from being trampled to death.

I was grabbed rather viciously by the arm and yanked to my feet. A far cry from the gentle hands that had helped me once before.

I fumbled to find my footing and then was brutally pushed. I stumbled again and would have fallen if not for my renewed sense of balance. I peered into the murky darkness and recoiled when I caught sight of the last people I ever wanted to see.

April and Evan, the maladjusted couple from the addictions support group, stared back at me. April half smirking, half guilty. Evan sneering and hateful.

I started to back away, not wanting any sort of confrontation, but found that I was boxed in by swaying dancers.

"All alone tonight, huh?" Evan shouted, the light flickering in his soulless eyes. His hand was wrapped around his girlfriend's wrist like an iron snare.

"What?" I asked, realizing I was saying that a lot this evening. I felt the prickling of instinct telling me to run. Evan gave off the aura of someone who delighted in hurting others. And for some reason, since day one, he had taken a particular dislike to me.

Evan let go of April and leaned in close. I tried to back away, but was again met by a wall of bodies. "Your boyfriend, Maxx. Where is he? I haven't seen him around for a while, and I have some business to take care of with him." I blinked in shock. Did *everyone* have freaking business with Maxx? He sure did get around.

And then I realized exactly what Evan was asking me.

Shit.

He knew.

"I don't know what you're talking about," I denied, shouting over the music. Evan bent his head until his lips were right next to my ear, and I shuddered in revulsion.

"I knew you were nothing but a slut. You should have thought about who you were spreading those pretty legs for. A lot of bad shit can happen if you're not careful. But you've already figured that out, haven't you? People just aren't very understanding when it comes to certain relationships."

I reared back as if Evan had hit me. He watched me with a sadistic joy, licking his lips and leering at me.

April had disappeared into the crowd, and I felt as though I was alone with Evan, even though we were surrounded.

Realization dawned on me. And I knew exactly who had told Kristie about Maxx and me. And it wasn't Brooks. I had been wrong about that one.

"Watch your back, bitch. I've got your number." Evan hurled his words like a weapon, every syllable a clear and undeniable threat.

Using my elbows, I pushed my way through the crowd even harder. Without slowing down, I ran all the way back to my car, not sure I had gotten the closure I was looking for.

chapter six

aubrey

I had always been a dedicated student. I was the weirdo who enjoyed writing research papers and staying up until four in the morning cramming for an exam. But my passion, my *enthusiasm,* for counseling, my chosen career path, had waned.

Knowing that the people who had championed you were questioning your dedication and abilities had a way of shaking you up. I sat in Dr. Lowell's office one weekday afternoon, waiting for her to finish with her class so we could have our first one-on-one meeting since I had received my official reprimand.

I was dreading it.

I looked around her familiar space, noting how different my feelings were about being here than they used to be. I still felt nothing but respect for my adviser, but there was an awkward tension that had never been there before. Nothing like ruining someone's perception of you to fuck up a relationship.

I fixed the wide cuff bracelet on my wrist, fingering the engraved silver. The small infinity symbols were rough on my skin, and I wondered what had possessed me to wear that particular piece of jewelry this morning.

I remembered how excited Jayme had been to give it to me for my sixteenth birthday. She had been working all summer at the local frozen custard stand to save up for this present. We had been at the mall almost six months before, and I had seen the cuff bracelet in the window of a small shop. I had loved it, but when I saw the price tag, I knew there was no way I could afford it.

So Jayme, who was only fourteen, had taken it upon herself to make sure I had it. That was the way we had been together. We would have gone to the ends of the earth for each other. We never fought. We were best friends. Which is why it had hurt so much when all of that had changed.

Because eventually, and rather suddenly, our relationship had soured and she had stopped caring what I thought about anything. Strangely, over the last month, it had become easier to remember the good times with Jayme rather than wallowing in the bad memories. I still felt her loss as acutely as ever—that was the sort of pain that never really went away. But somehow, I had started to readjust my mind to allow for more room to focus on the happy memories. After everything with Maxx, I realized that concentrating only on the negative would slowly destroy me. I had experienced more than enough destruction for one lifetime. I needed to reacquaint myself with the better parts of my past.

I smiled as I thought about the way Jayme's eyes sparkled as I unwrapped the gift. If I concentrated hard enough, I could still hear her laugh when I tried it on and did a dorky little dance in my excitement.

My mom had taken our picture as we hugged, and then my dad had called us into the kitchen to eat some cake. Mom had ordered my favorite, chocolate buttercream with raspberry filling.

Mom had framed that picture and given it to me a few weeks later. I had left it behind when I had gone to Longwood, thinking rather idiotically that by leaving it at home I could escape the memories.

Now I wished I had brought it with me. I had purposefully not taken any pictures of family when I had left. Remembering it now, I knew I had been incredibly shortsighted. I realized what I wanted, more than anything, was to look at my sister's face again and to remember her for the way she was *before* the drugs. *Before* Blake.

Before having to identify her body on that cold morgue table.

That birthday had been significant in so many ways. It was the last one I remembered where my family was happy together. That September when school started, Jayme met Blake, and nothing would ever be the same again. I hadn't picked up on the subtle changes in Jayme's personality that now, looking back, I could see so clearly. Hindsight and all that. But for that moment, things had been perfect. And it was that moment I was content to focus on now.

"I hope you haven't been waiting long." Dr. Lowell's voice took me out of my memories and threw me solidly back into the present.

I sat up a little straighter in my chair and smoothed my skirt nervously before tucking my hair behind my ears.

"No. Not long," I said, lying. I had been there for over twenty minutes already. But no sense in pointing that out.

Dr. Lowell acknowledged my answer with a nod. She made herself a cup of coffee, and I noted how she didn't offer me one. This one tiny omission hit me hard. It epitomized everything that had changed between Dr. Lowell and me. She walked around her desk and sat down in her chair, reaching for a manila file that sat on top of a stack of papers.

There was no polite exchange of pleasantries. No easy chitchat or questions about my week. Only cold silence and grim anticipation. I picked at the skin around my fingernails anxiously, unable to curb the obsessive tic. Habits were hard to break. I knew that only too well.

After a few minutes, Dr. Lowell looked up from the folder and pushed up the glasses perched on the edge of her nose. She smiled. A tight caricature of what I was used to from her.

"How are you?" she asked gruffly.

I blinked a few times, wondering how honest I should be with the woman who had been my mentor. Dr. Lowell crossed her hands in front of her and leaned forward. "You look as though you haven't been sleeping," she observed.

I cleared my throat and twirled the bracelet on my wrist as though it were a talisman of some sort. And strangely, it did help calm my twisting stomach.

"I haven't been, really," I admitted, having a difficult time making eye contact.

"And you've lost weight," Dr. Lowell continued, her hawkish eyes taking in every detail. She was entirely too observant for my peace of mind.

I cleared my throat again, wishing I had a glass of water. "Yeah, I guess so," I said.

"I'm concerned about you, Aubrey," she remarked, her voice softening marginally.

"Concerned?" I asked, not exactly sure how I was supposed to take her proclamation.

"I know you've been through a lot in the last few weeks. You've lost your way. Veered off course. Am I using the correct euphemisms?" Her lips quirked into a more natural smile, and even though I appreciated her effort, I couldn't reciprocate.

It was disconcerting to be read so clearly. "I suppose I have," I said softly.

"How did you get to this point, Aubrey?" Dr. Lowell's question was startling in its straightforwardness. I knew exactly what she was doing. She was shrinking me. She was looking at me as a patient. A client. It was mortifying to know that the strong, competent exterior I had been developing for years was nowhere to be found. I wasn't fooling anyone anymore, least of all Dr. Lowell.

What *had* led me to this point? Christ, I had been wondering the same thing since I had watched Maxx fight for his life on that disgusting bathroom floor.

A thousand unanswered questions had flitted through my mind in that small space of time. In the split second it took for me to realize the man I loved was dying because of his own demons and my inability to see them, I had realized that I really didn't know myself at all.

I rubbed the cuff bracelet with a bit more ferocity.

"I'm not sure, Dr. Lowell," I answered, trying not to be vague, but only honest.

Dr. Lowell rubbed a red spot on the bridge of her nose from her glasses. She looked as though she had a headache. I knew my actions had affected more people than just me. That she, being my adviser, had most likely received a lot of flak for not picking up on the situation. I had put more than my future at risk by making the choices that I had. And I had been too selfish and self-absorbed to realize that.

But then, at the time, nothing had mattered but the love I had discovered with the worst possible person.

"You're a smart young woman, Aubrey. You have a lot of potential. I've always appreciated how open and honest you've been about your history. About the ways in which your sister's death has affected you. But perhaps we're here through failings on my part. I put you in a position where you would be opening yourself up to things that could possibly trigger you. It was unfair of me to put that kind of pressure on you. I saw the red flags. Kristie had brought to my attention some incidents that I was too quick to dismiss. I think that at the end of the day, I'm just as culpable in this situation as you are, Aubrey." Dr. Lowell looked tired and sad, resigned.

"Dr. Lowell, that's not true. You've been nothing but supportive. I can't thank you enough for putting faith in me in the first place. I'm the one who messed up, not you. I did something I knew was wrong and hid it from everyone," I said, glad I was able to get that out without crying.

Dr. Lowell sat back in her chair and looked at me over the rim of her glasses. "And that, right there, is what sets you apart, Aubrey."

"What do you mean?"

"You can't undo what happened. The only thing I had hoped was for you to take responsibility." Dr. Lowell took off her glasses and slowly put them down on her desk.

"I remember reading a quote back during my undergrad years that said, *Adversity is the first path to truth.* Over the years, I've found this to be the truest statement I've ever heard. You have to go through the hard stuff to find exactly where you need to be. And I believe that how we react in our bleakest moments is a testament to the person we really are."

Dr. Lowell smiled again, and this time it was genuine and maybe tinged with something that looked like pride.

"You've impressed me, Aubrey."

I had to be hallucinating. Was she for real? Impressed with what? My ability to make really shitty decisions?

"It would be easy for you to blame Maxx. Or to use a myriad of excuses to justify your behavior, but you haven't done any of that. You've stood up and accepted your punishment and taken the lashing. It shows a true strength of character, in my opinion."

I cleared my throat, not entirely sure what to say.

"Well, thank you," I finally said.

"During your hearing, it was briefly discussed that you can earn your spot back in the program. I assume you're auditing the Boundaries and Ethics class that is required of you."

I nodded. I had handed in the necessary paperwork just that morning. My first class would be next week.

"If you follow through on the class and the supervision hours with me, the department will reassess your place at the end of the year." Dr. Lowell looked up from the folder in her hands and met my eyes. "In spite of everything, Aubrey, I truly think that you have a place in this program." Dr. Lowell gave me a long and steady look. "If that's what you still want."

I thought about what she was asking me. At one time the answer would have been a resounding yes. But my confidence had been shaken to its core. So now . . . I wasn't so sure.

"You're hesitating. I thought being a counselor was what you wanted to do," Dr. Lowell said.

I looked out the window and watched students rush by on their way to classes. I had been like them once. Confident and sure in my path. But how could I be assured that my path was the right one when I had veered off course so badly?

"What if I'm not cut out for it? You said yourself that given my past, I'm easily triggered. How can I possibly help other people when I haven't been able to help myself? What sort of person falls in love with a patient? What kind of counselor does the things I've done?" I asked in an agonized rush.

Dr. Lowell's face became thoughtful.

"I'm going to use some therapy mumbo jumbo and turn this around on you." Dr. Lowell leaned forward, her hands folded on her desk, and she peered levelly at me, her eyes dark and serious. "How would you answer those questions? Do you think you are equipped to help someone else, given your own experiences? What does your gut tell you?"

I smiled involuntarily. "It says that it's because of my experiences that I can help someone else." Dr. Lowell nodded in agreement. "But," I continued, "that doesn't change the fact that I crossed the line, Dr. Lowell. What if I mess up again?" And there was the root of my problem. I had lost confidence in myself, and I wasn't sure I could get that back.

"I can't answer that for you, Aubrey. But what I can tell you is if you take your future seriously, if you're willing to work for it, then we can try to get things back on track for you. It'll take a lot for you to prove that you're able to resume your spot in the program. And you have to take it very seriously." Dr. Lowell took a sip of coffee while I thought about what she was saying.

"Are you ready to do that?" she asked me.

Despite the twinge of apprehension I felt at possibly failing again, I knew that I couldn't let this opportunity slip by. "I am," I said, and I meant it.

After my meeting, I felt encouraged. I had a long road ahead of me, and I knew that there was a lot I needed to do in order to prove that I deserved my spot in the program back.

I just hoped I was up to the challenge. A lot was at stake. Everything I had worked for had been taken away from me. Dr. Lowell had dangled the possibility of getting it back.

That gave me something to work for.

It gave me motivation.

It would allow me to focus on something that wasn't Maxx Demelo.

✦

As I walked up the steps to my apartment, I could hear laughter filtering down the hallway. I paused, listening to the familiar lilting of my best friend's giggle on the other side of the wall. I hadn't heard Renee laugh like that in a long time. Too long.

I stood outside for a moment, enjoying the sound. I almost didn't want to open the door and ruin whatever moment she was enjoying. But it was cold and I had homework to start, so with reluctance I slowly opened the door and instantly wished I could quietly creep back out again.

Renee was on the couch, sitting close to a guy I didn't recognize. Her head was thrown back, exposing the long, white column of her throat in a signature flirty move I hadn't witnessed since freshman year. It threw me to see this side of her again. It was like coming face-to-face with someone you had forgotten you knew.

The guy, who was cute in a geeky sort of way with thick black-framed glasses and curly dark hair, watched her with a sweet smile on his face. Renee leaned in close to him, her grin infectious and genuine. She looked years younger. It was as though pounds of baggage had been lifted from her frail shoulders.

Seeing her like this was both inspiring and oddly painful. Because while it was a relief to see her bouncing back from her horrific heartache, a small, ugly part of me was jealous. Jealous that it was Renee making those positive steps forward. That she was the one with the smile on her face and joy in her eyes. I wanted that so much for myself and I worried I'd never have it again.

I tried to close the door quietly so as not to interrupt them. The soft click as it shut, however, told them they were no longer alone. Renee stopped laughing. She covered her mouth as though she had been caught doing something wrong.

"Aubrey, hey!" Renee looked sideways at the guy beside her, an almost guilty look on her face.

"Hey," I said back, dropping my bag onto the chair. Cute guy with glasses sat up straighter and gave me a shy smile.

"Um, this is Iain. He came over to help me study," she said, looking at him through her lashes. The flirty glances the two were throwing at each other made me wish I could slink back to my room and marinate in this awful feeling of selfish bitterness that was bubbling up inside me.

I hated that I felt that way.

But it was there all the same. How could I begrudge my best friend a chance to move forward? Why would I want her to be trapped here with me in the charred remains of our former relationships? I had hated Devon Keeton, the man responsible for her tattered heart and broken trust. He had used and abused her. He had threatened and nearly ruined her.

Seeing her laughing and flirting was a relief. Right? So why did I want to scream at the sky in anger? Why did I want to wail, "Why not me?"

And then I gave myself a sharp mental slap. Because I *could* have that. I just needed to fight for it. I couldn't sit by passively and wait for it to happen. Even if my heart constricted at the thought of loving anyone other than Maxx Demelo.

"Hi, Iain, nice to meet you. I'm the roommate, Aubrey," I said, walking toward the couple and holding out my hand.

"It's nice to meet you, Aubrey," Iain said with sincerity, shaking my offered hand with a firm grip. He seemed to be the polar opposite of Devon in both appearance and personality. He watched Renee with a worshipful expression, his eyes following her every movement. Renee flushed in an endearing way, and I couldn't help but smile, pleased when all traces of jealousy subsided as I watched my best friend teetering forward toward this thing blossoming on unsteady feet.

"I'd better get going," Iain announced as I continued to stand there like a creeper. I had been very obviously staring for an inordinate amount of time. Renee gave me a look that was hard to read, but probably had a lot of *stop embarrassing me* undertones, before getting to her feet and ushering her guest to the door.

"See you later," I called out, hurrying toward the kitchen so I could give them some privacy.

I heard the front door close, and then Renee appeared in the doorway of the kitchen, a soft smile on her face. She thankfully didn't mention my weirdness, and I luckily wasn't forced to explain it. "So . . ." I began, waiting for her to fill in the gaps.

"So . . ." Renee said, raising her eyebrows.

"When did all that start? You haven't mentioned an *Iain*," I said.

Renee shrugged.

"There's really nothing to tell," she said, evading. She went to the refrigerator and took out a bottle of water. I watched her closely while she took a drink, though the smile never left her face. She really was the worst liar. Worse than me, if that was possible.

"Is it serious?" I asked, and then hated myself for it.

Because the smile disappeared instantly. Renee's shoulders stiffened and the same haunted expression I had become used to in my own reflection drifted over her face.

"I can't even think about anything serious. My heart just isn't ready for that," she said quietly.

The Aubrey of six months ago would have prodded and nagged her for more information. The Aubrey of six months ago would have chided Renee for being hung up on the asshole that hurt her.

The Aubrey of six months ago really didn't have a fucking clue. So this Aubrey, the Aubrey with a heart full of painful experience, didn't push, didn't prod. This Aubrey simply nodded her head and let the silence that drifted through the room after Renee's soft answer be enough. Because this Aubrey understood.

All too well.

chapter seven

aubrey

I woke up feeling oddly rested.

I had finally slept through the night without dreaming of a homicidal Maxx.

I didn't know if it was my surprisingly productive meeting with Dr. Lowell earlier in the week or my staunch resolve to move forward, but for whatever reason, I had been given a reprieve from my anxiety-inducing nightmares.

And that, for me, was cause for celebration. Or at least my customary indulgence of Krispy Kreme doughnuts on the way to my first class.

I munched on strawberry glazed goodness as I walked the two short blocks to campus. It was warmer than normal for early spring. The campus was alive with students taking advantage of this first sign of good weather.

The warm air felt like a fresh start. As though even Mother Nature was on board with me getting my act together and putting the past behind me.

"Someone looks like they woke up on the happy side of the bed."

I glanced up to find Brooks beside me. He looked good that morning in a casual T-shirt and distressed denim. He hadn't bothered to shave, and the light stubble gave his face a rugged appearance that worked for him.

Not for the first time I was reminded of why I had been attracted to him when we had first met.

"Yeah, feeling pretty great today. It's amazing what a good night's sleep will do for you," I said, giving Brooks a smile. His face lit up and it was sort of infectious. My smile spread into a cheek-splitting grin. It was easier to feel normal with Brooks again after realizing that he hadn't gone behind my back to Kristie.

I now knew, after our encounter at Compulsion, that Evan had informed on me and that my anger toward Brooks had been unfair and misguided.

"It's nice seeing you like this. It's been too long," Brooks said, grabbing the other half of my doughnut and popping it into his mouth.

"You always have had a problem with grabby hands," I teased, elbowing him in the side.

"At one time you sort of liked my grabby hands." Brooks wiggled his eyebrows and I laughed off his flirting.

"Yeah, well, that was a long time ago. And I've learned a thing or two about the importance of personal boundaries since then," I joked back, enjoying our easy banter.

Brooks licked sugar from his lips, shrugged, and grabbed my hand, pulling me up short.

"I'm taking you out tonight. I think it's time to get you drunk and to have those normal college experiences all the kids are talking about." Brooks let me go and I took a step back.

"Uh . . . I don't know . . ." I began, but Brooks cut me off.

"Just sit back and enjoy the ride, Aubrey."

I involuntarily shuddered at his words. Sitting back and enjoying the ride is what had gotten me into trouble in the first place. But he was right. What could it hurt?

"Sure. Why not?" I said, shrugging.

"Wow. Your enthusiasm is contagious," he joked, rolling his eyes.

I playfully punched his shoulder. Maybe he was right and I just needed a good night out to forget about everything.

"When should I be ready for our night of wild and crazy shenanigans?" I asked, walking through the door Brooks held open for me. Our shoulders brushed and I felt a strange mixture of hesitance and pleasure.

Not because it was Brooks touching me. It had nothing to do with that. It was more about the fact that *anyone* was touching me. My body missed even the casual touches of intimacy.

I realized that I hadn't done myself any favors by living an isolated life.

Brooks walked close beside me, his arm rubbing against mine as we moved. And I allowed it.

"I'll be by around eight thirty. Get ready to have some fun, Aubrey. I'll pull a good time out of you if it's the last thing I do," Brooks threatened good-naturedly, and I couldn't help but smile. It felt good. *I* felt good.

What a concept.

✦

"Wow, going out on a school night? What's come over you?" Renee joked as I pulled a conservative sweater dress out of the back of my closet. It was cute, with a slightly scooped neck and fitted sleeves. It fell midthigh and was a flattering purple.

Before thinking too much about it, I grabbed my knee-high boots and lacy tights to wear beneath my dress. I didn't get dressed up often, but I was in the mood to look pretty.

"Yeah, Brooks convinced me to go out," I said, stripping down to my underwear and bra and then sliding the dress over my head. Renee didn't bat an eye. We had been living together long enough that modesty had lost its place in our relationship a while ago.

Renee gave me a smile. "That's good, Aubrey. I haven't always been Brooks's biggest fan. His collection of button-down shirts kind of gives me hives. But he's been a good friend to you. And who knows, maybe you'll find someone to get a little wild with."

I nearly choked.

"What?" I shrieked.

Renee held her hands up and laughed at my expression. "Jeez, calm down, Aubrey. I'm just saying that you've been tied up in knots for a long time now. Something simple might be good for you."

"And you honestly think hooking up with a random someone is *simple*? Are you serious?" I asked incredulously.

My face flamed hot and I felt an uncomfortable flip in my stomach at Renee's suggestion. It wasn't that I was against the idea of ever being with someone else. But I had the inexplicable feeling that I was betraying Maxx by even contemplating it. Which was ridiculous.

"I'll save releasing my inner hoochie for another night, I think," I joked, pushing aside my unease.

Renee playfully swatted my arm and grinned.

"It doesn't have to be a full-on sexcapade. You could just . . . you know, kiss someone a little. Find a hot stranger to whet your appetite," Renee teased, trying to break the heaviness in both of our hearts.

Her words had me recoiling at the thought of the last hot stranger I had been drawn to. I swallowed around the lump in my throat.

I forced a dry laugh from my mouth. "I appreciate your efforts in facilitating random hookups for the night. But I think just a beer and some nachos will be all that I need," I said.

"And probably a lot less drama," Renee quipped.

On a whim, I grabbed her hand and squeezed. "Come out with us," I said.

"I'd rather not be on hand to witness the Brooks Hamlin drool fest, thank you very much."

I rolled my eyes. "It's not like that anymore, Renee. Brooks and I are friends. He isn't looking to get into my pants," I swore, though I felt a twinge of doubt at the truth of my words.

"Yeah, well, it would still be kind of third-wheelish. You and Brooks have all those dork jokes you think are funny and no one else does. And when you start reciting Adam Sandler movies, it makes me want to slit my wrists. Just sayin'," Renee teased, and I tossed my hairbrush at her.

"Would you rather have us quote *Magic Mike*? I know how obsessed you are with that particular cinematic masterpiece," I laughed.

"Do not mock Channing Tatum," she warned, shaking my hairbrush in my face.

I snatched it out of her hand and pulled my hair up into a ponytail.

"Go get dressed. You're coming with us. I won't take no for an answer," I told her, shooing her out of my room.

Renee groaned. "One *Happy Gilmore* quote and I'm taking a cab home," she yelled from the hallway.

I grinned as I finished getting ready.

I was going out . . . with my friends.

I felt pretty damn good.

Of course, I should have known that it wasn't meant to last.

chapter eight

aubrey

We ended up going to a bar downtown that was a regular hangout for the LU crowd. I hadn't made a habit of frequenting the place, because I wasn't much on socializing in general.

I had never been the type of student to play beer pong at frat parties or do keg stands until I passed out. When we were freshmen, Renee had dragged me to several parties, but I had typically spent my night hanging awkwardly by the door like the stereotypical wallflower.

I was on my third Sam Adams and was experiencing the fuzzy light-headedness that meant I was slightly inebriated. A little sloppy and very giggly drunk.

"God, they suck!" I yelled into Brooks's ear as we watched a crappy band play their instruments really badly on the small stage at the back of the room. They were butchering Led Zeppelin's "Tangerine" into something almost unintelligible.

Renee's new "friend," Iain, had shown up and they had gone off to play a game of pool. She hadn't answered me when I had asked her whether she had called him. She played it coy, refusing to acknowledge that she was enjoying his company as much as it seemed that she was.

I knew that to acknowledge that she was opening herself to someone who wasn't Devon seemed impossible right now. But I was happy to see that she was trying.

So maybe I should follow her example.

The suggestion to find a stranger seemed entirely too daunting. But that didn't mean I couldn't enjoy the company of the person I had come with. And right now, with more than a little bit of alcohol in my system, I found myself pulled in by the comfortable familiarity of the man who sat on the stool beside me.

Brooks bobbed his head up and down in time to the music. He had also had several mixed drinks, though he didn't seem to be remotely drunk. It was clear that he was a lot more used to it than I was. Brooks looked over at me, his eyes twinkling. "They're not so bad. At least they know who Led Zeppelin is," he joked, referencing my lack of rock history knowledge when we had first started dating.

He had been horrified when he had played Zeppelin's *Houses of the Holy* album and I had asked who they were. As I was growing up, my parents had subjected me to all manner of country music. As a teenager I was more likely to listen to Top 40 than to the Rolling Stones. After that he had made it his mission to educate me on the finer points of rock and roll, forcing me to know every song by Jimi Hendrix and the names of every member of the Who.

And I could now consider myself properly schooled. I smacked his leg and then let my hand rest there, not moving it away. "Shut up. I know who they are now," I slurred a bit. My hand felt clammy against the fabric of Brooks's jeans. I thought I felt his muscles clench beneath my palm and I dug my fingers in slightly.

Leaning in toward Brooks, I reached over his arm, purposefully brushing my breast against his bare skin, and grabbed his Jack and Coke and took a drink. I made a face and handed it back. "That's disgusting," I sputtered, licking my lips in a slow, exaggerated gesture. I was being shameless. But I was committed to throwing myself into a good time with my very available friend if it killed me.

Brooks laughed, his face looking almost pained. He placed his hand on top of mine. For just a moment, he lingered, and it felt strange. I didn't understand what I was doing or why I was doing it. But I did know that for right now, that horrible emptiness inside of me had disappeared.

I tried not to feel embarrassed when Brooks lifted my hand and placed it carefully on my own leg. He didn't move away, but he didn't touch me again, and I felt myself flush in silent mortification.

"Brooks—" I began, but he cut me off.

"You think they'd play 'Cinnamon Girl' if I asked them to?" Brooks had gone back to bobbing his head in time to the music.

I looked at him and knew exactly what he was doing. He was giving me my out so that I wouldn't feel weird about whatever strange pickup move I had just attempted on him. I wanted to be ashamed, but there was something about Brooks that wouldn't let me be.

"Maybe. But do you think your ears can handle the massacre of your favorite song? Because that dude up there ain't no Neil Young," I said, moving past my discomfort.

"Let's go ask. Come on." Brooks hopped down from his stool and headed toward the stage. He took my hand and tugged me through the crowd. We were able to convince the wannabe rockers to play "Cinnamon Girl," and then we were dancing. Very, very badly. Because dancing and Neil Young ballads didn't really work.

I remembered seeing Brooks dance with Courtney at Compulsion and thinking how horrible his moves were, even in a place where style and technique weren't required. But I didn't care. Because we were having fun.

Renee and Iain joined us, and even though they danced with us in a group, I could see the way they turned toward each other. Iain was smitten, and it was obvious that Renee was losing the battle to not be smitten in return. Things were pretty freaking awesome.

And then it all went to shit.

My phone started buzzing in my pocket and I looked around at my friends, knowing they were the only people who ever called me. I pulled it out and looked down at the screen in the dim lighting and frowned at the unfamiliar number. It was local, but not one that I recognized. I hit ignore and shoved it back into my pocket, thinking it must be a wrong number.

"Who was it?" Brooks asked.

I shrugged. "No clue," I said as he swung me around in a circle. I laughed, feeling the threads of something that felt distinctly like happiness curl around me.

Then my phone started buzzing again.

I pulled it out of my pocket and saw the same number flash across the screen.

"Maybe you should answer it. It might be important if they keep calling," Brooks said.

"Yeah, okay. I'll just go outside for a minute. See if they'll play some Backstreet Boys when they're finished," I said, grinning, knowing Brooks's aversion to all things pop.

"Never!" he yelled as I started to push my way through the crowd.

My phone stopped buzzing and I waited to see if whoever was trying to reach me would leave me a message. I paused by the back entrance to the bar, staring down at my phone, feeling strangely apprehensive. Then it lit up again as the number blazed across the screen. I walked out the back door and into the cool night air, feeling some of the alcohol haze clear.

"Hello?" I said, sounding a little out of breath. There was an endless moment in which no one said anything and I wondered whether I was right and it was a wrong number.

And then the person spoke and I wished like hell I had never picked up the damn phone in the first place. Followed by the inevitable self-loathing for thinking that at all.

"Hey, Aubrey," Maxx said quietly, though I could hear him as clearly as if he were standing next to me.

I didn't say anything.

I couldn't say anything.

I wanted to ask him where he was. To demand answers to the questions that had been plaguing me. I wanted to yell at him, to know why he was ruining the first night in forever where I was actually feeling normal. A thousand uncontrollable emotions flashed their way through my mind, flittering in and out before I could figure out what I was actually feeling. Though I recognized homicidal rage and bone-deep desire mixed up with the rest.

"Are you there?" Maxx asked, sounding small and unsure. I leaned against the wall, needing it to hold me up before I fell.

"I'm here," I answered. The weight of those words was not lost on me. Nor how much of a lie they really were.

"Oh, well, that's cool. I thought you might have hung up. Not that I'd blame you," Maxx said, clearly nervous. We fell into silence like we had so many times before. But there was nothing comfortable about this quiet. The heaviness of unspoken words pulled us both down. What did he want me to say to that? Did he want me to disagree with him? Because that wasn't going to happen.

I had every right to hang up on him. Just as he had every right to be angry with me. We both had a right to be a twisted, complicated mess of angry, bitter, and hurt feelings. But instead I felt this sad sort of numbness, as though all of my emotions had been bled out of me.

I looked around the dingy alleyway behind the bar and thought of how much it looked like the place where Jayme had been found. What a strange time to think about that. But of course I thought about her as I heard Maxx's voice for the first time in weeks. They had become intricately twined together in my mind. The loss of each merging together until it was hard to differentiate one from the other.

"What do you want, Maxx?" was all I could manage to say. I sank to the ground, my head falling back and connecting with the concrete behind me as I slumped against the wall. The sharp bite of gravel underneath my legs cleared the last of the alcohol from my head.

"I just needed to hear your voice. I wanted to know how you were doing. I hoped you'd want to know how I was. I'm in rehab, you know. I decided to check myself in. Just like you wanted me to." The relief that I felt at his words was violent and almost painful. Maxx was in rehab. This is what I had hoped he'd do.

I wanted to cry. I wanted to shout out in jubilation. And I wanted to run far away from the momentary elation his admission brought me. Because while I was glad to find out the reason for his prolonged absence, I was also scared that this inopportune phone call would completely throw me.

"So how are you, Aubrey? I think about you every second of every day. I miss you," he breathed out softly.

He missed me. Why were my traitorous lips smiling at his confession? I blanked my face and then sighed, feeling the prick of anger take the place of irrational pleasure at hearing his voice again. "Do you want me to lie and say I've been great? That I've taken up yoga and have finally finished that crossword puzzle I had been struggling with?" I spat out, my voice layered in bitter sarcasm.

Maxx chuckled nervously. "No, I want you to tell me the truth," he said, sounding less and less like the confident man I had known before. I thought back to that day months ago when I had first seen him. He had been a force of nature. Magnetic and irresistible. A man who was self-assured and in control.

And while I had been drawn to his confidence, it was his vulnerability that had made me fall in love with him. That very same vulnerability that was now coming through the phone.

I should hang up.

I shouldn't sit here on the dirty ground listening to his sad voice and feeling the way my heart flipped over in my chest.

But I couldn't get over the fact that I felt as though I owed him something. That after everything he had been through, he needed some sort of compassion from me after I had refused to stay by his side.

But that didn't mean I couldn't give him a taste of exactly what he had put me through.

"The truth is, Maxx, things suck. Does that make you feel better?" I asked coldly.

"No, it doesn't, Aubrey," Maxx said quietly, and the sound of my name on his tongue made me shudder involuntarily. "I hate that I've made things worse for you. I hate that you wouldn't give me the chance to prove to you that I can make things better." He didn't sound angry or upset. He just sounded resigned, and that was almost worse.

I swallowed back the tears that I wouldn't allow to fall. I stared up at the streetlight until my eyes burned. I bit my lip so it wouldn't tremble and I wouldn't speak until I was sure I could do so without wobbling.

"I can't do this, Maxx. I told you before that I can't. I'm not sure what you're looking for from me, by calling after all this time, but I can tell you I can't give it. I *won't.*" I sounded so sure. So steady. It was all a goddamned lie.

"Is this some sort of 'making amends' assignment? Because I can assure you it's not necessary." I sounded hard and unforgiving. Which I knew was the last thing he needed, given what he was undoubtedly experiencing. But I also knew that if I opened myself up to him, that if I showed him a moment's kindness, that it would be a quick and ferocious fall right back to where I was a few short weeks ago. And I just couldn't do that to myself.

The back door of the bar opened and Brooks poked his head out. He raised his eyebrows when he saw me sitting on the cold ground, my phone pressed to my ear. I could only imagine what my face looked like.

"You okay?" he mouthed. I forced myself to smile and nod my head. I covered the phone with my hand.

"I'll be back inside in a minute. Order me another beer, would ya?" I said, trying to act normal and unaffected.

Brooks, of course, wasn't fooled. He took a step out into the alleyway. "Who are you talking to?" he asked, a little louder this time.

"Aubrey, are you still there?" Maxx's voice danced into my ear, bouncing around in my head.

I removed my hand from the receiver. "Yeah, just hang on a sec," I told him a bit tersely before turning back to Brooks.

"Just my mom," I whispered to my friend, rolling my eyes and affecting a grimace.

Brooks pulled a face. "Ugh, sorry. I'll order you *two* beers," he said with a smile that I really appreciated right then.

I gave him a thumbs-up as Brooks left me alone.

"Look, I've got to go," I said, returning to Maxx, who had waited silently on the other end.

"Who was that?" he asked quietly, and I recognized the tone clearly. He was jealous. And hurt. And there was a hint of betrayal as well. Which pissed me off.

"That was Brooks, all right? Not that I should have to explain that to you," I replied grumpily.

"Oh, your friend. Right," Maxx said, sounding relieved.

"Well, if you're finished asking about my social life, I really need to go," I said, wanting to get off the phone. And also *not* wanting to get off the phone. I wanted to run away and I wanted to stay exactly where I was.

Which had always been the strange dichotomy of my feelings for Maxx. He instigated a swirling, manic sort of confusion that consumed me.

I was trying really hard to be a woman who could learn from her mistakes. Not dive headfirst back into them.

I had also hoped that three weeks would harden my heart a bit more than they had.

"Aubrey, please. I know this will sound incredibly selfish, and I know you will probably say no, but I want to see you. I want to look at you and tell you how sorry I am. I need to see you and know that I didn't ruin everything." His words were a plea that was incredibly hard to resist.

His request both shocked and thrilled me.

I couldn't see him. It would undo everything I was fighting so hard to rebuild.

What would be the point of reopening wounds that were only just now starting to heal? I was walking on this path with a clear and distinct destination. And as things stood, there was no place for Maxx Demelo in Aubrey Duncan's new world order.

But . . .

Ugh! There it was . . . the doubt. The second-guessing. The brief hesitation and unwillingness to say no.

He's doing exactly what you wanted him to do. How can you punish him for that? the obnoxiously romantic girlie voice inside of me trilled loudly.

You're making a life for yourself without him. Don't let Maxx derail you now that you've finally made peace with your disastrous choices! the stern, rational voice yelled, drowning out my other arguments.

"I know you made your decision . . . but it doesn't change how I feel about you. It doesn't change the fact that I have a hole in my heart where you belong. I miss you. I just . . . I want to see you. Just to say a proper good-bye, I guess."

My jaded bitterness cackled in disbelief. He was so full of shit. His words smacked of emotional manipulation. But my heart could only remember the way he made my pulse race when he touched me.

"I don't know, Maxx." I heard the wavering.

"Please. Visiting hours are on Sunday afternoons, one to three. It really would mean a lot to me."

I chewed on my lip and rubbed at the sore spot in my chest. "Where are you?" I asked tiredly, wanting a few more answers before I ended the call.

"I'm at Barton House. Do you know where that is?" he asked, and I nodded, though I realized he couldn't see me.

"Yeah, it's that place outside of the city. On the farm, right?"

"Yeah, on the farm," Maxx confirmed.

"So do they have you raising chickens and herding cows or something?" I asked, and tried really hard not to smile at the sound of Maxx's deep, rich laugh.

"Thank God, no! Can you imagine me in shit kickers growing wheat or something? I'm not cut out for that crap." I started to laugh, too, and it felt good.

Too good.

And I realized that was something we hadn't done much of during our short yet intense relationship. We had been together for only a few months, but in some ways it had felt like years. We hadn't had a whole lot of time for laughing and joking and just being two people enjoying each other. We had been consumed by things far darker.

"I don't think I can, Maxx. I'm working really hard to move on.

And this phone call, going to see you, that would be the worst thing for both of us," I said finally, breaking the moment of easy familiarity we had been dangerously close to slipping into.

"The worst thing for me? Or the worst thing for you?" he asked, sounding a little angry but as if he was trying hard not to be.

"For *both* of us. I don't see how seeing me can help you right now. We did nothing but hurt each other. That isn't a place you need to revisit when it seems like you're trying to get yourself together," I said, wishing I didn't have to put voice to that painful truth.

But it needed to be said. Even if stating the obvious hurt just as badly as the first time I had left him. "I can't save you, Maxx. I never could."

"I'm not asking you to *save* me, Aubrey. I'm just asking you to come and see me. To give me *something*—" He cut himself off and there was a brief moment of silence, and in that quiet I regretted ever answering the phone. "I'm sorry. This isn't fair. I don't know what I was thinking. I'll let you go. Forget I called," he murmured.

I snorted in disbelief. Unfortunately for me, forgetting was something I'd never be able to do. Then, because I couldn't stand the thought of Maxx berating himself, I had to say something. "Maxx, it's okay. I understand . . . I'm just not ready . . . I just think—" I was making excuses when I shouldn't. I was trying to justify things that shouldn't need justification.

"No, it's fine. Take care of yourself, Aubrey. And I'm sorry. For everything." His voice broke. "I love you, Aubrey. Always," he whispered, and then I heard the soft click and the line went dead.

I dropped the phone on the ground and covered my face with my hands. I didn't cry, but I couldn't stop shaking. And I felt the loss of him all over again.

chapter nine

maxx

"Is your brother coming today?" Pete asked, and I had to stop myself from groaning out loud. Why did he ask me that every single Sunday, when the answer was always the same? Today was visiting day. My most dreaded day of the week. And the need to flee was there, prickling my insides.

I didn't bother to answer him. I swallowed my annoyed hurt and continued to focus on the notebook in my lap. My hands were coated in oil pastels. Having the time and focus to immerse myself in my art was one of the most positive things to come out of this experience. It had never been a habit I spent a lot of time developing. I wasn't the tortured artist who slaved over a picture to hang on my wall or something. The whole street art thing had happened purely by accident.

When I was young and fucked up, I had been hanging out with a bunch of dudes who thought tagging buildings downtown was a fun use of our time. They had handed me a can of spray paint and had left me to my vandalism. They had been busy writing dumb shit like *Born in East LA* and pathetic versions of gang signs. I painted a dead tree with fire for leaves. It wasn't great by any stretch of the imagination, but it was a hell of a lot cooler than the stuff my so-called friends were spraying on the walls.

We had been chased away by a store owner who threatened to call the cops. The next week we had been walking by and I noticed all of the tagging had been erased—except for my tree. The store owner had never painted over it. In fact, it stayed there for years, until it had finally faded away.

I remember feeling a huge sense of pride in that. Even though, to most people, it would have been vandalism, that shop owner had seen *something* in my crude, amateurish drawing that he had liked. And that guy had made me feel, without ever saying a word to me, like maybe what I had created was worth something. To a fifteen-year-old boy who had recently lost his parents and was struggling with his sudden responsibility of caring for and worrying about a younger brother, that sort of confidence boost was a big deal.

But for some reason, I could never let myself get lost in painting on a canvas or drawing on a piece of paper. I had actually failed art class in high school. My teacher had called me uninspired and lacking focus.

It was the story of my fucking life.

But then enter Gash and the club, and that strange talent for graffiti took hold once again and it allowed me to express myself in a way I had never been able to before. And again, people took notice. Gash had loved the visibility it gave the club and the increase in revenue my little scavenger hunt produced. It had become the one bright spot in that whole ugly, sordid world.

A few gallery owners had even put the word out that they were looking for X. My secret identity. My alter ego. The man who had drawn the women on fire and the hands of God that were strewn about the city. Street art was edgy and dark and oh so hip. And these guys wanted a piece of that culturally relevant pie. I had even called one of them once, just to hear what he had to say.

The guy was with a local gallery. He had tracked me down through the club, and because I was a greedy bastard, I had jumped at the chance to make some serious scratch. He wanted me to bring a sampling of my art. I had thrown together a pathetic mess of crappy canvases that barely represented what I was capable of, high on my own ego and confident that my talent was unparalleled.

I remember taking a handful of pills before hopping into the taxi. I stumbled my way into the gallery, barely aware of what was going on. The guy, Tatum Randall, had been displeased when I had thrown my shitty work down on a table and slurred, "What'll you give me for these?"

I had to give Mr. Randall some credit. He didn't laugh at me or throw my sad ass out on the street. He picked up each canvas and looked at it. I was so fucked up I barely recognized the look of disappointment on his face. And more important, I really didn't care.

"I'm sorry, X, I'm not interested in these," Mr. Randall had said, putting the canvases back on the table.

I had scoffed and pointed to some of the paintings on the wall. "I could shit on a piece of paper and it would look a hell of a lot better than this stuff." I remember having a hard time keeping my eyes open.

Mr. Randall had frowned at me. "Are you all right?"

I waved off his question. "So are you going to pay me or what?"

Mr. Randall had shaken his head. "I contacted you because when I saw your street art, I knew there was something special there. But this—" He indicated the pile of half-assed work I had produced. "This is not something I could promote. And clearly you aren't prepared to take this seriously."

I had tried to sit up straighter, but my bones were like liquid. I remember feeling as though I could sink into the chair. I was having a hard time focusing on Mr. Randall or the fact that I was flushing this perfectly wonderful opportunity straight down the toilet.

Mr. Randall had sighed. "I'll call you a cab."

And right before I left, using Mr. Randall as support because my legs had stopped functioning at some point, the middle-aged gallery owner had looked at me with mild disgust. "If you ever get yourself together, maybe we could have a conversation." He had practically shoved me into the back of the cab.

"But I can't invest in someone who won't invest in themselves. Good luck, X, or whatever your name is." And that had been the last I had heard from Mr. Tatum Randall.

I hadn't thought much at the time about how monumental that rejection was. I was fixated on the drugs. And the club. And being the god of the dark and seedy. But now I cringed as I remembered what an ignorant fool I had been.

After that, my art had returned to being that thing I did to get noticed. It was firmly entrenched in the world of Compulsion.

But then Aubrey came along and I found that my art could mean something else.

It could be *about* something else.

Confining my art to paper had never been something I was particularly good at. It had always looked like shit. And I wasn't really accustomed to creating anything without being stoned. I couldn't remember the last time I had picked up a brush when things weren't fuzzy.

At first it had been a major trigger. The counselors here were big into art therapy and so we were made to spend a lot of time drawing our feelings. I had hated it. It felt wrong.

And every time I had tried, I felt the shadows of withdrawal. I never flipped out. I never lost my head. But I couldn't draw anything.

Until I thought of Aubrey. And then words alone weren't enough to express how I was feeling.

I remembered the time I had taken gallons of paint and drew the broken mirror on the sidewalk out in front of her apartment building. I remembered how pathetic and desperate I had felt. I had needed her to see how much I loved her. How much I needed her. How essential she was to my very existence. I also remembered how fucking high I had been.

But now, being stone cold sober, drawing her released the stuff pent up inside of me. All of the anger and disappointment and longing that I couldn't give voice to. I had been conditioned over my short lifetime to keep it all bottled up and tucked away. Feelings were messy and I didn't have time for all of that.

But then I had met a woman who had made it impossible for me to hold anything back. And now, here at rehab, struggling to make things work, all I wanted to do was draw it. To put out there all the things I couldn't say. For the first time in my life, my art *evolved*. It was about me getting my head together. About focusing on what I was going to do with my life. How I could change for the better.

And I became sort of addicted to my art, like a placeholder for the drugs or something.

I smoothed the shadowed edge of the round cheek I had just drawn. My fingers caressed the lengths of long blond hair on the page. The picture was so accurate I could almost imagine Aubrey was here. In the flesh. It filled me with warmth to draw her. To paint her. To see her in my mind and to let my fingers create her. I could hold her close like this.

Forever.

I continued to smudge the line of Aubrey's jaw I had just put on paper. If I closed my eyes, maybe I could pretend it was her. Delusions were my new best friend.

"Whatcha workin' on?" Pete asked, clearly not getting the hint that I wasn't in the mood for company. I was trying really hard to keep my mind off the fact that I had asked Aubrey to come today and she had said no.

I closed the notebook and tucked it under my pillow.

"Nothing," I remarked, getting to my feet.

"Where are you going? The garden is off-limits; that's where visiting hours are being held today," Pete told me, putting some authority in his voice.

"Okay, thanks for letting me know." I walked past Pete, ignoring his continued attempts at conversation. The common room was empty. Either everyone had visitors, or those who didn't were holed up, depressed, in their rooms. It sucked being one of the few people without anyone to see them. But I refused to feel sorry for myself. I had lived most of my life alone. What else was new?

Unfortunately for me, I had been given a taste of what it felt like to share your life with someone who loved you. And I had gravitated toward it. I had held on to it, crushing it in my hands. And ultimately I had destroyed it.

Now I was left with the memory of what might have been. And that was so much worse than not knowing it at all. I looked at the clock on the wall. It was already 2:00. Only one more hour and I could pretend that visiting day had never happened. At least until next week, when I was reminded once again that no one would be coming to see me.

"Maxx, there you are."

I looked up to find Stacey standing in the doorway.

"You looking for me?" I asked, flipping the channels on the television, already cursing myself for choosing such an obvious place to hide out for the next hour.

"Yes! You have a visitor. She's waiting out in the garden," she said, waving a hand for me to follow her.

I sat there, staring at her like an idiot.

She's waiting.

"What?" I asked, not quite believing her. I couldn't wrap my mind around what she was saying. When I had been admitted to Barton House, I had put only two names on my allowed visitors list.

Aubrey Duncan and Landon Demelo.

That was it.

"Who is it?" I asked, almost scared of the answer I would be given.

"She said her name was Aubrey. We checked your file and she's an allowed visitor. Is that okay? Are you all right with that?" Stacey looked at me with concern.

My heart thudded in my chest and for a moment I thought I might pass out.

Fucking hell, she came. I looked at Stacey, who was watching me closely. I knew she was waiting for me to freak the fuck out.

And she had every right to be worried, because I was feeling mildly hysterical. On the inside, of course.

"Yeah, that's fine," I said, not sure I was telling the truth.

Aubrey had come.

Fuck. Fuck. Fuck.

I followed Stacey down the hall and out to the garden. I squinted in the bright afternoon sunlight and shivered in my thin T-shirt. Damn, I should have grabbed a coat. It was cold out here. And then I forgot about the cold. I forgot about the counselor who still stood beside me analyzing with her squinty eyes. Because there she was.

There was Aubrey.

My eyes drank in the sight of her. My senses were ravenous for her. And the gaping open wound in my heart oozed fresh.

She was looking down at her phone. Her long blond hair fell on either side of her face. I couldn't see her expression, her hair obscuring her. But I could tell by her body language that she was uncomfortable. That maybe she didn't want to be here at all.

I thought about turning around and walking back inside. That maybe as much as I wanted to be, I just wasn't ready for all of this.

The sight of her set off a thousand urges I had been trying hard to suppress. The need for the drugs. The desire to lose myself in the soft waiting oblivion of a handful of pills. Anything to feel numb. But the loudest urge of all was the one that practically begged me to grab her and run far, far away. To forget all of this stupid rehab shit and to bury myself in her and never let go again.

"Are you all right?" Stacey asked, and I felt annoyed by the question. Fuck no, I wasn't all right! I was losing my goddamned mind!

I nodded though and headed across the grass toward the table where the woman I loved sat oblivious to the insanity she had let loose inside me simply by showing up as I had asked her to.

She was still peering down at her phone when I approached the table. I pulled out the chair opposite her and sat down. Finally she looked up and I could see her face for the first time. Her blue eyes widened as she took me in.

I knew what she saw. I had lost a lot of weight. Withdrawals will do that. My face had always been angular, but now my cheekbones were more pronounced. My hair was longer, almost hitting my collar. But at least I had lost the dark shadows that had always ringed my eyes, and the sallow pallor of my skin had disappeared.

"Hey," she said softly, and the knot in my stomach loosened a bit.

"You came," I said, smiling. I glanced down at her hands and saw that they were clenched tightly around her phone as if she would break it. She looked terrified. I wanted to reach out and take her hands but figured that would be pushing things. We weren't together anymore. Aubrey wasn't my girlfriend. I had no right to touch her, no matter how much I wanted to.

"I did. Though I'm not sure I should have," she muttered, looking away. She fidgeted in her seat. Her anxiety was putting me on edge.

"Well, why did you?" I asked her pointedly, wanting to get past this awkward discomfort as quickly as possible.

"Because I needed to see you . . . one last time. You know, to make sure you were all right," she said, rushing through her words as though they would bite her.

One last time . . .

I held my arms out. "Well, look away, Aubrey. Because I'm alive and breathing." I wished I could curb the sarcasm, but her answer bothered me. What had I expected? Her to tell me she couldn't stay away from me? That she had been wrong and wanted to be with me again? Had I really thought this would be our new beginning?

"You look . . . better," Aubrey said, taking in my appearance. I wanted to know what she thought as she looked at me. I wanted to know whether when she saw me, she remembered everything as clearly as I did. I wanted to know if when she looked in my eyes she saw the man she loved or if she even felt that way toward me at all anymore.

"I guess so. I feel . . . better," I responded.

She gnawed on the skin around her thumbnail, not making eye contact. "This place is nice. I always thought they were kind of like hospitals. Not like—"

"Hotels?" I filled in for her.

Aubrey shook her head. "Yeah. It's very Holiday Inn." She chuckled and then cleared her throat as if catching herself doing something she wasn't supposed to.

"So, how's school going?" I asked, trying to think of something to say that was safe. More important, I wanted to see her smile again. I wanted us to find our way back to that laid-back easiness that had let me fall in love with her so fast and so hard.

Aubrey snorted, her eyes narrowing. "Is that really why you

wanted me to come out here? To ask me about school?" I was taken aback by her anger. I had expected it, but I was still surprised by its ferocity.

"No. I just wanted—"

"You want to talk about the weather? Would that make this whole thing less awkward? What the hell are we supposed to talk about? How about the way you fucked up the last few months of my life? Or would you like to tell me how horrible I am for leaving you? Because I can assure you that any guilt trip you lay on isn't nearly as bad as the one I've laid on myself," she hissed, and I had to sit back in my chair. Her words were like bullets and they hit swift and sure.

"I get that we've got a lot to talk about. We don't have a whole lot of time to get into all that," I said calmly. I clenched my teeth and tried to rein in the frustration that I felt bubbling to the surface.

This isn't how I wanted this to go at all.

Aubrey slammed her hands down on the plastic table with enough force to knock the ugly fake flower arrangement on its side. Neither of us moved to catch it as it rolled off the surface and fell to the ground.

"I can't do this with you anymore, Maxx. I tangled myself up in knots over you! You took what I gave you and threw it back in my face. You lied! To my face! Over and over again! But it tore me apart to walk away from you! Yet I did. Because I knew that if I stayed you'd kill us both! But here you are, pulling me right back in! And here I am *letting you*!"

I held my hands up in a placating gesture. "Whoa, Aubrey, hang on a sec." I was thrown off balance by her vehemence. There were a lot of bottled-up issues coming to the surface that I had been in no way prepared to hear.

Waking up in that hospital, alone, had been rough. Rougher in some ways than the withdrawals. But I was here, wasn't I? I was making an effort. Didn't that prove that I had taken her ultimatum seriously?

"I get that you're upset with me. But I wanted you to see me. To see what I was doing here," I said softly, looking around me, noticing that we were making quite a spectacle among the other patients.

Impulsively I reached out and grabbed one of Aubrey's hands and held it tightly. I dug my fingers into her skin as though that would make her listen to me. To hear me. "I wanted you to see that I took your words to heart. That I *am* trying!"

Aubrey's face softened for a moment and I felt her hand slacken beneath mine. Our eyes met and clung to each other and I thought that maybe, just maybe, I was finally getting through to her. But then her mouth set into a firm line and she yanked her hand away. "It takes more than a thirty-day stint in rehab to prove anything, Maxx."

I sighed and ran my hands through my hair. I didn't know what the hell to do. I was so used to being able to talk myself out of anything. Even Aubrey, I was ashamed to admit, had always been easy to manipulate. And although I loved her more than was good for either of us, I had used that skill on her one too many times before.

"That doesn't change *anything*," she hissed, lowering her voice so as to not be overheard. She sighed and covered her face with her hands. She looked tired. Exhausted, really. And I knew I had done that to her.

When I had practically begged her to come and see me I had only really thought about how great it would be for her to see this new, changed man. That then she could let down her guard. I had been angling for my way back in. But looking at her now I knew I didn't have a right to be let back in. At least not yet. I had a lot of proving to do.

I reached out again, unable to help myself, and gently laid my hand on her arm. She tensed, but finally dropped her hands from her face. Her eyes were wet and I hated myself all over again.

"I want you to get better. I really do. I wanted you to stop using. I wanted you to *want* to stop. Not for me. Not for your brother. But for *you.* This is amazing, Maxx. You being here." She waved her hand around her to indicate the facility where I had been begrudgingly living for the last three weeks. "But it's only the first step. You get that, right?"

I pulled my hand away, hating to hear the words of the counselors being echoed from her mouth. "Yeah, I get that," I said sharply, annoyed that we were back to this.

Aubrey grabbed my hand and squeezed before dropping it and pulling away. That momentary physical contact left me buzzing.

"Five minutes, everyone!" Stacey called out to those of us still sitting in the garden.

Crap. We had wasted almost an hour of not really saying anything. There was still so much I needed to tell her. I felt panicked. Scared that this was it. The only chance I had to say how much I loved her and how I was trying to change. For her.

"I finish up here in a week, Aubrey. I'm coming back to school. I'm hoping to finish up my degree if they let me. And then, who knows. Landon's going off to college in the fall and I have to figure out how to help him. But I'm going to do things legit this time. I'm not going to fuck up again," I said quickly, trying to get it all out while I still had a chance.

Aubrey was shaking her head, as if to stop me, but I ignored her.

"I want to know if you'll let me see you. When I'm back. If just maybe you would give me the chance to show you that things will be different."

I didn't know much. I was an ignorant fool in so many goddamned ways. I had always thought I was so freaking smart. But at the end of the day, I didn't really know a thing. I didn't know how to make a relationship work. I didn't know what it took to make a woman like Aubrey happy. I didn't know how to be someone who wasn't messed up and ruined.

But I did know one thing. That I loved this woman in front of me in a way that I would never be able to love anyone else. It was a deep-in-my-bones, drowning-in-it sort of love. It was desperate. It was obliteration. It was total anarchy in my heart. It was mine. It was all that I had.

Aubrey got to her feet, slinging her purse over her shoulder. She didn't answer me. I had laid my soul at her feet and she didn't say a fucking word.

I stood, too, and stared at her, not really believing that this was how our time together was ending. That after three weeks of thinking about nothing else, here we were, going our separate ways like strangers.

"That's it, then?" I asked her almost bitterly. I wanted to freaking cry. I wanted to scream. I wanted to shake Aubrey and demand that she reciprocate my wild, out-of-control feelings.

But then I saw the tears start to slip down her face, and I knew that I wasn't alone in any of this. I reached out to catch them with my finger. I brought the pad of my thumb to my mouth and tasted her salty pain.

"I don't know, Maxx. I just don't know," she said, her broken words piercing my gut.

"Just don't turn me away when I show up at your door. Don't tell me to leave when all I want is to talk. I have to know that when I leave here, I'll have something to come home to. Because I promise you, I won't give up on us. I can't."

I was fighting dirty. It's what I did. But I needed to know there was something for me out there. It was the only way I'd make it through any of this.

"That's not fair. You're not being fair!" she shouted, and then cast an embarrassed look around, realizing how loud she had been.

"This was a mistake. I've got to go. Good luck, Maxx. I mean that. Really," she said, pushing past me and heading toward the side gate that led out to the parking lot.

Then she was gone.

And I was left with nothing.

Again.

chapter ten

aubrey

Idiot!

What in the heck was wrong with me? Why did I continue to give him that sort of power over me? Why couldn't I ever say no to him?

Well, I'd just have to learn to. Because Maxx planned to come back and I needed to prepare myself for how I was going to handle that.

I had already learned how easy it was for me to fall back into that place where Maxx mattered. When I saw his face again I could see how much he wanted me. And I felt it—the thrill. The excitement. The overwhelming desire.

In that moment I had *wanted* him to want me. When I had dressed that day before going to see him, I had taken the time to pick out a skirt that I knew was flattering. I had chosen a shirt he had complimented me on before. I had made sure my hair was perfect and my makeup subtle but pretty. God, what was wrong with me that I was drawn back into the web of his manipulation and emotional games once again?

I had come home angry and determined. It would be all too easy for him to suck me back in.

"You look like you're ready to kick some ass and take some names," Renee commented after I had slammed through the front door and threw my purse onto the couch. I kicked off my shoes and collapsed down beside her. Renee hastily put the letter she had been reading on the coffee table before turning to me.

"I just saw Maxx," I told her, my voice hard.

Renee pulled her legs up underneath her. "Are you serious?"

I nodded. "He called me when we were out at the bar. He asked me to go and see him. I wasn't going to. But then—"

"You just couldn't help yourself," Renee interjected, sounding strangely angry.

I frowned at her response. "Well, not exactly. I just knew that if I didn't I'd drive myself crazy wondering how he was. I figured it was the only way I could put this madness behind me once and for all."

"Did it work?" she asked me.

I shrugged. "I hope so. I don't feel as though I have any other option."

"Is Maxx trying to move on as well?" Renee cocked her head to the side and regarded me.

I let out a breath and leaned my head back, closing my eyes. "I don't think so," I admitted softly.

"So when he gets out and comes back for you, telling you how much he's changed, how things will be different, will you be able to walk away?" Renee asked as she passed me the bag of Hershey's Kisses.

I wasn't able to come up with an appropriate response, so I stuffed my face full of chocolate instead. Renee grabbed her own handful of candy. "It's not so easy, is it?" she stated, giving me a sad sort of smile. I reached down and picked up the paper she had laid on the coffee table.

"What's this?" I asked, smoothing it out.

"My baggage," Renee answered, unwrapping a chocolate and popping it into her mouth.

"From Devon?" I asked, not reading the letter but instead handing it back.

Renee nodded, balling the paper up and throwing it across the room. I grabbed my roommate's hand and got to my feet. "Let's get out of here. Sitting around and feeling sorry for ourselves isn't how we should spend our Sunday. We're better than that."

Renee grinned and squeezed my hand. "Let's go tear some shit up."

We laughed together, knowing that our version of tearing shit up involved a bucket of popcorn and a nauseating chick flick. But it felt good. Better than good. It felt great.

And yet, for all of my strong talk, Maxx was on my mind, and I couldn't get rid of him.

✦

"What is up with you? You look like you're about to have an aneurysm," Brooks observed, tapping my foot with his as we sat on my couch and I pretended to watch the really bad made-for-TV movie on the Syfy channel.

"Wow, you sure know how to sweet-talk a girl," I joked, rolling my eyes.

Brooks dropped a few kernels of popcorn into his mouth and looked at me thoughtfully. "Something's up. What is it?"

I sighed. I had messed up our friendship once by lying to him, and I couldn't afford to lose Brooks again. Especially not now, when I needed my friends' support more than ever.

"It wasn't my mom on the phone that night at the bar . . ." I said, grabbing the bowl of popcorn from his lap and stuffing my face. "It was Maxx," I mumbled through a mouthful of the salty snack.

Brooks's frown deepened and he turned back to the television. "That explains why you lied about it," he muttered.

"Ouch," I said, grimacing.

"Whatever, you know I'm right," Brooks said.

"Well, it's not like he's the best topic of conversation between us, Brooks," I said, turning the TV down so that he would look at me.

"Okay, and that's probably my fault. I can be a bit . . . judgmental when it comes to Mr. I'm-such-a-badass-when-I'm-not-choking-on-my-own-vomit," he quipped, his mouth turning down, letting me know he was trying really hard not to snap at me.

"Brooks, come on. Can't you take off your sarcasm pants for just one freaking minute?"

"Sure, as soon as you stop losing your fucking head over a jackass who isn't worth your time," Brooks fumed, his choice of words shocking the hell out of me.

"I'm not losing my head, Brooks," I replied, completely offended. I thought I was doing pretty darn well, given the situation.

Brooks let out a long, tortured breath and took the remote from my hand and turned off the television.

"That wasn't too cool of me. Here you are, being all honest and stuff, and I'm being a jerk. Go ahead, tell me about it," he said, turning to face me.

I eyed him warily, not sure how truthful I should be. But I figured if our friendship was ever going to recover, I needed to tell him everything.

"Well, he asked me to go and see him at the rehab center where he's been for the past few weeks . . . and I went," I said matter-of-factly.

Brooks closed his mouth and his face went still. "You what?" he demanded.

"I went to see him on Sunday." I threw my hands up in the air in defeat. "It was a mistake and I don't know what the hell I was thinking. I guess I just thought that seeing him would help me shut the door on that part of my life. That I could be assured he was doing okay and then walk away."

"And did you?"

"Did I what?" I asked, confused.

Brooks's lips thinned as he answered. "Shut the door. Walk away."

"Well, I'm here, aren't I?" I said defensively.

Brooks didn't say anything for a really long time, though I could tell there was a lot that he wanted to say but was surprisingly holding his tongue.

"I guess, though I think that explains the staring off into space you've been doing," Brooks said after a while.

"I have not been staring into space," I argued.

Brooks only shook his head.

"So what did Maxxy boy have to say? Did he show off his healing track lines or his new and improved hypodermic needle collection?" Brooks spat out hatefully.

"Wow. What happened to not being judgmental?" I demanded, frowning.

"I just don't want you to forget who he is, Aubrey. Or what he's done. I have no doubt he wanted you to come and see him to prove that he's changed. To show you he's trying. I have no doubt he gave you a song and dance about being a better man and that he wanted another chance. Am I right?" Brooks asked, sounding both tired and bitter.

My mouth popped open, then closed again. I didn't say anything. There was no point. Brooks was right.

Brooks shook his head, looking sad. "For such a smart girl, you really can be so damn blind about stuff." He dropped the TV remote onto the coffee table with a clang.

"I just . . . I needed . . . closure. I needed to know that he was all right. That I could move on without worrying about how he was and what he was doing!"

"Well, now you know, Aubrey. The best thing you could have done was to walk away from Maxx. He would have eventually dragged you down further into that hole with him."

"You're not saying anything I don't already know, Brooks. God! Going to see Maxx was about *me*! I needed it for *my* peace of mind! I had turned my back on my sister and look what happened! I couldn't live with myself if the same thing had happened to Maxx. I could never go on and live my life with that weighing on my mind!"

"Jayme was not your fault, Aubrey! Shit, it was a horrible, horrible thing that had absolutely nothing to do with you!" Brooks grabbed ahold of my shoulders, digging his fingers into my flesh. "And Maxx isn't your fault either! You need to stop blaming yourself for things beyond your control! You couldn't change anything. Not for Jayme and not for Maxx. No matter how much you try to convince yourself that you could."

Brooks could never understand how badly I needed to hear those words in that moment. Brooks cupped my face between his palms, his fingers warm against my wet face. His thumbs ran circles over my skin and I leaned in, needing the touch. Needing to feel the connection even if it wasn't the one I still craved.

"You're a good person with a big heart. I love how you want to take care of everyone. But you can't. Some people can't be saved. And that doesn't mean there's anything wrong with *you*." I leaned in, my nose an inch from his. "Aubrey, you have to let go of this thing you had with Maxx."

"That's what I'm trying to do!" I whispered.

"Okay, but you also have to let go of the guilt. You're putting on a brave face. You're playing the part of the girl who is moving forward. But I can see that you've only been willing to go halfway," Brooks admonished gently.

"You really need to forgive yourself, Aubrey. For Jayme. For what you think happened with Maxx. For all of it. Until you do that, you'll be stuck."

Shit, he was right. He was so, so right.

"Stop trying to save everyone else and worry about saving yourself. Don't you deserve that?"

I should have wanted to pull out of Brooks's hold on my face. But I didn't. I wanted to lean in and drink in the comfort he gave me. I wanted to lose myself in the sensation of someone else. I needed to remember what it felt like to touch someone who *wasn't* Maxx. Otherwise, I was terrified I'd never be able to truly move on.

I pushed myself into Brooks's personal space and he stilled instantly. He held himself rigid and I could feel his breath on my cheeks. Slowly and purposefully I brushed my lips against his and I heard his audible gasp. It had been years since I had kissed him.

But it was familiar. Did I want this kind of familiar?

Yes.

No.

I was horribly confused.

But I pushed myself into it, pressing my lips harder against Brooks's. I kissed him with a heart that was empty but wanting so desperately to feel something again. I tried to open my mouth and invite him in but realized that Brooks wasn't responding. I pulled back slightly and opened my eyes. The eyes that looked back at me were dark. He was angry.

"I'm sorry—" I began, but Brooks cut me off.

"What the hell, Aubrey?" Brooks demanded, getting to his feet and rubbing his hand over his mouth as though to wipe my kiss from his skin.

My cheeks flushed in humiliation. Brooks's rejection ripped a hole straight through me.

"I just thought you wanted to . . ."

"Not like this! Not with you crying and miserable over some other dude!" he practically shouted.

I stood up and reached out to touch him, trying to make this better. But he recoiled instantly. "Brooks, I never meant to—"

"Use me? Try to make yourself feel better?" Brooks spat out.

I felt sick. He was right. That's exactly what I was doing and that wasn't fair. To him or to me. "You're right. That's exactly what I was doing," I said quietly, running my hands over my face in agitation. What was wrong with me?

I knew, on some level, Brooks had feelings for me. And I had counted on those feelings to help me force something on the both of us. I cared about Brooks, but my heart still belonged to someone else, whether I wanted it to or not. You can't give away something that wasn't yours to give in the first place.

Brooks blew out a noisy breath and looked as upset as I had ever seen him. I couldn't believe that I'd screwed up everything between us all over again. Because of Maxx. It was always because of Maxx. I felt like a total idiot.

"I think I should go," Brooks said, grabbing his keys from the coffee table.

"Wait, Brooks, please! Don't hate me!" I pleaded.

Brooks stopped just before reaching the door. "I don't hate you, Aubrey. I could never hate you. I just want more for you than *this,*" he said as he opened the door.

I wasn't sure exactly what *this* was. Maxx? Brooks? My pathetic attempts to use my best friend to feed my ego and make me feel better? Before I could say anything else, Brooks left.

chapter eleven

maxx

I was going home. I couldn't decide if I was glad or freaking the fuck out. Part of me was ready because I had to be. But then I thought about what leaving meant. All the old temptations, all the old impulses, would be there, ready and waiting to pounce. I hoped I was strong enough to resist them this time around. I had spent the last thirty days convincing myself that I needed to stay, and now, here I was, convincing myself that I needed to *leave*.

Escape had always been my vice, and in many ways rehab had been just that. Clean and sober escapism. Now it was time to man up and face the music of what lay out there . . . in that place I couldn't avoid forever. I folded my shirts into neat piles and then put them into the duffel bag I had brought with me. Dominic sat on his bed, looking morose.

"I'm really gonna miss you, man," he said, his head hanging low. I had gone out of my way to not make any connections, knowing that wasn't what I was there for. But my roommate had latched on to me anyway. He wasn't a bad person. He was just more than a little oblivious.

"You'll be all right. You don't have much longer in here yourself. You'll be out in no time," I said, trying to be nice, even if I really wanted to tell him to stop being such a pussy and suck it up. But then I looked at Dominic. Really looked at him. He was that kid in high school who hung on the fringes, wanting to be liked and taking the teasing even though he knew people were laughing *at* him and not *with* him. This was a person who didn't need anyone else giving him shit. Definitely not me, who wasn't in a position to look down on anyone.

"I don't know. My parents want me to do the full ninety days. They say I'm not ready to leave. That I'll relapse," he said miserably.

I rolled my eyes, wanting to smack the shit out of his ridiculous parents. They hadn't a clue what real addiction looked like. If Dominic was addicted to anything, it was Ding Dongs and Doritos. The only thing his drug of choice had done was to make him gain about fifty pounds and fanatically watch reruns of *South Park* for hours at a time.

I zipped up my duffel bag and threw it over my shoulder, determined that I would never make the Barton House my home again. "Look, Dominic, you seem like a decent guy. Don't let *anyone* decide your future for you. You're in charge of what happens, no one else. If you think you need to be here, then stay. If you don't, then check yourself out. And good luck. I mean that."

Dominic gave me a watery smile. "Thanks, Maxx. That means a lot coming from you." He sniffled.

I turned and headed down the hallway, my steps lighter than they had been in a long time.

I stopped outside a closed door and knocked loudly and with purpose. I squared my shoulders and stood up straight. I was ready for this.

I had to be.

"Come in," a voice called from the other side. I pushed open the door and walked into Stacey's cramped office. It smelled like blueberry muffins and was filled with enough frilly shit that made me wonder whether she farted rainbows.

"Maxx. Come in, have a seat." I did as I was told, choosing the only option available, a chair covered in bright orange upholstery. "I see that you're all packed and ready to go," she commented, indicating the duffel at my feet.

I kicked it with my shoe and nodded. "Yep. Just here to get the official sign-off and then I'm out of your hair."

Stacey typed something on her computer, and then papers started coming out of the printer. She looked up at me as she waited for the last of the paperwork to finish. "You're sure you're not interested in the full ninety-day program? Thirty days, while a great start, isn't nearly as effective as the more intensive in-patient treatment plan," she said, giving me the same shit she had been forcing down my throat for the last week.

I knew that she and the other counselors at Barton House thought I was making a huge mistake by not staying on for the longer program. And there was that small part of me that agreed with them. The whispering in my ear that told me that I wasn't ready. The self-doubt was almost crippling. But the truth was that the longer I stayed, the harder it would be for me to fix what I had messed up *out there.*

There was one thing I knew for sure, deep in my bones: I was going to take my newfound sobriety seriously.

"I'll call on Monday and set up an intake at the clinic downtown. I'll stick to the outpatient treatment plan," I promised, taking the pile of paperwork Stacey handed me.

She nodded, handing me a pen. "That's good to hear, Maxx, though you understand that coping with addiction triggers is much harder once you're back in your own environment. You have to make sure you have strategies in place to deal with them.

It'll be tough. There will be days you will want to use. So it's extremely important that you keep those numbers on that last sheet handy, if you ever feel like you're about to turn to drugs."

I flipped to the last page of the pile she had given me. There was a list of numbers, including the statewide hotline and a crisis number at the rehab facility. Christ, she acted as though my failing was inevitable. Which sort of pissed me off. Because there was that voice again telling me that it *was* inevitable.

I'll be there waiting for you. You can't stay away from me forever.

I clenched my fists and worked on breathing through the sudden paralyzing apprehension. Maybe I should stay. Maybe I couldn't do this.

I can do this! For Aubrey. For Landon. For myself.

I folded the paper and tucked it into my pocket and finished scribbling my signature on the required forms. When I was done, I handed them back to Stacey with what I hoped was a confident smile. "Thanks for everything," I said, picking up my bag and getting to my feet.

"Don't be afraid to admit you can't handle things, Maxx. You can't control addiction. Addiction controls you. The second you forget that, you've lost," she said ominously, and I felt myself bristle defensively. But I didn't bite her head off. Because her words were ones I had thought a thousand times already.

Stacey gave me a wan smile and shook her head. "I really hope we don't see you again, Maxx."

I chuckled. "Well, thanks," I replied blandly.

Stacey patted my back. "If we don't see you again, then that means you're doing all right. I really hope you succeed, Maxx."

"Thanks," I said again, wanting to get the hell out of there as fast as my legs could carry me.

Stacey walked me toward the front door. Hal, the security detail on duty, handed me a bag with my cell phone and a set of keys, the things they had confiscated when I had checked myself in.

"Take care, Maxx," Stacey said, holding the door open for me.

"You, too," I replied, actually meaning it. I walked down the front steps and out into the driveway, where a cab waited to take me back to the real world. I slid into the backseat of the cab and gave the driver my address. He grunted in acknowledgment, and then we were driving away from Barton House and I refused to look back as we left.

I was ready to put that part of my life behind me.

✦

I turned on my cell phone and it started to ding loudly in my hands. My screen lit up with a hundred texts and missed calls. Most of them from Marco and Gash.

Shit.

That was one piece of my world I wasn't eager to have to deal with. Because I couldn't go back there. That was obvious. It would be too easy to fall back into everything I had vowed to stay away from.

I was five minutes out of rehab and I was already hit with the strong urge to go back. Because fuck if Stacey wasn't right. It *was* harder out here. Inside you could pretend these things didn't exist. It made it easier to ignore the cravings. The desire to lose yourself all over again.

I erased every single text message without reading them. It felt good to do that. I thought about calling Landon, letting him know I was out of rehab. Maybe try to bridge that gap, but I didn't think a phone call would erase the weeks of bad blood that had built up between us. And truthfully, I didn't have it in me to be rejected all over again.

The cab pulled up in front of my apartment building. I gave him my last ten-dollar bill and got out, duffel bag in hand, and walked up the narrow steps to the place where I lived but had never really been a home.

I dreaded going inside, knowing it was probably a mess. I had been in a rush when I got out of the hospital. I had come home, grabbed some clothes, and left, checking into rehab before I lost the nerve. I unlocked the door and was hit by the smell of lemons.

Lemons?

I turned on the light and looked around in shock. I had never seen my apartment so clean. The floors had been swept and the furniture dusted. All of the clothes I remembered being strewn across the floor were gone and there were even pillows on my couch. I didn't even realize I *had* pillows.

I dropped my bag and walked into my kitchen, where the shock continued. The dishes had been washed and put away. There were dishrags folded and hung on the hook by the stove. The cabinets had been scrubbed and the refrigerator gleamed white. Further inspection revealed that the rest of the apartment was the same. The bathroom was spotless, the tub had been cleaned, and the mold that had been a permanent fixture in the corners was gone. I could eat off the floor, it was so damn clean.

Only two people had a key to my apartment, and I was pretty sure my landlord wouldn't have bothered to do all this. He gave new meaning to the term *slumlord*. No, this was Aubrey. She was the only person who would think to come here and do this.

I walked into my bedroom and knew instantly that I was right. All of my clothes had been washed and sat in the basket I didn't even know that I owned. My sheets had been changed and the covers pulled up. And in the middle of the bed I could see the outline of an impression where someone had lain. I ran my hand along the concaved pillow, indented where her head had been. Aubrey had come into my apartment and cleaned it. Then she had lain down on my bed.

I kicked off my shoes and slowly lowered myself down on the

exact spot where she had been. I pulled the pillow to my face and thought I could smell her there. I didn't know when she had done this. It could have been weeks ago. Or it could have been yesterday. I wasn't exactly sure what it all meant except that she had come into my apartment and made it a home.

It was no secret that I wasn't much of a cleaner. And I was also aware of Aubrey's OCD when it came to neatness. The knowledge that she had thought about me at some point to come in and do this gave me a hope I hadn't felt in a while. As I lay on clean sheets and looked around my spotless bedroom, things suddenly didn't appear so bleak.

I must have dozed off, because I woke up sometime later. The sky had turned dark and the only light came from the soft glow of the clock on my dresser. Hit by a desire that had become very familiar over the last few weeks, I jumped up and opened my closet, rooting around inside until I located a large container of sidewalk chalk. I didn't bother trying to find my paints, knowing that I had used up the last of them before I had gone into rehab.

I looked for my car keys, finding them in the same spot I had left them. Driving my car after so long felt a bit like hanging out with an old friend. It was a piece of shit, but it was *my* piece of shit and I had a crazy love for the clunking of the engine and the squealing of the brakes, even if these meant that it needed some serious maintenance.

I drove through town until I parked down the street from a particular brick building I knew all too well, though I had been inside only once. I made sure to position my car behind a tree so I wasn't immediately visible. It wasn't that late, but I noticed that the lights in the apartment on the third floor were out.

Feeling brave, I grabbed the chalk and walked down the street and stopped in front of the steps that led inside. Dropping to my knees, I dumped out the chalk and grabbed the color I needed and started making long, harsh strokes. It was hard to see, not the best environment to draw. But I didn't need to see what I was doing. My hands didn't need light to know what they were creating.

I didn't know how long I was out there. It could have been hours or it could have been only minutes. People walked by, some stopping to watch me, others asking what I was doing. I ignored them.

When I was finished, I sat back on my haunches and squinted in the darkness at the final product. It was hard to see, but what I could make out, I was pleased with. My knees ached from kneeling on the hard concrete; my hands were covered in chalk dust. It was caked under my nails. My jeans were streaked with it.

I gathered the chalk that I had left and put it back into the container. It wasn't my normal medium, but I had to admit that it was easier to work with. I just hoped it didn't rain before morning. I took one final look up at the darkened apartment and wondered if she would understand what I was trying to say.

Who was I kidding? She had always understood me better than I understood myself.

The picture wasn't much. But in this crazy, fucked-up world I found myself in, it was the only way I could get her to see *me.* And right now, that was something.

chapter twelve

aubrey

"We need a girls' night," Renee declared, walking into my room. I looked up from the book I had been reading, but not really absorbing.

"A girls' night?" I asked.

I noted the almost frenetic energy Renee exuded and wondered what was up. She was in a good mood, but it was a crazy sort of good mood that I hadn't seen in a long time. It was the kind of mood that used to result in Renee getting loaded and dancing on tabletops.

"Yes. You. Me. Drinks. Eating. Laughing. I think we could both use it," she commented, fingering the row of sticky notes in varying colors I had arranged on my desk.

"Okay, as long as you stop touching my stuff," I said, shoving my textbook back into my bag and swinging my legs off the side of my bed.

"We can call Brooks if you want, see if he's up to hanging out," Renee suggested. I raised my eyebrows.

"Wouldn't that defeat the purpose of a girls' night?"

"Yeah, well, I didn't know if you'd like an excuse to mend fences. What better way than with pizza and beer?" Renee said.

I had made every attempt to make things up to Brooks after being a total asshole and kissing him for all the wrong reasons. Like the good guy that he was, he hadn't held it against me, but I still felt a tension between us. We continued to exist in this complicated ebb and flow of discomfort and I didn't really know what to do about it.

"He acts like a girl, anyway. With all the feelings and sensitivity and stuff." Renee chuckled and I snorted.

"Yeah, I'll text him."

Hey, heading out for food and drinks. Do you want to come?

Only a few minutes passed before my phone chirped in my hand.

Sure. Time and place?

"He's game," I said, smiling.

"I told you he wouldn't stay miffed with you. It's impossible for Brooks Hamlin to stay away from Aubrey Duncan."

I threw a pencil at my roommate. "Go and let me get ready," I told her.

Renee laughed in that slightly forced way of hers. "Well, hurry up, I'm hungry."

✦

I laughed so hard I thought beer would shoot out of my nose. Brooks and Renee were trying their hand at impersonations, and Renee's Pee-wee Herman was scarily accurate.

"This is disturbing on so many levels," I said, once I was able to breathe and Renee had stopped to eat a spicy wing. She waved her hand and bowed slightly.

"I'm a woman of many talents," she preened. Brooks balled up his napkin and tossed it at her, where it bounced off her shoulder and onto the floor.

"You've been hiding that one, Renee Alston. You're a sneaky, sneaky girl," he joked.

We had opted to get pizza and wings at a place not far from campus. By the time we got ready and out the door, it was already almost nine. The place was packed by the time we arrived and we were lucky to find a tiny table near the back.

Brooks had been slightly standoffish at first, but once he had a few beverages in his system he had relaxed considerably. Renee and I shared a pitcher of beer, and after an hour we were all laughing and enjoying ourselves.

"I've gotta pee," Renee said after polishing off the last of her pizza. She hopped down off the stool, a little wobbly on her feet.

"Need help?" I chuckled.

She narrowed her eyes and pursed her lips. "I'm fine," she said, and headed toward the bathroom.

Brooks's easy smile faded slightly as we were left alone in our awkwardness.

"Brooks—" I began.

"Aubrey—" he said at the same time.

We both stopped and laughed a little nervously.

"This is weird, isn't it," he stated rather than asked.

"Maybe just a little," I agreed, sipping on my beer.

"I'm still kind of pissed at you," he grumbled, wiping up a puddle of beer that had spilled from the pitcher.

"I'm picking up on that," I said tightly.

Brooks looked at me finally and what I saw wasn't anger. It was hurt. And that made me feel ten times worse.

"But I hate staying mad at you. It doesn't feel right. Just promise me something," he said firmly.

"Anything," I promised.

He dropped his eyes to the slice of pizza on his plate. "Next time you kiss me, mean it."

I swallowed my surprise, not sure what I should say. "Okay," I finally said after a beat, giving him a small smile. His lips quirked upward in response.

"What'd I miss?" Renee asked, appearing beside me.

"Not much. Just listening to the frat guys at the next table talk about the waitress's boob job," I replied blandly.

I looked around the crowded bar and saw a familiar face looking in our direction.

"Hey, Renee, isn't that Iain?" I asked, nodding my head toward the bar. Renee's jaw tightened and her shoulders went rigid.

"Probably," she said quickly.

Brooks had turned in his seat and was chatting with a group of people at the table behind him. I leaned in close to Renee.

"Are you going to go say hi?" I asked. Iain, who was with a few other guys, was looking rather pointedly toward our table.

"I don't think so," she said, downing the rest of her beer. She seemed uncomfortable.

"I thought things were going well with you two. Did something happen?" I asked, bewildered by her attitude.

"Yeah, I happened," Renee muttered, lifting the pitcher and pouring the rest of the beer into her mug.

"Does this have to do with Devon?" I asked. Renee stiffened instantly. My suspicions about Renee's crazy mood this evening were confirmed. Something was up. I could tell.

"Why would it have anything to do with Devon?" she demanded, sounding defensive.

This was not the place to interrogate her. I looked over at Iain again, but he had turned back to his friends. And I felt a little sad for him. And for Renee.

I lifted my glass. "Tonight is about fun and forgetting. Fuck the drama!"

Renee's shoulders relaxed and she lifted her glass in return. "Fuck the drama!" she yelled back, giggling when people around us looked at her.

"What are we toasting to?" Brooks asked, giving us his attention again.

"To living a drama-free life," I explained.

Brooks lifted his mug and nodded his head. "Now, that's something I can toast to." He smiled at me and I smiled back.

"Absolutely," I agreed.

✦

We ended up staying at the bar until it closed at 1:00 a.m. I drank just enough to feel good without losing control. Brooks remained relatively sober and chose to head back with his friends to the frat house instead of going home.

"You ready to get out of here?" Renee asked, coming out of the bar.

"Yep. I'll talk to you on Monday, Brooks," I said, looping my arm through Renee's. He lifted his hand in a wave as we headed down the street in the direction of our apartment building.

"Tonight was good. Thanks for making me go out," I said, reaching for the bottle of water in her hand and taking a drink.

Renee squeezed my arm. "I needed it as much as you did."

I hadn't thought about Maxx once. I had, for the first time in a long time, been able to enjoy myself, stress free.

"What the hell?" Renee asked, coming to a stop. We were out in front of our apartment building. The street was quiet and empty.

"What is it?" I asked, wondering why she had stopped.

Renee pointed to the pavement at her feet. "Look."

I looked down at the sidewalk. I was surrounded by a swirling, vibrant pattern of colors. A pair of giant hands seemed to be reaching up from the ground. A purposeful, violent punch to the gut. The fingers seemed to be grasping for something that I couldn't see. I knelt down on my haunches and traced my fingertips along the curves and bends.

"It's beautiful," Renee said from behind me, taking a step back to get a better look. I could see that the entire thing had been done in chalk this time, not paint. I rubbed the edge of a complicated geometrical pattern with my thumb, strangely satisfied to see it smudging beneath my finger.

"Unbelievable," I muttered, standing back up and feeling my anger ignite as I took in the very obvious statement laid out before me.

"It *is* unbelievable. I've never seen anything quite like it," Renee exclaimed. I had never told her about Maxx's art. For some reason it hadn't come up. It was another one of those mysteries I had kept to myself. But looking down at this intricate drawing, I knew that Maxx was back. He was home. And he was making good on his promise to not give up. Standing there, coming down from the high of a good night with friends, I didn't quite know what I was supposed to feel.

Without realizing exactly what I was doing, I unscrewed the top of the bottle of water in my hand and poured it out over the drawing, watching as it splashed and spread across the drawing, erasing it, ruining it.

"What the hell, Aubrey?" Renee screeched, jumping backward as water splashed her jeans. I didn't say a word as I watched the liquid destroy Maxx's visual pronouncement of his feelings.

"Why did you do that?" Renee asked, following me as I walked into our building.

"Because it didn't need to be there," I said, knowing I hadn't really explained anything.

"Stop dodging, Aubrey. What's up?" she asked.

I felt dangerously close to screaming. After such a wonderful night, having it end like this infuriated me. "It's Maxx. That was him," I told her.

"Maxx? What are you talking about?"

"That's his artwork. He must have done it while we were out.

Which also means he's out of rehab." I let myself into our apartment and turned on the light. I kicked off my shoes and collapsed on the couch, draping my arm over my eyes.

"Is he X, then? The one who used to do the graffiti for the club?" Renee said, the pieces obviously falling into place.

"Yep, that's him," I replied shortly, my arm dropping beside me. I was exhausted. The late hour and Maxx's sudden reemergence back in my life had me wanting to crawl into bed.

"Why didn't you ever tell me that? I mean, wow. He's kind of a big deal," she said, sitting down beside me.

"Yeah, I know. But who the hell cares that his talent is off the charts? It doesn't change the fact that he can't have any place in my life anymore. No matter how many pretty paintings he leaves outside my front door," I stated emphatically, though my words rang somewhat false and I wondered who I was trying to convince. Renee or myself.

"But from that painting I'm guessing he doesn't plan on going away anytime soon."

"I guess not," I agreed.

"And how do you feel about that?" she asked, and I couldn't help but laugh.

"Isn't that my line?" I snorted.

Renee chuckled. "I've seriously been hanging out with you entirely too long," she said.

I sobered and sighed. "I'm not sure how I feel, Renee."

My friend pressed in close and put her arm around me. I rested my head on her shoulder and closed my eyes. "It'll be all right," Renee said, and I wondered if she was speaking for me or for herself.

"I'll be all right," I parroted her, trying to believe it.

chapter thirteen

aubrey

"Hey, ladies!"

I glanced over my shoulder to see Brooks jogging toward Renee and me as we walked across campus.

I hadn't slept well the last two nights. The dreams that had all but disappeared in the last two weeks were back with a vengeance. While I couldn't remember the exact nature of my nightmares, all I knew was that I woke up soaked in sweat and feeling a knot of dread in my stomach so tight I felt sick.

When Renee and I left home this morning, I refused to look at the remnants of the chalk drawing that still marred the sidewalk. And I refused to think about the possibility of seeing Maxx again now that he was out of rehab.

Nope. Wasn't thinking about it at *all.*

"What's up?" Brooks asked, a little out of breath once he slowed down to walk by my side.

"Nothing," I said at the same time that Renee responded, "Maxx." I shot Renee the look of death. She widened her eyes innocently and mouthed, "Sorry."

Brooks's jaw clenched marginally, but then he smiled.

"Well, let's go get a doughnut before class. That'll put you in a better mood." Brooks began to steer me toward the small coffee shop.

"I'm heading to the library. You want to meet up for lunch?" Renee asked.

"Uh, I think I'll just head back home to eat," I said, knowing that what I was doing was running away and hiding.

Because after the unexpected artwork outside my door, I wasn't comfortable with the possibility of seeing the artist.

Renee gave me a look but didn't comment. When she left, Brooks and I continued on to the coffee shop. The place was heaving by the time we got there, full of students getting their dose of caffeine before class. We got in line and waited.

"I have a study group tonight; do you want me to come over afterward?" Brooks asked. I nodded absently, not really hearing him.

"Sure, sounds great," I said, giving Brooks my attention and pushing away any twinges of misgiving brought on by too little sleep, not enough coffee, and a particular drawing in chalk gracing the gray pavement outside of my apartment.

"I'll bring the new Nicolas Cage movie—it looks awesome," Brooks continued, and I groaned playfully.

"Your Cage obsession is becoming concerning," I quipped.

"No more concerning than any of yours," he lobbed back. I smiled wanly at the barb, feeling its sting even if it hadn't been calculated to hurt.

We approached the cashier, who knew us by name and began to punch in our orders before we could give them. Brooks and I had been coming most mornings for the past three years.

After we got our orders, Brooks and I left and stood on the path for a few minutes before we headed in opposite directions.

"There's a party this weekend at Sigma Kappa. I thought you

might want to go," Brooks ventured, sipping on his coffee. I made a face. Brooks wasn't in a fraternity, but he was friends with several of the brothers at the Sigma Kappa house.

I snorted. Brooks should know better.

"Why would you even ask that?" I gaped.

"Because I saw how much you ended up enjoying yourself this past weekend. Admit it, you had fun," Brooks said, poking me in the side and making me squirm.

"Yeah, I guess," I muttered, not needing to add that my perfectly enjoyable evening had been shot to shit once I got home. No sense in being Debbie Downer.

"So you see, mingling with society isn't a *bad* thing. And maybe if you're not sitting around your apartment all the damn time, you'll stop moping about someone you shouldn't be moping about."

I drew myself upright. "I am *not* moping!" I stated firmly.

"But you can't deny that you're a bit antisocial," he countered.

"And you can't deny that you're a bit of a dickhead," I threw back.

Brooks laughed and reached out, pulling me into his chest, wrapping his arms around me. "You're the most awesome chick I know, Aubrey," he said with genuine affection.

I felt my cheeks heat up and moved out of the shelter of his arms, remembering how easily I had used him to fill the gaping hole in my chest. I couldn't use Brooks as a fill-in. It wasn't fair. "So does that mean I'm off the hook, then?" I asked, my mouth quirking up into a smile.

"Come on, Aubrey. Pretty please with a beer keg on top?" He folded his hands together as he begged.

I laughed. I couldn't help it.

"Ask me next week when I'm not feeling so *mopey,*" I joked, sticking my tongue out.

Brooks rolled his eyes good-naturedly. "Fine, your loss. But I won't give up," he warned, and I felt a prickle of apprehension.

Not because of Brooks's words per se, but because of similar ones spoken by someone else entirely.

"I have to get to class. I'll see you later," I said.

"I'll see you this evening," Brooks called out as he walked toward the library.

I started down the pathway toward the psychology building, when I felt someone come up close behind me.

Students were everywhere, but this particular presence had me feeling nervous.

And with good reason, apparently.

"Aubrey."

My name, spoken in that familiar way, like a mixture of a curse and a prayer, made me feel uncomfortably weak in the knees.

Should I make a run for it?

It was too late. I was already stopping and turning around before I could think better of it.

"Maxx. You're here," I said blandly, as if I weren't torn in two at the sight of him.

It had only been a little over a week since I had gone to the rehab facility, but somehow seeing him here, on campus, was so much harder. It felt wrong and familiar at the same time.

Maxx, the student, had always felt like such a contrast to the Maxx I had met in the support group and later the Maxx I knew at the club. He had been a man with many lives who lived in many different worlds. It had taken me a long time to reconcile myself to the person he was in each and how they all coexisted inside of the same body.

I stared at this Maxx and wondered which one he was. The look in his eyes reminded me of *my* Maxx. The man who loved me. But there was a tired vacancy that was reminiscent of that *other* Maxx. The one who had needed his drugs more than he had ever needed me.

Maxx rubbed his finger along the bridge of his nose and gave me a shy smile that was completely out of character. "Yeah, well, I have a meeting with my adviser. I had to withdraw from classes, you know, when I went into rehab. Now I'm hoping to sort out some summer-school classes and see how far behind I really am. I have a feeling I'm screwed no matter what I do," he said matter-of-factly, without a hint of self-pity.

"That sucks, I'm sorry," I replied lamely, not really knowing what I was supposed to say. It felt weird having random small talk with him like this.

Maxx kicked at a piece of gravel, and the surprisingly juvenile action tugged at my hardened heart. "Well, I only have myself to blame," he said, putting his hands into the pocket of his hoodie.

This time I didn't respond. It wasn't the time or place to have the conversation that statement warranted.

I nodded my head toward his jeans, which still showed traces of colored chalk at the knees.

"You've been busy," I said, sounding irritated.

Maxx looked almost embarrassed.

"Yeah, well, when the muse strikes and all that," he muttered, not meeting my eyes.

"And the muse struck outside my apartment building?" I questioned.

"It always brings me back to you, I guess," he said softly, and my heart thumped wildly and threatened to explode out of my chest.

"*You pierce my soul. I am half agony, half hope*," Maxx murmured, almost under his breath.

Christ, Maxx was quoting Jane freaking Austen. I had to get out of there, and fast.

I cleared my throat and pulled my messenger bag farther onto my shoulder.

"I'd better get going," I said, trying to sidestep him.

He reached out, his hand catching mine, his fingers loosely grasping. I startled at the contact. It was such an innocent touch, but I felt it in my bones.

"I told you last week that when I got out I hoped you wouldn't shut the door in my face if I showed up. That drawing was my way of asking you if you would. If it was okay if I ended up there."

My hand shook a bit as I pulled away from his hold.

"And I think it's too soon to tell, Maxx. You need to focus on you. Not on me," I told him sharply.

"What if I said there was no me without you?" he asked, chewing on his lip. An innocent movement that spoke volumes about his lack of confidence. I swallowed hard and clenched my hands into fists so I wouldn't throw my arms around him. Or smack him in the face. The jury was still out.

"Then I'd tell you that it was time you figured out who you are on your own. That you can't base your future on something that won't happen. Because you and me, Maxx, we're over. We have been for a while now." I knew I didn't sound as convincing as I wanted to. Damn it!

Maxx shook his head. "You don't mean that. I won't let you mean that."

"You won't let me?" I scoffed. "I don't think you have much of a choice in the matter."

"We always have a choice, Aubrey. And this time, mine is you. I know you need me to prove to you that things will be different. That *I'm* different. I also know it'll take time. I'm going to work on being patient. And even though every fiber of my body wants to drag you back to my apartment where I can spend the entire day showing you exactly how much I love you, I'll wait. Until you're ready." Maxx's eyes heated and burned into mine. He reached out and softly stroked his finger along the length of my face, and I flinched. He dropped his hand instantly.

"I won't give up on us, Aubrey. I can't," he said with a promise.

That's what I'm worried about, I thought, but didn't say out loud.

"I've got to go," I said again, needing to leave. Needing to flee.

Maxx didn't say another word, but I knew without having to look that he watched me as I hurried down the path toward my class and away from him.

chapter fourteen

maxx

I wasn't lying when I told Aubrey that I was screwed. Because I was royally and truly fucked. Before I had gone into rehab I had been on the cusp of flunking out of LU. My adviser, the pretentious prick extraordinaire Dr. Ramsay, had been all too eager to let me know how much I had messed up.

It seemed that most of my financial aid was contingent on my GPA, and with my previous grades and my ultimate withdrawal from my classes for the semester, the university had pulled the scholarships and grants I depended on to pay for school. Without them, I couldn't afford to stay on at Longwood University.

"You can make an appointment with the financial aid office and find out if you are eligible for any other types of assistance. But, Maxx, given your academic record, you will be hard-pressed to find much out there to help you. I warned you months ago that you were perilously close to losing your financial aid. It's a shame you didn't take my warnings seriously," Dr. Ramsay said, and I wanted to punch that self-satisfied smirk right off his face.

The old Maxx would have knocked some shit off his desk and

threatened to shove his stapler up his ass, then gone straight back to his apartment to get as fucked up as humanly possible. I started to pick at my jeans, trying to distract myself from the almost overwhelming desire to get loaded. Did I still have any pills left in the apartment? I was pretty sure I had an *in case of emergencies* stash somewhere. Where the hell would I have put them?

I found myself sitting there, thinking about all the places I could have left some drugs. In the back of my closet? Nah, I'd cleared that out months ago. In the bottom of my top drawer? Maybe. I tended to lose a lot of stuff among my socks. Under my bed? In the couch cushions? In the medicine cabinet?

I barely heard Dr. Ramsay when he said my name. "Mr. Demelo, did you hear me?"

"Yeah, I get the picture. My days at Longwood University are officially over. You've made that crystal fucking clear," I said, getting to my feet.

Dr. Ramsay looked taken aback by my venom. "That's not at all what I said, Maxx. You could still have options."

"Look, Dr. Ramsay, I know I messed up. I own that. I accept that I wasted this opportunity. Now I just have to figure out what the hell I'm going to do with my life."

"Mr. Demelo, I understand you're upset. But let me call over to the financial aid office, see if I can get you an appointment this afternoon," he said, picking up his phone. I was surprised he was making the effort, but he needn't bother. One thing was obvious. I had never been cut out for college, no matter how much I had hoped that being at Longwood would lead me to something better.

I had been playing the role of student to fulfill some crackpot promise I felt that I owed my dead parents. I had thought by getting a degree I could prove that I could do something right and that Landon wasn't completely misguided in his hero worship. But was I ready to give up on a dream that had never been mine to begin with? Could I let go of that last shred of the Maxx I had been trying so hard to be?

Even though I was angry and wanted nothing more than to tell Dr. Ramsay and Longwood University where to shove it, I swallowed my pride and nodded. “Sure, that would be great,” I said.

Dr. Ramsay lifted the phone to his ear and spoke to someone on the other end. After a few moments he hung up and wrote something down on a sticky note and passed it to me: *Leah Fletcher @ 2:30.*

“They may be able to help, but the rest will be on you. You’ve got to come back next semester ready to work. Otherwise all of this will have been a waste of both of our time,” Dr. Ramsay said, pursing his lips.

“Well, I wouldn’t want to be a waste of anyone’s time,” I muttered, stuffing the slip of paper into my pocket.

✦

I had a few hours until my meeting at the financial aid office and I didn’t want to go back to the apartment. I knew that being alone right now was the worst thing I could do. In rehab I was always surrounded by people, whether I wanted to be or not. Now I realized that had kept me from thinking too much about the very thing that had put me there in the first place.

The lull was the most dangerous time for me. Because when I was alone, I would think. Then I’d want to stop thinking. Stop hurting. And the only way I knew to do that was to use. To take so many pills that my mind would go blank and my heart would go numb.

God, I missed it. I missed the perfect moment when the drugs hit my system and I stopped feeling altogether. Because feeling meant bleeding. And I was almost bled dry. So I headed to the library and figured I’d use the time to get on the computer and start looking for a job.

I had a mountain of bills stacked on the counter, unopened. I still had some money, but it wouldn't last long. It seemed my drug-dealing lifestyle wasn't profitable enough to pay my bills and support my habit while saving for that rainy day. I was damn close to being completely broke.

The library was busy and the low buzz of conversation was exactly what I needed. I found an available computer and sat down. After fumbling around for my wallet, I found my student ID card and typed in the seven-digit number by my name.

I browsed local newspapers for job listings online. After a few minutes it became obvious that my options were severely limited. I didn't possess much in the way of a skill set, though I wondered if my drug-dealing past could be construed as "marketing and sales." I snickered to myself as I thought about how I'd explain that during an interview.

The more I clicked through Web sites, the more frustrated I became. Unless I wanted to spend my days slinging fast food, I was out of luck. I ran my hands through my hair in frustration. My phone vibrated in my pocket, and I pulled it out, seeing another text message from Marco. I was surprised he hadn't come pounding on my door. But I had a feeling he had already done that. And not finding me, he had resorted to phone stalking.

I didn't know how long I could get away with avoiding him. Marco was my oldest friend and my link to that world I was trying to leave behind. And I knew that if I called him back, the temptation to return to my old job would be too hard to resist. So I erased the text without reading it.

"Maxx! Hey!" I glanced up at a pretty girl with long black hair who looked vaguely familiar. She was smiling at me like we definitely knew each other. And she knew my name, so our having some sort of connection was obvious.

I wondered absently if we had fucked. I sure as hell hoped not. The last thing I needed was a stage-ten clinger.

"Hey," I said noncommittally.

The girl pulled up a chair and sat down beside me, ignoring the annoyed look from the guy who sat at the computer beside me as she squished herself into the small space. "Where the hell have you been? Group has been such a snooze without you there!" she exclaimed, and it dawned on me that she must be in the addictions support group on campus.

I looked at the girl again and tried to remember her name, but it just wasn't coming to me. She must have sensed my lack of recognition, because her face fell a bit. "It's Lisa. Remember? I sat beside you every week."

"Oh, yeah, Lisa. Hey, how've you been?" I asked, not really caring.

"Not so good. Twyla got busted last week for having a bottle of Oxi in her room. Her parents pulled her out of school," Lisa said, and I tried to remember who Twyla was.

"Oh, well, that sucks," I said, turning my attention back to the computer screen as I scanned the want ads.

"Yeah, it really does, now I don't have a roommate. So anyway, where have you been? Are you not coming to group anymore?" she asked, and I was three seconds away from telling her to take a hike.

"Nope," I answered shortly, grabbing a pen from the cup on the desk and writing down a few numbers of jobs that could have potential.

"I understand, it's so boring. Kristie has a new guy in there helping out now that Aubrey is gone. And he sucks even worse than she did."

Her flippant comment caught my attention. "Wait, Aubrey's not helping out in the group anymore?" I asked.

Lisa's eyes widened. "Oh, that's right! You guys were involved! But you're not anymore, right?" she asked, frowning slightly.

How the hell did this chick know that Aubrey and I had been together? Aubrey had gone to a lot of trouble to make sure that no one ever found out. Hell, I was hammered in the head over and over again about how bad it would be if anyone ever knew. It had never occurred to me that Aubrey had to face any repercussions as a result of our relationship. "What are you talking about?" I demanded, not confirming or denying what Lisa was saying.

"So, it's not true? Twyla had told me that she heard you two were together and that's why Aubrey wasn't helping out anymore. Got kicked out or something. Whatever, she was way too straight edge. Don't you remember how she flipped out on Kyle?"

I got to my feet so abruptly that my chair was knocked over. I didn't bother to pick it up as I left.

chapter fifteen

aubrey

After Boundaries and Ethics class, I ended up blowing off the rest of my day. My run-in with Maxx that morning had rattled me, and all I wanted was a bubble bath and to rearrange my closet. I needed to get my equilibrium back. I was proud that I'd been able to walk away with my head and heart intact, but I still felt unsettled.

Renee was in class until early evening, so I had the place to myself. I turned my music on, blasting old-school Nine Inch Nails and pulling all of my shoes and sweaters out of my closet. I was knee-deep in shoeboxes when the doorbell chimed. I stood up and wiped my dusty hands on my jeans, pulled my stringy hair into a low bun, and headed out to the living room. The doorbell rang again and I growled in frustration. "Hold your horses," I muttered as I turned the lock and opened the door, not bothering to look through the peephole.

And then I froze. I should have known walking away from Maxx had been too easy.

"What are you doing here?" I asked shortly, thinking about shutting the door in his face.

He frowned, the lines between his eyebrows deepening. "We need to talk."

"Well, I'm sort of busy—" I began, but Maxx cut me off. He stepped forward, forcing me to back up and let him into the apartment.

He shut the door behind him and stared at me with an intensity that made my stomach drop into my scuffed sneakers.

"No. We need to talk *now,*" he said, his words strong and brooking no argument.

I crossed my arms over my chest and leveled my hardest glare in his direction.

"Uh, excuse me? Where do you get off?" I fumed.

Maxx closed his eyes, clearly frustrated.

Well, that makes two of us, buddy.

Maxx opened his eyes again, the blue blazing with a ferocity that made me take another step back. "What happened after I went to rehab?"

Huh?

"What are you talking about?" I asked, confused.

Maxx advanced toward me and I backed up until my legs hit the side of the couch and I was forced to sit down on the arm, a position that gave him too much of an advantage, but I couldn't move.

"You're not leading the support group anymore. Why?" he asked, his words clipped and harsh, as though the thought really pissed him off.

Why would he be angry about whether or not I was facilitating that stupid support group anymore?

"Why?" I snipped. I leaned back, trying to get some distance, but I was in danger of sliding down the arm of the couch and onto my back. That inelegant move would have made me look even more ridiculous than I already felt.

"Can you give me a little space here? You're making me feel claustrophobic," I said, holding my hands out, making sure not to touch him.

Maxx looked at the shrinking space between us and muttered, "Sorry."

"Can I sit down?" he asked, looking suddenly unsure. For all of his bluster only moments before when he had barged into my apartment, his confidence seemed to have waned.

"Sure, it's not like I'm going to be able to make you leave, am I?" I threw back at him.

Maxx winced and I felt a little bad for being so hateful. But only a little.

"I didn't mean to just march over here like this. But I heard some stuff today and I needed to see you. To hear from you that it wasn't true. Because if it *is* true, God, if it is . . ." He trailed off and stared at me again, his eyes wide and suddenly anguished.

I felt that uncontrollable pull toward him again. But I ignored it. It was a matter of survival to pretend it didn't exist at all.

"You're not making a whole lot of sense, Maxx," I said wearily. He seemed . . . *tortured,* and that need to take care of him reared its traitorous head. It took everything inside of me to not pull him close and hold him the way I would have done without reservation once before.

"I heard—" He stopped abruptly and swallowed audibly before speaking again. "I heard that you were kicked out or something. I didn't get the whole story. But I heard it was because of me. Because of *us.* That you got in trouble as a result of our relationship. Is that true?"

Maxx's insistence irritated me. I was unsettled having him here, in my space like this. He enveloped. Took over. Consumed.

"Why would it matter if it were true?" I asked sharply in an attempt to hide my unease.

Maxx covered his face with his hands and scrubbed his fingers down his cheeks as he raised his head to meet my eyes.

"Because the last thing I have ever wanted was for you to be brought down with me. I never wanted what I *was*, what I chose to do, to impact your life like that."

"Are you serious?" I scoffed.

Maxx reared back as though I had slapped him. "Yes, I'm serious!"

"Because if you *ever* thought for one *second* that your habit . . . that who you *are*," I spat out, "wouldn't affect me, then you were even more deluded than I thought." Maxx opened his mouth as if to argue, but I shook my head, cutting him off.

"C'mon, Maxx! I loved you! We were together! We made the decision to share our lives, for whatever that was worth. I warned you about the risks for both of us! But I made my bed and now I'm lying in it. Because that's life, Maxx. When we make bad decisions, we have to deal with the fallout!" I yelled. I was getting worked up. I couldn't help it.

"I know there are consequences, Aubrey! I'm one big, walking consequence! You think I don't realize that? But, God, I never meant for any of this to happen!" We were both breathing rapidly. Maxx's face was flushed and his eyes were a little wild. I knew that I must look the same way.

"I need to make this right. For you. For us," he stated emphatically.

I shook my head. "There is no *us*, Maxx. I told you that," I said tiredly.

Maxx's eyes flashed with fury. "I don't believe that, Aubrey, and I don't believe that *you* believe that! There will *always* be an us!"

Good God, I actually wanted to believe him.

"I don't want to do this right now. You need to leave," I said in a shaky voice. I lacked any real conviction, but I hoped the words would be enough.

They weren't. Maxx dropped to his knees and crawled across the space between us until he was kneeling in front of me. He looked up at me and brought his hand up to my chest, placing his palm over my heart, which beat erratically.

"I feel it, Aubrey. Right there, where it matters. You want me here." He grabbed my hand and brought it up to his chest, where I felt the frantic thud beneath my fingers. "Do you feel that? That's where you are. That's where you will always be. And as long as this heart beats, I will never give up on what we had. I will make you see that I can change. I can be the person you need me to be."

I tried to pull my hand away but he held me firm, the flat of my palm pressed to his chest.

"Please, Maxx. Stop it! Stop talking to me like this! You've already done enough! I can't survive you again!" I beseeched, feeling myself start to panic. If he stayed much longer, speaking to me like this, my control would slip.

He dropped his hand to my leg. "I hate myself for everything I've done to you. What I've put you through is my biggest regret. Aubrey, you were the only beautiful part of my nasty life. And to know that just by loving me, you lost so much . . . I don't think I can deal with that."

The anxiety in my gut twisted painfully. I felt the press of his hand on my leg and could see the wetness on his face. We were so close. Achingly so. If he kissed me now, I wasn't sure I had the strength to resist him.

Because I wanted him to kiss me. Because as much as I was trying desperately to believe otherwise, I knew that I loved this man, as much as I ever had. It was a love without logic. It was a love without sense. It was a love that had no real place in the world I was trying to build for myself.

You can't move on from a love like that. Even if it was destined to only bring you pain.

I stared down at his face and saw the way he was tearing himself apart. Over me. Over everything he had done. I couldn't sit there and let him beat himself up like that, even if a part of me yelled, *He deserves this!*

I covered his hand with mine, squeezing lightly. "I made my choices, Maxx. I knew what I was getting into the first time we kissed. I made the decision to cross that line. I knew what was at stake by loving you. But even after everything, I can't regret it. Not ever. I'm angry with you. So damn angry, Maxx. But I don't regret you. Not even a little bit," I whispered, having lost the ability to speak any louder.

Maxx dropped his forehead to my knee and wrapped his arms around my calves. "I'm so, so sorry, Aubrey." His voice sounded broken.

I lifted my hand and let it hover for a moment over the back of his head, not sure if I should touch him. I didn't know what to do. I was torn in half. I dropped my hand to my side and leaned back. "Maxx. Please, stop it," I said gently, making my choice.

Maxx released me from his hold and moved backward, furiously wiping his cheeks with his hands. "I shouldn't have come here. I'm sorry, Aubrey. I just keep doing the wrong thing when it comes to you," he apologized, looking embarrassed by his breakdown.

I couldn't help it. This time I did the only thing my hurting heart would allow. Even if it was wrong and stupid.

I touched him.

I reached out and put my hand on the side of his face, reveling in the contact I had denied myself. I was disgusted that I was enjoying it, but I didn't pull away. Maxx leaned into my palm.

"The one thing you don't have to be sorry about is the future of my academic career. I'm dealing with it. It's handled. It really has nothing to do with you," I told him.

Maxx let out a chuckle. "I must sound like the worst kind of narcissist, insisting that everything in your life has to do with me."

"For a little while, it did," I admitted before I could stop myself.

Maxx grabbed my hand, the one cupping his face, brought it to his mouth, and tenderly kissed my palm. His lips lingered on my skin as he stared into my eyes. His kiss burned like a brand. We gazed at each other, the air sizzling and electric. I couldn't move. I couldn't breathe.

Then he got to his feet. "But not anymore," he said, wiping the last of the tears from his face. He pulled out his cell phone and looked at the screen. "I've got to get going. I have a meeting at the financial aid office," he said, tucking his phone back into his pocket.

"Oh, okay," I said, feeling completely off balance.

"It seems I lost most of my financial assistance for school. I have to go and figure out whether there's any chance that I can come back next semester to finish my degree," Maxx said on a sigh.

"I . . . I hope it works out," I said sincerely.

"Me, too." He turned and walked to the door and I followed him.

"I'm sorry I came here like this. I shouldn't have done that," he said as he opened the door.

I shook my head. "Don't be. It's . . . it's fine." I had resorted to insincere niceties, having nothing else to say.

"Thanks for not shutting the door in my face," Maxx said, giving me a weak smile. I opened my mouth to respond but my voice failed me. And then he was gone.

chapter sixteen

maxx

Some mornings I would wake up and the first thing I'd think about, even before my eyes had a chance to open, was drugs.

What it felt like to be stoned. Where I could get them if I really wanted them. Who I had to call to score as soon as possible. How soon it would be until I was so fucking high I thought I'd never come down again.

Then I'd get up and start my day, and those brief instances of exhilaration, thinking about my long-lost love, would evaporate under the weight of my new life. And I'd start feeling depressed. These were dark times, when I thought about the person I was before I had gone into rehab and how far I was from the confident, self-assured man I had thought I was. For some odd reason I couldn't conjure up the bad and horrible about the person I used to be.

All I could remember in those bleak moments was how I had felt on top of the world. My body craved that feeling again. The physical addiction had subsided in the weeks since I had last used.

What I fought against now, every second of every day, was all in my fucking head.

It was the memory that was the danger now. Everything was a trigger. Everything reminded me of what it was like when I was high. At times, particularly when I was alone, with only my wretched self for company, it was almost impossible to ignore the cravings.

With Marco continuing to blow up my phone the temptation was tantalizingly close. So I kept myself as busy as possible. Not being in school made that hard, but I filled my hours with legal things. Because Maxx Demelo had officially turned over a new leaf.

I had gone to the meeting with Leah Fletcher, who had walked me through the process of applying for some grants for "disadvantaged students." She had me complete new paperwork and was able to scrounge up enough government aid to cover tuition for next semester. That would be enough time, if I busted my ass, to finish my degree.

But I still needed money to live. Pay bills. Keep a roof over my head. Food in my stomach. All of those necessities that were essential in order to stay alive so I *could* graduate. It would be such an easy fix to call Gash and jump back into the club and my role there. The money was good, the adrenaline rush was even better.

But I couldn't. I *wouldn't.*

So I had entered the world of the gainfully yet miserably employed. When I wasn't shoveling horseshit at the stables just outside of town—a job I found on Craigslist—I was burning off my skin at the local coffee shop. The whole thing really sucked.

But I'd stick it out. I had to. Though one thing was for sure, walking the straight and narrow was much harder than I ever thought it would be.

In my efforts to be Maxx Demelo, Recovering Addict, there was one thing I still hadn't done: go downtown to make an intake appointment for my outpatient counseling. I knew that I needed to. I had a meeting with my probation officer next week and it was important I show that I was continuing with treatment.

He had known I was in rehab but not that I'd almost died on a bathroom floor from a drug overdose. If he had been privy to that knowledge, I wouldn't be sitting here on the outside. I'd be sitting in a jail cell feeling pretty damn sorry for myself.

It was Saturday morning and I woke up with four hours to kill before I had to be out at the horse stables. Kenny Wyatt, who ran the place, hadn't been exactly impressed with my lack of general horse knowledge when I had called him up and asked him about the job. Luckily the horrible pay and even worse duties didn't make "stable hand" very popular for those seeking employment. Kenny had hired me on the spot, though he was less than pleased about it.

There was nothing less attractive than coming home smelling like you had spent the day rolling around in manure. Feeling restless and unwilling to sit around my apartment chewing on my nails, I grabbed my car keys and headed out, no real destination in mind.

It was a sunny day and the streets were busy. My car petered along, clunking noisily. I looked in my rearview mirror and saw black smoke billowing out from the back.

I wished I had somewhere to go. I felt displaced and isolated. The only real connections I had ever had were with people who now wanted nothing to do with me. I picked up my phone but then dropped it again, knowing that I had no one to call. I felt a sharp pain in my chest that was a lot like loneliness. A memory resurfaced unbidden.

"I hate living here, Maxx." Landon's voice was small and timid. We had only been living with our uncle David for a few weeks, but I could already tell it was not going to be a good situation. Two hours after dropping us off at his house, he had left, with no indication of where he was going.

He had been gone for three days.

When he came back, he reeked of stale booze and looked as though he hadn't showered in a month. He hadn't acknowledged either of us and had instead gone to his room, where he proceeded to sleep for the next twenty-four hours.

This was our life now. But at least I had Landon. And he had me.

He was the only thing in my stupid, messed-up life that made me feel good. Even if the responsibility of taking care of him felt like a noose around my neck sometimes.

I threw my arm around Landon's shoulders. "Yeah, me, too, buddy, but we've got each other. We'll be all right," I promised, meaning it.

Landon was small for his age and barely came up to my shoulder. He was a clingy kid who followed me around everywhere. A normal teenage brother would have been annoyed by his tagalong brother. But we weren't normal.

"Okay, Maxx," Landon replied.

I knew he missed our dad. Even though he hadn't been the best parent at the end, he was still the only parent Landon had ever known. He didn't remember Mom. And I hated that.

Now I was the only parental figure that he had.

"You wanna learn how to check the oil in a car?" I asked, wanting to distract the poor kid from our shitty life.

Landon's face brightened considerably. "Yeah!" he enthused, eager to spend time with his big brother.

"Come on, then, let's go out in the garage. Dad's old Mustang is out there."

Just as I was about to get up, Landon wrapped his skinny arms around me and squeezed. "You're the best brother ever, Maxx," he said, his voice muffled as he pressed himself into my chest. I stiffened for a moment but I didn't pull away.

I hugged him back, not caring that I looked like a total pussy for embracing my brother.

He needed the affection.

I did, too.

I shook my head, clearing my mind of the memory.

I missed Landon. I missed the relationship we used to have. I needed him back in my life.

So I turned down a side street and started to pass familiar houses. I pulled up in front of the one-level brick house where I had spent my bleak formative years, and killed the engine.

I hadn't called Landon since leaving rehab, knowing that what I had to say was better said in person. Though I was terrified that the kid who I had practically raised wouldn't want anything to do with me.

I was sweating bullets, which wasn't like me at all. Well, it wasn't like the old me, anyway. This new me seemed to get freaked out over everything.

I walked up on the porch and put my hand on the doorknob and then thought better of it. Ringing the doorbell, I stood back and waited.

Landon appeared after only a few seconds and looked irritated at seeing me standing there.

"You're out, I guess," he said coldly, crossing his arms over his chest like the teenager he was.

I shoved my hands into my pockets and shrugged. "Yeah, I am."

"I thought you'd call," my brother said bitterly.

"I would have if I thought you would have answered," I threw back.

Landon rolled his eyes.

"So are we going to have this conversation out here or can I come inside?" I asked.

"David'll probably be back soon, so maybe another time." Landon started to close the door and I stuck my foot out, wedging it in the jamb.

"Look, Landon, I know you're pissed at me, but there are things I need to say, that you need to hear. I fucked up, buddy. Big-time. Give me a chance to make it right."

I saw Landon waver and he dropped his eyes. "Okay. But not for long. I've got stuff to do."

I wanted to laugh at his petulance, but I knew that would be a bad move, given the state of our relationship.

"Not a problem." I walked into my uncle's house and for the first time I didn't feel angry and resentful toward the man who had begrudgingly taken us in after our dad's death. What was the point in wasting the energy to hate him? It hurt me more than it hurt him. And I couldn't focus on that sort of bullshit. Not now when I was trying to make the people I cared about see how much I had changed.

And holding on to bad blood kept me stuck. And stuck was not something I wanted to be.

"Can I get something to drink?" I asked, noting how unchanged everything was. The same green-and-tan sofa that had been there for the last decade was pushed against the wall. The stained rug that had been my grandparents' laid haphazardly on the floor.

"Yeah, you know where everything is," Landon said, sitting down on the couch and turning up the volume on the television. He wasn't going to make things easy, that's for sure.

I went into the kitchen and opened the refrigerator, surprised to see that it was full of food. I checked the cabinets and found that they, too, were full. I grabbed a glass and filled it with water from the tap and returned to the living room.

"You doing the grocery shopping now?" I asked.

Landon didn't bother to look at me as he answered, his eyes still trained on the cartoon that played on the screen. "Nah. David's been home a lot more. He got a job at the county office building doing maintenance."

"Are you shitting me? Is he on something?" I asked, hardly able to believe that David had turned over a new leaf. Though if I was capable of change, why not my dickhead uncle?

"No, I think that's your thing, not his," Landon said blandly.

"Okay, I deserved that," I stated.

Landon flipped the channel, still not looking at me.

"I'm sorry I didn't take your calls while you were gone," Landon said gruffly, as though the apology was cutting into his throat.

"You don't need to apologize. I get it," I told him.

"Yeah, I don't think so," Landon said, his voice rising.

"Seriously, I do. I know you're upset with me—"

"Maxx, stop it. Just listen to me. For once." He threw the remote onto the coffee table and finally turned to look at me. Sometimes he reminded me so much of our dad. They had the same sandy-colored hair and pronounced jaw. And even though Landon was young when our father died, he had somehow adopted so many of his mannerisms that it was sometimes unsettling. Like the way his eyes flashed and his jaw ticked when he was pissed off.

Even though I was on the receiving end of my brother's ire, I was glad to hear the strength in his tone. He had finally grown a pair.

"Okay," I said.

Landon clenched his hands into fists, and two red splotches spread across his cheeks. I felt tense, with no idea what was coming next.

"I . . . I can't believe how much you lied to me. You're . . . you're such a hypocrite . . . this whole time you've just been this . . . this *drug addict*." He spat the words at me like they were dirty.

"You were the only person in my life I knew would always be straight with me. No matter what. But I can't ever trust anything you say again. You're just a big, fat liar."

I felt wounded. He didn't get it, didn't understand that things weren't so black and white. Suddenly I was pissed that he was attacking me like this. How quickly he forgot that I was the one who had always made sure he had dinner. I was the one who had always gotten him up for school and made him do his homework. Yeah, I had fucked up. Big-time. But that didn't negate the years of bullshit I went through making sure he was taken care of.

"Now, hang on a sec. I know that I let you down. I get that you feel betrayed. But don't for one second think that lying to you was easy. And everything I did was for you. You could be a little more fucking grateful," I snapped, feeling my patience for his surly attitude hanging by a thread.

Landon gave an incredulous snort that made me want to hit something. "So this is my fault? That's messed up, Maxx, even for you," he scoffed.

I opened my mouth to speak, but he cut me off.

"What if you'd *died*, Maxx?"

My angry defensiveness fizzled out. Landon looked stricken, and I felt like an ass for trying to defend myself at all. Talk about a fucking punch to the gut.

Shit. He was right.

I had almost *died*. Then where would Landon have been?

I was a fucking hypocrite. I was so damn selfish.

"Landon. I . . . I thought I had everything tight and controlled. I was such an idiot. I didn't really think about what I was doing to you. Because, honestly, I didn't even know what I was doing to myself."

"What about Aubrey? How about what you did to her?" Landon asked, and my heart stopped and then started up again painfully.

"Yeah, I messed up with Aubrey, too," I admitted, feeling weird talking about my girl problems with my kid brother.

"So I'm guessing she dropped you on your ass?"

"It wasn't like that," I argued, though that's exactly what had happened. I took a deep breath. I wasn't prepared for a conversation like this with Landon, of all people.

"Look, Landon . . . I get that you're mad at me. You have every right to be. But you're my brother. We've got to work this stuff out. I'm trying really hard here. I just want you to see that." Landon refused to look at me.

"I'm working at the coffee shop on campus. Landon . . . I'm making fucking coffee! That should tell you how serious I am to do things right," I said.

Landon's lips quirked. Just the slightest movement, but it was something. "You could come by sometime and I'll make you a latte or some froufrou shit." I was trying to be funny, but it sounded pretty strained.

My brother snorted. "If you make coffee like you cook, I think I'll pass."

"Hey, it's not that bad. I've almost figured out how to use the espresso machine without burning myself," I joked, my laugh sounding rusty and unused.

Landon's face softened. Just a bit. "Seeing you in that hospital sucked, Maxx. I don't think I've ever been that scared," he admitted gruffly. I knew talking about feelings wasn't something he liked to do, being a teenage boy and all.

"I know, man. I'm sorry. Really, really sorry. I was . . . I *am* . . . an addict." It hurt to admit that out loud. To confirm the words he'd spat in my face, to confirm what I had denied for so long. And to my brother. The one person I had tried so hard to hide it from.

But I also felt relieved that finally, after all this time, I could admit it. Own it. Move on from it.

"So you've stopped, then?" Landon's voice sounded small and it reminded me how young he really was. It reminded me of that little kid I had taken care of all those years ago.

"Yes, God, yes. But I can't lie and say I don't want to. Because I do. All the time. But I'm going to fight against it. Because you deserve better from me, Landon."

Landon nodded and turned back to the television. I didn't say anything else, not sure if I should stay or leave. Landon wasn't giving me much to go on.

When his show was over, Landon got to his feet and I figured that was my cue to go. I was disappointed that things felt so unfinished. I couldn't tell if Landon was willing to forgive me or not. I didn't know if this was it. Whether I'd lost my brother for good.

Landon started to walk out of the room and then stopped, not quite turning back to me. "You wanna help me change the oil in the 'stang?" he asked, his tone noncommittal.

I felt something that was a lot like hope spark inside me. "Sure, buddy. I'd like that," I told him, getting to my feet and following him out to the garage.

chapter seventeen

aubrey

As far as weeks could go, I'd had better. I had been working hard to keep my nose down and focus on my schoolwork, staying late on campus to study. I went to class and then I went home, not lingering too long in between. I had to limit the chances of a run-in that would only leave me bruised and wanting.

I was walking home from class that particular afternoon, thinking about everything and nothing all at the same time. I was trying to concentrate on the stuff that mattered. School. Getting back into the counseling program. My friendships with Renee and Brooks. Anything but Maxx Demelo.

I had my eyes trained to the ground, moving quickly. I started up the steps to my apartment building, when a movement out of the corner of my eye caught my attention. I paused and turned and then wished instantly that I hadn't.

Tucked into the shadowed alcove between my apartment building and the shop next door were two people locked in a passionate embrace. The man had the woman pressed against the wall, her hands gripping his shoulders as he held her tightly.

He lifted her up and she wrapped her legs around his waist without once breaking the kiss that was consuming them both. My stomach rolled and I felt an inexplicable guilt as I watched the scene in front of me. Ugly emotions surfaced about my own warring emotions about Maxx.

I watched my roommate run her fingers through Devon Keeton's short red hair and for a moment, I hated her for not being stronger. For falling right along with me. Because clearly I wasn't the only one who was tempted to open a door that was better off left closed.

I turned my back on Renee and her ex-boyfriend and walked inside.

✦

Renee breezed into the apartment half an hour later, a mess of hair and frenetic energy. Even if I hadn't seen her in the alley with douchebag Devon, I would have instantly known something was up. Her face was flushed, her eyes bright, and her hands shook when she turned the lock in the door.

"Hey," I said, going for blandly neutral.

"Hey," Renee said back, not quite meeting my eyes like the guilty girl she was.

"Where've you been?" I asked, digging a bit for information, testing the waters to see whether she'd be honest and forthright.

It seemed my dear roommate and best friend opted for a renewed relationship with dishonesty and distance.

"Library," she responded vaguely.

"Really. Did you get a lot of reading done?" *Reading* being a euphemism for dirty, wrong spit swapping.

"Yeah, I'm going to nail that microbiology test tomorrow," she said, and if I hadn't known she was lying I would have been fooled. She was that convincing.

"Or nail something else," I muttered.

"Excuse me?" she asked, looking flustered.

"I saw you," I said.

I had to give my friend credit, she played confused well. She tied her disheveled hair up into a ponytail and gave me a bewildered smile. "Oh yeah? Where?"

"With Devon," I told her, trying not to sound as disappointed as I felt. In her. In me. In our obvious inability to really move on from the person who hurt us so badly.

Renee's face paled, and she began chewing on her bottom lip. "It's not what it looked like—"

"Is that why things with Iain didn't work out? Because of Devon?" I asked, not because I couldn't believe she would be so stupid, but because I understood her choices all too well.

But that didn't make them any easier to swallow.

Renee narrowed her eyes. "Don't, Aubrey," she warned.

I held my hands up in a placating gesture. "I'm not judging, Renee! I just want to know what's going on. Talk to me, please," I begged, desperate for us to not fall back into that horrible place where our friendship used to reside. Full of secrets and mistrust. Laden with tension and false smiles. And all because of the very man I had seen her kissing minutes before.

"I don't know what's going on. Just please drop it!" she pleaded, heading back to her bedroom.

I didn't chase her. I didn't demand answers. Maybe I should have. But I couldn't. Not when I could only look at her and see my own failings.

We woke up the next morning and drank our coffee together as if nothing at all had happened. We walked to school and talked about the weather and every other mundane, boring topic we could think of. And for the most part, we were pseudonormal. Except for the unspoken words that lay between us.

Except for the truth.

I walked in the door of my classroom later that day and promptly stopped in my tracks. April, Evan's emotionally beaten girlfriend from support group, stood in front of the professor's desk, handing him a slip of paper. She looked up as I came in, her face a mask.

I scurried to my seat and pulled out my textbook, burying my nose into the reading, my earlier feelings of goodwill vanishing quickly. I refused to look up when I saw a pair of ratty sneakers in my peripheral vision walking past and sitting at the desk directly beside me.

I chanced a glance to my left and saw April sitting beside me despite several other available desks around the room, chewing on her thumbnail. I kept reading until the professor started his lecture, ignoring her.

"Do you have an extra pen?"

I practically jumped out of my seat at the sound of the soft, yet husky voice of the frail dark-haired girl I had never heard speak before. "Uh, sure," I said, not knowing what possessed me to respond to her at all, especially given her involvement with Evan. I dug around in my bag and found another pen and handed it to her. She blew her hair out of her face and gave me a timid smile. It never reached her eyes, and I thought that she looked incredibly sad.

"Thanks, Aubrey," she whispered, turning back around in her seat. The entire exchange had lasted a whole thirty seconds, but it left me feeling strange.

I had a hard time focusing on the rest of the class. When April leaned over to return my pen, she thanked me sincerely. "I guess I need to be a little more prepared next time." Her voice startled me again. It was pleasing to listen to. Soft but with a slight rasp. She had been mute the entire time I had facilitated the support group.

Even during that one, terrible run-in at Compulsion, she had never uttered a single word, letting her boyfriend do the talking for them both.

I slowly reached out and took the pen from her, tucking it back into my bag. "I didn't know you were in the counseling program," I said, not able to help my curiosity about what she was doing in this particular class . . . with me. It felt like too much of a coincidence, given Evan's threats only weeks before.

April got to her feet and slung a tattered purse over her shoulder. She seemed to be unwilling to make eye contact, choosing to look over my shoulder instead. Her dark hair, which had remnants of purple dye at the tips, looked tangled and slightly unkempt. She gave off the little-girl-lost vibe; not your typical student.

"I'm not. I needed to take some extra classes to fill in the semester and this looked sort of interesting," she mumbled, and I wasn't sure I entirely believed her.

"Okay, then. Well, see ya later," I said, not wanting to prolong any sort of interaction between us. I walked out of the classroom and felt her presence behind me as I left the building.

As I left I saw Evan sitting on the steps, obviously waiting for his girlfriend. He looked up as I walked toward him, and his hateful sneer froze my blood. "Hey, Aubrey," he said, saying my name like a curse. I looked away, not responding. I heard him laugh, and apprehension curdled inside me.

✦

When I met up with Brooks for our usual morning coffee the next day, I was not in the best mood.

"I recognize that look," Brooks said, pointing his finger at my face.

I batted his hand away and scowled. "What look? And play nice," I warned.

Brooks chuckled and held the door open for me. The Coffee Jerk was crowded, which was typical for a weekday. Everyone was looking for the required caffeine to get through the day.

"The look that says you didn't sleep enough, so tread carefully," Brooks quipped, getting in line.

"I guess that's accurate," I conceded. I was starting to forget what a good night's sleep felt like.

Brooks slung his arm around my shoulders. "Do I need to come over tonight and make you a cup of chamomile tea and tuck you in?" he cooed sarcastically.

I elbowed him in the gut and he dropped his arm. I smiled at him in a way that was more a baring of teeth. We continued to edge toward the counter. Brooks was talking about a research paper and I half listened. I was tired. I was irritable. And I needed my coffee.

And then I saw him.

Maxx stood behind the counter in a brown Coffee Jerk T-shirt, manning the industrial-sized espresso machine and looking harried.

Why did he have to start working at the only place in town that makes coffee the way that I like?

I was irrationally annoyed. But then I felt a smidgen of something else. Joy? Because at least Maxx was working. He had a job that paid him legal, honest money. He was trying.

My jaw hardened and I instantly stepped out of line and exited the coffee shop without another word. Brooks came after me with a confused look on his face. He had obviously not noticed the new barista on duty.

"What's wrong?" he asked, and I only shook my head, not wanting to get into it. Not now when I was feeling edgy.

"Nothing, I just realized I needed to get to class early," I lied, feeling marginally guilty for not telling Brooks the truth.

"Oh, okay. Well, I guess I'll just see you later, then," Brooks said, still looking bewildered. I forced a smile and nodded, hurrying to class.

✦

Later in the day I had yet to meet my caffeine quota and things were getting scary. I had practically yelled at the girl sitting in front of me in statistics when she had asked for a pencil.

I knocked over a TA as he came through the door with an armful of papers. I had been charging ahead, full of piss and vinegar and with no attention to those walking around me.

By the end of the day I was a twisty mess of irritation not fit for human company.

Knowing I needed a coffee shot stat, I decided to chance a return trip to the Coffee Jerk. I hoped and prayed that Maxx's shift would be over by now. I was relieved when I entered and didn't see him behind the counter. I gave my order to the girl who wasn't my ex-boyfriend and felt myself relax once I sat in a booth near the back, finally getting my coffee fix.

"Hey," a deep voice said to my left.

The universe hates me, I thought drolly, quickly followed by a firm, *Don't look up, Aubrey!*

I looked up.

Of course I did.

I was nothing if not consistent when it came to Maxx.

"Hey," I muttered, my mouth turning down at the sight of Maxx, still in his work uniform. His blond hair was disheveled and he looked tired.

"Can I sit down?" he asked, indicating the empty seat across from me.

"It's a free country, isn't it?"

Maxx's jaw stiffened as he slid into the booth opposite me. We sat in awkward silence. I would have laughed at our discomfort if I were in a laughing mood.

"How's the coffee?" he asked, indicating my now almost-empty mug.

"Coffeelike," I replied shortly, swallowing the last gulp of my beverage.

"You're not going to make this easy for me, are you," Maxx said, frowning.

This time I did laugh. But it wasn't because I found his remark particularly funny.

"Oh, I'm sorry. Is my standoffishness a problem for you?" I asked, my words icy cold.

Maxx cleared his throat. "That's not what I meant," he said softly.

"Well, you can't expect anything from me, Maxx. You just can't," I told him truthfully.

I thought about Renee and Devon in the alleyway outside of our building and felt frigid inside. I looked at the man responsible for my own heartache and felt a hardening inside.

"I know that you think you have to stay away from me because I hurt you. I know you're trying to build a life without me. But I also know that the only life worth living is the one we can have together."

He slowly reached across the table and took my hand between his palms and held it.

"I know what you look like when you love. And it's right here. In your eyes. On your mouth. I look at you and know, without a doubt, that you feel the same way I do." Maxx ran his thumb along my bottom lip, and I jerked back.

I felt my face flush and pulled my hand from his restraining grasp.

"I've got to go," I muttered, getting to my feet.

"Will you come in tomorrow? I'm working. I can buy you a coffee. I know how much you need your caffeine in the morning," Maxx said, sounding a little desperate.

I pulled my book bag up onto my shoulder. I wouldn't look at him.

It would be too easy to give in. I should start avoiding this place. I should ignore him and leave before I did something stupid. So what do I do? I give him the answer that I know I shouldn't. I found myself saying, "I come in every morning, Maxx. So I guess I'll see you then."

I'm not caving, I told myself. *I'm just telling him the truth. I do come in for coffee every morning. It didn't mean anything.*

Maxx's smile was as bright as if I had offered him the moon.

"Okay, well, I'll see you then."

It didn't mean anything! I yelled to myself over and over again.

What a lie. With Maxx, it meant *everything.*

chapter eighteen

maxx

Lately, talking to Aubrey felt a lot like banging my head against the wall. I was getting nowhere . . . fast. Didn't she see how much I was attempting to change?

I tried not to get frustrated, because I saw in her eyes how much she still loved me. But being kept at arm's length was maddening when the connection between us was still as intense as ever.

I hated working at the coffee shop. The pay sucked and the hours were even worse.

Working at the stables was a little better. Sure, shoveling shit for ten dollars an hour wasn't the best use of my time, but I got to be outdoors and no one really bothered me. I put my feelings aside because working my ass off was for a greater purpose. These were all steps in proving myself.

"You're a hard worker, Maxx. I have to say that I'm impressed," Mr. Wyatt said, watching me as I cleaned out one of the stalls.

I had gone straight from my shift at the coffee shop to the

stables. I didn't have time to change, so I was still wearing the brown T-shirt from earlier. I would have had time to run home and put on different clothes if I hadn't stayed to talk to Aubrey.

Well, I had stayed only to be *rejected* by Aubrey. Again.

It was becoming a sad, pathetic pattern. "Thanks," I grunted, lifting a shovel full of hay and manure and dumping it in a wheelbarrow. Mr. Wyatt patted a pretty gray horse named Harvey and inclined his head toward me. "Have you ever ridden a horse?" he asked.

"Sure," I lied. I had never been on a horse in my life.

"Well, if you ever want to ride one of our beauties, come on out. You're always welcome," he said with a final pat on Harvey's neck. Mr. Wyatt was a gruff fellow but he seemed decent. I knew that the offer wasn't made lightly.

"Thanks, Mr. Wyatt. Maybe I will," I said, wiping sweat off my forehead, knowing I left a smear of dirt behind.

"These guys could use the exercise. You'd be helping me out," Mr. Wyatt continued, seeming embarrassed by his kindness.

"Of course," I agreed, not letting on to the fact that I knew the old guy actually liked me. Mr. Wyatt reached into his pocket and pulled out some cash. "Here's your first week's pay. I don't do checks."

I took the money. "Thanks," I said genuinely.

Mr. Wyatt nodded and left. I quickly counted the money and felt my stomach drop. It was only $250. I couldn't pay bills and buy food with this meager amount. I was working my ass off and barely surviving. I left work feeling completely disheartened.

I walked into my apartment twenty minutes later and flipped the light switch, relieved when the lights turned on. I wasn't sure how long I'd get by without paying my electricity bill before they cut my power. I collapsed onto the couch and let out a long, agonized breath. I needed to do something. I had to find a way to make some money.

There's one place I could go for some quick scratch, my subconscious teased.

It was tempting. I missed the club. I missed the dark world where I was king. I missed the adrenaline rush of doing something I knew was wrong and getting away with it.

God, I missed the drugs.

I'll always be here, waiting for you, my addiction whispered seductively in my head. My hands began to shake and something that felt dangerously like physical withdrawal racked my body. My heart started to pound and sweat dribbled down my back. I felt sick and dizzy. The need to use was overwhelming.

Get it together! I screamed silently to myself.

I needed to lose myself in something safe. I got up and rushed back to my bedroom and threw open my closet door. I dug around inside with my heart slamming angrily in my chest.

Get a grip, Maxx!

I finally found my sketch pad and a box of charcoal. I sat down cross-legged on the floor. The lighting was shit, but I didn't need to see. I needed to feel.

My fingers moved almost mechanically at first, but then the fluidity of drawing took over. My breathing began to slow. My heart calmed down. The sweat dried on my skin. Minutes turned into an hour, my fingers never stopping.

When I was finished, I straightened my back, feeling stiff from sitting in the same position for so long. I stretched and held up the pad in front of my face and couldn't help but smile.

The style was uniquely mine. Tangles of long hair becoming snakes as they reached down from the sky. Fingers sprouting up from the ground like talons.

It was warped. It was fucked up.

But it looked pretty freaking awesome.

I knew that I was good. Enough people had told me throughout the years that I believed it.

I thought with regret about that meeting with Mr. Randall all those months ago. I had really messed up something good.

It was the story of my life.

I walked over to the corner of my room where I had stacked at least two dozen canvases. I slowly went through them, pulling out the ones that stood out. The ones that best demonstrated my ability.

Feeling impulsive, I pulled out my wallet and found the card Tatum Randall had given me over six months ago. I was actually surprised I had kept it.

Maybe there was a part of me, even when I was bombed out of my mind, that held on to this small possibility.

I quickly dialed the number on the crisp, white card before I could talk myself out of it. I chewed on my thumbnail as the phone rang and rang.

"Bellview Gallery, how can I help you?" a woman's voice chirped in my ear.

"Um, hi, is Mr. Randall available?" I croaked.

"May I ask who's calling?"

"Maxx— I mean X," I fumbled, sounding like a moron.

"X?" the lady asked incredulously.

I gritted my teeth. "Yes, X. He'll know me," I said through clenched teeth.

"Okay, then, hold on. Let me see if he's still here."

I was put on hold and had to listen to five minutes of really bad elevator music.

Just when the horrible strains of John Tesh were about to send me over the edge, the phone clicked.

"X. Hello. I must say I'm rather surprised to hear from you," Mr. Randall said. He sounded cold and less than thrilled.

"Yes, I understand. I didn't make the best impression when we met," I said, hating to grovel, but what other choice did I have?

"I believe that is an understatement," Mr. Randall scoffed.

He was starting to piss me off and I had to work hard to rein myself in.

"Yes, well, I wasn't in a very good place back then. Things have changed considerably since then." I paused a moment, mentally preparing myself to beg.

"I wanted to know if you'd still be interested in seeing my work. I've put together some amazing pieces—"

"X, after our last meeting, I think it's safe to say that you wouldn't be a good fit for my gallery."

I felt myself bristle at his automatic rejection.

"Sir, I get that I was a bit of a mess. I was dealing with some stuff. Not that that excuses my horrible behavior. But I don't think it's exactly fair—"

"Look, I'm sure there are a lot of other galleries out there that would be interested in you and your . . . *eccentricities.*" The jackass wouldn't let me get a word in. "But Bellview Gallery isn't that place. I'm sorry."

I felt what little hope I had about possibly using my art to generate a livable income dwindle away.

I crumpled up my pride into a tiny ball and shoved it away. "Sir. Please. Just give me another chance. I think you'll change your mind if you just see my work. My real work." I sounded desperate. He had to hear it in my voice.

Mr. Randall was quiet for a bit. I chewed through the skin on my lip and tasted blood, the sharp sting keeping me grounded.

"I'm sorry, X. When I saw your street art I thought you were a different artist. I thought you were someone I could promote and nurture. Unfortunately, the impression you gave wasn't one of someone ready to work hard and take their talent seriously. I just can't take that risk. Not right now." He actually sounded a bit sorry.

But he wasn't as sorry as I was.

I couldn't beg anymore.

"Okay, then. Well, thank you for your time." I felt despondent. Dejected. Lost.

"Best of luck, X. I really mean that," Mr. Randall said, sounding sincere.

I wanted to tell him where to shove his unnecessary well wishes.

But I held my tongue.

I hung up the phone and looked at the canvases propped against the wall.

I was quickly getting tired of being kicked when I was already down.

In a fit of anger I hurled the pictures across the room.

The one of Aubrey I had painted after getting out of rehab was split down the middle.

Broken and ruined.

Just like me.

chapter nineteen

aubrey

I was drinking so much coffee that I threatened to float away. My caffeine drive had kicked up a notch now that I was making random stops at the Coffee Jerk throughout the day. I swear I was going to have to start earning stock options, given how much money I gave them.

"Hello again. Here for round two?" Maxx asked, cocking his head to the side.

"Yep," I said, my mouth popping around the word.

"Caramel latte, extra foam?" he asked, already punching in my regular order.

"Yep," I said again, feeling suddenly embarrassed. Our eyes met and clung for a moment before I broke the heated stare off. I looked away and pointed to a table near the door. "I'll be over there," I said quickly.

I sat down and put my bag on the table. I pulled out a packet of information and laid it out on the table. I looked down at the glossy pages. The words *Department of Education* stood out in a bright yellow. I opened up the catalogue and started thumbing through, looking at the offered classes: Teaching Principles, Classroom Learning Assessment, Classroom Management.

I had been thinking about my future a lot lately, and whether I was on the right path. My confidence in my ability to be a professional counselor had been shaken, and despite my efforts to put my best foot forward, I was terrified of failing again.

"Here ya go," Maxx said quietly, sliding the steaming mug in front of me. "Department of Education certification in elementary teaching?"

I wanted to tell him to leave. To mind his own business. Instead I found myself telling him the truth. "I don't know. I guess I'm just thinking through some other options."

Then Maxx was sitting down across from me. "I thought being a counselor is what you wanted to do." He looked concerned and I had a hard time meeting his eyes. I worried he'd be able to see straight through me as he had always been able to do.

I shrugged. "When I was a kid I wanted to be a teacher. That only changed after Jayme died. I just think that maybe I made my career choice based on the wrong reasons." Why was I vomiting up honesty all over the place? And to Maxx, of all people? The last person I wanted to see into the heart of me.

"How is wanting to help people the wrong reason?" Maxx argued, frowning.

"How is this any of your business?" I asked coldly. Maxx sat back in his chair and crossed his arms over his chest, not put out by my pissy attitude.

"It's not, I guess. But that doesn't mean I don't want to know anyway. I'm here if you want to talk."

He was being sincere. I could see how much he wanted me to accept his offer. It would be so easy to open my mouth and tell him everything. To forge a type of intimacy that we had never really experienced together. We never had the chance to connect on a level separate from the angst and turmoil.

But I didn't say anything.

I ignored him, my eyes trained on the booklet in front of me, not really seeing it. After a few awkward moments, Maxx cleared his throat. "Okay, well, enjoy your coffee. I'll talk to you later."

Aubrey, you are an idiot, I chastised myself. I turned to look at Maxx, who was walking back to the counter, his shoulders slumped. I opened my mouth to say something.

To call him back? I had no idea what I was going to do.

"Hey." I was startled by the sudden appearance of my roommate. Renee sat down in the chair Maxx had just vacated. Her hair was windblown and wild, her cheeks flushed as though she had just run across campus.

"Hey," I said back, resisting the urge to look at Maxx again. She took off her coat and draped it over the back of the chair. She glanced up at the counter, her eyes widening. "I didn't realize Maxx worked here."

I grunted noncommittally. She pushed my cup with her finger. "Is that why you've been walking around like a tweeker on a meth binge? Caffeine overload?" Renee narrowed her eyes.

"I'm just indulging my love of lattes. Nothing more."

Renee shook her head and sighed, pulling the Department of Education brochure toward her. She frowned again. "What in the world is all this?"

"I'm thinking of changing my major," I remarked breezily, as though it wasn't a huge deal. Because it *was* a huge deal.

If I were to change my school trajectory, I would be essentially going back to square one. But the harder I worked to fight my way back into the counseling program, the more my doubt grew. I was beginning to question absolutely everything. It was unsettling.

"Change your major? Did you drink some crazy juice this morning?" Renee asked in disbelief. I understood why she was confused. This was completely out of character for me. But since meeting Maxx, out of character had become *in character.*

I glanced at Maxx out of the corner of my eye, unwilling to admit that perhaps he was a major reason for my change of heart.

"I just have a lot of thinking to do."

Before Renee could respond, her attention was pulled to the light tapping on the window beside us. We both turned in unison. Devon Keeton stood on the other side of the glass, his red hair sticking up all over his head, his hands shoved into his pockets. Renee swallowed, her eyes darting to me.

"What's that all about?" I asked, jerking my thumb in Devon's direction. He tapped on the window again, seeming a little agitated when Renee purposefully turned her back.

"It's no big deal," she mimed, giving me a loaded look.

Renee fidgeted in her seat and continued to look through the course catalogue as though her ex-boyfriend, the same guy I caught her making out with only days before, wasn't standing there, staring at her beseechingly.

"Is he just going to stand there all day?" I asked, unsettled by Devon's stalker behavior.

Renee blew out a breath and rubbed her temples as though she had a headache. "I just want to ignore him. I don't want to look at him. I just want to forget about him." My friend looked tired, sad, and more than a little conflicted. Finally she got up and stormed angrily out of the coffee shop.

"Who's that?" Maxx asked, wrapping a dish towel around his hand. We both watched Renee and Devon's obviously heated exchange.

"He was her mistake," I said with a clear edge to my voice. Maxx's eyes flashed and he looked at me, picking up on the innuendo.

"Is that why you come in here three times a day for coffee you don't really want? Because I'm *your* mistake?" Maxx asked, sounding angry.

"I like coffee," I muttered, looking back out the window. Devon tried to reach for Renee, but she put her hands up, stopping him. I could see that she was crying. She shook her head violently, her red hair flying around her face.

"Aubrey," Maxx said softly, grabbing my attention as surely as if he had shouted it. "We're not them," he said quietly, picking up on a thought I had mulled over more than once.

He still stood there, twisting the damn dish towel around his hand. He was gnawing on his bottom lip again, a sign he was anxious.

"We're us. And that's not such a bad thing, you know," he continued quietly.

I sighed, not responding. Because, really, what could I say? He was right. We weren't all bad. Even though there was some really messed-up stuff between us, there was also some beauty as well. Because of Maxx, I had been able to open myself up in a way I hadn't been willing to do in three years. Because of Maxx, I started to become the Aubrey Duncan I used to be. Spontaneous. Open. Vulnerable.

I had to find a way to get past this anger I felt toward him. This bitterness was clawing a hole through my gut. "I know," I finally admitted, watching as Renee shouted something at Devon and turned away, walking quickly down the path toward the parking lot. Devon stood there, looking at a loss. If I didn't know what an asshole he was, I might have felt sorry for him. Because he seemed honestly heartbroken.

Serves the abusive fuckhead right!

"How about, instead of coming in here three times a day, you let me take you somewhere?" Maxx said, startling me.

"What?" I asked, my mouth gaping open like a fish's.

"What would you say if I wanted you to spend the day with me? Out of the coffee shop, that is," he said, his mouth curving upward in a hesitant smile.

I was hit by a wave of déjà vu that had me sucking in a painful breath.

Spend the day with me, I recalled him saying that first morning we had spent together. I remembered exactly what we were doing when he had asked me to blow off classes and be with him.

Just for today. No classes. No work. Just you. Just me. Just us together.

"Yeah, that's not going to happen, Maxx," I said, showing both of us exactly how different things were between us now.

Because that time, all those months ago, I had done exactly as he had asked, no hesitation.

Maxx stopped twisting the towel in his hands and dropped it onto the table.

"I'm not asking you to run away with me, Aubrey. I'm just asking for a few hours. I could come by after you go to the library and take you out to the farm where I work. The stable manager said I could ride the horses sometime. That's it. If you have a horrible time, I'll never ask you to come out with me again," Maxx stated.

Horseback riding? The randomness of it reminded me yet again of how much I missed that spontaneous side that only Maxx brought out in me. "You just won't give up, will you?" I asked, feeling myself giving in. Because I already knew the answer. And I hated that the part of me that still loved him didn't *want* him to give up. Ever.

I sighed and looked up, meeting the eyes of the man who stood in front of me with his heart in his hands, hoping that I would reach out and take it.

"Okay," I whispered. I felt as though I were standing on a precipice, ready to topple over.

"Really?" Maxx asked, his smile turning into a full-blown grin. He looked as though he had just won the lottery.

It was sort of irresistible.

And by the sinking feeling in my gut, I knew I was in trouble.

chapter twenty

aubrey

Why had I accepted Maxx's invitation?

I had a strong feeling that the world I had only just gotten back on track was about to change all over again.

I sat on my couch only an hour after leaving the coffee shop, the brochure for the Department of Education in my lap and a thousand different possibilities for my life floating around in my head. I was feeling completely and totally overwhelmed.

Renee walked through the door in the middle of my silent freak-out looking much calmer than she had earlier. "Are you all right?" I questioned her.

My friend collapsed on the couch beside me. "I've made a mess of stuff," she said, her admission rough in her mouth.

"You want to talk about it?" I asked, giving her the opportunity to share with me what was going on with her. My curiosity was killing me. I wanted to know what Devon said to her. I wanted to know what exactly she was doing with her abusive ex-boyfriend. I wanted to grill her more about Iain and what had happened between them. Renee put her hand over mine that still clutched the course catalogue and squeezed. The comforting gesture was clearly for her as much as for me.

"I do want to talk about it, Aubrey. I really do. Just not right now. My head sort of feels like it's going to explode." She gave me a wry smile that I returned.

"This is definitely a head-explosion zone," I agreed.

"So, Maxx . . ." Renee's voice trailed off, letting me fill in the gaps for her.

"He asked me to go horseback riding with him," I told her, grimacing.

"Horseback riding? Since when are you Annie Oakley?" Renee scoffed.

I rolled my eyes. "Since never. But I told him okay," I said in a rush, putting the truth out there as quickly as possible.

Renee squeezed my hand again and dropped her head onto my shoulder. "What's wrong with us?" she asked, giving voice to the very question that had plagued me for months.

"We love too hard and too recklessly, I think," I murmured.

"Let's just hope we can walk away in one piece this time," Renee said softly. And we sat there, supporting each other as heartbroken friends do.

✦

I was pacing holes in the living room carpet when Maxx finally arrived. I opened the door and slipped out into the hallway, not letting him inside.

"Ready?" he asked, and I nodded.

"Ready," I said, giving him a thin smile. Maxx ran his hands through his hair, and I found myself really looking at him. My misgivings kicked up a notch as I took in his appearance. He was wearing worn jeans that hung off his narrow hips. His chest strained under a red button-down shirt. He had rolled up the sleeves to his elbows. His hair fell in haphazard curls across his forehead.

He was thinner. His face more angular, his cheekbones more pronounced. His eyes were clear and steady. Absent was the bloodshot haze I had been used to seeing. He looked happy. Excited, even. It was a look that could prove lethal to my wishy-washy heart.

Because this was a new Maxx. Someone I had only seen in glimpses between withdrawals. Someone who had shown his face only briefly while I had loved and been consumed by him.

A stable Maxx. Calm. Competent. Together.

Angry, bitter Aubrey wondered if this, too, was an act. And if it wasn't, I wondered how long it could last. *Enough with the negativity!* I chastised myself.

This Maxx smiled with shy reservation, as though he wasn't sure whether he should or not. He spoke with consideration of his words. He thought before he acted. He was so completely different that it was hard to believe he was the same person. The connection we had always shared was still there, yet it strained and stretched in this strange new world we coexisted in.

We walked to his car silently.

"Do you want to listen to the radio?" he asked, fumbling with the ancient dials on his dashboard once we were buckled in.

"I don't care," I said, situating myself so I could get comfortable on the crunchy leather seats.

Maxx flipped to a rock station and pulled away from the curb in front of my apartment building.

"How are the jobs going?" I asked him, feeling like conversation was required.

"Not bad. But they're mind-numbing and sort of pay the bills."

"Sort of?" I asked.

"Well, they don't pay as much as I wish they would," Maxx said with a hint of bitterness.

I didn't know what else to say. I had never struggled so much with small talk before. Perhaps it was because there were a million things I felt I *should* be saying. Things I should ask him.

Should I talk to him about rehab? Should I ask him how he was getting along now that he had been discharged? Should I ignore the topic altogether and for just one day pretend that that particular darkness never had a place in our lives?

"I was thinking the other day how little I really know about you," Maxx said suddenly, surprising me.

"What?"

Maxx shrugged. "You know some about my parents and you've met Landon, but I don't know anything about where you came from. And I don't think we've ever really talked about your family before. Not once in all the time we spent together did you ever tell me about your parents or your sister. The one that died."

"Well, that's the only one I had," I retorted.

Maxx shook his head. "See, I didn't even know that. What's wrong with me that I never thought to ask you such fundamental questions like how many siblings you have or what your parents are like?"

I knew he was right. As deep and wild as things had been between us, it was startling to realize that I had never shared such simple things with him. On one hand, he knew things about me that no one else did. They were the sorts of things that could only be wrenched out of someone at moments of absolute vulnerability. I had opened up to him about my feelings of guilt and grief about Jayme. But when it came to the little things boyfriends and girlfriends knew about each other, we were completely deficient.

It felt strange to backtrack now. Particularly since we were no longer playing those roles in each other's lives. I wasn't sure I wanted to give him those tidbits of truth. I didn't know what purpose it would serve. I was adamant that I wasn't here with him in order to pursue a continued connection, yet I was here all the same.

Would it hurt to let him in . . . just a little bit?

"I guess we haven't. My parents aren't really a subject I like to talk about. We haven't had much of a relationship since my sister, Jayme, died. They blamed me. *I* blamed me. It worked out better to have as little to do with each other as possible." I kept emotion out of my voice. I was blandly neutral, giving nothing away.

He didn't badger me for details; he just let that piece of information sit there between us. "What was she like? Your sister? Was she like you? Too smart for her own good?" Maxx asked, shooting me a sideways smile.

I stiffened instantly, not exactly prepared to dive into this particular subject. "Umm . . ." I began, my throat feeling suddenly tight.

"It's okay, you don't have to tell me," Maxx said softly, his smile slipping.

And then, just like before, I was talking. Without even realizing what I was doing, I opened myself up a little bit more. And it felt good. I *enjoyed* sharing my memories of Jayme. I needed to.

"No. She and I were nothing alike. Even though we looked alike, our personalities couldn't have been more different. I've always been a little school-crazy. Good grades and getting into a decent college were really important to me."

"Big surprise that you were always the overachiever. You were probably on the debate team and ran for school council, too," Maxx deduced, chuckling.

"I was *not* on the debate team," I huffed with feigned indignation.

Maxx made a point to control his laughter. "I'm sorry. I won't make that assumption again." He tapped his fingers on the steering wheel in time to the music. "But I totally called the school council. What were you? The president?"

"Vice president," I muttered under my breath, grumbling but without venom.

"I knew it," Maxx said, smacking his hand against the steering wheel.

"Well, Jayme was always more interested in hanging out with friends and going out, even though our parents were pretty strict. I had a ten o'clock curfew until I left for college," I told him.

"Wow. I never had a curfew. But that's because David never gave a shit where I was or what I was doing. Sometimes I would wish like hell he'd tell me to be home by a certain time. Then I would know that someone cared if I ever came back at all," Maxx said, his smile now brittle.

My heart couldn't help but twist a bit at the thought of Maxx growing up unloved and alone. So much of that sense of disconnectedness had formed the person he eventually became. The guy who had thrown himself into the club scene in an effort to belong *somewhere.* The guy who used drugs to stop feeling anything at all.

These tiny pieces of his past helped me understand him a little bit better. It certainly didn't excuse everything that he had done, but I was better able to get the motivations. Maxx cleared his throat and forced a smile back on his face. "So Jayme was the party girl and you were the homebody, right?"

"Not entirely. I went out with friends. I had a life. I just had my priorities," I said.

"I have no doubt you were the girl in high school I would never have had a chance with. You have always been way too good for a guy like me," he said, chuckling in that self-deprecating way of his.

I didn't respond. What would be the point?

Our coming together all those months ago was a perfect storm of circumstance. Maxx had walked into my life at a moment when I needed the chaos and insanity that he created, whether I had realized it at the time or not.

"Jayme was . . . unique. She had these crazy toe socks that were all of these different colors. When she was in a bad mood, she'd wear them, swearing they were the key to having a good day." I shook my head, snorting. "I have no idea why I just told you that," I said, feeling embarrassed.

"That's cool, I had a pair of those toe sock things, too," Maxx remarked, and I arched my eyebrow in disbelief.

Maxx shrugged. "Seriously. My mom got them for me when I was a kid. When it was really cold out I'd wear them around the house. They were ugly as hell, but fuck if they weren't comfortable," Maxx said, turning down a gravel road, rocks hitting the underside of his car with audible clangs.

"Jayme and I used to dress up in our mom's skirts and blouses and would put our hair up in buns. We'd pretend that we were Amish. Our parents had taken us to Pennsylvania Dutch country one summer, and we became sort of obsessed. I don't know why. Maybe it was the awesome horse and buggies or those kick-ass bonnets." I rolled my eyes and Maxx smirked. "We'd spend all weekend refusing to watch television or turn on lights. We'd light candles in our rooms and do stuff like try to sew scarves. It was kind of ridiculous." I couldn't believe I was admitting this to him. I wasn't used to talking about Jayme like this. Not in a positive way, focusing on the good memories. But it felt good.

Better than good.

How was it that the man who had shrouded me in so much darkness was now giving me nothing but light?

Once we had started sharing these seemingly random stories, it was like neither of us could stop.

Maxx told me about sneaking into his dad's bedside table and finding his nose hair trimmers and proceeding to shave baby Landon's eyebrows off. I then told him about pretending to be mute for an entire day and how Jayme insisted on being my interpreter. We had developed our own version of sign language that we used until she died.

Soon I was chuckling. A deep, from-the-gut laugh that I hadn't experienced in a long time. I barely realized Maxx had parked the car beside a large brick stable.

"We're here," Maxx announced, shutting off the engine.

I got out of the car and followed Maxx around the side of the building. It smelled like hay and horses and a lot like manure. I crinkled my nose.

"Mr. Wyatt?" Maxx called out, unlocking a gate and going inside. He held out his hand, and I took it without thinking. He pulled me after him, and I jogged a bit to keep up.

"Hi, Maxx." A balding man with a threadbare plaid shirt and dirt-streaked jeans came out from one of the stalls, a shovel full of horse crap in his hand.

"Is it all right if we take out Brandy and Earl?" Maxx asked, still holding my hand tightly, almost as though he was worried I'd run off.

Mr. Wyatt nodded and swung the shit-laden shovel toward the stalls at the back of the stable. "Sure thing. Now, you said you had riding experience, right? What about your friend?" he asked. Maxx nodded and squeezed my hand. I nodded, too, though the truth was, I hadn't ridden a horse since I had gone to summer camp when I was twelve.

"Okay, well, those two are gentle beasts; I don't think you'll have any trouble. Just stay in the corral," Mr. Wyatt instructed.

Maxx tugged on my hand, and we walked in the direction of Brandy and Earl's stalls. "Have you ever ridden a horse before?" I asked, arching an eyebrow.

Maxx nodded his head, his lips splitting in a huge grin. "Nope."

"Figured," I muttered, snickering.

"How hard can it be?" Maxx shrugged, and I finally saw some of that easy confidence of the boy I used to know.

"I think you're about to be pretty surprised," I warned.

"I'm a quick learner. I've helped Wyatt put on saddles a few times. I've got this." Maxx pulled two leather saddles off the wall and lugged them over to a pretty gray mare with kind black eyes and the softest ears I had ever felt.

I cooed to her, scratching her neck. Brandy was a sweet and gentle horse, which was good, because I was beginning to think this experience was going to end up with either Maxx, me, or both of us falling on our asses.

Maxx hefted the saddle onto Brandy's back, and she stood there patiently as he fumbled with the buckles.

He grunted as he repositioned the saddle several times before getting it right. I peered at it nervously. "Are you sure it's on there correctly?" I asked.

"Of course." Maxx stepped close, leaning down until his mouth was next to my ear. "Don't be scared, Aubrey. I won't let you fall," he said softly, his voice low.

I shivered at the feel of his breath on my neck. I couldn't help it. It was an involuntary reaction to his proximity.

I helped Maxx drag the second saddle over to the next stall and put it on Earl's back. Earl seemed stressed. He pawed at the ground and didn't act overly thrilled to have Maxx attaching the saddle to his back.

"This one seems kind of hard to handle, Maxx," I said, eyeing the horse apprehensively.

"Nah, Earl's awesome. Wyatt rides him all the time."

"Mr. Wyatt has also been riding horses for years. He probably makes it look pretty easy," I offered, not trying to be a negative nelly. But the last thing I wanted was to take Maxx to the hospital with a broken neck.

"You'll see, Aubrey. I'll be riding this horse like a pro in no time," Maxx stated with enough self-assurance that I almost believed him.

He was able to attach the saddle to the back of his horse a bit more easily than he could with Brandy, but when it came time to mount Earl, the ornery horse wasn't having it. Earl moved around, not letting Maxx get a strong grip on the reins so he could pull himself up.

"Uh, I don't think he wants you on his back, Maxx." I chuckled, watching Maxx try to control the uncooperative horse.

"He's just being moody," Maxx griped, trying to put his foot in the stirrups again. Earl took a step forward, and Maxx lost his balance, falling into a pile of horseshit.

"Fucking hell!" he yelled, and I lost it. I started laughing so hard that I couldn't breathe. Maxx struggled to his feet and promptly lost his footing again and fell onto his back.

"You could help me out here, Aubrey," Maxx said, holding out his hand.

"Sorry, it's just you're in a literal pile of shit there, Maxx," I pointed out.

"You're so damn funny," Maxx muttered.

I grabbed his hand and started to pull him up, when he gave my arm a hard tug and I fell beside him in the manure.

"I'm going to fucking kill you!" I shrieked, trying to stand up but losing my footing, just as Maxx had. The crap seemed to be sucking me down.

It was Maxx's turn to crack up, but the humor of the situation was now lost on me.

The smell was atrocious, and the squishy feeling between my fingers was making me nauseous.

I looked down at my ruined clothes and at Maxx. His eyes were twinkling, and he was grinning even though we were sitting in horse poop. He looked happy. Maybe the happiest I had seen him since that day we had gone sledding.

And then I wasn't pissed anymore.

We managed to help each other up just as Mr. Wyatt came in to see what all the commotion was about.

"Well, that's not exactly how you ride a horse," he said dryly, and that set us off again.

"I'm guessing the two of you are going to need a shower," Mr. Wyatt mumbled, shaking his head at us.

"If you don't mind, sir," Maxx said, calming down.

"Come on, then. I have some extra clothes. And I'm sure I can find something of my wife's for you," Mr. Wyatt said, inclining his head in my direction.

"Thank you, Mr. Wyatt," I said, biting on my lip to stop from snickering.

The head stable hand led us to a shower cubicle at the back of the building that had several towels hung over the door. It was a little grimy and looked as if it hadn't been cleaned for a while.

But it was either wash myself in there or smell like horseshit.

I'd choose the moldy shower.

"It's going to be cold. But I'm not letting you in the house smelling like that," Mr. Wyatt said, leaving us to our shower.

"Uh, can you turn around, please?" I asked Maxx, feeling silly, considering how many times he had seen me naked in the past.

But things had definitely changed in that department.

Maxx did as he was asked. I quickly stripped and got into the shower, turning on the water and screaming when the frigid water hit my skin.

"Fucking hell!" I screeched.

I hurriedly rinsed off and wrapped myself in a towel, exiting the shower. Maxx was still standing there, now with a pair of linen trousers and a pink frilly shirt in his hands. His eyes heated as they took in my state of undress.

"Doesn't exactly look like your style," I joked, feeling uncomfortably hot under Maxx's gaze.

He blinked, as if realizing that he was blatantly staring. He handed me the clothes. "Uh, yeah, these are for you." He cleared his throat and then went in the small shower cubicle.

I quickly got dressed and realized Mrs. Wyatt must be several sizes bigger than I was. The shirt gaped open, and I had to tie a knot in the bottom so that it fit properly. I was just putting on my socks and shoes when Maxx got out. He had wrapped a towel around his waist, and I couldn't help but stare at the droplets of water that clung to his chest.

In my efforts to get over my feelings for this complicated man, I had conveniently forgotten the intense physical attraction we shared. The lust. The desire. The longing that made it hard to breathe.

But I felt it now. It reached out and squeezed my insides, making it impossible to move.

He looked at me, his wet hair slicked back away from his face, his blue eyes hooded.

I licked my lips, and Maxx's eyes dropped to my mouth. I remembered this feeling. This wanting and waiting that had always consumed me.

"Here you go," I said, breaking the moment by handing him a pile of clothing Mr. Wyatt had left for him.

"Thanks," Maxx said, taking the shirt and jeans from my hands, his fingers brushing against mine.

I pulled my hand back and shoved it into the pocket of my oversized pants, trying to ignore the tingles in my fingertips.

Our horse-riding adventure pretty much ended after that. As soon as we were finished getting dressed and awkwardly avoiding each other's eyes, Mr. Wyatt called Maxx over.

"Just give me a minute. Let me see what he wants and then we can get out of here," Maxx said. I nodded and watched him go over to his boss, who had lowered his head and spoke to Maxx with an apologetic look on his face.

Maxx's face shadowed and his mouth turned down. Whatever Mr. Wyatt was saying, it didn't make him very happy.

What was going on?

After a few more minutes, Maxx came back, not even trying to hide the look of frustration on his face.

"What's wrong?" I asked, after thanking Mr. Wyatt for letting us use the facilities.

Maxx didn't answer until we were in his car and driving down the long driveway away from the stable.

"It seems that he doesn't need me at the stable as much as he thought. He's cut my hours. Which means I either need to find another place of employment or take on a third job if I want to keep my electricity on," he said resentfully, jerking the steering wheel as he drove through the streets back toward town.

"Maybe the coffee shop could give you more hours," I suggested. He looked deflated, and I knew this had to be a major blow for him. I could see how hard he was trying.

"I doubt it. They're scraping together hours to give me as it is." He gave me a pained smile. "I'll figure something out. I always do," he said.

We didn't say anything else to each other. The surprisingly enjoyable day appeared to sort of fizzle out, as neither of us seemed in the mood to try to continue making useless conversation.

"Do you want to come over for a while?" he asked, and I found that the suggestion didn't irritate me in the slightest. It was actually almost appealing. But I knew that I couldn't. No matter how much fun I had with him today. I shook my head.

"I should get back. I have homework I have to get done for tomorrow's class," I said as an excuse. Maxx's face darkened briefly before smoothing out. He gave me a short nod and didn't say anything else.

A tension radiated from him that made me nervous. I opened my mouth several times to say something to dispel the uneasy energy, but could never think of anything to say.

I was relieved when he pulled up in front of my apartment building. Maxx's change in mood reminded me so much of the man that I remembered.

I turned to say thank you for our day, when he reached across the seat and cupped his hand around the back of my head.

I pulled back from his grip, ready to push him away. My heart slammed in my chest, and my breath came out in short, erratic puffs.

"What are you doing?" I demanded. Why was he ruining our perfectly good day?

Maxx's hand curled around the back of my neck, his fingers threading into the hair at the base of my skull, the slight pressure causing my pulse to race.

"Don't tell me to stop. I just want to remember what it feels like to get lost in you, back when it all made a crazy sort of sense," he begged, pulling me toward him, capturing my lips before I could object.

I startled in response, tensing, ready to pull away again.

"Please, Aubrey. You can deny what's between us later. You can tell yourself that you've moved on. That you want nothing to do with me. But you and I both know that's not the truth. And I had hoped we had finally stopped lying to each other," Maxx murmured against my mouth.

Then he was kissing me again, and I didn't stop him.

The fight left me. The anger, the bitterness, the purposeful isolation disintegrated instantly.

Kissing Maxx was like waking up. Like stepping through the mist into a clearing. It was love and lust and passion. It was pain and anguish and gut-wrenching turmoil.

It was everything.

My lips parted almost involuntarily, and his tongue swept in, tangling with mine. He moaned, intense and low, and wove his fingers in my hair, burying deep. I couldn't help my body's response as I melted into him.

My lips had missed kissing him.

My fingers had missed touching him.

My heart missed beating only for him.

I gave up fighting the inevitable and wrapped my arms around him, holding him as tightly as he held me.

The feel of him in my mouth was familiar and intoxicating.

This is what oblivion tasted like.

Slowly, his lips became less frantic until he stopped kissing me altogether and he rested his forehead against mine.

"I know you've said you don't want this. But I'm all in, Aubrey. I always have been."

I closed my eyes and tried to get my breathing under control.

"I have to go," I whispered, trying to move and failing. Finally, I was able to unwrap my arms from around Maxx and pulled myself away.

With shaking hands I opened the door of his car and got out. I walked up the steps to my apartment building, escaping to the safety of my own four walls.

Escaping the truth that reverberated through my body.

I loved Maxx.

What was I going to do with that?

chapter twenty-one

maxx

I didn't want Aubrey to go home. I knew that if I let her leave when I felt like this, I couldn't trust myself alone. Having my hours cut at the stable had left me reeling—I had no idea how I was going to manage to scrape by without that money. My immediate thought after receiving the unwanted news was that I wanted to get high. Really fucking high. And forget about how much my life sucked.

I could have called a hotline or one of the numbers the counselors at Barton House had given me. But I didn't want to call a fucking hotline.

I only wanted Aubrey.

And so I'd kissed her like a man drowning. And she hadn't pulled away. She took everything that I gave her.

I felt it. That moment when she surrendered herself to me all over again. The taste of it was sweet on my tongue as I took exactly what I wanted.

It had been a while since I hadn't asked permission to fucking breathe. I grabbed her, and I held on like my life depended on it. And maybe it did.

But then it was over and she was leaving and I was left alone.

Always alone.

I drove home, feeling depressed and not entirely sure what the hell I was going to do and whether I had the energy to try.

I walked up the stairs to my apartment trying to figure out my next move. Finding another job seemed like the most sensible plan. But the thought of pounding the pavement attempting to find someone who would be willing to give me a chance made me want to smash stuff.

I thought again about the art gallery and how royally I had screwed it up. I had been holding the golden goose in my hand, and I had lost it. And now here I was trying to find a way to survive without falling back on the easy solution. The club. The drugs. Quick cash in my pocket.

But what would be the price?

"Where the fuck have you been?" a voice growled from the shadowed recess beside my door. Marco stood up from where he had been sitting on the floor and gave me a look that could break bones.

"What are you doing here?" I asked, wondering about my chances of knocking his ass out and getting into my apartment. The last thing I wanted was to deal with Marco and whatever he had come here to say.

"Oh, I don't know. How about the fact that you dropped off the fucking Earth and Gash is ready to roast your ass on a pike?" Marco shouted, his voice echoing down the hallway. My meth-head neighbor opened his door a crack and peeked out. I could see one bloodshot eye watching Marco and me as we squared off outside my apartment.

"I'm not doing this shit out here," I replied, shouldering past the guy who had been my friend for over five years, and put my key into the lock.

"Then we'll talk about this inside. But I'm not fucking leaving until you give me some goddamned answers!" Marco roared, pushing past me and into my apartment.

I flicked on the light and figured I might as well have this out with him now. I had avoided it long enough, and I knew Marco wasn't going anywhere until he got what he wanted.

And right now that was a small dose of truth.

Marco tossed something at me and it smacked my chest. I grabbed it before it could fall to the floor. I held it up and saw that it was a plastic bag with a dozen or so pills of all different colors.

My only salvation and my greatest nightmare.

"I don't want this shit, Marco," I said, holding out the bag for him to take.

Marco shook his head. "I figured you needed some incentive to tell me what's been going on with you," he said, sitting down on my couch and putting his dirty boots up on the clean coffee table.

My hand shook as I held the pills. My ears buzzed, and I couldn't see anything but the drugs in my hand.

"Have you become a housekeeper or something? Your place is seriously clean. I'd be impressed if I didn't want to rip your nut sack off and shove it up your ass," Marco was saying, though I barely heard him. My mouth had gone dry, and my heart started to pound.

I'm right here, Maxx. I've never really left you. Not like everyone else. You can always count on me.

The goddamned voice was back. I heard it as clear as if it were a real person whispering in my ear.

I could barely control my fingers as I twisted the bag into a knot and shoved the pills into my pocket. Nausea erupted in the pit of my stomach, and I felt bile crawl up the back of my throat.

"Have you gone deaf as well as stupid since I saw you last, fuck face?" Marco threw a pillow at my head, and I didn't even bother to catch it.

"I don't have time for your crap, Marco. Say what you want to say and get the fuck out." I gritted my teeth and swallowed the urge to punch him in the face. This guy had been my closest friend for years. But it wasn't what you'd call a "healthy" friendship. Our relationship had thrived on the worst of each other. He was the one who could undo everything I was trying to accomplish. And he didn't even realize it. And I doubted he'd even care.

Marco's face darkened, and I knew that we were dangerously close to coming to blows.

"You're a dick, Maxx. You disappear for over a month, leaving me in the fucking lurch. You took off with Gash's money *and* his fucking drugs, and then you don't answer my calls? I've been by this shithole every week since you up and took a trip to la-la land and this is the crap I get from you? I've had your fucking back for years, X. You and me, we had an agreement. And you flaked. Pretty hard core, too. I deserve some answers as to where the hell you went." Marco swung his feet to the floor and sat up, no longer lounging like he owned the place.

I thought about telling him where I had been. That I had almost died and had gone to rehab. I probably should have. It would have been the smart thing to do. To be honest with the only pathetic excuse for a friend I'd ever had.

But Marco wouldn't get it. And more important, he wouldn't give a shit, because in the end, I had bailed. There weren't enough excuses in the world to make him okay with that.

"I had stuff going on with Landon," I lied, hoping it would be enough of an answer to let me off the hook without going into specifics.

"What was up with Landon?" Marco asked, as cold as ever. Of course he knew my brother. He had spent time at my house before I had graduated high school and Landon had been much younger.

"It was a bunch of drama with David. You know how it goes. I had some things to sort out and square away." I had forgotten how good I was at lying. It was effortless, like sugar on my tongue.

Marco's face smoothed out marginally, and I knew he had bought my story. "Well, you'd better get your kneepads ready, because you're going to have to do some serious sucking in order to make it up to Gash. And I hope like hell you have his money. Otherwise you'll be eating out of your asshole for the rest of your life."

It was good that I had put the wad of cash from that last night at the club in my dresser before heading to rehab. I had sold the entire supply Gash had given me to sell. I had made the fucker his money before taking enough smack to stop my heart.

I walked back to my room and got the bundle of cash I had stuffed into a sock in the back of my drawer. I came back out to the living room and handed Marco the money.

He quickly counted it and looked relieved it was all there. "Shit, you actually did what you were supposed to for once. You're damn lucky, X. Gash has been livid since you pulled your Houdini act. He wants you back at the club immediately. Like, *now.* He's been on a hair trigger lately. He fired Randy and got rid of three of the bartenders. He's tearing through staff like crazy. Someone's lit a fire under his ass, and he's ready to rip us all a new one." Marco scratched the douchey goatee he had grown in my absence, looking as nervous as I'd ever seen him.

"I don't think I'm going back to the club, man," I said, ready for the fireworks.

And Marco didn't disappoint. His face went molten red, and he looked like he was ready to spit nails. "What the fuck are you talking about?" he demanded.

"Just what I fucking said! I'm done with the club! I'm gonna try to play it straight for a while," I said, hating that I sounded like such a pussy. And hating that I wished I could take back the words as soon as I had said them.

"Why in the hell would you want to do that? We're making a mint! So because you've developed some sort of sudden moral fucking center, I'm going to have to suffer because of it? You really are a selfish prick, you know that?" he yelled, kicking over my coffee table.

"Dude, if you're going to break shit, go somewhere else and have your hissy fit," I told him dryly.

Marco gave me a dirty look, but leaned down and picked up the overturned table. He sighed and pulled at the silver hoop in his lip. "Do you have something against cash, Maxx? Because I know you can't be so stupid to think you can get that sort of scratch at a nine-to-five. We've got a great little operation going on. And now that Gash is cutting down on people, he's less focused on what I'm doing at the door. He's more interested in his other side projects. He's been meeting a lot with those dudes from Mexico. He won't give a shit about some money missing from the door every night. We could even increase the amount if we're careful. This is the time to make some serious coin, man." Marco's eyes snapped, and he was a man with some intense conviction. He made it damn hard to say no.

Because he was right. I couldn't make the kind of money I did at the club anywhere else. I'd had my chance to make something of myself and had blown it. My art, even school, had become nothing more than wasted opportunities in the wreckage of my life. I fingered the bag of pills in my pocket, feeling their familiar round smoothness.

"Just come by the club this weekend. Talk to Gash. See what he has to say. If you tell him what was going on with your brother, he probably won't use your face as a punching bag," Marco suggested, and I smirked.

"Golly gee, you make that sound so appealing," I responded sarcastically, even as I was already considering his offer.

"Just come by. Don't fuck yourself because of some newfound scruples. Screw that shit. That's not who you are. You're fucking X, dude. Don't forget that." Marco pointed at the bag of pills I had unconsciously taken out of my pocket and held between my fingers.

"You need to take the edge off. I can tell it's been a while," he said, and walked out the door.

I crumpled the bag in my hands and headed to the bathroom, before I could talk myself out of it. I lifted the toilet lid and held open the bag, watching as a handful of pills fell into the water. Before the last of them could fall, I quickly stuffed it back into my pocket.

I flushed the toilet and then hurried down the hall to my bedroom, shoving the bag into the back of my drawer.

I slammed it shut and fell back against the dresser, breathing heavily. My skin was clammy with sweat, and my throat felt tight with the overwhelming urge to swallow the last two pills in the bag. I wanted them.

I didn't think I had ever wanted anything so much in my entire sad fucking life. I couldn't. I wasn't going to crawl back to that, no matter how much I craved it with every cell, every molecule, in my body.

I'll be here whenever you need me, they whispered.

I covered my ears with my hands and wanted to scream for them to leave me the hell alone! That I wasn't that guy anymore! That I wouldn't let myself be him! I had people who were counting on me. People who needed me to be someone different.

I slid down to the floor and closed my eyes. And then I leaned over and threw up onto my carpet. Acidic bile dribbled from my mouth, and I wiped it away with the hem of my shirt. My head was pounding and my ears were ringing as I forced myself to forget about the drugs I had stupidly hung on to.

The drugs, now that I had them again, I couldn't let go of. I wanted to, but I had learned a long time ago that want and need were two entirely different things.

chapter twenty-two

aubrey

I was confused. No, I was more than confused. I was *disoriented.*

Maxx's kiss had thrown me. I should have predicted it. What had I expected would happen? That we'd sit around and knit a freaking sweater?

He had seemed so upset after getting the news that his hours were being cut at the stable, and I hurt for him. He'd pulled me in with his sad desperation, just as he always had. So much for my so-called hardened heart. Now here I was, several days later, still bothered by his sadness.

I showed up early to my Boundaries and Ethics class so I could have my weekly slip signed off for Dr. Lowell. I suppressed my abject humiliation at being treated like a naughty grade-schooler who has to have her work approved.

"Hey, Aubrey."

I looked up to see April taking her now-usual seat beside me. I had spent the last few classes trying to ignore her to keep my distance from Evan intact, but I was too tired to maintain my active silence. "Hey, April. How are you?"

April gave me a startled look. "Uh, fine, thanks. How are you?" she asked, the conversation stilted. April didn't seem to know what to say, and I wondered when was the last time she had been asked that question.

"Not bad. Did you do the reading last night?"

"Yeah, but I'm not sure I understood any of it. This stuff is over my head. I audited this class thinking it would be an interesting filler. I quit my job, which I wasn't happy about. But I realized I had some time to kill, so I thought why not. But it's way more work than I thought it would be," April said on a sigh.

"Sorry about the job. That sucks," I said sympathetically with a grimace.

"Yeah. It does. But I should have probably quit a long time ago. It's for the best," she said, as though repeating something she had been told many times before.

My curiosity was piqued. "Why is it for the best? Where were you working?"

"I was a cashier at the independent bookstore on Maple Drive," April said.

"I love that place! That sounds like a great job! Why in the world would you want to quit working there?" I asked.

April chewed on her bottom lip, sucking the small silver ring into her mouth. "Evan didn't like my boss. It created . . . problems," she answered hesitantly.

I could imagine what sort of problems Evan created. I got the feeling that April didn't want to talk about it, and I wasn't going to press her for personal details.

"Yeah, so this class is no cakewalk, that's for sure," I continued, as though she hadn't mentioned Evan or her job.

"Yeah, I've heard," April said, giving me the hint of a smile.

"I barely scraped by with a B the last time I took it," I told her without thinking.

April frowned, cocking her head to the side.

"You've taken this class already and passed? Then why in the world are you taking it again?" she asked incredulously, and I realized my mistake.

"You're just a masochist like the rest of us, huh?" She giggled, and I couldn't help but wonder if we might have been friends under different circumstances. I could see a glimmer of the person she could be if she wasn't with Evan, and I wondered why she stayed with someone who sucked away all elements of her personality.

My mind immediately went to my best friend and the girl she had become when she had been dating Devon.

"Damn, my cover's been blown," I joked, smiling back. April laughed, and it was an infectious sort of sound that made me hate her boyfriend more than I already did for taking that joy away from her. The professor began his lecture, and I was pulled from my surprisingly enjoyable conversation.

At the end of class, I packed up my stuff and noticed that April was waiting for me. I gave her a questioning glance. She picked at her textbook and started sucking on her lip ring again. "So, we have that test next week," she began.

"Yeah, it's going to be a killer, too. So I recommend studying your ass off," I replied offhandedly, throwing my bag over my shoulder and heading out of the room.

April scurried behind me to keep up with my longer strides. "Do you think we can study together? Because I'm lost. I don't understand any of this," she suggested, a note of pleading in her voice.

I stopped before leaving the building. I could see Evan standing impatiently just outside the door, a cigarette hanging from his mouth and a glower already pinned to his face.

"Yeah, I don't think that would be such a great idea," I said pointedly, nodding my head toward her boyfriend on the other side of the glass.

April noticeably deflated and seemed to shrink in on herself at the sight of Evan. Her shoulders sagged, and her eyes focused on the floor. "Yeah, you're probably right," she muttered, barely audible.

I felt myself get angry. Really, *really* angry.

It wasn't right that April was allowing herself to be controlled by this guy. I thought of Renee kissing Devon, and I felt an almost murderous rage. At April. At Renee. At every girl who let herself be dictated by the moods and whims of the person who claimed to love her.

And that included *me*.

I squared my shoulders and shook my head. "You know what, let's study together. We can meet at the library. That shouldn't be a problem, right?" I asked, and April looked up through her eyelashes. She seemed so small and timid. Like a dog that had been kicked one too many times.

"I would really like that, Aubrey," she said, her lips trembling, as if afraid to smile. I wanted to punch the abusive dick standing just outside.

"Great. Then let's get together tomorrow evening—"

"What the fuck is taking you so long?" a voice barked, the door slamming open and ricocheting off the wall.

April instantly recoiled. Her eyes glazed over and her shoulders went up, her chin tucking into her chest as though bracing herself for a blow.

Evan glared down at his tardy girlfriend, clearly expecting an immediate answer. But April had gone mute, incapable of speaking, let alone explaining herself.

Then he realized I was also standing there.

"What the hell do you want, bitch?" he asked, his lip curling up in a disgusted sneer.

I looked him straight in the eye. "None of your damn business," I responded slowly, succinctly.

Evan's face flushed red, his jaw ticking, his eyes darkening. I had pissed him off. I got the impression he wasn't used to having anyone talk back to him.

"You'd better watch your mouth, girlie. I'd hate to see it wiped right off your face."

Was this guy for real? A month ago I would have most likely trembled at being confronted in such an aggressive manner. But not now.

I crossed my arms over my chest and arched my eyebrow. "You do know that sort of language can be construed as threatening and abusive. And someone with your colorful legal history should know that you can get into quite a bit of trouble for that sort of thing."

Who is this girl? I barely recognized her. But I really, *really* liked her. Evan looked apoplectic. April's face had paled, and her eyes pleaded with me to shut up. To stop goading this very angry tiger.

Fuck that.

"You *will not* speak to me in a threatening or derogatory way *ever again.* I'm not sure who pissed in your cornflakes, but it certainly wasn't me. And whatever hard-on you have for me, you need to check it before I decide to report to someone exactly how you've been harassing me." I inclined my head just the slightest and dropped my voice until it was soft, barely above a whisper, but the words held a strength as though I had shouted them.

"You're not the only one who can make threats. And you're not the only one who can report things and mess up someone's life."

Evan opened his mouth, and I had no doubt a string of violent profanities was ready to spew forth, but I wasn't about to hear them. I looked at April, needing to communicate a silent apology for whatever my tirade would mean for her later, but she was looking staunchly at the floor.

Knowing I had only seconds to make my escape, I pushed open the door and started down the stairs, proud of how well I had handled that extremely unpleasant situation. Then I was grabbed by the back of my shirt. My hair was caught in the tight fist at my back and my head jerked viciously. I was then wrenched down the steps until we both stood on the sidewalk.

"You fucking bitch!" Evan roared, and I knew that he had every intention of using the fist he had digging into my back on my face.

I looked around, hoping to see someone . . . *anyone.* But unfortunately we were alone. It was getting later, and the campus was growing quiet as people left for the day. I silently cursed the tiny campus community. Normally I appreciated the lack of crowds, but not now. Not when I was terrified.

I opened my mouth to scream, but the sound got lost in my throat as I saw the murder in Evan's eyes. He was one scary dude, that's for sure.

"You act like a bitch, you get treated like a bitch," Evan spat into my face, leaning over me.

"Evan! Stop it!" April screeched, and even though I was most certainly facing extreme bodily harm, I couldn't help but be shocked by the fact that she had finally found her voice.

Evan was beside me, breathing loudly, and he pointed at his girlfriend, who stood at the top of the stairs, trembling. "You're fucking next!" he shouted.

How could no one hear what was going on? Shouldn't the sound of shouting alert someone to a situation? I had never felt so horribly alone. And so absolutely petrified.

Evan swung back around to look at me, his face nauseatingly close to mine. I could smell the nachos he must have had for lunch as well as the putrid stench of stale smoke. There was a good chance I would vomit. And I wanted to. I wanted to be sick all over the fucking bastard.

"You've messed with the wrong guy, you prissy cunt." He sneered, and then he was stumbling backward.

Because Evan wasn't standing in front of me anymore. He was on the ground, and there was someone standing over him, fists colliding with skin. Over and over again. Evan tried to get to his feet to defend himself but was promptly dropped back on his ass with a punch to the jaw.

"I warned you once and you didn't fucking listen!" Maxx yelled as he brought his arm back and let it fly, fist connecting with face. The sickening thud of flesh and bone made my stomach turn, and April screamed again.

Evan scrambled backward and held his hands up, trying to protect himself. He had given up on trying to fight back, and now he was simply trying to stop himself from bleeding any more.

Maxx was a machine of violence. He kept hitting Evan. I experienced a horrible sense of satisfaction seeing Evan whimper in the dirt, but then I realized the potential implications of what was happening.

The last thing Maxx needed was to get into any more trouble. Particularly since he was most likely still on probation. I chanced grabbing ahold of his arm. "Maxx! Stop!" I yelled, pushing myself up against him. Maxx fought against my grip, still trying to get to a cowering Evan, who wasn't so big and threatening anymore.

Now he was a crying heap of pathetic.

"You do *not* need an assault-and-battery charge. Please, just stop!" My voice was shrill in my own ears, and I was feeling adrenaline rush through me. I started shaking as I realized everything that had just happened.

Shit, I was going to lose it.

Maxx seemed to instinctually recognize my changed demeanor. He dropped Evan and immediately turned, his hands coming up to frame my face. "Are you okay? What did that fucker do to you?" he demanded, his voice harsh, but his touch gentle.

His thumbs stroked the tender skin of my jaw, and I felt the sharp sting of tears in my eyes.

"I'm going to kill him," he whispered, his eyes narrowing, and I knew he meant it. Before Maxx could go after Evan again, I gripped his arms as hard as possible.

"I need to go home," I said in an agonized whisper, my hands shaking so badly that I could barely hold on to him anymore. My bag fell from my limp hands and dumped out onto the ground at my feet. Maxx's eyes clouded with concern, and I saw smears of red on his knuckles as he reached down to collect my things. The sight of Evan's blood on his hands caused my stomach to heave.

"I need to leave," I repeated, and swallowed bile thick in my throat.

Maxx put his arm around my shoulders, holding me up. "Of course. Let's get you home," he said softly in my ear, steering me away from Evan, still lying on the ground. I looked up to where April had been standing and saw that she was gone.

"Will he be all right?" I said. I don't know why I cared. But Evan hadn't been moving, and I really only worried about Maxx getting into trouble for intervening. Though my mind wouldn't let me even begin to think about what would have happened had Maxx not shown up when he had.

"Fuck him," Maxx said with a vehemence that shook my already trembling body. I didn't say anything else as we walked across campus toward the south-end parking lot. "My apartment's back that way," I said, pointing in the direction we had come.

"I know. But I'm driving you. You can't walk home right now." Maxx held his car door open for me as I got in. I wasn't about to argue with him, because he was right. I didn't think my feet could make the journey.

I leaned my head against the window and closed my eyes, not opening them again until Maxx pulled up in front of my apartment building. I got out, not wanting to feel like a complete loser by having him help me up the stairs. Even if I was shaking so badly my teeth were chattering.

Shit.

Evan had wanted to hurt me. I had never seen such cold hatred in someone's eyes. I should report him to campus police. But what would that mean for Maxx? Evan wouldn't let himself go down alone. He'd pull Maxx right down with him. Of that, I was certain.

Maxx fished my keys out of the side pocket of my bag and unlocked the door. He took my messenger bag and dropped it onto the couch. I didn't say anything. I pushed open my bedroom door and kicked off my shoes. I sat down on the edge of my bed and stared blankly at the wall.

Maxx stood just inside the entryway, as though not sure what he should do.

"I think I just want to close my eyes for a bit," I said tiredly.

I didn't wait for Maxx to say anything. I crawled up onto my bed and tucked my hands underneath my head, curling into a ball. My body shook and I felt like I should cry. But I didn't want to give Evan any of my tears. That asshole didn't deserve them.

After a few minutes, my bed dipped and I felt Maxx lie down beside me. He didn't touch me, but I could feel his body heat against my back. The sound of the hypnotic rhythm of his breathing lulled me to sleep.

chapter twenty-three

aubrey

I woke up feeling groggy and winced as I moved my arms. My muscles felt bruised, and it took me a minute to remember everything that had happened earlier.

Evan and the horrific scene after class. And Maxx.

I sat up abruptly, pushing aside a blanket that hadn't been there when I had fallen asleep. My room had grown darker, and I could see the soft glow of my alarm clock displaying the time. It was just after eight in the evening.

Crap! I had slept for almost three hours!

I heard a soft exhale of breath, and I looked over to see Maxx curled onto his side. His hair was messy and fell onto his forehead. He had one hand tucked beneath his cheek and the other reaching outward.

He looked incredibly young. Vulnerable, even.

My heart twisted and turned painfully as I watched him sleep. Love that had never gone away re-ignited unobstructed in my chest.

I knew I should push it away, seal it back into the box I had tucked it away in. But I couldn't.

Not now.

Maybe I was still in a state of shock. Maybe I wasn't thinking clearly, given the horrific experience I had just gone through. Whatever the reasons, I found myself once again drawn toward the very person I knew I should stay away from.

Without thinking about what I was doing, I slowly lifted my fingers and let them hover above his skin. I wanted to sweep his hair back and feel the soft strands.

But I couldn't let myself touch him. Even as my fingers tingled with the need to.

I wanted to lie back down beside him. To press myself against him the way I had done so many times before. To fall back into that crazy, passionate place that had dominated my life.

My heart demanded that I never let this man leave my side again. That he belonged there. He would *always* belong there.

But my head said something else entirely. It warned me of the price of loving him.

But was it a price I'd be willing to pay?

I thought about Renee. And Brooks. And Dr. Lowell. The people who believed in me. The ones who gave me my second chance.

I wouldn't be disappointing just myself if I allowed this to happen.

But having him here, after what had happened, made my emotions run high. Irrational emotions that had always gotten me into trouble.

I wanted to be smarter. I wanted to be strong and turn away.

I was struggling.

Maxx's lips quirked into a sleepy smile, and his eyes slowly drifted open. "The whole watching-someone-while-they-sleep thing is a little creepy, you know."

I blushed, embarrassed at having been caught.

I cleared my throat and looked away. "Yeah, well, you have drool caked to the side of your face."

Maxx frowned and wiped at his cheek, and I couldn't help but grin. He rolled his eyes. "You're hysterical, Aubrey," he deadpanned.

I smirked, chuckling to myself before sobering. "You shouldn't have stayed," I told him firmly but quietly.

I sounded ungrateful, and I knew that. But it was my last-ditch effort to keep him at arm's length. Because I knew all too well there was a very big difference between doing what was right and doing what *felt* right.

Maxx sat up. His hair was mussed, and there were fine red lines along his jaw from the crease of the pillow. There was something rugged and raw about his face that made it impossible to look away.

"There was no way I would have left you, even if you had tried to make me." His eyes flashed vehemently, and I believed him.

"I know," I sighed.

Maxx ran his hand over his face before looking at me again.

"I think you need to report Evan."

"If I did, what would happen to you?" I asked. Maxx frowned, looking confused.

"You beat the crap out of him, Maxx. You don't think he'd jump at the chance to take you down with him?" I continued.

"That's ridiculous, Aubrey!" Maxx fumed.

I held my hand up, silencing him. "It is what it is, Maxx. You know I'm right."

I hated remaining silent about what Evan had done. It felt wrong, and in a way like I was letting him win.

I thought about April and knew without a doubt that what I had experienced at his hand was most likely mild in comparison to what she had been through.

An abusive bully like that needed to be dealt with. But I knew sacrificing Maxx to do it wasn't an option I was okay with.

Maxx looked at me like I had lost my mind. "Do you think I honestly give a rat's ass about that? I can handle what happens to me. But you sure as hell can't let him get away with what he did to you. It's not right!" he said emphatically, as though reading my mind.

I shook my head, knowing he wouldn't be able to change my mind. "I don't think he'll mess with me again. Not after you nearly put his head through the concrete," I said with a small smile, trying to lighten the mood. If that was at all possible.

Maxx let out an exasperated breath. "You have to stop trying to save me, Aubrey," he said, his words hanging in the air with the weight of uncomfortable truth.

"That's not fair, Maxx, and more than a little messed up for you to say!" I bit out, feeling tears that had refused to fall earlier prick my eyes, even as I fought against them. I was exhausted. I was exposed. I was going down fast.

Maxx slid across the bed until only inches separated us. He slowly reached for my hands, enfolding them between his.

"No, that wasn't fair. But it's the truth. You can't help me at the expense of yourself. You have to come first . . . not just this time, but all the time. I love you too much to have you throw away your safety to protect me. I wouldn't be able to live with myself." He was impassioned and emphatic. He was trying to be selfless. I got that.

Then I got angry.

I reared back and stumbled to my feet, almost falling over in my need to get away from him and his touch.

"Don't you dare," I warned, holding my hands out as if that would stop him.

Maxx looked bewildered and extremely hurt by my reaction. He didn't understand that I resented his sweet sentiments and his efforts to be a guy who would put me first.

But where the hell was this guy when I was throwing my life away in order to jump off the cliff with him?

Where was this sensitive person when I was watching him fight to breathe on a disgusting bathroom floor, a used hypodermic needle at my feet?

And where was this caring, compassionate man when he had used every element of emotional manipulation in his arsenal to get me to stay with him, no matter the cost to me?

"What did I say?" he asked, getting to his feet but not walking toward me. I was having a hard time breathing. I was enraged.

"You sit there being all emotive and . . . *perfect.* Saying all the right things," I hissed, barely able to look at him. "You can't do this to me! I can't sit on my bed with you after what just happened and have you tell me that I need to *protect myself,*" I all but shouted. "I'm in this fucking mess *because* of *you*! I'm still trying to claw my way to the surface after you decimated my *entire life*!"

We both recoiled at my words. But somehow, these things I had thought but never really said needed to be said. I had shared some of this at the rehab center when I had visited him, but obviously there was still more that I needed to say.

Maxx opened his mouth but I shook my head, silencing him.

"Don't. Just don't. You drew me in, you made me love you, and I was willing to do anything for you. But that wasn't enough, was it? I threw away my career to watch you freak out every time you couldn't find your pills fast enough! I watched you *die,* Maxx!" I screamed, and Maxx flinched.

"You *died*! And I had to give you CPR! Do you even begin to understand what that was like? To put my mouth to yours and breathe for you, watching your chest rise and fall and then wait for you to do it on your own? And when you didn't, putting my fingers to your neck to try and find a pulse that wasn't there? I thought you were gone! Just like Jayme. Just. Like. Jayme!" I shrieked, gripping my hair at my scalp and pulling hard.

Welcome to Nervous Breakdown Land. Ticket, please.

Maxx reached for me, his palms outward, trying to placate me. "Aubrey, please, just calm down so we can talk about this," he begged, tears coursing down his cheeks as he watched me slowly fall apart.

"You *knew* what I had been through with Jayme! You *knew*!" I agonized, my voice softening as I crumpled down onto the bed again. Maxx stayed where he was, watching me with hesitation, not sure if he should comfort me or leave me alone.

"I was a selfish bastard, I know that! I didn't care about how you were feeling. All I cared about was getting what I wanted. What I *needed*," Maxx stated without any hint of denial. His plain and unobstructed truth cut through the red haze of my anger.

"You *were* a selfish bastard, Maxx. Which is why I walked away. I couldn't lose you. Not to drugs. Not to an addiction I had no control over. I was going to start my life over. But here you are. In my room. You saved the day like a fucking superhero. And I should want you to leave. I should open the door and kick your ass out. But I *can't*. Because my heart *aches* for you, Maxx!" I pulled at the shirt over my chest as though I could pull the beating organ from my flesh and hand it to him.

"I'm so sorry, Aubrey! God, I'm so fucking sorry!" Maxx sobbed, his face soaked with tears, his eyes bright with pain.

"You keep saying the same old shit, Maxx! You're *sorry*. You're *different*. You've *changed*. But it comes down to the fact that I don't *trust* you. How can I?" I spat out.

"I don't know." Maxx hung his head.

"I want you to leave," I said.

"If that's what you want," Maxx replied, heading to my door. He looked shattered.

He had looked like that before. When he had been coming down from the drugs. When he had been at the edge of the abyss and ready to topple over.

I hated that look.

But this time it wasn't because of the drugs.

I had put that look on his face. The desolation in his heart.

I had worked so hard to figure out what I needed to do if I was ever faced with this moment again.

I needed to tell him to leave. To turn my back and walk away. Again.

I was strong. I was in control.

But I loved him.

And watching him leave was tearing me apart.

When it came down to it, I was tired of hurting. Tired of fighting. Tired of everything.

Holding on to him had always been hard. But losing him was worse.

"Wait," I called out, feeling a definitive snap in the air between us. Maxx looked confused. Wary. But hopeful.

"I want you to leave. I do. I know it's what I should say. But it's a lie." Maxx took one small, tentative step toward me. Our eyes met and I saw my past. My present. My future.

"I want you to leave, Maxx, but I *need* you to stay. *Please*." My lips trembled. "I'm such an idiot. I want the one thing that can hurt me the most. But I can't help it. You're in my blood, Maxx. You're everywhere. In everything. I can't escape you. I don't *want* to escape you. You've destroyed me. But I want you to put me back together. Can you do that? Can you make everything right again?" I asked, and I knew I was asking too much. That I shouldn't put the pressure of this on his unstable shoulders. But I was also tired of carrying the weight alone.

It was time that he started sharing the burden of our twisted love.

Maxx collapsed beside me on the bed, his hands coming up to frame my face. "I will if you let me," he promised, running his thumbs along the curve of my lips.

"I will do everything I can to make it up to you. I swear it, Aubrey," he whispered, and then his mouth was on mine and there was no holding back anymore. My hands came around to grip the back of his shirt as we devoured each other in a frenzy of pent-up emotion and desire.

I parted my lips beneath his and moaned deep and low in the back of my throat. Maxx pushed me backward and he lay over me, his hands coming to the front of my shirt and pulling anxiously at the buttons.

He was wild. I was ravenous. We were desperate and lost and could only be found in each other.

I pulled his shirt up and over his head and threw it onto the floor, then fumbled at his belt buckle. We were clumsy, our fingers shaky, our kisses intense.

Maxx pulled back, bracing himself on his arms above me as he looked down at my fevered face. His eyes burned into mine, and I felt myself shudder at the heat I saw there. "I've dreamed every day of this moment. When I could touch you like this." He hastily unzipped my jeans and then dipped his hand inside, his fingers teasing my wet opening. I groaned and arched my back.

"When I could taste you on my tongue," he murmured, bowing his head to take my throbbing nipple into his mouth. He sucked hard and teased the sensitive bud with his teeth. I was a writhing mess beneath him, my hands touching everywhere, trying to get closer.

"Oh my God, Maxx!" I breathed in an agonized rush. He pushed aside the flimsy material of my panties and plunged his fingers deep inside my body. I stretched around the wanted intrusion.

"Of what it feels like to be so deep inside of you that I never want to leave," he spoke into my skin, his tongue caressing the soft, vulnerable flesh between my breasts.

His words set me on fire. In an almost violent movement,

Maxx ripped my jeans and panties down and threw them aside. I reciprocated by doing the same to the rest of his clothing.

Soon we were naked and panting and kissing and touching every inch of each other as though we'd never have the opportunity to do so again.

Maxx fit himself between my thighs, and I felt the tip of him against me as he pressed a soft kiss to my mouth. The hot pressure teased me as I moaned loudly.

I was so close to losing my head completely. All I could think about was experiencing that perfect moment that I had only ever experienced with him. Being so close to someone that you didn't know where you ended and the other began.

Maxx slowly started to push himself inside of me. Tentative, almost, but with careful precision.

And then, suddenly, some of the fog lifted from my lust-addled brain and I pulled my hips back slightly, stopping him.

Maxx lifted his lips from mine and looked down at me. Sweat dripped from his forehead, and his hair matted at the sides from the effort it took for him to stop.

"What is wrong?" he asked, his voice rough.

Something hit me with the force of a freight train. A realization that I had never, *ever* thought about until just now.

"You're not wearing a condom," I told him, hardly able to believe that I had never, in all the times we had been together, thought to ask him to protect us. How could I have been so stupid? I knew Maxx's history, so how had I never stopped to ensure something so vital? I had let my desire and my intense feelings for him overshadow absolutely *everything.*

Maxx pulled out of me and reached for his pants that hung halfway off the side of the bed. "You're right, I'm not. I'm . . . I'm sorry," he said, sounding contrite and almost embarrassed. His fingers were shaking as he found his wallet and produced a foil packet from the folds inside.

He sat there, staring down at the tiny square in his palm, looking strangely lost. I sat up and pulled a blanket over my chest. "I've never worn one with you before," he whispered, and I could tell he was hurt and confused by my insistence that he wear one now.

I slid over until I was pressed up against him and placed my hand over the one that was holding the condom. "No, you haven't. I never asked you to. But you and I have never even talked about past partners and whether we were clean and safe. That's a little scary, don't you think?" I asked.

Maxx looked up at me, his face flushed, the sweat drying on his skin. "I'm clean. I've never been with someone without one. I get tested regularly. I had to," he said quietly, empathetically.

"I'm clean, too," I said, just as quietly. "And I'm on the pill."

Maxx nodded, chewing absently on his bottom lip. "I can't believe we've never talked about this. Seems pretty fucked up, right," he stated rather than asked.

I didn't say anything.

Because it *was* fucked up. We had been so willing to get lost in each other, even at the cost of common sense and reason.

It was a scary sort of crazy.

"I just think if we want stuff to be different this time, then *we* have to be different. And that includes things like this," I said, lifting the wrapped condom from his palm.

"Are we trying to do it differently, then? Are you saying you'll give me another chance to make things right with you?" Maxx asked in the barest of breaths.

I thought about what he was asking me. Whether I was willing—whether I was *able*—to throw myself back into his world. Back into the messy chaos that had dominated our relationship in the past.

I knew I couldn't.

I couldn't be the girl living in denial. Or even worse, the girl living in a constant state of anxiousness waiting for him to fall off the cliff.

But I also knew that I didn't have the strength to pretend that he could exist on the periphery of my life. That he wasn't the center of it. That he wasn't the steady, thumping pulse at the heart of who I was.

I ran trembling fingers through his hair, feeling the soft texture of his curls as they tickled my skin. "We can't go back to who we were. To *what* we were. But maybe . . . we could try to be something better," I offered hesitantly, hardly able to believe that I was doing this.

That I was back here again. Loving him beyond sanity.

Maxx leaned into my touch, his lips curving upward into a smile that was blinding in its brilliance. "Something better," he murmured before leaning in and kissing me softly but with more passion than any kiss I had ever experienced before.

Maxx pulled the blanket away from my chest and pulled me flush against him. Skin to skin.

Heart to heart.

He carefully laid me back down onto the bed, never breaking the contact of our mouths. We weren't rushed as we had been before. Something had changed.

And I knew instinctively that *we* had changed.

That I wanted to trust him. With all of me.

Eventually our slow, languid touches became more heated, and soon I was burning alive in Maxx's unquenchable flame. I heard the rip of the foil packet and then the slight pressure as he pressed himself against me once more.

This time I didn't stop him. I spread my legs to accommodate him. My fingers dug into his back as he pushed deep inside me. We both gasped as he buried himself to the hilt.

Maxx looked down at me, his eyes surprisingly bright. Were those tears?

I reached up and brushed away the stray wetness on his cheek.

He didn't move as we lay there, as close as two people could possibly be, our noses touching, our lips brushing against one another.

"I love you, Aubrey. I love you so much," he said in a tormented sigh, as though the words were somehow painful.

I curled my hand around the back of his neck and brought my legs up to wrap around his hips. Maxx groaned as I moved just a fraction of an inch.

"I love you, too, Maxx. More than anything," I said, giving him the words he had always needed to hear.

chapter twenty-four

aubrey

Afterward, we lay in bed, trying to catch our breath, silent and heavy from the moment we had just experienced together. We were both exhausted, tangled together in my sheets. Maxx traced lazy circles on my back, making me giggle. The air was warm with renewed promises and tangible hope.

"*To love or have loved, that is enough*," he whispered into my hair.

"Where's that from? I like it," I asked, smiling into his skin.

"*Les Misérables*. It's a personal favorite."

I smiled, my eyes drifting closed. This moment was as close to perfect as I could imagine.

Then my bedroom door flew open, and we were scrambling to cover ourselves.

"Aubrey, do you have a moment, I need to talk—" Renee's words drifted off as Maxx quickly pulled the blanket over his body.

"Uh, can you give us a minute, Renee?" I said, my voice sounding strangled as I saw the look of total shock on my best friend's face at the sight of Maxx . . . naked. And me . . . naked.

"Yeah, okay. Sorry," she mumbled, and closed the door with a decisive slam.

"Shit," I muttered, getting out of bed and rooting around for my clothes. Maxx watched me pull on my pants and shirt.

I struggled with my buttons, already trying to think of how I could possibly justify having Maxx here, like this. How was I going to explain to Renee and, dear God, *Brooks*, that I was willing to give Maxx another chance?

That we were together, after I had been adamant that he would never be in my life again?

I felt like a total hypocrite. A liar.

My postsex euphoria was murdered on the spot.

And then I felt Maxx's hand on my arm, and I startled at the contact. "It'll be okay," he said, once again reading my mind.

I gave up on trying to fasten the buttons on my shirt and pulled it back over my head, opting for a simple T-shirt instead. I was feeling edgy, not sure what I was going to have to face when I left my room.

"Will it, Maxx?" I asked with venom.

Maxx grabbed my hands and pulled me toward where he still sat on my bed.

"I don't know," Maxx said after a beat. But he gave me a beautiful smile. "But we'll try our damnedest to make it okay."

He got to his feet and wrapped his arms around me, pressing his lips to mine.

"I love you, Aubrey Duncan," he murmured against my mouth, his blue eyes twinkling wildly.

I sighed and couldn't help but smile back at him. "I love you, too, Maxx Demelo."

He squeezed me tightly, and I let myself enjoy it for a moment longer. "Let me go talk to Renee. Give us a few seconds before coming out, okay?"

Maxx nodded. "Go do what you need to do," he urged me.

I walked out into the hallway, softly closing the door behind me with a quiet click. I stood there for a minute feeling apprehensive.

"Stop acting like you're heading to the firing squad," Renee called from the living room, and I rolled my eyes.

She knew me too well.

I found her sitting on the couch, her feet propped up on the coffee table, her chemistry book open on her lap. Her eyebrows arched when I walked in, and she patted the spot beside her.

I sank down onto the couch, and she closed her book. "So, first of all, sorry about that," Renee said, jerking her thumb in the direction of my bedroom.

I felt my face flush.

"And second, what the hell is going on?" Renee asked, getting straight to the point.

I couldn't really tell if she was angry, but I saw her obvious concern.

"What happened to *I'm never going back there again*? What happened to that woman who realized how destructive a relationship with Maxx was? How do you go from *I won't let him in my life again* to hopping into bed with him? I'm a little confused." Renee frowned and looked exasperated.

"I guess we're both doing things that surprise us," I countered. Renee flushed, her eyes narrowing slightly.

"If this is about what you saw . . . Just because I chose to do something stupid doesn't mean you can," she argued.

"This has nothing to do with that, Renee. God! It's just . . . things feel different."

Renee snorted in disbelief, and I straightened my back defensively, knowing how ridiculous I sounded.

"Okay, I know how that sounds. I also know that it looks like I'm just another silly girl allowing herself to be led around by her vagina," I grumbled.

"From what I just walked in on, I'd say that was an accurate description," Renee agreed.

"I'm going into this with my eyes open this time. No more head in the sand, living in denial. I promise. I know I was adamant about keeping Maxx out of my life, but what if my head is wrong and my heart is right? I don't want to find myself five years from now wondering what if I had given him another chance. What if this was my time to be happy. *Finally!*"

"Okay, I understand that. I really do, but have you even thought about what this will mean for your chances of getting back into the counseling program? What will you tell Dr. Lowell the next time she asks how things are going? Will you just come out and say, *Well, you know that guy I'm supposed to stay away from? Well, we're bumping uglies again. Ain't love grand?*" Renee's hardened sarcasm surprised me. I hadn't expected her to be so bitter.

I reached out for the Department of Education catalogue that still lay on the coffee table. "Yeah, I've already thought about that," I said, holding it up.

"Is that why you're talking about changing your major? I was joking when I suggested that in the coffee shop. I had no idea it was the truth!" Renee looked stricken.

"Yes and no, I guess. I just think that I went forward with counseling to fix something broken inside of me. That's a really selfish reason for wanting to help other people. And, yeah, being with Maxx is a huge ethical violation. One that if I was dedicated to my chosen career, I wouldn't be making." I dropped the booklet back onto the table.

"But that's not really the point of all this, is it? Because you can't be this pissed about Maxx. Sure, I get that you're disappointed and worried, but you seem pretty freaking angry." I crossed my arms over my chest.

Renee's shoulders had sagged, her mouth turning down. "I guess I just wanted one of us to be strong enough to keep on walking."

Her words hit me straight in the heart, and I wanted to ask her more about what had happened with Devon. It was obvious it was weighing heavily on her. But just as I was about to broach the subject, Maxx came out of my bedroom. He stood out in the hallway and watched us uncertainly.

Renee looked up at him, her face unreadable. She got to her feet. "I hope you know what you're doing, Aubrey. I don't want to watch you fall apart all over again," she said firmly before walking past Maxx and into her bedroom, the door closing with a slam.

"I'm guessing that didn't go as well as you'd hoped," Maxx deduced, coming into the living room and sitting beside me on the couch.

"I have a feeling that had to do more with her than with me. But she's right about one thing, Maxx. I won't fall apart over you again. I can't let myself. You've ruined me once already."

Maxx pulled me in close, his arms wrapping around me, his forehead resting against my neck.

"Losing you almost killed me, Aubrey. I won't willingly go through that pain ever again. I can promise you that," he murmured before kissing me softly but thoroughly.

His words rang in my head, not entirely assuaging the anxiety in my gut.

I won't willingly go through that pain ever again.

One thing I had learned from Maxx was that when it came to his addiction, nothing was *willing.* It was always beyond his control.

✦

"Can I see you later?" Maxx's voice was like velvet in my ear. I gripped my phone tightly in my hand. I wanted to see Maxx. So much. But there were things I had to do first.

Namely, talk to Brooks.

I hadn't seen my friend in a week. His schedule was hectic, and it had given me time to think about how I would give him the news about Maxx and me.

So when Brooks had called last night and asked to hang out, I knew I couldn't put him off. I wouldn't avoid him, and I wouldn't keep secrets. That's what the old Aubrey would have done.

I had agreed that we could get together, feeling empowered by the need to be honest. Things with Renee were strained, and I only hoped Brooks would be more understanding. I couldn't expect him to be okay with my decision to give Maxx another chance; I only hoped our friendship was stronger than his disapproval.

"I can't tonight. I told Brooks we'd hang out."

"That's fine, I'm wiped anyway. I'm still trying to find another job now that the stable doesn't need me anymore. I really wish I could find something that didn't involve animal shit or fry grease," he said, sounding a little defeated.

Maxx never complained about money, but I knew he was stressed about it. I knew he was barely getting by, but I didn't know how to help him.

I hated to admit that I wondered whether he would go back to the club. Whether he would slide back into a world of quick cash and easy drugs.

I wanted to trust that he wouldn't. He had sworn that was behind him. But that was what he knew. And I worried when I saw the tension on his face as a result of his struggles. And then I hated myself for worrying.

"You'll find something," I said brightly, though I, too, wondered what his possibilities were.

"Yeah, I just hope it's sooner rather than later," Maxx muttered, and I could hear his exhausted sigh.

"Have you thought about calling around to other galleries to see if they'd be interested in seeing some of your work?" I suggested.

Maxx had told me about Mr. Randall at the Bellview Gallery in town. I knew it was embarrassing to admit how much he had messed up such a great opportunity.

"Yeah, I don't think that's such a great idea," Maxx said shortly.

"But you're so talented—"

"Aubrey, please, just drop it." His voice sharpened, and I knew it was a touchy subject.

"Have you called to set up your intake for counseling at the addictions center?" I asked, bringing up yet another topic I knew he was uncomfortable talking about. Maxx had mentioned that he was supposed to follow an outpatient treatment plan after his stint in rehab. It was a condition of his probation, now that he was no longer attending the group on campus.

"Not yet. I'll do that tomorrow," Maxx said, sounding testy.

"It's important, Maxx," I told him, not backing off, though trying not to sound like a self-important nag either.

"Yeah, well, so is finding a job so that I don't end up homeless," he snapped, and I tried not to get pissed by his attitude.

He's stressed. Give the guy a break, I thought.

Maxx let out a sigh.

"I know you're only trying to help. I'm sorry. I shouldn't bite your head off for looking out for me. I just don't want you to start worrying about me. I'll figure something out. Though I have to admit money's tight. Bills have to get paid," Maxx remarked.

Maxx's candor was both a surprise and a relief. The fact that he was talking about these things with me was a big deal. I was so used to him keeping me in the dark. I had always felt like the last person to know what was going on in his life. I had been ignorant of so much that hearing him speak openly left me unsure of how to respond. This was new, uncharted territory for both of us, and it would take some getting used to.

"I get it. And I shouldn't be hassling you about the counseling. I've got to trust you to do what has to be done," I said.

Trust.

There was that word again.

"How's that going?" Maxx asked.

"How's what going?"

"Trusting me?" Maxx responded quietly.

"I'm getting there," I answered, reciprocating his honesty with some of my own.

"I suppose that's all I can really hope for," Maxx said, and I wished I could give him more than that. But I couldn't. Not yet.

"So, what are you and this Brooks guy going to do, and should I be jealous?" Maxx asked lightly, clearly changing the subject in an effort to dispel the sudden tension that had arisen between us.

Even though he was trying to be funny, there was an element of seriousness to his question. I had never told Maxx about my past with Brooks. But I also knew that Maxx was insecure. About himself. About me. About our unstable relationship.

And now that I was with a new Maxx, one who didn't try to disillusion me with false confidence, I was more aware than ever of how unsure he was about everything. And particularly about me.

"He's just a friend, Maxx," I assured him.

"You must think I'm such a fucking pussy." Maxx chuckled in that self-deprecating way of his that was very new and a little off-putting.

I didn't like to admit that I sort of missed the cocksure guy with the swagger who acted as though he owned the world. But that person had been a result of the drugs. They were the reason he had felt so untouchable. It made me angry with myself for missing any part of that person he used to be.

But I couldn't help it.

Because that was the guy I had fallen in love with first.

No matter how destructive he was, I had been drawn to his insanity.

"Don't be ridiculous," I scolded. "Brooks and I have been friends for years. He helped me a lot, after—" I stopped abruptly.

"After you left me," Maxx filled in, and I thought I could hear a trace of bitterness.

"After you almost died," I volleyed back, not able to stop myself from setting him straight.

"Yeah, after I almost died," Maxx agreed, the resentment leaking out of his voice to be replaced with a dull wretchedness.

"Maxx." I said his name softly, reassuringly.

"It's fine . . . *I'm* fine," he said, and I knew he was trying to sound convincing.

I wasn't sure how much I believed him. Though I was trying.

"I just want to see Brooks to tell him about us. I owe it to him. I won't hide it. Not this time," I said.

"Because this time is different," Maxx finished.

I smiled, even though he couldn't see me.

"Because this time is different."

chapter twenty-five

aubrey

"Take this stuff before I drop it," Brooks huffed, shoving bags of Indian food into my hands after I opened the door to his knock.

"Well, hello to you, too," I said, kicking the door closed and following my friend into the kitchen.

"What is all this stuff?" I asked, indicating the bags Brooks was dropping onto the table.

"Instead of watching a movie, I brought over my PS4. I have the new racing game, and I thought you'd be down to get your ass handed to you," he joked.

I was nervous about talking to Brooks. He had always been very vocal with his Maxx-is-a-druggie-loser opinions. And they had only grown louder after Maxx had ended up in the hospital and I had ended up in front of a disciplinary panel.

Considering he had been the one to help me put together the pieces after I had fallen apart, how could I even begin to expect him to be okay with me not only forgiving but reuniting with the guy who had almost destroyed me?

But Brooks was in a good mood, which was a plus. I only hoped it made him less likely to hate me when I finally told him.

"Sounds great And I see you even went to my favorite Indian place," I pointed out, opening one of the cartons of steaming rice.

"Of course. Like I'd ever come here empty-handed. I know better," he said.

I snorted and grabbed a samosa from another carton.

"So, I have some big news," Brooks announced, grinning.

My mouth was full, so I waved a hand for him to continue.

"I got into LU's graduate program. So that means you're stuck with me next year, babe." Brooks grinned, and I felt a sinking in my stomach.

He looked so happy. And for a moment, I wished I could rewind to that less-complicated time when it was just Brooks and me, eating chips on my couch and watching horrible B movies. Before there was a Maxx.

I found myself wanting the easy simplicity he offered, just by being who he was.

"Maxx and I are back together," I said without preamble. I hadn't meant to say it like that, but the truth was burning a hole on my tongue. The words sort of tumbled out like vomit.

Way to be smooth, Aubrey.

Brooks blinked and frowned as though he hadn't heard me correctly. "Excuse me?"

I took a deep breath and blew it out noisily. "Just don't hate me, please. I don't think I can take another round of Brooks Hamlin's icy disapproval," I said.

Brooks sat down on one of the kitchen chairs and looked at me as though I had sprouted an additional head. "Did you seriously just tell me that you're with Maxx again? The guy you got kicked out of the counseling program for? The guy who loved his drugs more than I love shitty movies? That Maxx?" he asked, his voice turning hard and brittle.

I sat down across from him at the table. I started to pick at my nails in nervousness, but promptly stopped.

"He's trying to change," I started, but Brooks's disbelieving laughter stopped me.

"Oh my God! Will you listen to yourself? I swear I feel like I'm stuck in a goddamned time warp! Or at least a really bad Lifetime movie. Weren't we having this conversation only a couple of months ago? Seriously?" Brooks laughed again, but his eyes told me there was nothing funny about the situation.

"Look, I'm telling you because you're my friend and after everything that happened before . . . I didn't want to lie to you."

"Oh wow! Don't I feel special!" Brooks sneered. "Do you want me to give you a round of applause for jumping back into bed with the guy who ruined you once already? How about I pat you on the back and say *Way to go for making the same mistake twice, buddy!*"

I started to fume. I couldn't help it. Brooks's condescending moral superiority had always pushed my buttons.

"Give me some fucking credit, Brooks! I'm not going into this blind! I know what it looks like to you! I know you think I'm a fool. But I'm not. I'm not going to pretend that he doesn't have problems. Because he does . . . in spades. But so do I. I'm a damn mess! I'm a big ol' jumbled pile of issues! Love isn't conditional. Or at least the real kind isn't. What kind of person would I be if I expected him to accept me for my faults but I won't accept his? I know what happened before. I know what I'm putting on the line by loving him, but it is what it is. So either accept it or don't, I don't really give a shit!" I yelled, my anger taking over.

"You're on academic suspension, Aubrey!" Brooks smacked the surface of the table with his palm, the sound echoing around the kitchen.

"I know! And I'll tell Dr. Lowell, and we'll see what happens. But maybe the counseling program's not what I'm supposed to be doing," I said with a shrug.

Brooks looked stunned. "What are you talking about? You've wanted to be an addictions counselor for as long as I've known you! Don't you see how messed up it is that you're thinking about throwing all of that away over some *guy* . . ."

"No, Brooks! This has nothing to do with Maxx! I came to LU thinking I could make things right after Jayme's death. I think . . . maybe I went into my major for the wrong reasons."

Brooks rubbed his eyes with the heels of his hands as though he had a headache. "I just don't even know what to say to that."

Well, this was going just about how I expected it to. Though I had hoped I'd be wrong.

Brooks dropped his hands and looked at me, his eyes sad. "What do you want from me, Aubrey?" he asked tiredly. "My blessing? Because I can't do that. Not after I saw the way he hurt you. Not after watching you turn yourself inside out over him."

He grabbed my hand, lacing his fingers with mine. The physical contact shocked me. "I know you think this is what you want. That you have this amazing, epic love. But you don't. What you have, what you've always had, is an unhealthy obsessive dependence. You feed off the worst of each other. You deserve so much more than that," Brooks said, his words sounding more like a plea.

What he said had been true . . . once.

He painted a picture of the Maxx and Aubrey we had been months ago. Not the Maxx and Aubrey we were trying to be now.

But how could I fault him for calling it like he saw it?

"I understand that you can't accept it, Brooks. I just hope you'll still be my friend." I was probably being incredibly selfish, but I couldn't stomach the thought of losing him again.

"Why does it matter if you have me in your life when you have *him*?" Brooks spat out, rather immaturely.

I widened my eyes. "Because you're my friend and I love you," I told him.

Brooks shook his head, his dark hair falling into his eyes. "You just don't get it. I love you, too, Aubrey. So much," he said, his voice cracking.

"I know you do, Brooks—"

"No, Aubrey, you don't get it. I *love* you. I'm talking a give-you-a-kidney-if-you-needed-one kind of love here. It's an elope-to-Vegas-tomorrow-and-love-you-for-the-rest-of-my-life kind of thing." Brooks laughed, but he looked like he was in pain.

I thought I might throw up.

This is not how I pictured this conversation going at all. Though I should have guessed.

I remembered how desperately I had thrown myself at him only a month before. What had I expected him to feel after I had been playing with his emotions to make myself feel better?

Next time you kiss me, mean it, he had told me.

I was such a jerk.

"Brooks—" I started, but he held his hand up, stopping me.

"Yeah, so I never thought I'd be telling you this after you just finished telling me you were in love with another dude. It definitely sucks. But I just needed you to see you have options. That you have *me.*"

Brooks got to his feet and gathered his bags, leaving the food he had brought with him.

"Where are you going?" I asked, feeling a little panicky. I didn't know where this whole *I love you* thing was going to leave us. This felt so much worse than when we had stopped talking the last time.

That had been done out of anger. This time he was leaving because of rejection.

My rejection.

Because I couldn't return his sentiment, and he knew that.

"I'm thinking hanging out would be a little weird and I kind of have to process the fact that I just confessed to my best friend that I'm ridiculously in love with her." Brooks gave me a sad half smile.

"You don't have to go . . ." I began.

"Yes I do. Because you *love* Maxx. You're with *him*. And I can't be a silent, supportive friend about that right now. Maybe one day I can, but it will take me some time. Please be cool with that, Aubrey."

I followed him to the door, wanting to reach out and stop him. But I couldn't touch him. Not now. Not after his confession and my realization that I had brought this entire thing on myself by being completely inconsiderate of his feelings.

"Does this mean we're not friends anymore?" I asked, sounding small.

Brooks turned around and looked at me, his eyes unreadable. And then he hugged me. A tight, chest-to-chest, folding-me-into-his-body hug. I could hear his heartbeat beneath my ear.

When he pulled away, I felt alone. "I'll always be your friend, Aubrey. I love you too much to ever push you out of my life again. It hurts more to not talk to you than it does to have you love someone else. I just have to deal with the fact that I may have made a complete jackass of myself here tonight." He laughed again, this time a little lighter.

"You're not a jackass, Brooks. You're amazing, and I have never deserved your loyalty," I told him, meaning it.

Brooks mussed my hair in a platonic gesture. "Yes you do, Aubrey. You deserve the world." He cleared his throat, and his smile was a bit more natural this time. "Save me some chicken korma. I'll eat it next time I come over."

"Okay," I said quietly, watching him leave.

chapter twenty-six

maxx

Hitting rock bottom was easy.

It's the climbing back up that I was finding to be near impossible.

My life had made so much sense back when I could take a few pills and pretend that the stuff that I really had to worry about—school, Landon, paying bills—didn't matter.

Because when life got tough I had the best friend in the world to make it all better.

And she was always there when I needed her.

I missed her.

The drugs.

Even now when I was trying to live the right sort of life, I found that when I went to sleep at night it was with the memory of *her* taste in my mouth.

But when I woke up, the first thing I saw was Aubrey's face in my mind, and that helped me get out of bed and walk through the rest of my day, firm in the knowledge that I was better off without *her*. The pills.

But then the night would come and I'd miss *her* all over again.

And it wasn't just the drugs and the high. It was the club. And the euphoric sense of power that came from being X. I missed Compulsion. I missed knowing I mattered and that I was important.

But now I had Aubrey. And Landon, whose icy demeanor was gradually thawing. And my art that was slowly evolving into a real passion. I still stung from the knowledge that I might never be able to make money off it the way I wanted to. But I loved it for what it was: the only escape I could count on right now, when I had denied myself the one I really wanted.

That had to be enough for me now. And it was. In my heart I knew that. But in the dark hours before sleep, the vicious hunger was my only company and I wanted so much *more.*

"How's school going?" I asked Landon on our now daily phone call. For the first few weeks, my brother had been distant. Even after we had made headway during my visit, I knew he was purposefully keeping me at arm's length.

However, I was persistent. It was one of my better qualities, actually. And even though giving him space may have been the more considerate thing to do, I couldn't sit back and wait for him to come around.

So I had pestered. I had bothered. I hadn't let up in the slightest. It was my vow after leaving rehab to not allow either Landon or Aubrey to slip out of my life again.

I had called my brother every day until he answered and begrudgingly spoke to me. It was still uncomfortable, but we were getting there.

"Not bad. Trying to finish up my end-of-the-year art project," Landon answered vaguely. I could hear him banging around in the background and tried not to get frustrated by his lack of engagement.

"Oh yeah? What's your project on?" I asked, pulling details out of my brother the way I could imagine pulling teeth. Slowly and painfully.

"You know. Art stuff," Landon said. There was a muffled sound, and I could hear Landon speaking to someone on the other end.

"Why don't you explain the art stuff then," I said through gritted teeth. I loved my brother. But his teenage resentment, even if it was totally deserved, was frustrating.

"Just some three-dimensional piece I have to work on. Look, I've got to go. I'm hanging out with some friends. I'll call you later," Landon said distractedly.

"Sure, Lan. But I'd really like to see you this week. Maybe we could grab something to eat. I'll even take you to that pizza place you get such a hard-on for," I joked, forcing a laugh.

Landon snorted. "No, you're the one that gets a chubby for the Hawaiian. Don't put that on me."

I chuckled. "Whatever, man," I muttered.

"Okay, yeah, that sounds good. Maybe Friday. You're paying, though," Landon said, and while he still sounded distant, I knew that he, like me, was trying in the only way that he could.

"Friday it is. I'll swing by and get you after school. We can go by the mall and get you that new Xbox controller I owe you." I was clutching desperately, but I'd say and do just about anything to get my brother to stop looking at me like I was a failure.

"It's about time," Landon said. "I've been collecting interest, and I think you owe me a game or two as well."

I laughed again, though this time it was strained. I had broken Landon's game controller months ago in a freak Call of Duty accident. I pulled out my wallet and opened it. I could almost imagine flies buzzing around its vacant emptiness. I was broke, but I'd scrounge up the money somehow if it meant spending time with Landon.

"Yeah, yeah," I said, though sounding a lot less enthusiastic than I had before.

"Okay, Maxx, I'll see you Friday after school. Later."

I dropped my phone onto the table and stared down at my empty wallet. I'd get paid on Friday, but my coffee shop wages were barely covering my electric bill. I was a month behind in my rent, and I knew it was only a matter of time before my skeevy landlord would be handing me an eviction notice. I had whittled away the last of my savings, and I was living off fumes by this point.

As if on cue, there was a pounding from the front of my apartment. "Hey, we need to talk," Marco said, pushing past me. I clenched my teeth.

"I thought we were done talking," I said, closing the door.

Marco headed into the kitchen and began to open up the cupboards. "You need to go shopping, there ain't crap to eat in here," he said, slamming the doors closed. He grabbed a stale bag of chips from the counter and started stuffing his face.

"Why the fuck are you here, Marco? If you're not going to give me grief, then I can't think we have anything to say to each other," I said shortly.

"Damn, when did I become your public enemy number one? You and me have always been tight. Now I'm starting to feel like a stalky ex-bitch trying to get you to call me back. That stuff don't fly with me." Marco spoke around a mouthful of chips. Dude had zero manners. It was disgusting.

"Chew with your goddamned mouth closed, you're grossing me out." I narrowed my eyes at him, wary and on guard.

"So, we had the club at the industrial complex on Delany last weekend," he said suddenly, changing the subject completely.

"Okay. So?" I asked, not getting his point.

"What do you think of the location?"

I thought about the place he was talking about and shrugged. "It seems way too obvious for one. Too out in the open. Did the police show up?" I had to ask.

Marco upended the chip bag into his mouth and chewed noisily. "Yep, around midnight. A bunch of people got busted for possession, and Eric got caught fucking an underage chick in one of the back rooms. Gash is pissed."

I wasn't surprised in the least. I knew the location was a bad one. Too public.

"Who was the scout, and is he still breathing?" I chuckled, knowing all too well how Gash would respond to that sort of screwup.

"It was some newbie that Gash brought in. I think the guy was attached to one of his side ventures. Not a whole lot of brains obviously. As for the breathing part, I really don't give enough of a shit to find out." Marco crunched the bag in his hand and threw it toward the trash can, missing it completely. Of course he didn't bother to pick it up.

"Sucks for Gash," I said unsympathetically.

"Well, what do you think about coming back?"

I wanted to roll my eyes. Marco was one dense fucker. "I'm not slinging that shit—"

"Yeah, yeah, heard you loud and clear. I'm talking about coming back as a scout. Gash knows you're the best. He's willing to pay you pretty well to do it, too. A lot more than you were making before." Marco sniffed and gave my sad apartment a disgusted look. "And it looks like you could use the extra scratch. This place is depressing."

I opened my mouth to shoot down the offer but stopped.

Because the idea was really tempting.

"Come on, Gash isn't asking you to dirty your pretty little hands. Just find the location. Maybe show up every now and then and just be your badass self, dude. Compulsion is your playground, man, you know you miss it," Marco said with a smirk.

"I don't know," I said slowly, knowing the offer was almost too easy. Too perfect. There had to be a catch. There always was with Gash.

"How about this. I have to go out and find a spot tonight. Right now, actually. Why don't you come with me? You've always had a better eye for the shady shit than I did. It'll be like old times." Marco pulled his keys out of his pocket and nodded his head toward the door.

Just like old times.

What could it hurt?

It's not like I was going to the club. I wasn't going to put myself back into a situation that could trigger me.

So why not?

I looked down at the newspaper on the coffee table opened to the want ads.

"Yeah, sure."

✦

"Gash is going to be stoked," Marco said with a grin as we pulled away from an old mill on the outskirts of town. It was a spot I had found months ago but knew instantly it was perfect for the club. It was out of the way. It was quiet. And best of all, it was far away from the police.

Gash would love it.

"Yeah, well, you just have to know where to look for these places," I said noncommittally. The truth was that I had enjoyed doing this small thing that had once been a part of my life.

Though it made me crave more than I should. More than was good for me.

"So why don't you come back? Just to do the scouting thing. You don't need to do the other stuff unless you want to," Marco proposed, beating the subject to death. He had repeated this same sentiment at least a dozen times in the two short hours it took us to find the spot for Compulsion. He should have recorded himself so he'd stop wasting his damn breath.

"God, you're like a fucking broken record, Polo," I moaned, hating to admit how appealing his suggestion was.

I already found myself justifying it in every way that I could.

I need the money.

It's better than drudging it at a crappy minimum-wage job.

I don't have to even go to the club. I wouldn't be putting myself back in a position where I'd be tempted to do anything like what had gotten me into trouble before.

Marco sensed my hesitation and grinned, knowing he had me. He must have been happy with my lack of denial, because he didn't threaten to make me swallow my teeth for using my patented piss-off-Marco nickname.

"Yeah, but you want to do it. I just don't see what the big fucking deal is. You've done a total one eighty and it makes no sense. You want to finally tell me what happened? What made you go all straight edge?" he asked me, parking in front of the convenience store where I lived.

Yeah, like that was going to happen.

"Maybe I'm just sick of playing skeevy douche bag," I told him.

Marco snorted. "But you're the fucking king of skeevy douche bags, dude."

"You really are asking for my fist to make nice with your face," I said.

"Whatever. I'll come by next week and bring you your cash. Then we can do this all over again. Should be a blast," Marco said, then made a high-pitched squeal.

"I haven't said I'll do it," I pointed out.

"You haven't said you won't either," Marco threw back.

I felt it. That moment when I started to move backward was almost imperceptible, but it was there all the same. I felt almost powerless to stop it.

"Yeah, yeah," I agreed finally.

"Cool, man. It'll be good to have you back," he said, and he sounded like he actually meant it.

"Sure," I responded, and knew that deep down I agreed with him.

I walked back up to my apartment and picked up the letters that had been delivered through the mail slot. Bills. And more bills. In a sudden flash of rage I crumpled them into a ball and tossed them across the room. I sat down on the couch and turned on the television, only to find static. I tried to flip the channel, but they were all the same.

I figured that somewhere in that pile of overdue notices was my cable bill. Unpaid.

I turned off the television and threw the remote against the wall. I watched with satisfaction as it smashed into pieces, the batteries rolling across the floor.

I picked up the newspaper I had left on the coffee table. There was nothing there. Nothing for a guy with limited work experience and no college degree. Even with the financial aid I had scraped together to cover the rest of my classes, I'd still be short to cover the total cost. I was getting really tired of worrying about money and whether I'd be forced to eat ramen for the fifth night in a row. Or whether I'd have enough to help Landon the way I wanted to.

How did I think I'd ever be able to start a life with Aubrey if I had nothing real to offer her? I was slowly becoming a pathetic fool living on delusional dreams and nothing else. I thought of Gash's offer to come back to the club, and I knew I had very few choices. And having no options was a dangerous position for me to be in.

I'm still here, Maxx. In the back of your drawer. I'm not going anywhere.

The voice teased me. The need crawled like a snake up my throat, making it hard to breathe. I got to my feet and went into the bathroom, quickly running the water in the sink. I splashed cold water on my face and rubbed my eyes.

I braced myself against the smooth porcelain of the base and stared at the man looking back at me from the mirror. I wished I could say I liked the person I saw there. But I couldn't.

Sure, my eyes were clear. Gone was the sickly sallow pallor of my skin. I had gained some weight since my stint in rehab, mostly because I was eating cheap shitty food full of fat and chemicals, because that was all I could afford.

But the person I saw there, in the smeared glass, looked tired and lost and more than a little depressed.

He looked defeated.

I pushed away from the counter and rushed back to my bedroom, slamming the door shut.

I ripped open the drawer and pulled out my socks and boxers, throwing them onto the floor. I found the tiny plastic bag I had put there weeks before. The two pills taunted me.

I wanted them so much it hurt. I wanted to cry and shout and kick shit. Then I found myself running back down the hallway with that bag clenched tight in my fist, as though the devil himself were chasing me.

I pushed open the door to the bathroom and dropped to my knees in front of the toilet. I dumped the remaining contents of the bag into the water and with shaking hands flushed. I fell to my side, curling my knees to my chest, and sobbed.

I hated myself for still wanting them, and for being so weak that I had almost given in.

Most of all I hated myself for the brief moment when I had felt that those drugs were my only choice. That they were all I needed.

Trembling and sick, I crawled out to the living room and found my phone. I dialed a number I had programmed and had never used.

I put the phone to my ear and listened to it ring. "Recovery hotline, this is James. How can I help you?"

I took a deep breath and didn't say anything. I thought about hanging up.

The road stretched out ahead of me, and the choices I made now would define how I moved forward.

It terrified me.

"Hey, James, I'm an addict and I feel like using . . ."

chapter twenty-seven

aubrey

I wasn't expecting my day to end with a decision to go home.

It had started like any other typical day.

I had gotten up. Gotten dressed. Had a cup of coffee. Made small talk with Renee. I had met Brooks in the library, careful to avoid any reminders of our awkward conversation in my apartment. I had gone to class, eaten lunch, spoken to Maxx on the phone.

And then my mother happened.

My phone rang just after I settled into my evening of homework and required reading.

I answered it without looking at the number on the screen. I assumed it would be Maxx or Renee.

I was the queen of repeat mistakes.

"Aubrey, I'm so glad you picked up." I paused, in shock to hear my mom's voice on the other end. We hadn't spoken since our last phone call weeks before, and by my calculations I shouldn't hear from her again for at least another two or three months.

Her voice sounded strange. Husky and thick, as though she had been crying. I was instantly on edge.

"Is everything all right?" I asked, thinking something must have happened to my dad. That could be the only reason for her calling me again so soon.

"Yes, everything is fine," she said, her voice muffled. Then there was silence. Was I supposed to fill in the gap?

I had forgotten how to have a normal conversation with my mother years ago, so I was completely at a loss.

"Is there a reason you're calling?" I finally asked, going for blunt instead of beating around the bush.

I waited for my mother to chastise me. To tell me that I was being rude and should watch myself. She did neither.

What was going on?

"Your dad and I were going through Jayme's room this week. Finally cleaning out her clothes and donating them to Goodwill. I . . . I almost couldn't do it."

I frowned. Why was she calling to tell me this? She sounded weak and tired and nothing like the aggressive, antagonistic woman she had become since my younger sister's death.

I was equally surprised that she and my dad were disturbing the shrine they had built to Jayme. Her room had been left virtually untouched since she had last been in it, over three years before. The only time I had been home after starting college I had found my mother changing the sheets on Jayme's bed as though she were still sleeping there.

"She told you everything! You had to know what was going on! How could you not tell me? How could you not do anything to help your baby sister? What sort of person are you?" my mother had screamed at me the night before I had left to go back to Longwood. It had been the last time I had slept under the roof of my childhood. The last time I had been in my parents' company.

I had become so used to my resentful mother it was easy to

forget the other sides to her personality that had all but been obliterated.

"I'm sure that was hard," I ventured slowly, feeling as though I was walking into a trap.

My mother sniffed loudly on the other end, confirming that she was indeed crying.

"We found some things I thought you might like to have. Some pictures and keepsakes I know Jayme would want you to have."

I swallowed thickly around the lump that had formed in my throat. "Oh, well, you can mail them—" I began, but my mom cut me off.

"Actually, I was wondering whether you'd come down for a visit. I asked you last time we spoke and you never really answered me. But your dad and I would really like to see you. It's . . . it's been too long," she said in a rush.

The air was sucked out of my lungs. "You want me to come for a visit? Why?" I practically shouted into the phone.

My mother hissed in a breath, and I waited *finally* to be yelled at.

But instead she remained calm. "I'm your mother. Do I need a reason to see you?"

"Yes. Considering you haven't bothered in the last three years." I sounded angry. And I was. I thought I had made peace with my lack of parental relationship. But with my mother dangling the carrot of her company in front of me, a part of me I thought was dead resurfaced. The part that longed for her parents' affection. The part that had once been loved and adored by her family.

"There's a lot I think we need to talk about. We can come to you if that would be easier. Your dad and I could get a hotel room. Take you out to dinner—"

"No!" I said loudly. I knew that having them here at Longwood was the last thing I wanted. I couldn't have them invading the space that had become my escape. From home. From Jayme's memory. From them.

"Okay, I understand," my mother said, sounding sad, which was perplexing on so many levels.

I had no defense against this person. This ghost of my childhood that I thought long gone.

I didn't know what had precipitated this dramatic change, but I was wary and distrustful. I had hardened myself against my family because they had hurt me deeply already. But my heart strained to open up to her. It wanted to. It needed to love her again.

I had spent years avoiding going back to that place. I had worked hard to put it behind me, even if the memories of my sister and the family I had lost still clawed at my insides every day. I had been firm in the belief that I couldn't go there. Ever again.

But hearing the soft regret in my mother's voice had me doing something I thought was impossible to do.

It made me miss home.

"But please think about it. I think it would be important. For all of us," my mother said quietly, the lack of resentment in her tone louder than her words.

"I will," I promised.

I hung up the phone feeling conflicted.

✦

"Ugh!" I yelled, throwing down my pencil in frustration. Jayme snickered from across the kitchen table, and I threw her a nasty look.

"What's wrong, Aubrey?" my mom asked from the back door. She had just come in from getting an armload of firewood that Dad had cut up last weekend. It was the end of fall, and the first signs of winter were appearing. North Carolina was experiencing an unseasonable cold snap, catching everyone by surprise. The

forecasters were even calling for a few flakes of snow before the week was out.

"I hate algebra! I just can't get it!" I complained, picking up my pencil again.

I should have listened when people said high school was a lot harder than middle school. But I thought I would be fine. I mean, I was smart. I got straight A's. What would be the problem?

Algebra with Mr. Foltz was the problem.

"You look really funny when you want to cry," Jayme teased, though it wasn't malicious. I stuck my tongue out at my little sister.

"You just wait, Jay. In two years you'll be exactly where I am, and then I can make fun of you," I threatened, though there was no real bite to my words. We both knew that when the time came, I'd be helping her with her homework anyway.

Mom opened the refrigerator and pulled out a jug of iced tea she had made earlier, pouring some into glasses and bringing them over to the table. She sat one down in front of me and handed me a chocolate chip cookie.

"Brain food," she said, smiling and sitting down beside me.

I took the offered snack and ate it, thinking there was nothing better in the world than my mom's homemade chocolate chip cookies.

"Okay, so what's the problem?" she asked, leaning over my textbook, a concentrated frown on her face.

I pointed to the gobbledygook on the page. "Mr. Foltz told us one way to do it and the book is saying to do another. Neither of them make any sense!" I moaned, burying my head in my crossed arms in a fit of teenage melodrama.

I could hear Jayme giggling again and Mom quietly shushing her. Then her hand was on my back, a calm, comforting touch. I lifted my head and looked at my mother. Even though I was a teenager and quickly outgrowing the idea that my parents were the coolest people on the planet, I still believed that my mother had the answer to everything. I held on to that belief with a strength of conviction I didn't think I'd ever lose.

My friends had always been so jealous of the relationship I had with my mom. They thought she was the coolest. She'd take me shopping, talk to me about boys, help me apply makeup that looked great. I was lucky.

Mom put her finger underneath my chin and lifted my face. "Sometimes we just need to look at something another way. Things are never so simple that there's only one answer."

I smiled. She smiled. Jayme smiled from across the table.

My entire life up to that point was made up of moments like this.

And I felt completely and totally loved.

✦

I waited for Maxx after his shift at the coffee shop. I had been sitting in the same booth for over an hour, pretending to look over my assigned reading when actually I was simply watching him work.

He looked tired. There were dark circles under his eyes. His smile was strained as he greeted customers. The bright blue of his eyes was dull and listless even though they still lit up when he looked at me.

I could see Maxx talking to the other girl on duty. She smiled a sickeningly sweet grin and flipped her hair. He picked up a plateful of chocolate fudge cookies and inclined his head toward me.

I quickly ducked behind my book but peeked out over the top. The girl's expression soured, but she nodded.

"I see you," Maxx said, dropping down into the booth across from me.

"Didn't realize I was hiding," I teased, though feeling embarrassed at having been caught staring like a psycho girlfriend. He slid the plate of cookies toward me, his exhausted face softening as he looked at me.

"What was it you said about chocolate?" he teased.

"That I'd do just about anything for it," I responded, picking up a cookie and taking a bite.

"That's what I'm counting on," he said, his voice husky and rich.

I cleared my throat, feeling my face flush and my belly twist in that slightly painful way that meant I was completely turned on.

"So, I have a proposition for you," I announced, putting the rest of the cookie back onto the plate.

Maxx reached across the table and took my hand, his thumb sliding back and forth over mine. "Well, that *was* the point of the chocolate," he said with a smirk.

I rolled my eyes but had to clear my throat again before continuing.

"I'm thinking about going home for the weekend. To see my parents," I said quickly, needing to say it before I lost the nerve.

Maxx frowned and dropped my hand, sitting back in the booth. "Okay . . ."

"I haven't been home in three years." I glanced out the window and then back to Maxx. "I haven't seen my parents in three years," I went on.

"Wow. Okay. So why are you going now? Is everything all right?" he asked.

"Everything's fine. My mom called and said she'd like me to come home. She has some things of Jayme's she'd like me to have. I just think . . . that it's time."

Maxx nodded. "Well, if that's what you need to do. Then absolutely you should go."

"I'd like you to come with me," I stated, not quite able to look at him. I hadn't really thought about Maxx coming with me until that moment. But I realized that if I was going to do this, I wanted him with me.

Maxx blinked a few times, looking shocked. "You want me to

come to North Carolina with you? To meet your parents?" he asked incredulously.

Shit.

This would be that "meet the parents" moment.

It was too much too soon.

He was going to balk and freak out and God knows what else.

The niggling doubts that always worried at the back of my mind when it came to Maxx roared to life.

He's going to go get high. You've pushed him, and now he'll need to turn to the pills. It's all he knows. He will always disappoint you. How can you have a relationship when you don't even trust him?

I became enraged at myself for letting that horrible voice in my head drown out everything else.

"It's cool. You don't have to. I just thought I'd ask. I was only thinking it might be nice to get away—"

"Of course I'll come, Aubrey. If you need me, I'm there. Always," Maxx said earnestly. He reached back across the table and took my hands again, and I relaxed marginally.

"I know it's a big step, meeting the parents and all. Particularly my parents, because they've sort of sucked. And if this freaks you out or makes you want to—"

Maxx leaned across the table and wrapped his hand around the back of my neck, gently tugging me toward him. He kissed me. A hard pressing of lips that effectively silenced my worries.

When he was finished, he rested his forehead against mine, our noses touching. "I'm ready for any and every step, Aubrey," he whispered, and I shivered.

I sat back in the booth and gave Maxx a shaky but genuine smile.

"Okay, then. I guess we're heading to North Carolina."

✦

My heart seized up the moment we entered the city limits. Marshall Creek, North Carolina, hadn't changed a bit. There was something both comforting and exasperating about that.

I drove through the familiar streets, past the diner where Mom took me to celebrate winning the school election. Past the local library where Jayme volunteered during middle school. And right by the high school where I had graduated.

I didn't look at any of it. I didn't need to. The memories of this place were imprinted on my mind whether I wanted them there or not. And strangely, it still felt like home.

I had expected to feel nothing. A numbness. An emotional disconnect. But the warmth that spread outward from my heart to be back in this small country town was something indescribable. It felt good.

Maxx hadn't been very talkative on the two-and-a-half-hour ride to my hometown. He had spent most of the time staring out the window and chewing on his bottom lip.

After agreeing to come with me to see my parents, he had seemed to retreat into himself. He was present but absent at the same time. I began to second-guess my decision to ask him to come with me in the first place. Because it seemed to weigh on him in a manner I didn't understand. I just wished he would tell me why.

"I always pictured you in a place like this," Maxx murmured, half under his breath.

I looked through the window at the nondescript brick houses and well-manicured lawns. The white picket fences and random joggers with their dogs on the sidewalks.

"Really?" I asked, turning off the main road and onto a side street lined with red maple trees. In the fall they turned a bright, almost violent red, and Jayme had always loved to walk by them.

"It's sort of perfect," Maxx said, finally looking at me. "The streets are clean, the houses are painted, the people are smiling. You deserve to live in a place like this."

I didn't know what to say to that, so I gave him a small smile in return, which quickly faded. I slowed down the car as I approached the end of a cul-de-sac and the house with light blue siding and tan shutters flanked by the familiar red maples. I could still see the frame of the tree house my dad had made for Jayme when she was six among the bare limbs.

I pulled my car into the driveway. I thought I was going to be sick. And then I started to panic.

"I can't do this," I said, my voice hoarse as my throat tightened.

I gripped the steering wheel as though I would break it in half. "I have to leave. I can't go in there." I heard the rising hysteria in my voice and knew I was three seconds from losing it. I closed my eyes and tried to breathe in and out of my nose, trying to slow my erratic breathing.

I was jolted out of my downward spiral by a gentle touch on the back of my neck. Fingers buried into the hair at the base of my skull, a firm pressure that had an instant calming effect.

"It'll be okay, Aubrey," Maxx whispered, and I felt his lips on my temple, the soft whisper of his breath as he spoke in my ear. "It'll be okay."

I opened my eyes and turned to look at him. Blue eyes burned into mine, and I knew he was right. I leaned in and kissed him, unable to put into words how much his presence meant to me. Maxx Demelo had become *my* savior.

"Okay, let's do this," I said, a little louder than I meant to. I pulled away from Maxx and opened my door, getting out before I could talk myself out of it.

"I'll get our bags," Maxx said as I started heading toward the porch. I took in a million details in the seconds it took me to approach the house that had once been my home. My parents had replaced the old, battered porch swing with a small, wrought iron patio set. My mother's old rosebush on the side of the house had been dug up, and a wooden lattice now stood in its place.

It was obvious my mother was still compulsive about her gardening. Now that the weather was getting warmer, I could see she had been working to get her flower beds in order.

My eyes traveled over the well-worn steps I had climbed countless times. And then I was standing in front of the door, now dark blue and no longer a gleaming white. There were so many changes, yet it still felt the same. The soothing familiarity of *home* fought to overwhelm the nerves in my belly.

I stood there, staring at the door, not knocking. I wasn't sure what I was waiting for, but I couldn't bring myself to raise my hand to the wood.

"Do you want me to do it?" Maxx asked quietly, dropping our bags on the floor by his feet.

I nodded. This was it. I was home.

chapter twenty-eight

aubrey

Maxx knocked, steady and loud. Then, as though she had been waiting by the door, my mother was suddenly there, standing in the open entryway.

"Aubrey," she murmured, her voice a hoarse whisper. She was surprised. I hadn't told her I was coming.

Her face looked so different than I remembered, and she didn't seem exactly pleased to see me. I started to think this idea of mine was a huge mistake.

"Mom," I replied, looking up at the woman who had loved me and then thrown me away.

We didn't move toward each other, but I could feel her gaze as she looked me over, and I wondered how much I was coming up short.

My mother had aged since I had seen her last. Her blond hair was streaked with gray, and her once unlined face was punctuated with wrinkles. Her eyes looked tired and sad, and her shoulders were slightly drooped. She seemed weary and . . . *old.* It shocked me.

Maxx cleared his throat and thankfully broke the tension. "Hello, Mrs. Duncan. I'm Maxx Demelo, Aubrey's boyfriend," he said, holding out his hand.

My mother offered him a polite smile. "Aubrey never mentioned a boyfriend," she said, and I wanted to roll my eyes.

"Which is crazy, given how often we chat," I said with icy sarcasm.

Maxx widened his eyes, and my mother's jaw tightened, though I could have sworn I saw a flash of hurt on her face before she smoothed her expression.

Mom shook Maxx's hand and then moved aside, waving us inside. "I wasn't exactly expecting company, so you'll pardon me if things are a bit of a mess," she said, sounding slightly flustered. I realized how unfair it was to spring my visit on her, with a boyfriend no less, without giving her time to prepare.

I guess I had worried that if I had actually spoken to my mother again, I would have chickened out. That she would have said something to piss me off, and I would never have made this necessary leap to bridge my past with my present.

I had avoided this town, this house, this woman, for so long, and I was tired of running. If Maxx was making an effort to move beyond his past, then I owed it to him—to us—to do the same.

So I took a moment to breathe in and out, collecting myself, before following my mother into the house. Maxx put a hand on my lower back, and the slight pressure, the smallest reassurance, was all I needed to calm my trembling nerves.

I reached down and laced my fingers through his, finding strength in the man who had always needed me to be his rock. Now he was slowly becoming my foundation.

We stepped together over the threshold, and I stopped, looking around. I almost thought I could hear the echoes of my baby sister's laughter in the air around me. The memories of a thousand mealtimes and movie nights. Years of holidays and those infinitesimal moments that make up a life. They were everywhere. All around me. Threatening to drown me in the agony and joy of remembrance.

It was the same house but different. The furniture was all as I remembered, though it looked as if the walls had received a fresh coat of paint sometime recently. But the atmosphere was what had changed. It felt . . . *empty.*

The heart, the love, the center of this home had disappeared. It was a shell of the happy place I remembered as a child. It had been buried in the ground with my sister.

I hated it.

It seemed wrong that three years later, we were still imprisoned by our grief that had almost destroyed us. I looked at my mother, and she was straightening the cloth runner on the dining room table. She looked edgy and uneasy with my being here, even though she had requested that I come.

For the first time since my sister's death, I allowed myself to let go, just a tiny bit, of the anger and resentment that had taken up a painful residence inside me. I was tired of being the emotionally disconnected, righteously furious woman who felt wronged by her parents and betrayed by a sister who had hidden secrets that had ultimately killed her. Holding on to that was exhausting.

Maxx still held my hand tightly in his. His eyes scanned the space I had once inhabited, and he appeared to be taking it all in, though his face revealed nothing.

I wondered what he was thinking. Did this conjure memories of his own family? Would this trigger something dark inside of him?

Before I could start to panic at that thought, my mother finished her fretting and turned back to us. "I really wish you had told me you were coming. I haven't even made up your room." She inclined her head toward Maxx. "I hope you're comfortable with sleeping on the couch. Aubrey's father and I aren't those liberal parents that are okay with their daughter sharing a bed with a man while unmarried." I covered my snicker with a cough. I found my mother's stern words humorous. It felt good to laugh instead of becoming angry at her blatantly judgmental tone.

Maxx cleared his throat and gave me a sideways look before turning back to my mother and her pursed lips. "Yes, ma'am. I would never expect that. The couch is fine."

My mother nodded her head into the living room. "You can leave your stuff in there." Then her eyes flickered to me and the hard set of her mouth softened slightly. "Aubrey, let me take you up to your room."

"I know where my room is, Mom," I pointed out, not sure I was ready to be alone with her.

There it was again, that flash of hurt that was there and gone before I could be sure I had seen it at all. She looked as though she wanted to say something. I wasn't sure exactly what to expect. In the last few years, our interactions were few and fraught with tension and unresolved bitterness. But right now, while those feelings were still there, it seemed they were being smothered by something else.

Tentative hope.

"Okay, then. Well, I'll go put some coffee on. Come down after you drop your things in your room." Then she was gone, and I took my bag from Maxx, who seemed unsure as to what to do. I knew I was putting him in an extremely awkward position. It was unfair of me to lean on him like this when he was only just learning how to cope with his own issues.

But I needed him. I needed to be able to rely on him.

Maybe I was testing him. Testing us. Testing the strength of this new relationship we were foraging for ourselves. I wanted to see if we'd shatter or whether we could survive the weight of the baggage of both of us.

Looking into his eyes, I wasn't entirely sure where we'd end up.

Broken and bleeding, or strong and together. "Do you want me to come with you?" he asked. It was on the tip of my tongue to say no. To go it alone, as I'd forced myself to for a long time now.

"Okay," I said, my voice cracking slightly.

We climbed the stairs, and I could smell the brewing coffee wafting from the kitchen. A smell that should have been comforting and familiar, but seemed lost in the deafening silence of the house around me.

Once I reached the landing I started to head down the hallway and hesitated the barest of seconds as I passed a room with the door closed.

"Jayme's room?" Maxx asked, picking up on my unspoken panic.

I nodded and continued forward. I pushed open the door leading to the room I had slept in for the first eighteen years of my life and was sucked through a time warp.

I looked around in complete wonder as I took in all the ways the space hadn't changed. I had truly believed that by now my parents would have boxed up my stuff and put it in the attic. Maybe turned the room into an office or used it for storage. Given the less than civil relationship we had endured, I hardly expected them to hold on to anything that was mine.

They had been clutching madly to the threads of their dead daughter's life, so I figured they wouldn't have enough room for what was left of mine.

I was completely wrong.

"It's the same," I mused, turning in a circle, taking in every detail of the room I had forgotten about.

"You had a serious thing for pink, huh?" Maxx asked, fingering the frilly drapes covered in pink polka dots.

"I was a different person," I said softly, walking to my dresser and picking up a framed photograph.

It was the picture of Jayme and me after she had given me the silver cuff bracelet. My sister's arm was flung around my neck, and we wore identical toothy grins.

I ran my finger along the smooth and dust-free glass, wishing I could touch my sister's face one more time.

"Wow, you weren't kidding when you said the two of you looked alike," Maxx said, looking over my shoulder at the photo.

I glanced back at him and smiled. "Yeah, but she was prettier."

"I don't think that's possible, Aubrey," Maxx murmured, placing a soft kiss to the side of my neck before resting his chin on my shoulder, his arms wrapping around my middle. I pressed back against him, appreciating his solid warmth.

"You guys look happy," Maxx observed.

"We were." I put the picture down and turned in Maxx's arms, twining my wrists around his neck. "Thank you for being here. I don't think I could have done this on my own," I whispered.

"You don't ever have to thank me. I'm glad to be here for you. You've been my rock for so damn long, it's about time I returned the favor." I reached up on my tiptoes and touched my lips to his.

He clutched me tightly and opened his mouth under mine. Our tongues stroked and teased as we deepened the kiss. It was so easy to get lost in Maxx. Even here, in the middle of my childhood bedroom with my mother just downstairs.

Maxx's fingers wove through my hair, and I pressed myself against the length of him, wishing I could disappear inside of him.

"Whoa, hang on a sec," Maxx said breathlessly, pulling back. His face was flushed, and his eyes were bright. "I don't think getting you naked would endear me to your parents. And if you don't stop right now, that's exactly what will happen," he warned lightly.

I smiled. "Okay, later though." I kissed him one last time before taking a step back.

"We should go back downstairs, I guess," I said, feeling the heaviness in my chest return.

"Yeah, we should," Maxx agreed, giving my hand a squeeze.

My dad had come home in the few minutes I had been upstairs, and I wondered whether my mother had called him.

Dad looked as though he had aged twenty years. His hair had turned completely gray, and his face was lined and tired. Gone was the strong, always smiling man of my youth.

"Hi, Dad," I said in a small voice. Dealing with my dad had in some ways been harder than dealing with my mother.

Maybe because the disapproval and shame were absent from him. From my dad, there was *nothing.*

After Jayme had died, he had retreated from me completely, and it was as though, for him, I no longer existed.

And that hurt, perhaps more than my mother's coldness.

"Aubrey," he said, with a gentleness I hadn't heard in years. And then he did the most surprising thing. He walked across the kitchen and enfolded me in a tobacco-scented hug.

"I'm so glad you're here," he said quietly into my hair. It had been so long since I had been hugged by my father. And I had missed it. A lot.

I felt like crying, but wouldn't. Not now.

I pulled back, putting some distance between myself and the man who had raised me. "Still smoking that pipe, I see," I commented, trying to smile but finding that my mouth wouldn't cooperate.

My dad's smile was just as rusty. "Busted."

"I keep telling him to quit. To try one of those e-smokers, but you know how stubborn he is," my mom spoke up, fixing several cups of coffee.

I wanted to argue that I *didn't* know how stubborn he was. Not anymore. The truth was that these people in front of me had become strangers.

Maxx came forward and held out his hand. "Hello, Mr. Duncan, I'm Maxx Demelo. Nice to meet you, sir," he said politely.

My father looked surprised to see him but shook his hand. "And you are?" my father prompted, his brows furrowing.

I grabbed Maxx's hand and pulled him close. "He's my boyfriend," I answered.

My dad's smile slipped, and a silence rose between us.

I wasn't sure what I was supposed to say or do.

"Let's take our coffees into the living room," my mother interjected, waving her hand toward the hallway. She handed me a steaming mug, and this time my smile came without effort.

"You kept it," I mused, holding it up to see the faded blue writing. Maxx peered over my shoulder.

"That's pretty funny," he chuckled, indicating the OCD mug Jayme had given me all those years ago.

"Yeah, it is," I said in agreement.

"Are you coming?" my mother asked, already in the hallway.

Maxx cleared his throat. "If it's okay with you, I need to run to the store and grab some things I forgot to bring." I frowned at him.

He met my eyes. "I'll be back soon," he said, and I felt a momentary panic at the thought of being left alone with my parents. Maxx was my buffer! He couldn't leave!

"Of course. There's a Target just off the highway," my mom offered.

"I saw it as we came into town, I think I can get there." Maxx smiled. My parents went on to the living room, and I rounded on my boyfriend.

"You can't leave me here with them! What the hell, Maxx?" I demanded in an angry whisper.

Maxx kissed my forehead. "You need to talk to them . . . alone. Give yourself this time with your parents, Aubrey. Trust me when I say if you don't you'll regret it." His eyes were filled with pain, and I knew he was thinking of his own parents, whom he'd never be able to talk to again.

"I don't know," I said.

"Do this for yourself." He buried his nose in my hair and held me tightly for a moment before pulling away.

"Can I have your keys?" he asked, holding out his hand.

"Don't drive over twenty-five miles an hour and make sure you brake for all stop signs," I instructed, dropping the keys into his hands.

"Yes, ma'am. I'll take care of your baby," he laughed.

He kissed me one last time and gave me a slight push toward the living room. "Now go and talk to your parents."

✦

"We were cleaning out Jayme's room and we've put some things aside that we thought you'd like to have," my mother said after I joined them in the living room.

I felt awkward and uncomfortable sitting on the same sofa that had been there since I was a kid. The frayed arms had worn over the years.

My mom passed me a shoebox, which I took gingerly.

"It took us a long time to sort through her things. We had been putting it off, neither of us willing to do it," my dad said, taking a sip of his coffee. After his initial hug, he now seemed almost reserved.

I took the lid off the box and looked down into the random treasures from my sister's room that my parents had collected. I pulled out a ratty, pale pink teddy bear that sat on top. Why in the world would my parents give me Mr. Swizzle? My sister had slept with this ugly thing until she went to high school. And I suspected she hid him under her pillow after that, still holding him while she slept.

"Uh . . . thanks?" I held the bear in my hand, not sure what else to say.

My mother let out a tense laugh. "You don't remember, do you?" she asked. I frowned.

"I don't remember what?"

My parents exchanged a wistful look, and my mom shook her head. "Of course you wouldn't. You were so young. But you picked that out for Jayme when she was a baby, just before we brought her home from the hospital. Your dad took you shopping for a welcome-home gift for her, and you insisted on Mr. Swizzle. Jayme slept with it every night after you gave it to her. When she was in her crib, we'd put it in the corner and she'd stop crying. It worked every single time," my mother told me, and I stared down at the worn stuffed animal in my hands.

"How did I not know that I was the one to pick it out?" I asked incredulously.

"It's yours now. I think she'd want you to have it." Mom wiped at her eyes, and I knew she was getting weepy.

I put the bear down, and my fingers began to hesitantly sift through the remaining items in the box. I realized that my parents had carefully chosen things that they knew would be meaningful to me.

I saw the coral necklace I had helped her pick out when we went to the beach one summer during middle school. We had argued over that particular necklace, but in the end I had let Jayme have it because she was my sister and I loved her more than a stupid piece of jewelry. Jayme had worn it all summer.

I found an old spiral notebook with a ripped cover, and I realized it was our "secret club" notebook. I thumbed through the pages to find my childlike scrawl and Jayme's crude drawings as we detailed our secret missions and important secrets we didn't want anyone else to know.

My mother leaned over me and reached into the box. "Do you remember this?" she asked, pulling something out and putting it in my hand.

"I *knew* she took it! That sneaky brat!" I gasped through a choked laugh. Lying in my palm was the silver locket on a chain my grandmother had given me for Christmas when I was ten. Jayme had pouted all day because she had wanted one, too.

Then two days later it had mysteriously disappeared, and I never saw it again. I had accused Jayme, but she denied it and I had gotten into trouble for insisting my sister was the culprit.

My mother shook her head. "I guess we owe you an apology for not believing you." She smiled.

"I told you guys she took it! Where was it?" I asked, holding up the locket and attaching it around my neck.

"It was in a box at the back of her closet. I'm guessing she hid it and completely forgot about it. There were old Pokémon cards and chains made from Tootsie Pop wrappers as well," my dad said.

"I can't believe her. If she were here, I'd shake her silly," I muttered. Our conversation died down, and we sat in heavy silence.

I put the lid back on the box and set it down at my feet. "Thanks for this. I appreciate it," I said sincerely, surprised that they would think to do this for me, given our relationship the last few years.

"Aubrey, I know things have been hard since Jayme died—" my mother began.

"That's a bit of an understatement, don't you think?" I threw back at them, not able to keep the vicious spite out of my voice.

My mom bit down on her bottom lip and closed her eyes.

"What your mom is trying to say is we've been unfair to you. We haven't been the parents that you needed us to be. It's inexcusable and wrong. After Jayme died, we shut down, and in the process we lost not one but both of our daughters," my dad said, leaning forward.

My eyes began to burn with unshed tears. How long had I thought about them with only resentment and bitterness at emotionally abandoning me when I needed them most?

"You hurt me, badly," I whispered, staring down at my hands.

I startled at my mother's hand touching mine. "We know. We

were in so much pain, and it was easier to blame you than to accept our own culpability in what happened to Jayme." I felt the first tears escape down my cheek, and I hurriedly wiped them away.

"But you weren't wrong. I should have told you what was going on with Jayme. I should have done more to save her." My voice was broken, and I could barely hear myself over the thudding of my heart.

My dad came to sit beside me, and my mother gripped my hand tightly between hers.

"That's where we failed you, Aubrey. Because you were a child, too. We should never have put that sort of responsibility on you," my father said firmly.

"But—" I began, but my mother cut me off.

"No! We were the parents. Not you. *We* should have seen what was going on with our daughter. That was *our* responsibility. And it was our guilt and shame that made it impossible for us to see how we were treating the only child we had left. I'm sorry, Aubrey."

I let out a choked sob and couldn't hold back the tears any longer.

"Why now? Where did this sudden realization come from?" I demanded, feeling my tears mix with years of anger.

"We were in the kitchen drinking our coffee one Saturday morning and made the decision to go through Jayme's things. Neither one of us had been able to do it in all the years since she had been gone. But something clicked that Saturday, and we grabbed a few bags and went up to her room," my dad stated.

"Going through her things brought up the hurt and pain all over again. And as we cried and laughed with each new discovery of who our daughter had been, we realized that we weren't just missing Jayme, we were missing you, too," my dad finished softly.

"Then we heard from your school about your suspension from

the counseling program, and we knew that all of it was our fault. That we hadn't been the parents we should have been. That we allowed you to go off to school only months after losing your sister, alone in your grief. We should have helped you, but we didn't, and we will never be able to forgive ourselves." My mom's words were punctuated with her muffled sobs, and we cried together. My mother and me. And our mutual tears began to heal the brokenness inside of me.

Tentatively, my mother wrapped her arm around me, and I let her hug me, unable to hold on to the anger I had felt for so long. I needed this. I needed to feel the love that only my parents had ever been able to give me.

I had been defined by my grief and regret for years. They had weighed me down and pulled me under. It was time to let some of that go.

My dad's arms came up to encircle both my mother and me, and I felt warm from the inside out.

They held me for a long time, my mother and me continuing to cry and my dad holding us both.

chapter twenty-nine

aubrey

I felt right.

Perfect, even.

I had made peace with my parents. It was only the first step, but it was an important one. We still had a lot of baggage, but I felt we were finally putting the painful past behind us.

My mother wanted to know about my apartment and my friends. My dad asked about my classes and what the food was like at the commons. I was a junior in college and it was the first time my parents had asked about any of this. But at least they were asking now.

But then they wanted to know about the details of my suspension.

"The letter didn't go into specifics. Only that you were found guilty of an ethical violation," my mother stated, her brows furrowed in confusion.

"What does that even mean?" my father asked.

I sighed, wishing I didn't have to go into this right now when we were starting the process of mending our relationship.

"I was facilitating a support group on campus to work toward my volunteer hours. I became . . . *involved* . . . with a member of the group," I admitted, figuring it was best to be up front rather than drag it out.

"Involved?" my mother questioned.

"Yes. As in we were together. He was my boyfriend."

My parents digested that piece of information. I looked at them and waited for their attack. They looked concerned. Upset. But not appalled.

"Is this person still in the picture? What about Maxx? I thought he was your boyfriend?" my father asked, confused.

I took a deep breath. "Maxx is the guy, Dad."

My parents recoiled a bit in shock.

"You're still involved with him? What about the counseling program? What about your future?" my mother asked, seeming horrified.

"Maxx *is* my future, Mom. And as for the counseling program, I'm . . . I'm not sure that's where I belong anyway."

Just then, at the worst possible moment, the front door opened, and Maxx came in with a shopping bag.

He lifted his hand in a wave, recognizing the strange tension in the room. My mother gave him a tight smile, but my dad called him into the room.

Maxx gave me a questioning look.

"We were talking about my suspension," I filled in, and Maxx tried to cover his look of panic.

"Oh," he replied shortly.

"Please have a seat, young man," my father said, and I found that I had missed his overprotectiveness. Because I could see as clear as day he was about to go papa bear on poor Maxx.

"Our daughter was just filling us in about your history. And we have to say, we're very concerned. Are you aware what

Aubrey is putting on the line by continuing your relationship?" Mom asked.

Maxx squared his shoulders and faced my parents. "I know that Aubrey is an amazing woman that I love with my whole heart. And while I know to most people our relationship doesn't make any sense, to us, it does. I'm a better man because of your daughter, and I have to believe that if she is willing to take the risk by being with me, then I have to do everything I can to be worth it."

God, I loved him.

There wasn't much more to say after that, and my parents had reluctantly dropped the subject.

The next day, after breakfast with my parents, I had decided to give Maxx a tour of Marshall Creek. He had seemed more than ready to get out of my parents' house for a few hours.

"I don't think I've seen you smile so much . . . ever," Maxx commented after I had shown him my high school and the church where Jayme and I had been baptized.

"I don't think I've smiled this much since I was seventeen," I admitted, turning in to the small parking lot of a tiny diner in the center of town. Maxx held the door open for me as I walked into Sunset Café, a Marshall Creek staple that had been slinging burgers and fries since the fifties.

After we grabbed a table, I looked up automatically at the chime of the bell above the door and noticed a tall, thin young man with dark hair to his shoulders walking in. He moved with a swagger that indicated total self-confidence.

He hadn't changed.

Not in three years.

I hated him for it.

Because Blake Fields deserved to have the weight of his actions destroy his life the way they had destroyed my sister's.

But there he was, looking healthy and *alive.*

God, I fucking loathed him.

"Aubrey," Maxx was saying, but I barely heard him.

All I could do was watch the person who was responsible for the death of my sister turn to a girl who had followed him into the diner and put his arm around her, pulling her close.

He smiled down at her, and she reached up on her tiptoes to kiss his mouth. He smoothed the hair back from her forehead and smiled down at her in a way I had never seen him smile at Jayme.

"Aubrey!" Maxx said again, but I ignored him.

Before I realized what I was doing, I was on my feet and moving toward the front of the diner. Blake and his girlfriend were looking around, obviously trying to find a place to sit. Neither saw me approach. It wasn't until I stopped in front of him that Blake bothered to look at me at all.

I saw his puzzled frown and knew he was trying to place me. I could see that I was familiar to him, but he couldn't figure out how he knew me.

"Uh . . . hey?" he said, posing his statement more as a question. His girlfriend looked at me, then at Blake, seeming confused.

I swallowed, feeling suddenly nauseous.

I wanted to punch him in his smug face. I wanted to rip the hair from his head. I wanted to break every bone in his pathetic body and leave him to die in a dirty alley just as he had left my sister.

I thought of a million ways to kill the man who stood before me. A million horrific, painful ways to inflict on him the same torture he had unwittingly inflicted on my family by simply being the person he was.

A manipulative, cowardly drug dealer.

I still hadn't moved. I blocked their way into the diner. I opened my mouth to scream. To yell. To hurl insults and threats into his face.

Blake cocked his head to the side, looking more and more confused.

He was alive.

My sister was dead.

And there was no changing that.

"I'm Aubrey Duncan," I said, my voice soft and crushed. Blake frowned, uncertain, still not able to figure out who I was.

I felt Maxx come up behind me and put his hand on my arm. "Who is this?" he whispered in my ear, but I shook him off.

Blake's girlfriend gripped his arm and looked up at him. "What's going on, Blake?" she asked, seeming irritated.

Blake's frown deepened. "Am I supposed to know you?"

"I'm Jayme's sister," I said, choking on the words as they passed my lips.

My statement hit Blake with the force of a punch to the jaw. He flinched, his face paling. He took a step backward, away from me.

I stared at him, wanting to say so much more. I wanted to tell him how I blamed his thoughtless actions for the destruction of my family. I wanted to remind him of his selfishness that had killed the person I had loved.

But seeing the look on Blake's face, I didn't need to.

"I'm sorry," he let out in an agonized rush, his face crumpling.

We stood there, Blake and me, two people irrevocably connected by the girl we had both lost.

"Why did you leave her there?" I asked. Because that was what haunted me the most. The thought that this asshole had left my baby sister to die. Alone.

Blake's girlfriend tugged on his arm, trying to get his attention, but he was focused on me. I knew we were making a scene. I could feel people looking at us, but I didn't care. I was vaguely aware of Maxx's warm hand on my skin, but I couldn't look away from this pathetic man in front of me.

Blake moved forward a step, then stopped. He dropped his girlfriend's hand, as though he didn't remember she was still there. We were both stuck in a quagmire of heartache.

"I didn't know!" he implored, his hands becoming fists at his sides.

"What the hell is that supposed to mean?" I demanded, not caring that my voice was rising and I was the center of attention.

"Aubrey, this probably isn't the place to do this," Maxx said, curling his hand around my upper arm and trying to pull me back.

I resisted and continued to stare at Blake, who had gone white.

"We had gotten into a fight. She saw me—" Blake cast a quick look around. "I was doing some fucked-up shit that I shouldn't have been doing. And she got upset. I tried to get her to leave with me but she refused."

"So you left her there! Alone with a bunch of druggies!" I accused, feeling my throat starting to constrict painfully.

"I wasn't thinking! I was stupid and fucked up and I just thought we'd talk about it in the morning and everything would be fine!" Blake's eyes filled with tears, and I was shocked to see them drip down his face.

"I didn't know that would be the last time I saw her! I didn't know that the last thing she'd ever say to me was that she hated me!" Blake's voice cracked, and he ended on a sob.

I was rendered completely speechless. I had often wondered about that last night of my sister's life. I had hated and vilified the man standing in front of me for so long. But watching him wipe his tears, I could see that he, too, was broken. That even though there was a girl by his side, he still struggled with losing Jayme.

Just as I did.

"God, I'm so sorry! I know I should never have taken her there. That I should have made her leave with me! I wonder every day what would have happened if I had made a different choice that night."

"Well, she wouldn't be six feet under the ground, would she?" I asked coldly.

Blake made a choking sound and shook his head, his dark hair falling in his face.

"I loved her, too. I loved her so much," he half spoke, half cried, and suddenly it was too much.

I could see, all too clearly, that Jayme's death had destroyed something in him as well. Something he'd never get back, or ever recover from. Blake Fields, at the heart of everything, was just as messed up, just as damaged, as the rest of us.

But he was still an asshole. He was still the guy who had manipulated and degraded my sister.

Without saying another word, I pushed past Blake and ran out to the parking lot.

I pulled my keys out of my pocket and got into my car. Maxx barely had time to get in before I was throwing the gearshift into reverse and driving blindly away.

I felt the stickiness of tears drying on my face but did nothing to wipe them away. Images of my sister slammed into me like a freight train.

My grief ripped into me, tearing me open. The desolation I had felt so acutely in those first few weeks after her passing flooded over me all over again. This is why I never came home. This is exactly what I had been afraid would happen. I wanted to shove the pain back down where it belonged. Tiny, compact, and out of the way. I couldn't breathe. I couldn't think. I was in a mindless frenzy of grief.

This was the problem with suppressing emotion. When you finally allowed yourself to feel again, you were ill equipped to handle the good and the bad. You were left unable to cope with the ebbs and flows. You shattered too easily.

"Stop the car, Aubrey," Maxx said firmly but softly.

I kept driving crazily, not really seeing where I was going.

"Aubrey, seriously, pull over."

I jerked the steering wheel to the right and threw the car into park, not paying attention to where I was.

"It's okay. It's okay to let it go," Maxx was saying, but it sounded like he was shouting from the end of a tunnel. My blood rushed in my ears, and I worried I might pass out.

"I've hated him for so long. I've blamed him for what happened. He was a fucking drug dealer." I barely acknowledged the way Maxx balked at my brutal assessment.

"He got her hooked on drugs and then took her to that place where she *died*! I've never allowed myself to see him as anything other than a selfish bastard." I took a deep breath and looked at Maxx, who seemed to be bracing himself for something.

"And he's all of those things. Each and every one of them. But . . . what's the point of blaming him? It won't bring Jayme back. And it doesn't change the fact that Jayme made her own choices that night. Stupid, horrible choices that cost her her life. I can't walk around with this hole in my heart." I put my hand over my chest. "I hurt, Maxx. So much. Losing Jayme turned me into someone I didn't recognize. It destroyed my family. My relationship with my parents."

Maxx cupped my cheek with his hand, his thumb stroking the curve of my face. "I'm tired of it. I'm tired of the pain. The resentment. The bitterness. I'm tired of hating Blake and keeping my parents at arm's length." I bowed my head. "I'm tired of being scared of you and this thing between us. I'm ready to be happy. To live life the way it's meant to be lived.

"I can admit that there was a part of you that reminded me of Blake. Even as I loved you, I hated that side of who you were. It disgusted me even as I was drawn to you." I took a deep breath before continuing.

"But Blake was just a screwed-up kid. *You* were screwed up. You made some shitty choices. You were selfish. You were self-centered. But you were broken, too. And it's hard to resent someone who is as lost as I am."

And I felt it. That instant when the weight that had taken up residence in the center of my chest all those years ago actually started to lessen.

For the first time, I felt . . . *lighter.*

I looked up at the man I had gone to hell for. "I love you, Maxx. I went down this scary, dark path with you, and I thought you'd drown me." I sniffled rather inelegantly, but I didn't care.

I kissed his mouth softly . . . gently. "I was terrified of everything you were. Everything that you did. But I couldn't stay away from you. And then the worst happened, and I thought the best thing I could do was walk away and never look back." Maxx's eyes were reddened and wet, and I could feel the fine tremors in his hands as he held my face. He was silent, not saying anything, letting me say my piece.

"But I was wrong. And I've never been so glad to be wrong in all my life. We belong together. Today. Tomorrow. Forever. Because you made it impossible for me to shut down. You reached down inside of me and yanked the heart I had almost forgotten I had to the surface, dripping and bleeding but still beating." I closed my eyes, overcome with emotion. But when I opened my eyes again, I was smiling, tears staining my cheeks. "You've shown me what it means to truly *live,* Maxx."

He made a noise in the back of his throat, and then he was kissing me.

He was healing me.

He was giving me my future.

And I walked toward it happily and for the first time in a long time . . . with hope.

chapter thirty

maxx

Going to North Carolina with Aubrey had seemed like such a good idea.

But what I was left with in the end was a reminder of who I really was at my roots. In my dark, twisted heart.

I couldn't stop thinking about Blake, her sister's ex. He was a conceited little punk with an arm full of track marks and teeth rotting from meth use. He was obviously the worst kind of druggie. The forsaken kind. The type with no future.

I had looked at Blake Fields and seen myself.

The person I had been for a long time.

Aubrey had looked at him with so much disgust, and in that moment I didn't see a whole lot of difference between him and me.

And I hated myself all over again.

Aubrey left her parents' house happier than I had ever seen her. We talked the whole way home, but I couldn't get rid of the heavy weight in my chest.

The fear that I'd lose her. That she'd wake up one morning and remember that I was just like Blake. A sad, sorry loser.

I took Aubrey's bag as we walked up the steps to my apartment. The bass from my neighbor's stereo was blasting. I unlocked the door and turned on the light.

Aubrey dropped onto the couch and stretched her arms above her head. "I'm exhausted," she said with a yawn.

I joined her on the sofa and pulled her into my arms. It still amazed me how easily she fit against my body, like we were two pieces of the same puzzle. Yeah, it was cheesy as hell, but true.

"You seem happy," I observed, kissing the top of her head.

Aubrey pulled back and looked up at me. "I am, Maxx. I really am. I feel like finally, after all this time, things are falling into place. Don't you feel it?"

No, I didn't. But damn, I wanted to.

I woke up every morning with my stomach a knot of anxiety as my mind drifted to drugs. To bills. To a thousand ways I could fail.

But looking in Aubrey's blue eyes, shining and bright, I could believe that she was right. That maybe we were finally getting to where we needed to be.

I stood up and grabbed her hand, pulling her to her feet. "Whoa, what are you doing?" she asked with a lopsided grin.

I kissed her mouth, hard, and then practically dragged her down the hallway to my bedroom.

Once inside, I didn't bother to turn on the lights. I was too frantic for her. I made quick work of our clothes and soon had her naked on the bed underneath me. I looked down at her in the shadowed darkness and felt, for a moment, exactly what she had been talking about.

I felt myself coming together. I quickly put on a condom and buried myself deep inside her. There were times when I made love to Aubrey that I couldn't get deep enough. No matter how much I touched her, it was never enough.

Aubrey arched her back, and I lifted her hips as I glided in and out of her body. I leaned over and kissed a trail from her belly button to her breasts. I loved her body. I loved the way she made me feel like I was the only person in the world. To Aubrey Duncan, I mattered.

"Oh, God, Maxx!" Aubrey moaned loudly. Her flushed skin was hot to the touch and drove me mad. I slammed into her over and over again until I felt the moment that I could finally let go.

And I did.

Afterward, as the sweat dried and I lazily kissed her fingers, I thought that just maybe, everything would be okay. I felt optimistic about finding a job and making money. That I'd be able to provide for the woman I loved. That we'd make a life together.

I ran my hand down her back, listening to her soft breaths, and felt such an intense love I thought I'd strangle on it.

"I love you, Maxx," she murmured against my skin, placing soft kisses on my chest.

"We'll be together forever, right?" I asked a little desperately, holding her tight against me. I needed her reassurance. Needed it more than air.

Aubrey propped her chin on my chest and looked up at me through thick lashes framing hooded eyes. Her smile was tired but content. "Forever, Maxx. We'll be together forever," she promised before lying back down.

I stared up at my ceiling for a while after that, lost in half-crazy thoughts.

My heart clenched painfully and the optimism I had been feeling dwindled away.

"When did you come and clean my apartment?" I asked her suddenly.

Aubrey rolled off me and onto her back, her hair fanning across the pillow. She rolled her head to the side and looked at me with a bemused expression. "When did I clean your apartment?"

I reached out to trace a line between her breasts, flattening my palm over her stomach. I thought about putting a life inside of her. Of branding her in a way that was life altering and permanent.

I had never thought about being a father before. But with Aubrey I thought about it a lot. Of getting married and buying a house. Filling it with children.

What sort of father would I be?

How would I ever be able to provide for a family when I couldn't get more than a minimum-wage job?

"When I was in rehab you came by. You cleaned my apartment, didn't you?" I wasn't sure why I was pushing to know. Maybe I just needed a reminder that if Aubrey was willing to take the risk to be with me, then she loved me in spite of everything I had put her through. And I needed to take some risks of my own.

Aubrey stretched her hand out and ran her fingers up my side, making me squirm. "Yes, I came by. I was a wreck, Maxx. I had lost you. I had been suspended from the counseling program. It was a dark, dark time for me. But somehow I ended up here. And you know what?"

I grabbed ahold of her hand and pulled her close. "What?"

"I felt better just being here. I felt at peace. How crazy is it that after everything we put each other through, I would feel safest in your home?"

I ran my thumb along the curve of her jaw, her words hurting me, though I knew she hadn't meant for them to.

"It's crazy, all right."

✦

"Maxx." I opened my apartment door two days later to find my landlord standing on the stoop.

"Mr. Reese. Hi," I said, opening the door wider to let him come in.

"I don't need to come inside. I'm here to give you this," he said, handing me an envelope.

I didn't need to open it to know what it was.

It was my formal eviction notice.

"You've got thirty days to come up with the outstanding rent, or you'll have to vacate the premises. I've tried to be reasonable here, son, but I'm not in the landlord business out of the kindness of my heart. I've got kids. I've got a wife. I've got shit to pay for. So you'll need to cough up the cash or find somewhere else to live," Mr. Reese said gruffly.

I opened the envelope and looked down at the overdue amount that I owed him: fifteen hundred dollars. Shit. Shit. Shit. There was no way I was going to come up with that kind of money.

I had used the rest of my paycheck from the coffee shop to pay my electric bill and to take Landon out to dinner. I had stupidly bought him the controller I had promised, refusing to think about the thousand other things I had to pay for.

Because it had made my brother happy, and that was something I wasn't willing to pass up.

"I get it, thanks for bringing this by," I said with sarcasm.

Mr. Reese smoothed his greasy comb-over and grimaced. "Look, you seem like a nice kid, Maxx. I hate to do it to ya, but like I said, we all have bills to pay."

He wasn't telling me anything that I didn't already know.

After Mr. Reese left I sat on my sofa feeling numb.

What was I going to do?

I was failing.

Miserably.

And worse, I was disappearing in the process.

I had been forcing myself into becoming a changed man to the point that I was beginning to lose all sense of myself.

What the fuck was I doing?

I was in a pretty bleak place. Imminent homelessness will do that to you.

"Yo, Maxx! Open up!" Marco's voice yelled from the other side of the door sometime later.

I thought about ignoring him. But knowing Marco, he'd just stand out there making a racket until I let him in.

Stupid bastard.

"What the hell do you want?" I barked, wrenching open the door.

Marco held his hands up. "Dude, chill out!" He shoved a wad of cash into my hands.

I looked down at it in surprise.

"Now smile, because money puts everyone in a good mood," Marco said, pushing past me like he always did.

I stood there in the open doorway and counted the money: five hundred dollars.

"What's this for?" I asked.

Marco rolled his eyes. "Have all those drugs addled your brain? It's for the scouting last week. I told you I'd be bringing it by. You ready to go do it again?"

I stared down at the money in my hand. Five hundred dollars was a lot of money, but it wasn't nearly enough. I thought about my dead-end job at the Coffee Jerk and knew that I'd never be able to survive on what I was making.

I thought about Aubrey and all her talks of our future. I thought of Landon going off to art school next year.

I needed more.

A hell of a lot more.

"Yeah, let's go. Then can you take me to Gash's office? I need to talk to him," I said, grabbing my empty wallet and shoving it into my pocket.

Marco let out a little whoop. "Hell, yeah! You comin' back to the club?"

"Just come on. We'll talk about it later."

✦

"Well, if it isn't the prodigal son," Gash mused from behind his desk in his crappy office. I set my mouth and gave him a short nod.

Gash looked at Marco and narrowed his eyes. "You can wait in the hall. And shut the door when you leave," he commanded.

Marco looked surprised. "But—"

"But nothin'. This is between X and me. I don't want a fucking audience. Your ass buddy will be out in a minute."

Marco didn't argue. No one ever argued with Gash.

When Marco had left and shut the door, Gash pointed to one of the seats in front of his desk. "Sit," he ordered.

I sat down in the chair. "I was glad you took my offer to scout again. You have the best eye. The last dickhead didn't stick around for very long." I was shocked by Gash's praise. He wasn't one to give it willingly.

"Yeah, well, I needed the cash." No sense beating around the bush. I wanted to get to the point for my impromptu visit.

"So Marco tells me," Gash said, leaning back in his chair and crossing his hands over his belly, wearing a self-satisfied smirk. He knew my weaknesses. He had made a living on exploiting people. He knew he could get me through my vices: cash, power, and drugs.

"I'm guessing that while the money you get from scouting helps some, it's not nearly enough. Am I right?" he asked, his smirk irking me.

I cleared my throat, hardly able to believe I was groveling to this shit stain for help. I had sworn I'd never set foot in the club again. That my new life had no place for the world I used to live in.

But that was before I had been given an eviction notice. That was before I had been reminded of how impossible it would be for me to support the woman I loved in the way I wanted to.

I needed money. Desperately. I wanted to take care of the people I loved. How could I do that if I couldn't even take care of myself?

"Do you have any jobs around the club where I could make some extra scratch? Bartending? Bouncer? I'm not picky." I hated eating crow. I choked on it.

Gash's smile widened.

"I've cut a lot of jobs lately. I'm not sure if Marco told you or not."

I fidgeted in my seat. "Yeah, he mentioned something like that."

"I don't have any extra jobs like that to hand out. Particularly to someone who has proven they're not entirely trustworthy." Damn, he was enjoying this.

And it reminded me of how much I hated him.

"But . . ." Gash trailed off as he opened a drawer in his desk.

He pulled out a Ziploc bag and dropped it in front of me.

I didn't touch it, even though my fingers started to itch with the desire to grab it and run. I could see the pills gleaming white under the overhead light.

"I told Marco—" I began, barely able to get the words out.

"I know what you told Marco, and I respected that. I'm just telling you the only job I have left is the one you walked away from."

My nostrils flared, and I started to salivate.

This was a really bad idea.

I'm right here, where you left me, Maxx. I've missed you.

The voice taunted me just as it always had.

"No. I can't," I responded emphatically, proud of myself for turning down the temptation.

Gash opened the bag and pulled out a handful of pills. They were a variety of prescription narcotics, my drug of choice. He grabbed an envelope and dumped them inside, carefully licking the seam and closing it.

"You know as well as I do how much money you can make. It doesn't have to be a regular thing, X. Just once or twice. You know, to pay off your bills. Until you can find a better job." Gash pushed the envelope containing the pills across the desk.

"Just think about it. But not too long. I need to unload this shipment *this* weekend. This is some grade-A shit from California. It'll bring top dollar, and I'd like my best people getting it out there. And X, there's no one better than you, and we both know it."

His flattery didn't matter.

All I could see was the envelope containing those tiny, soul-destroying pills.

"Take 'em. Consider it your signing bonus." Gash laughed, a horrible sound.

"I'm not saying I'll do it," I hedged, hearing the weakness in my ears.

"We both know that's a fucking lie." Gash laughed again, obviously finding my hesitance really funny.

My hand darted out and grabbed the envelope, folding it in half and shoving it into my pocket.

I got to my feet and hurried to the door.

Going there had been a really bad idea.

But I was a man out of choices. And the worst ones were starting to seem like the best ones.

"Let Marco know by Thursday. But you can keep the pills, Maxx. You look like you need them," Gash called out as I pulled open the door.

I felt as though I had made a deal with the devil and there was no going back.

Not now.

Not ever.

chapter thirty-one

aubrey

I love you, I texted to Maxx as I walked across campus toward the psychology building.

I love you more, he texted back only a minute later, making me smile.

Since coming back from North Carolina more than a week ago, I hadn't been able to get over the nagging worry that something was different between us. The twinge of anxiety brought back nasty emotions I was trying hard to overcome.

Distrust being the most lethal.

The likelihood of relapse can be as high as 60 percent. Staying sober is a lifetime battle. What makes you think anything will be different?

That horrible voice taunted me with statistics and facts, reminding me of the likelihood that Maxx was indeed headed back down a dark path.

We had been back together for such a short time. I hated how quickly our respite had faded.

Suspicion was poisonous. It tainted everything.

I had experienced it once before, and I had sworn when I decided to try with Maxx again that it was a fixation I wasn't willing to reacquaint myself with.

Truthfully, Maxx had done nothing to warrant my wariness. He continued to work at the Coffee Jerk and look for other employment options. I hadn't seen anything to make me think he was using again.

So why the twinges of apprehension when we were together? I had convinced myself that my instinct was impaired. I needed to learn to trust him. To not question everything he said and did. But forgetting our painful past was hard.

Particularly as I headed to Dr. Lowell's office for my weekly progress meeting. I hadn't yet told her about Maxx, but I knew that I couldn't put it off any longer.

Today might very well change the rest of my life.

"Hi, Aubrey! Have a seat." Dr. Lowell waved her hand at me and I walked inside, dropping my bag onto the floor.

I handed her my signed slip from Dr. Jones, my Boundaries and Ethics professor.

Dr. Lowell checked it off and put it in my file on her desk. She crossed her hands over the folder and gave me a smile.

"I went to visit my parents a couple of weekends ago." I don't know why I felt the need to tell her this. Only that she had always been such an easy person to confide in. "I feel like we've been able to deal with Jayme's death and move forward as a family. Finally."

Dr. Lowell's smile broadened. "That's wonderful, Aubrey. I'm seeing a lot of positive steps forward for you, which pleases me immensely. I think we are definitely able to start talking about next semester and how to reestablish your place in the program."

This was it. My moment of truth. I froze momentarily, unable to say anything.

Dr. Lowell looked proud, an expression I hadn't seen on her

face directed at me in a while. She was handing me back the keys to my chosen kingdom. I had proven myself in her eyes, and she was willing to take me back into the fold.

But I couldn't enjoy the victory, because it was laced with lies.

"Why did you want to be a counselor, Dr. Lowell?" I asked her. She looked startled by my question.

"Hmm. Well, I suppose it was for the same reasons as you, to help people," she answered.

"Did you ever think that maybe it was a mistake? That you were traveling down the wrong path?" I continued, not entirely sure where I was going with this conversation but knowing I had some things to say before I chickened out.

Dr. Lowell sat back in her chair and seemed to think about what I was asking her. "No, Aubrey, I didn't. I've always known that this was my purpose in life. But it's totally normal to have doubts. It's part of growing up," she said, with kind and understanding eyes.

"I get that most people waver in their path from time to time, but for me, after everything, I've really been thinking if perhaps this all happened because I'm not meant to be an addictions counselor. That maybe I've gone into this for all the wrong reasons."

"Where is this coming from, Aubrey? If you need more time before coming back into the program—"

"It's not that, Dr. Lowell. When I was in high school I planned to go to college to become a teacher. It was my dream. Then my sister died and all of that changed and I became sort of obsessed with helping others the way I felt I had failed her. My old dreams faded under my guilt. And then I met Maxx." I paused and took a breath.

"And I realized that there was more out there than these so-called plans I had." I looked at my favorite professor. "Have you ever met someone who makes you question everything?"

Dr. Lowell frowned. "I'm confused, Aubrey. Are you telling me you don't want to be in the counseling program anymore?"

I bit on my lip and prepared myself to take the most significant step of my entire life. "Maxx Demelo and I are seeing each other again," I said, and watched Dr. Lowell's swift intake of breath and narrowing eyes.

"Aubrey—" she began, warning clear in her tone, but I cut her off.

"And I understand that this will impact my chances of reentering the counseling program. I thought I'd be more upset by this than I am. When I really thought about giving up on being a counselor, I found that I wasn't quite as devastated as I should be in giving up my dream. Because I realized it was never really my dream to begin with."

I sat up a little straighter and looked Dr. Lowell in the eye. "It was my attempt to fix myself, but that's not a reason to go into a profession whose aim is to help others. I think it's time that I follow dreams that will make me happy, not remind me of my pain."

Dr. Lowell looked at a loss for words, which was a first. She seemed flustered and tapped her pen against her coffee cup several times before responding.

"I can't say I'm not disappointed, Aubrey, because I am. I'm worried that you are making decisions based on a relationship that has already proven destructive and inappropriate."

I understood her concerns. But they were far from the truth.

"This has nothing to do with Maxx, actually. This decision, this choice, has to do with me. I've got to stop letting my past influence my future."

Dr. Lowell took a drink of coffee and sat quietly for a time.

"You do understand that by changing your major this late in the game, it will affect your graduation date. I'm not sure how you will graduate with your class," she said, sounding tired and maybe a little sad.

“I understand. I also understand that I’d have to find a new adviser in the education department.”

Dr. Lowell nodded. “Yes, you would,” she agreed.

We were both quiet for a time. This was a major turning point, and I felt a brief hesitation. What if I was making a huge mistake? Was I really doing this?

Yes. I was.

“I want to say thank you for everything you’ve done for me. When I came here as a freshman, I was lost and floundering. You gave me something to tether myself to. This program gave me a purpose for a little while, and for that I will always be grateful.”

Dr. Lowell got to her feet and came around from behind her desk. Before I realized it, my mentor, my favorite professor, was enveloping me in a hug.

“You’re an amazing young woman, Aubrey. I hope you always remember that.”

It felt like the end of an era. It was terrifying and exhilarating all at the same time.

For the first time in years, I was okay with not knowing what the next step would be. When I looked into my future, I didn’t see school and career.

I only saw Maxx.

He was my new dream.

And for that moment I did trust him. I believed in him. In *us*.

I just hoped I wouldn’t be proven wrong about him again.

✦

“Can I come over? I’ve got something for you,” I said to Maxx. It was Saturday, and I had hoped to spend the day with him.

I had called him to tell him about my meeting yesterday. He was supportive and just as enthusiastic as I was about the change.

“I think it’s a great opportunity for you. And we don’t have to sneak around, double bonus,” he enthused after I told him.

"Yeah, it's kind of scary, but I think it's the right move for me," I said. I felt a little sick when I thought about having to essentially start back at the beginning, but I knew that if I had continued on the counseling track I would have been doing it for the worst possible reasons. My career shouldn't be about proving myself. It should be chosen because it makes me happy and fulfilled.

And if I was truly honest with myself, counseling never made me feel either of those things. It had been about running from my past and making up for things that, now that I was thinking outside of the thick cloud of grief, were never really my fault to begin with.

Jayme's death wasn't my fault. It had taken me entirely too long to realize that.

The guilt, the shame, every snarled, tangled emotion that had weighed me down for the last three years, had slowly been dissipating.

I stared at the framed picture in my hands and grinned. I had discreetly taken Maxx's photo of his family from its spot at the back of his drawer. I had taken it downtown and gotten it framed.

After confronting my parental demons, I felt it was time for Maxx to do the same. He needed to see that his memories of his parents weren't something that he needed to hide away.

"Oh yeah? What is it?" he asked, sounding distracted.

"It's a surprise," I teased, annoyed by his lack of attention.

"I'd love to see you, but I can't tonight."

"Why not?" I asked, hearing the accusation in my tone.

"I'm going out to see Landon for a little while," he said, and I relaxed.

"I'm glad you guys are talking again," I said. I knew that Maxx was working hard to repair his relationship with his brother. If they were spending time together, then he was getting somewhere.

"Yeah, well, I'd better get going." He sounded sort of dismissive, but I chalked it up to his thinking about his evening with his brother.

That was all it could be.

Right?

"Okay, then," I said, a little disappointed. I put the framed picture in my bedside drawer.

"I'll come by in the morning to see you before heading into work. You can give me my surprise then," Maxx suggested.

"Okay, sounds good. Have fun tonight."

"I love you, Aubrey. Everything I do is for you. You know that, right?" Why was he asking me this? His question bothered me.

"Yeah, I know that. But I hope you're doing it for you too," I couldn't help but say.

"I love you," he repeated.

"I love you, too."

I hung up the phone strangely disquieted. I pushed the feeling aside and walked out into the living room, an evening of nothing spread out before me.

I saw that Renee was also on the phone, a smile on her face. "I'll see you in a little bit, then," she was saying, and I tried not to eavesdrop, but I was nosy.

She hung up the phone, and I scurried to the kitchen.

"I see you, Aubrey," Renee called out, following me.

I grabbed a glass and filled it with water, trying to act nonchalant. Renee entered the kitchen and gave me a pointed look, arching an eyebrow. "You want to know who I was talking to just now. Admit it."

"I'll admit no such thing," I said, lifting my chin.

"I was talking to Iain," Renee said, grabbing her own glass and filling it with orange juice.

Her answer surprised me. "Iain? I thought you had nixed that."

"Yeah, well, everyone has a change of heart now and then," she said blandly.

I emptied the rest of my water into the sink and turned to my blasé roommate. "What brought this on?" I asked.

"Don't act like you don't have your own ideas," Renee said.

"Devon?" I asked, and Renee nodded.

"Let's just say I realized the error of my ways and smartened up before I made an even bigger mess of things." She looked sadly resigned.

"Does this have to do with what happened at the coffee shop?" I asked. Renee had never talked about the day her ex had stood outside the window and the ensuing argument.

Renee leaned back against the cabinets, closing her eyes briefly before looking at me with a ferocity that shocked me. "I was a stupid, stupid girl. I thought love could fix a man like that. I was wrong. So fucking wrong. I let myself slip, Aubrey. And do you know what happened?"

"What?" I asked.

"He proved that he was the same asshole he always was. He won't change. I'm not sure he can. But I'm not going to be the girl to wait around and find out." She seemed so sure, so firm. I was happy to see it, but something bothered me.

"What exactly happened, Renee?"

Renee rubbed at a spot in the middle of her forehead. "His anger is an issue, Aubrey. It always has been. His jealousy is out of control. I thought he was different. He promised me that he was. But I found out very quickly that it was a lie. *We* were the lie."

"But what about Iain?"

Renee shrugged. "I like Iain. He's sweet, considerate, gentle. The complete opposite of Devon in every single way. And most importantly, he doesn't make my heart hurt for loving him. Because that will never happen again."

"I'm sorry, Renee," I said quietly.

She gave me a wan smile and straightened her shoulders. "Don't be. It was a lesson I had to learn all over again, I suppose.

But I can tell you one thing, I'm not letting my heart do the talking ever again."

She seemed so resolute. So sure her heart had led her astray. "Your heart won't always be wrong," I told her softly.

I thought my heart had loved the wrong person. But instead, it had led me home.

chapter thirty-two

maxx

I didn't think about what lying to Aubrey meant.

I couldn't.

I hadn't started my day thinking it would end with my deceit.

That I'd be perilously close to backsliding into my old life, my old world.

I had spent my morning at work and felt good when I had received higher than average tips. Sure, it wouldn't cover the cost of my rent, but it was a good start. I still had the thousand bucks from club scouting sitting in my bank account and planned to scout again next week. It was a decent job, and I was trying to stay optimistic about it.

If I was able to scout and not actually go to the club, then I didn't necessarily feel like I was keeping anything from Aubrey. I couldn't tell her about it, because I knew it would only worry her.

But in the back of my mind, Gash's *other* offer was a tantalizing possibility. As was the envelope of pills I still kept hidden in the back of my closet.

I was feeling somewhat upbeat, given my recent bout of pessimism.

And then my brother came for a visit.

"Landon! What are you doing here?" I asked, opening the door to him.

In all the years I had lived in my dinky apartment, Landon had never been by for a visit. And that had been completely intentional.

I had worked really damn hard to keep Landon away from the shit in my life. I never wanted him to see how I lived. But there was no point in keeping up pretenses anymore.

Landon came inside and looked around. "This is where you live?" he asked.

"Yeah, it is. Welcome to Casa de Maxx," I said wryly. I felt mildly ashamed when I saw the barely disguised look of disgust on his face.

"It's kind of ghetto," he observed.

"Yeah, well, the rent is cheap. So, did you come by to criticize my interior decorating skills?" I asked lightly, trying not to get pissed by my brother's comment.

Landon stopped snooping and sat down on my couch, pulling some brochures out of his backpack. "Well, I've been talking to my guidance counselor more about art school. You remember me talking about that with you, right?" he asked with an edge to his voice.

I knew what he was thinking. Did I remember or had I been too high to hear him?

"Yeah, I remember," I said a touch defensively, sitting down beside him.

He handed me a pile of glossy paper. "Well, these are brochures from three of my top picks. I was wondering if you'd look at them with me." He sounded kind of angry as he asked me. "You know, because I don't have anyone else to really ask. None of my friends want to hear about art school, and even though David is less of an asshole, he's still an asshole."

"And I was your choice by default," I said. Damn this kid and his ability to wound me. It made me want to shake him senseless.

Landon rubbed his forehead in an agitated gesture. "Yeah—" Then he looked at my face. "No, actually," he admitted grudgingly. "I wanted to look at this stuff with you. To get your opinion. Because even though you're a lying sack of shit, you're still my brother," he mumbled petulantly.

"Wow, you sure know how to sweet-talk a fellow," I deadpanned.

"Whatever," Landon said under his breath.

There was a long moment of silence, then I picked up the first brochure and started to skim the information. "So what is it exactly you want my expert opinion on?" I asked.

Landon shrugged. "I don't know, really. They're all good schools. I'd like to go visit them over the summer before filling out my applications in the fall. Maybe you could come with me," he suggested offhandedly, as though it were no big deal.

I shrugged and tried not to smile. "Yeah, sure, that'd be cool," I said just as neutrally. Landon nodded and pulled out another pile of papers, dropping them in my lap.

"This is information about classes and stuff. It's a lot and it sort of makes me crazy looking at it all."

"Well, let me help you out, then," I offered, starting to thumb through the information.

And then I came to the cost of tuition and almost lost my lunch.

"Shit, Landon, is this how much it fucking costs to go to one of these schools?" I couldn't help myself from saying.

Landon instantly froze, our period of thawing camaraderie now over. "I know how much it costs, Maxx. But I'm also working my ass off so I'm eligible for a crapload of financial aid. You know, so you don't feel like you have to help me out. We saw how great that turned out last time," he spat out hatefully.

I swallowed down my angry retort and tried to remember those super-helpful breathing techniques forced down my throat in rehab.

After a few minutes I was feeling better. "There's nothing wrong with my wanting to help you out, Lan," I told him.

"I just don't want you thinking you *have* to," Landon said glumly.

I looked down at the number blazing back at me from the page. Landon had always been my responsibility. I had always contributed toward his welfare. But now I could barely keep my water turned on and food in my stomach.

How in the fuck would I ever be able to keep myself afloat and feel like I was doing what I needed to do for the people I cared about?

"Okay, well, let's not worry about that right now and just look at these schools," I said, changing the subject, but the burn of failure raged in my gut.

"Okay, cool," Landon replied, giving me a small smile.

And I smiled back, even if inside I was screaming.

✦

The club was pounding in the distance as I pulled my car into the field. Marco and I had discovered the old airstrip by chance earlier in the week. It had been a real find. It had served as the regional airport in the sixties but had closed a decade later due to funding cuts.

Gash and company had set up shop in the old hangar. I could see lights flashing from the smashed windows, and the ground vibrated under my feet. There was no fear of being discovered this far out of town. There was nothing around for miles. It was perfect.

Marco saw me before I saw him. "X!" he yelled loud enough to be heard over the thumping music.

Every single person standing in line turned in my direction. I saw the widening of eyes and heard the whispering begin and I couldn't help but grin. It felt nice to be noticed. I missed the notoriety. The attention.

Marco clapped me on the shoulder and immediately ushered me inside. The hangar was a huge open space. Gash's crew had set up a bar at the very back and flickering strobes and laser lights hung down from the ceiling. The DJ booth was perched up on a platform in the middle of the room.

"What in the fuck are you doing here, man? I never thought I'd see your ugly mug on this side of the rope again."

I looked around for the signs of Gash's crew. He usually set up camp on club nights in some out-of-the-way location, close enough to keep an eye on things but far enough away that he didn't have to be a part of the festivities. For all of his shady dealings, he didn't enjoy the actual club.

"I'm here to talk to Gash," I said, shouting over the music.

Marco frowned. "Oh yeah? What about?" he asked, and I looked at the guy who had been my friend for years in surprise.

"What do you think, dumb-ass?" I snapped, annoyed that he expected me to say it out loud.

I thought Marco would have whooped when he heard I was rejoining the fray. He had been pressuring me long enough to dip my toes back into the scene. But he didn't seem very happy about my news. He seemed . . . worried.

"I'm not sure that's a good idea, man," he said, pulling me to the side and away from the rest of the crowd.

"What the fuck are you talking about, Polo? You've been up my ass for months to come back to the club. Remember your whole *you're the king of sleaze, X,* pep talk? What the hell is your problem?"

Marco tugged on his eyebrow ring, something he only did when he was nervous. He looked around and then dropped in close to my face, invading my personal space in a way I didn't appreciate.

"There's just been rumblings . . ." he began to say, but then I heard my name being called.

"X!"

I looked over to see Vincent, Gash's lackey, motioning for me to follow him.

I turned back to Marco. "I'll catch up with you later, all right?" I said.

Marco shrugged as though he hadn't been really weird only seconds before. "Whatever. See ya." And then he bled into the crowd, returning to his spot at the front door.

I followed Vincent to the back of the room and into a tiny office. Gash was inside with a handful of people, smoking a spliff.

"X! Good to see you, come in," Gash said, his voice tight with a lungful of smoke.

He waved the rest of the people out until I was left with only Gash and Vincent.

"I wasn't sure you'd be coming back," Gash said, though I could tell by the smirk on his face that he knew he'd see me again. And he knew exactly what I was here for.

"Well, I've been thinking about your offer," I started to say.

Gash nodded to Vincent, who reached into a leather satchel and pulled out two freezer bags full of pills.

I felt sick taking them from Vincent. They burned my fingers with guilt and shame.

I couldn't believe I had resorted to this. I had worked so hard to put this behind me, and here I was jumping back in with the sharks.

But I was feeling desperate and I was tired of not being able to provide for myself. I just needed to make enough to get by until I could figure something else out. This would *not* be a permanent solution.

I was dedicated to my new life. This would just help ensure that I didn't drown while I was trying to live it.

At least, that's what I'd managed to convince myself.

"It's important that you're here next Saturday with all of that. Be here no later than ten o'clock," Gash said firmly. I frowned. Gash had never given me such specific instructions before. It was always just sell the shit and give him the money.

"Any particular reason why?" I asked, dropping the drugs into the book bag I had brought inside with me for this very purpose.

"Because I fucking said so, that's why," Gash yelled.

What had him so wound up?

"Okay . . ."

Gash smoothed back his graying hair and gave me his trademark smug smile. "You're going to make us a lot of money, X. It's good to have you back in the fold."

I bristled. "I'm not back in the fold, Gash. This is a one-time thing. I just need some cash to help me get by. Times are tough, ya know."

Gash laughed, a disingenuous sound. "Of course. A one-time thing. No strings attached. I get it." Wow. He was being uncharacteristically agreeable. I had expected threats of bodily harm at the very least for not wanting to go back to dealing full-time.

"All right, well, I'm gonna go. I'll see you next Saturday," I said, backing up toward the door.

"Don't be any later than ten, X. I'm fucking serious. Otherwise things may happen to you and the people you love that aren't very nice. You get me?"

There was the Gash I knew and hated.

"Yeah, I get ya," I responded, hoisting my bag up on my shoulder.

I left Gash's makeshift office and headed to the front door.

Hands reached out trying to grab me. Girls pressed themselves up against me, begging me for the thing I had always been able to give them.

I used to love this. And I still felt the power of it. But it felt disgusting and wrong. I didn't stop until I was out of the club. I didn't bother talking to Marco again, either. Not when my shame was heavy on my back.

Just one more time, I repeated to myself the whole way home.

I went home and instead of sleeping, I thought about the drugs in my bag. How much I wanted them. How much I craved them.

Just one more time . . .

chapter thirty-three

aubrey

"I feel like we're ships passing in the night," I teased on a balmy Monday afternoon. Maxx gave me a tired smile, having just woken up, and kissed me as I walked into his apartment. I hadn't seen him all weekend, this being the first we had been together in days.

"How was Landon on Saturday?" I asked. I had only been able to speak to him briefly on Sunday, and the subject of his day with his brother hadn't come up.

"Huh?" he asked, rubbing sleep from his eyes. He seemed to be sleeping more and more lately. I worried he was getting depressed. I tried to keep him up and active, but he was resistant and grouchy.

I knew he was worried about his financial situation, and I also knew that I didn't have any way to help him. He had pounded the pavement trying to find more work, but he was coming up woefully empty-handed.

"Your brother. The kid you were hanging out with on Saturday," I prompted with a confused smile.

Maxx gave me a sheepish grin. "Oh yeah. He was good. He wants me to go with him to look at art schools this summer." He pulled out a box of cereal and dumped some into a bowl. He looked in the refrigerator, but there was no milk, so he started eating it dry. I thought about buying him groceries, but I knew that his pride wouldn't allow him to take money from me.

I wrapped my arms around his waist and nuzzled into his chest. "That's awesome, Maxx." Aside from the financial stresses, I knew that he agonized over how to make his relationship with his brother work again. Landon felt betrayed, and I completely understood where the younger boy was coming from. And in true teenage fashion, he held a serious grudge.

Maxx crunched on his cereal and swallowed before leaning down to kiss the top of my head. "I'd like to take you out sometime next week. Somewhere nice," he said suddenly. I pulled back and looked up at him.

"You don't have to. I'm just as happy staying here and hanging out with you," I protested. I didn't want Maxx wining and dining me when he could barely afford the bare-bones groceries in his kitchen.

"I'd really like to. I haven't had a chance to take you out on a date that you deserve."

I kissed his chest and laid my cheek over his beating heart, strong and sure beneath my ear. "You have other things you have to pay for. You don't need to take me to some fancy dinner," I argued.

Maxx put his bowl on the counter and wrapped his arms around me so that we held each other. "I haven't done much right by you, Aubrey, but let me do this. Besides, I'll be flush with cash after the weekend," he said offhandedly.

I leaned back, pulling out of his hold slightly, and gave him a questioning look. "Oh yeah? Why's that?" I asked.

"I've been given a chance to make some great money."

I brightened. "Did you take your stuff to a different art gallery?" I asked hopefully. I had, as subtly as possible, been suggesting he try to sell his art to other art dealers. The interest was out there for his work; he just needed to seize it. He had been adverse to it after his earlier rejection, but maybe he had finally come around.

Maxx scratched his temple. "Uh, no. That's not it. I don't really want to talk about it right now, but hopefully my days of living hand to mouth will be over soon and I can finally start banking on our future." He pulled out of my arms and dropped his now-empty bowl into the sink.

I wanted to badger him about this great new *opportunity.* The fire in his eyes worried me. But before I could say anything, he picked up the small gift bag I had brought with me and held it up.

"Is this the surprise you were teasing me about?"

"Uh, yeah," I said, feeling distracted.

Maxx grinned and began pulling tissue paper out of the bag. He lifted the heavy frame into his hands and stared down at the picture behind the glass. His face was carefully blank, and I wondered if I had overestimated his pleasure at receiving it.

"How did you find this?" he asked quietly, not looking at me, his eyes trained on the photograph of the four people in the picture.

"Actually, I found it one of the first times I was ever here. I know you kept it in the back of your drawer, and I just thought it was time you took it out of hiding, don't you think?" I asked quietly.

Maxx stood there for a long time, then without a word, he walked down the hallway. I followed after him, not sure what he was going to do. He approached his dresser and slowly put the framed photo in the center. He moved it until it was facing his bed.

"I hope it's okay that I did that. I wasn't trying to violate your privacy—" I started to say. Maxx grabbed me suddenly and hauled me up against him, his mouth claiming mine hungrily. He pulled back a moment later, both of us breathless.

"Thank you, Aubrey. Thank you so much. Every day you remind me of what it means to be given a second chance. And I swear to God I won't let you down."

Then we stopped talking for a while.

Sometime later, when we finally came up for air, we lay on our sides pressed together in his bed. Maxx played with my hair, and I stroked lazy circles on his chest. "Do you ever think about where we'll be in ten years?" I asked him.

Maxx ran his hand up and down my back. "All the time," he murmured. I rolled onto my belly and propped my chin on his chest, looking up at him through my lashes.

"What do you see?"

Maxx pulled me up so that I was eye level with him. "I see you. I see me. I see us living in a great big house with a dog that you insisted on naming Molly, though I liked the name Daisy." Maxx's eyes take on a faraway expression, and I watch him, fascinated as he recounts a life we hadn't lived yet.

"We have a little girl, five years old, who looks exactly like you, but she loves to paint, just like me. You're pregnant with our little boy and we spend our weekends fixing up the nursery. I paint a motorcycle on the wall and you hang blue curtains in the windows. Your parents come to visit on holidays and my brother stays with us when he's in town. You're a teacher and I'm an artist and we make it work because we love each other just as much, ten years from now, as we do right now."

His beautiful vision for our future gives me goose bumps. "Wow, you've really thought about this," I said softly, kissing his chin.

"Every day, Aubrey. It's what gets me through all the bad stuff. It's what kept me in rehab. Let me show you something." He carefully pulled out from underneath me and got out of bed.

He walked over to the pile of painted canvases that had slowly grown over the past few months. He pulled out a canvas toward the back. He brought it over to the bed and sat down, holding it in his lap.

I sat up and crawled over to him, looking over his shoulder, and was instantly speechless.

It was a picture of me in profile. In true X style, it was vivid and detailed. The colors were more muted than was typical of his artwork, but it punched me in the gut with its power.

In the painting, I stood in front of a window, looking over my shoulder, my long hair billowing behind me, bleeding into a large sun hanging in the imaginary sky. I wore a long, flowing dress that disappeared into a field of flowers at my feet.

The painted Aubrey held her hand out, and long, masculine fingers intertwined with my slender ones. Maxx had painted himself emerging from the shadows to grasp me. He had never painted himself before. I couldn't deny the significance of this picture. It took my breath away.

Maxx looked at me. "When I think of my future, this is what I see. You. Me. Together." I kissed his shoulders. He put the painting down beside him and reached around to cup my face. "Which is why I will do *anything* for you. I will walk through fire to give you the life you deserve. Do you trust me to take care of you?" he whispered, kissing my cheeks, my nose, my mouth.

Did I trust him?

I wanted to.

So I didn't answer him, choosing to kiss him instead and hoping that was all the answer he needed right now.

✦

I stared down at the course listing for the education department and was overwhelmed. There was a lot to choose from. And in doing the calculations, by changing my academic track midstream like this, I was pushing back my estimated graduation date by at least a year.

But I wasn't questioning my decision to move away from counseling. I truly felt it was the best choice I could have made. It just felt *right.*

I was sitting in the Coffee Jerk, sipping on my latte and poring over the catalogue. Maxx wasn't working, which was just as well, because I needed to focus on figuring out how I was going to make this whole change-my-major thing work.

"Whatcha lookin' at?" I glanced up as Brooks pulled out the chair opposite me and sat down. I hadn't seen much of him in the last few weeks. Not since his declaration that had left things feeling very awkward.

I lifted the course book in my hands. "Picking out classes for the fall."

Brooks frowned. "So you're really changing your major?" he asked.

I bit on my lip and nodded. "Yeah, I am."

I expected a lecture or at least a snort of disgust, but I got neither. Brooks simply looked at me thoughtfully.

"You're not going to tell me again how stupid I'm being to throw away the last three years? No berating comments on how far behind I'm putting myself by doing this?"

Brooks shook his head. "Nope. None of that. You can't force something that doesn't work, Aubrey," he said with a tinge of sadness.

I had a feeling that he was talking about more than just my major.

He took a sip of his coffee. "I've decided to go to the University of Maryland for grad school. I just accepted their offer last week," he said.

I dropped the course catalogue onto the table and looked at my friend. "What happened to staying at LU for your master's?" I asked.

Brooks took another sip of his coffee and looked at me, his eyes meeting mine. "I would be staying for all the wrong reasons. I think you were right when you said it'd be good to get away."

I felt a knot forming in my stomach as my guilt flared viciously.

I had treated Brooks Hamlin unfairly. He had been nothing but supportive and a true friend, and I had used him. Emotionally manipulated him. Then cast him aside when Maxx reentered my life.

I didn't like myself very much in that instant. Not at all.

"I know what you're doing over there," Brooks said, breaking me out of my self-loathing.

"Oh yeah? And what is that?" I asked tightly.

"You think this is about you and what I told you. That's pretty narcissistic of you, don't you think?" he teased good-naturedly.

"But you seemed so sure about staying on at LU," I countered.

"Yeah, and maybe I was hedging for something to happen between us. I love you, Aubrey, that hasn't changed. But it wasn't cool of me to put that on you when I knew you didn't feel the same way."

I clenched my hands into fists. "I led you on, Brooks—"

"And I knew why you were doing it. I knew you were in love with Maxx and nothing had changed. Even though I can't really stand the guy and think you can do so much better, that's where your heart is. I can't force you to feel something for me that isn't there. And to put that pressure on you wasn't right."

I reached across the table and grabbed ahold of his hand, squeezing it. "You are such a great guy, Brooks. You're one of my best friends, and I really hope that never changes, no matter where we end up. Because this—" I squeezed his hand a little harder. "This is the kind of friendship that lasts a lifetime."

Brooks squeezed back. "I know. I hope you realize that I only want the best for you. And even if I don't entirely understand why, you seem to think it's Maxx. And I have to be okay with that. I have to trust you to make the right choices for yourself and stop treating you like you're incapable of making your own decisions."

Trust.

There was that word again. It seemed that everyone was having trouble embracing it.

"I appreciate it, Brooks, I really do."

We smiled at each other in that easy, familiar way of ours, and then Brooks grabbed the course catalogue and flipped through it.

"There are some great classes in here. What's the track you've decided on?" he asked, changing the subject.

I let him steer our conversation into territory where we felt the most comfortable, and I knew that it would take some time and maybe some distance, but we'd be okay.

chapter thirty-four

aubrey

It was Saturday evening and Renee and I were walking back from the campus library. Maxx was spending time with Landon again, so Renee had asked if I wanted to keep her company while she finished up a project for her marketing class that was due on Monday.

"We're such wild and crazy chicks. Hanging at the library on a Saturday night," I laughed, slinging my coat over my shoulders. We were marching into the first week of May, the end of school just around the corner, and it was finally warm enough to walk around at night without a jacket.

I loved the summer. It was my favorite time of year. I planned to suggest to Maxx that we go down and stay with my parents for a few weeks after school let out. Marshall Creek was only an hour's drive from the Outer Banks. I wanted to have the time with Maxx to really unwind and relax after how stressful the last few months had been.

My parents and I were in regular contact since I had been to see them, and while things were still awkward at times, we were getting there.

"I can't wait until summer," I said.

"Me neither. My parents asked me to come home for a few weeks. I'm really thinking of taking them up on the offer." Renee picked up her book bag and followed me out the door.

"Are you going to see Iain at all over the summer? Is he sticking around campus?" I asked. I still wasn't sure what was going on with Iain. I knew Renee had gone out on a few dates, but I knew my friend and she was purposefully not investing in a relationship with the guy.

Renee shrugged. "I'm not sure. We haven't really discussed summer plans," she said, unconcerned.

"Maybe you could make some plans with him?" I urged. I hated seeing Renee close herself off the way I had always done. Renee was the impulsive, passionate one. I had been steady and emotionally stunted. I wasn't sure what to think about the role reversal.

I worried about Renee. Sure, she was doing great in school and seemed to be making a good effort of moving on from Devon, but there was a spark missing in her eyes that bothered me. Renee gave me a sideways look, knowing exactly what I was doing. "You're so pushy, Aubrey," she accused with a smile.

"I just want to see my best friend happy," I replied, nudging her shoulder with mine as we walked across campus.

"I *am* happy," Renee argued.

"Okay, I'd like to see you *happier*," I corrected.

"I don't need a guy to be happy, Aubrey. Give me a bit more credit for my personal growth," she scolded.

"I'm not saying you need a guy, Renee. I just don't want you to morph into the Aubrey zombie of emotional death," I joked.

"An Aubrey zombie, huh? Sounds pretty scary." She laughed.

"It is, trust me," I said soberly, meaning it.

"I know you think I'm shutting myself off because of what happened with Devon. And that's not it. I swear it. I'm just protecting myself from now on. And I don't think jumping into something serious is the way to do that. I can date Iain and have fun, but that's it. That's all I'm capable of right now."

"Okay, I understand, I won't push it."

"I don't mind you pushing, Aubrey. I know it's because you love me," Renee said, looping her arm through mine.

"Love you silly." I grinned.

Renee chuckled and shook her head. "You've got the silly part right."

"What's going on over there?" Renee pointed to a group of people congregated around the side of the gym.

"I'm not sure," I said, giving my friend's arm a tug.

My guts twisted with déjà vu.

"Let's go check it out," I said, my voice strangely rough.

"Whatever it is has gotten everyone pretty excited," Renee commented as we bounced on our tiptoes trying to see over the heads of the crowd.

"Let's go linebacker on these guys," I said, nodding my head toward the people milling around in tight clumps.

"I've got my elbows ready," Renee joked. Together, we pushed through to the brick wall that seemed to hold everyone's attention.

And then my heart dropped to the ground along with my belief in trust and love and hope.

"No," I breathed out, hardly believing what I was seeing.

A large painting took up most of the wall. The word *Compulsion* draped the clouds drawn onto the brick. It was a rather mundane drawing of a field of flowers and a tree, the address clearly written on the bark.

It wasn't the prettiest drawing I had ever seen, but its significance made me want to throw up.

"Isn't this what Maxx used to do for the club?" Renee asked from behind me.

I nodded, my mouth dry and my throat tightening dangerously. I pushed back through the crowd and leaned against the far end of the wall, trying to breathe through the nausea.

This couldn't be right. Could it?

Maxx would have told me if had he started working for Compulsion again. Right?

I didn't want to believe what my eyes so clearly saw.

Proof of his deceit and betrayal.

I slammed my hand into the wall in frustration, barely registering the pain that shot up my arm.

"Whoa, what's wrong?" Renee asked, frowning.

I pointed at the artwork that everyone was talking about. "That's the fucking problem!" I seethed, tears stinging my eyes.

"I don't get it . . ." Renee began.

I pushed myself off the wall and pressed the heels of my hands into my eyes. "Because if this is X, then that means he's working for the club again. And if he's working for the club again, then he lied to me. He told me he was never going back there."

"Oh," Renee said softly. I dropped my hands to my sides, feeling completely despondent.

I pulled my phone out of my pocket and dialed his number.

It went straight to voice mail.

"I can't do this again!" I agonized.

Doubt shredded my heart.

"You don't know that's him. I mean, look at that drawing. It doesn't even look like his other stuff," Renee said thoughtfully. But who else would have done it? That was Maxx's job.

It would explain his strange mood.

And his cryptic "job" that would earn him so much money.

I tried dialing Maxx's number again and growled in frustration when it went to voice mail again. I tapped out a quick text.

Where are you?

And then I waited.

And waited.

Nothing.

How could he do this?

I covered my mouth with my hand to stop the wail that threatened to claw its way out of my throat. I turned around blindly and started walking away, bumping into someone in my desperate efforts to flee.

"Sorry," I muttered, tearing my eyes away from the painting.

"Aubrey!" I found myself face-to-face with April.

I hadn't seen her since my run-in with Evan. She had dropped out of the Boundaries and Ethics class, and honestly, I had been too wrapped up in my own life to think about where she had disappeared to.

"April, hi," I said, casting a look around for her psycho boyfriend.

I turned back to April and was met with a shock. She smiled at me. A full-out grin. Because she looked . . . *different.*

Gone was the pink hair and facial piercings. Her hair was a nice, normal shade of brown, and her face was scrubbed clean of her usual heavy makeup. She had a nice face when it wasn't obstructed by all of the metal.

"I've wanted to talk to you," she said, casting a nervous glance in Renee's direction. My roommate got the hint and moved a few feet away.

"You haven't come back to class," I stated.

"No, I took some time to get things sorted out." She dropped her voice. "I left Evan."

I blinked in shock. "What? I mean . . . that's great. I'm really glad, April." And I meant it. I wanted to give her my attention, but involuntarily, my eyes were pulled back to the painting behind April. I stared at it for a moment. It was a crude drawing, not very detailed in any way. There weren't any symbolic figures or deeper meaning. It was only poorly drawn block letters with flames shooting out the side. It looked like juvenile tagging rather than legitimate art. April was still talking, and I had to force myself to concentrate on what she was saying. But my mind was in total turmoil.

Was this X?

Had Maxx really gone back to the club? Was that why he had been so distant and evasive?

I've been given a chance to make some great money.

And he hadn't told me exactly how he planned to do that. I stared at the painting a little longer, still hardly able to believe it.

He wouldn't do this to me. Not after everything we've done to get to this place together.

But my head argued against my romanticism.

The proof is right in front of you! He lied! He told you he had an opportunity to make money. What did you think he'd do?

I blinked and tried to clear my head, purposefully looking at April again.

"Yeah, after what he did to you I knew I couldn't sit by and take his shit anymore. I pressed charges against him for . . . well, some stuff that happened . . . he took off. I don't really know where he is. But I moved back in with my parents."

I stood there lost for a moment, trying to pull myself back into the conversation. Then I realized what she had said.

"I'm really happy to hear that. I felt horrible for leaving that day without knowing if you were okay—"

"Don't feel bad. I'm just sorry I couldn't stop him," April murmured, hanging her head.

I tentatively put my hand on her arm. "Don't blame yourself for his issues. It's easy to be fooled by pretty words and false promises disguised as love," I said, looking at the horrible graffiti again.

What will I do if he's at the club? What will I do if I find out he's lied?

Then an even more horrific thought smashed into my consciousness, threatening to send me to my knees.

If he can lie about this, what else is he lying about?

He was supposed to be with Landon tonight. My gut told me that wasn't true. I thought about the past week and how strangely Maxx had been behaving. I had been so quick to dismiss it. I had been falling back into the old pattern of denial and excuses without realizing it.

I felt a flash of white-hot rage. I clenched my hands into fists and tried to control the urge to scream.

"Are you heading to the club?" April asked suddenly.

"What?" I asked, barely listening.

"Compulsion. Are you going? Some friends and I were thinking of heading over. You and your friend could come with us if you want." She gave me a smile.

"I'm not sure," I said, my mind going a thousand miles a minute.

"I bet Maxx will be there, too," she said, snapping me back to the here and now.

"What?" I demanded.

April looked startled by my outburst. Renee put her hand on my arm to try and calm me down, but I was feeling decidedly *not calm*.

"Uh, I know he used to go all the time, and I saw him there a week or so ago," April said haltingly.

The world fell out from underneath my feet.

"I've got to go," I said, stumbling backward.

"Did you get the address first?" April asked, pointing to the horrible painting.

She pulled out a pen and wrote it on a piece of paper, handing the scrap to Renee, since I wouldn't take it. April stared at the picture on the wall for a moment. "Doesn't really look like X's stuff, does it?" she mused, but I didn't really hear her.

"Whoa, Aubrey, slow down!" Renee called out.

"I've got to get my car. Are you cool heading back to the apartment by yourself?" I asked, not slowing down.

"Wait a second, where are you going?" Renee wheezed, trying to keep up with me.

"Maxx lied to me. I have to know what's going on," I said through gritted teeth. I wasn't going to fall into a heap the way I would have done before. This time, I'd find him and I'd demand my answers.

"You can't go alone," Renee argued.

"You're not coming with me. What I need to say to Maxx is between the two of us," I bit out.

Then I stopped myself. I turned to my best friend. "I won't be long. And I won't be going down this road again. I'll be fine."

Then I was running toward my car.

chapter thirty-five

maxx

"If you don't want to come tonight, I'll take the stuff back to Gash, no worries," Marco said. He had come by my apartment just before seven. He was getting ready to head to the club and was decked out in his scary bouncer gear.

"Dude, why are you being such a pussy about me coming tonight? I don't get it," I said. My nerves were fucked as it was. Marco's sudden apprehension was getting to me.

"I heard what happened to you, you know," Marco said suddenly, grabbing a soda from the fridge and popping the top.

"What are you talking about?" I asked. The bags of pills sat on the counter. I had been staring at them for the last few hours wondering what the hell I was getting myself into.

I couldn't let myself touch them. Because then I knew I'd be lost. I tore my eyes from the drugs and looked at my friend.

"What do you mean you know what happened to me?"

"I ran into Landon last week. He's become a cocky little shit, hasn't he?" Marco asked, downing the rest of his soda and tossing it into the trash. I was impressed when he actually made the shot.

"He can be. Where'd you see him?" I asked, not sure how I felt knowing Marco spoke to my brother. But they knew each other from back in the day. I guessed it wasn't totally weird.

"He hangs out at the body shop on Fifth. My buddy Dan is a mechanic over there. Landon was helping Chandler do some detailing work. He's got a lot of talent. Must take after his jackass brother," Marco grumbled, though I recognized the compliment in the insult.

"Yeah, he's pretty good," I agreed. Marco and I didn't make a habit of talking about shit. This entire conversation was dangling into twilight zone territory.

"So he told me you were in rehab and that you had OD'd or something."

Well, shit.

"So you weren't dealing with Landon stuff. You were in fucking rehab," Marco said, scowling.

"Did he just come out and tell you that?" I asked, irritated.

"No. I asked him what he had going on that caused you to drop off the planet for a month. He didn't know what I was talking about. Then he told me where you had really gone."

"So I went to rehab. What's it to you?" I asked defensively.

Marco's scowl deepened. "You should have told me, man," he said, his voice gruff.

I laughed. "Why? So we could talk about our feelings and crap? That's not how we work. I wasn't going to tell you that kind of thing."

Marco actually seemed a little hurt.

"I would have understood, you know. My mom went to rehab when I was a kid. I would have gotten it."

I was shocked. I didn't know much about Marco's past. We weren't the type of friends to braid each other's hair and talk about deep stuff. I didn't know anything about his parents or where he came from. It had never mattered.

I had been so shallow.

"I didn't know. Sorry, dude," I said sincerely.

Marco waved away my words. "Whatever. It's no big deal. But I wish you had been up front with me," he stated.

"Yeah, well, it wasn't something I wanted to broadcast."

"Why in the hell are you doing this tonight then?" Marco asked, poking one of the bags with his finger.

"I need the money. I'm floundering big-time. I like the idea of food and electricity," I responded.

"You don't need to sling this stuff to make money, dickhead," Marco scoffed, crossing his arms over his chest.

"I'm running out of options, so if you have any ideas, please share them." I was getting pissed at his attitude. It was a little late to be spouting this BS. Marco tapped his fingers on the countertop, looking uncharacteristically unhappy.

"What about your art stuff? I mean, people love that stuff. Why not try and sell it to real buyers?"

I sighed in frustration, feeling like I was banging my head against a wall.

"Dude, don't you think I've already tried that? Let's just say I didn't make the best impression with the one gallery that I spoke with."

Marco frowned. "It was one gallery, X, there are more out there. Why don't you try with another one?"

I chewed on my lip, unnerved by his sudden interest in the legit parts of my life. "What's this about, Marco? Why are you working so hard to talk me out of doing this tonight? It's what I'm good at. It's what I know. I thought you'd be stoked to have me back."

Marco pushed himself away from the counter and started pacing the room. I had never seen him so worked up. Something major was happening. "What's going on, Marco? And don't feed me a line. Be straight with me," I said sharply.

Marco stopped his manic pacing and looked at me. "I've just heard some talk," he began.

"Yeah, you said something about rumblings at the club. What've you heard?"

Marco started playing with the ring in his lip. "Just some people have said that Gash has been marked by the cops. They've never bothered him before, but with all these fucking drugs he's bringing into the area, they can't ignore his operation anymore."

Well, damn. I hadn't expected him to say that. But that had always been part of the appeal of the club. The adrenaline rush that went with doing something you knew was wrong. "It's probably just talk, Marco—"

"No, I really don't think it is. I'm not one of those pussies who go on about their gut feelings, but I think there's more to it than just talk."

I picked up one of the bags of pills. It was heavy in my hands. I slowly unzipped it and took out one of the smaller bags containing ten tiny blue pills. I wondered if there would ever be a time when I wouldn't want them. I wondered if I'd ever be able to get through a day without wishing I was high.

I'm tired of craving something that could kill me.

I dropped the drugs onto the counter, even if my fingers itched to touch them again. "I just think you should look at other options besides the club right now," Marco said gruffly.

"I need the cash though, man. I mean, I really, really need it. It'll be a one-time thing. That's it," I swore.

Marco laughed bitterly. "Look who you're talking to, Maxx. You may be able to fool your chick with those words, but not me. I see the hunger on your face. You *want* it, dude. It's all over you."

At the mention of Aubrey I felt a little sick.

Is the quick cash really worth losing her?

I knew the answer immediately.

No.

But I didn't know what else to do. Marco shook his head and picked up the two bags of drugs. "What are you doing?" I barked.

"Let me take these to the club with me. I've got to get over there and help set up. *If* you come tonight, just find me and I'll hand 'em over." He stopped and looked down at the pills, an odd expression on his face.

"And if you don't, I'll give 'em back to Gash, no harm, no foul."

"He'll get pissed, Marco, you know that," I argued.

Marco dropped the bags into his satchel and shrugged.

"I can deal with Gash." He really was in a weird mood tonight.

For an instant I had the violent urge to tackle him and take the drugs back. *They're mine!* the dark voice snarled inside of me.

But I forced myself to ignore the self-destructive whispers.

"Yeah. That's cool," I agreed.

Marco started heading to the door and then turned around to look at me again. "Dude, I really hope I don't see you tonight."

And then he was gone, the door closing behind him with a bang.

What the fuck?

I hadn't expected Marco of all people to give me a way out. I just didn't know if I really wanted to take it.

chapter thirty-six

aubrey

I broke several speed limits getting to Maxx's apartment. My heart was beating angrily in my chest. I was feeling out of control as I pulled up across the street from the Quikki Mart.

I grabbed my purse and ran down the narrow alleyway. I took the steps two at a time, practically running over Maxx's meth-head neighbor, who was going down as I was heading up.

"Whoa, lady, where's the fire?" he asked, scratching at a sore on the side of his mouth. I didn't bother to answer as I rushed past him.

My hands shook as I fumbled with my keys, finally locating the one I was looking for.

What did I hope to find by coming here? I asked myself as I made several unsuccessful attempts to unlock the door.

Proof that he lied? Proof that he was being honest? Confirmation that I wasn't a total idiot for finally starting to trust him again?

I finally unlocked the door and went inside, noting that the place was dark and it was obvious he wasn't home. I turned on the lights and stood in the middle of his living room, wondering what I should do next.

What was I even looking for? I didn't honestly think that he'd leave a note saying "Out doing drugs, be back later."

I marched purposefully back to his bedroom, throwing open the door with enough force that it bounced off the wall. I was raging on suspicion. These feelings were dangerous. I looked around, but nothing stood out.

I walked across the room and sat down on his bed, my heart in jagged pieces at my feet. I stared up at his painting of us, which now hung above his bed, wanting to trust that he wouldn't throw away the possibility of that future.

Because Maxx loved me. I loved him. That should be enough for me to believe in him. But it was hard to overlook what I had seen and heard tonight: the painting for the club. April's innocent admission that she had seen Maxx at the club. The growing concern over his attitude and unwillingness to tell me about his mysterious job.

I got to my feet and walked to the center of his room. I clasped my hands behind my neck, doing a slow circle as I took everything in. Nothing looked different. But that didn't mean there wasn't something hidden. Something he didn't want me to see.

Compelled by distrust, I started opening his dresser drawers, rooting around in T-shirts and boxer shorts. My fingers clawed their way through his clothes, looking for the source of my unrest. I felt a momentary pang of guilt for violating his space like that.

What else am I supposed to do?

When I didn't find anything there, I began to rummage through his bedside table, searching. Dreading what I thought I might find. But as I continued my search, coming up empty with every drawer and crevice I searched, my heart began to feel lighter.

I started to chastise myself for not giving Maxx the benefit of the doubt. I felt angry at how quickly I had rushed to the worst possible conclusion.

"You should be ashamed of yourself, Aubrey Duncan," I muttered under my breath.

As I began to talk myself into leaving, I ran my hands along the spines of books lining his shelf. Old, tattered copies of Tolstoy and Dickens. Some Jane Austen and Robert Browning thrown in for good measure.

Then I saw it. The white envelope was wedged inside a worn copy of *Jane Eyre,* barely poking out of the top. I didn't really notice it at first, but something drew me back to it.

I pulled the dusty book off the crowded bookcase and carefully opened it to where the envelope was squished between the pages.

It was lumpy, and I could tell something was inside of it. I tore it open. Several small, round objects fell out, scattering across the floor. I bent over to retrieve them and froze, my fingers less than an inch from the offending objects.

Because it wasn't empty.

It was full of tiny, hateful pieces of betrayal.

I was staring at what I was sure was the source of Maxx's absence tonight.

Drugs.

I looked up at my painting over his bed, numb with the realization that that seedling of trust that had only just started to grow would never be able to take root. It started to die a painful death on Maxx's bedroom floor.

I picked the bag up with a shaking hand. I noticed that the envelope was still sealed. The pills hadn't been touched.

Maybe they were from before. My thoughts echoed with excuses and denial.

Then why were they still here? Why hadn't he gotten rid of them?

I wrapped my fingers around the pills I gathered off the floor, holding them tight in my fist, and walked over to his dresser. With my other hand, I picked up the framed photograph I had given him and stared down at the innocent face of Maxx as a child.

I thought for the thousandth time what his life would have been like had he not been tragically abandoned by the people in that picture. I knew you couldn't control death, but it was hard not to rail against a universe that orphaned two small boys and left them to fend for themselves.

I'm trying really hard not to be that guy anymore. The one who hurt you. Who disappointed you. Will you let me be that guy for you? Please?

Maxx's desperate pleas bounced around my head, goading me with their dishonesty. In a fit of rage I dropped the pills and stomped on them, digging my heel into the floor. The pills gave a satisfying crunch as I smashed them to dust.

When I was finished I looked down at them, wishing I could feel *something.* But I wasn't entirely sure what I was even supposed to feel. All I knew was I needed to face the man who had obliterated my heart—*again.*

And I knew exactly where I had to go.

I walked back through the apartment, slamming the door and heading down the stairs. Once back in my car, I sat there for a moment trying to gather my tattered thoughts.

I wouldn't curl into a ball and cry about my betrayal. I was going to get answers.

And that meant going to the club.

chapter thirty-seven

maxx

three hours earlier

After Marco left, I wasn't sure what I should do. I pulled out my phone and dialed Landon's number.

"Hey, Maxx," he said after answering on the second ring. It was nice not having long conversations with his voice mail anymore.

"Hey, how about I come by for a bit and we can work on some random shit in the garage?" I suggested. The club didn't open for a long time yet, and I couldn't sit around my apartment thinking about my horrible choices.

"Yeah, okay. I've got a scooter I've been putting together if you want to help me," Landon offered.

"Sounds good. I'll be there in fifteen."

I absently pulled an envelope of pills out of my pocket. I had begun carrying it around with me. In my mind, I thought of it as both a test and reassurance. If I didn't succumb to the urge, I'd be able to go to bed feeling like I had won a small victory. But I also liked knowing they were there if things got too tough. If the effort to live this life I had been carving out for myself became too much, I had my old friend to fall back on.

It was fucked up. I walked back to my bedroom, pulled out the old copy of *Jane Eyre* that had been my mother's, and stuck the envelope inside before putting it back on the shelf.

I'll throw them out later, I promised myself, not wanting to think about the reasons for not getting rid of them *now.*

✦

"Pass me the wrench," I said to Landon, holding my hand out. I was covered in grease, but it felt good to keep my mind busy. It kept me from thinking too hard about exactly what I was going to do later that night.

"So what's with the impromptu visit?" Landon asked, handing me the tool I had asked for. I started messing with the tiny engine, trying to fit my fingers in the tight space.

"I had some time to kill," I said dismissively.

"Time to kill before what?" he asked, hopping up on a stool and watching me work.

I wiped some sweat off my forehead. "Isn't this supposed to be your project?" I asked, avoiding his question.

"Yeah, well, you came in here and took over." Landon snorted.

I handed him the wrench and we swapped places. Landon easily fit his smaller hands into the space to loosen the gasket.

I hated lying to him about what was going on with me.

So why are you? I asked myself. The answer to that question wasn't making a whole lot of sense anymore.

"I'm gonna go grab a drink. You want anything?" I asked Landon, heading toward the kitchen.

"Nah, I'm good," he answered, focused on his task.

I went inside and grabbed a soda and then headed into the living room. I sat down and propped my feet up on the coffee table, needing a minute to myself.

I had to leave soon and head home to get ready for tonight. My stomach clenched with dread at the thought.

"Get your feet off my fucking coffee table."

My uncle David walked into the room, dropping his keys onto the same coffee table and glowering at me. Of course I didn't listen. I would never give David the satisfaction of making me do anything.

David kicked my feet off the table with the heel of his boot, and I tried to control my temper, but it was always hard to do when it came to my uncle.

"What, no threats to kick my ass? No big and bad posturing?" David sneered down at me.

I slowly got to my feet and looked him in the eye. We were the same height, but I had a good twenty pounds on him. We had had enough physical altercations over the years that I knew I could take him. David was a dirty fighter, but I was better. I had to be. Knowing exactly where to punch was what had kept me alive over the years.

"What is your problem with me, David? I get you're just an asshole, but you want to tell me what it is about me specifically that gets your panties in a bunch?" I said, low enough that my brother wouldn't hear me out in the garage.

David snickered. "I don't think enough about you one way or the other, *kid,* to get anything in a bunch." He tried to walk past me, but I grabbed ahold of his arm and stopped him.

"Get your hand off me," he growled.

"I don't get it. You were my mother's brother. Shouldn't that mean something? Why the fuck do you hate me so much?" I finally voiced what I'd wondered for years.

David glared at me through narrowed eyes. He chuckled humorlessly. "I don't hate you, Maxx. I feel fucking sorry for you."

I reared back as if he had hit me. "Excuse me?"

"Because you're exactly like me," he sneered.

"I'm *nothing* like you!" I said through clenched teeth.

David leaned in close, his face contorted with anger and bitterness. "You're *exactly* like me, Maxx. A waste of skin. Making the same stupid mistakes I did. Look around you, because this will be your life."

He pulled his arm out of my grasp and slammed out the front door. Landon came in from the garage a minute later, and I was still standing in the middle of the living room, hardly able to believe that my jackass uncle had just given me the ultimate wake-up call.

"Was that David? Is he home?" my brother asked.

"Uh, yeah. But he went out front. I think that's my cue to bounce," I told him, my chest uncomfortably tight.

"Yeah, you're probably right. I'm almost done with the scooter anyway," Landon said, wiping his hands on a towel and tossing it onto the table.

"I'll come by next week and see how it turned out, okay?" I said, picking up my keys to leave.

"Sure. Text me or something," Landon said.

I looked around David's house again before I left.

Look around you, because this will be your life.

I walked out to my car, but my uncle was nowhere in sight.

I pulled out my phone and tapped out a quick text to Marco.

I'm going to have a look at some other options.

✦

I went back home and started going through the pile of canvases that sat in the corner of my bedroom. Shit, I sure had done a lot of painting in the last few weeks.

Going through them, I realized that these were the best pieces I had ever done. I pulled out two paintings that caught my eye. One was of Aubrey standing on a bed of snakes that was done in long, vivid strokes. The second was a self-portrait I had only finished two days ago.

I didn't make a habit of putting myself in my art. I wasn't sure what had possessed me to do it. But when I had sat down in front of the canvas, this is what had formed.

In the painting, I looked sickly and tired. Strung out on drugs and dying on the inside. Miserable and weak. The shadowed image of my skull was visible through my wasted skin.

Looking at this painting, I saw death. A glimpse of what might have been.

I had exposed myself completely in this picture. It was raw, it was gritty, it was harsh.

Without thinking twice I grabbed both paintings and headed back to my car.

✦

"These are unreal!" A squat, bald man named Dandy Veers held up my self-portrait and stared at it in awe.

I had ended up leaving my apartment and driving into the next town, Blackham. From there, I had driven until I found an art gallery still open at this time on a Saturday evening.

If I had any common sense, I'd wait until Monday and make some calls. But the truth was, I was terrified that if I waited, I'd end up going to the club and find my way back to the Maxx in that painting.

I walked into a small gallery in the center of town. I carried my two paintings under my arm and asked if they'd be interested in purchasing my pieces.

The gallery owner had looked at me like I was a nut job. Which was understandable, given the impulsive nature of my visit.

But I had shown him my paintings, and then his entire demeanor had changed.

"And you're the artist?" Mr. Veers asked, peering at me as though he didn't believe it.

"That's me," I answered.

He stared at the self-portrait for a few moments, making indecipherable noises in the back of his throat before picking up the painting of Aubrey.

"This is incredible. The depth of the colors, the level of intimate detail . . . You actually have the aesthetic of that street artist X. His portraits share this . . . intensity." I couldn't help but grin.

"Uh, yeah. That's me," I told him.

"You're X? And you've never shown your work in a gallery?" Mr. Veers asked incredulously.

"Yeah, things haven't really worked out."

The man looked at me in disbelief. "I can't believe you actually walked into my gallery tonight. This is *amazing*! I'm . . . I'm a huge fan!"

He took another moment to examine my work. "Are you interested in setting up a show here? I know several people who'd likely be interested in these pieces, and they'd pay a handsome price for them."

"Really?" I asked, hardly able to believe my luck.

I hadn't expected anything when I had walked in. The idea to take my art into the city had been a whim. Mistaking my silence for hesitation, Mr. Veers waved his hands rapidly as he spoke, attempting to convince me.

"Look, we can keep it small. You choose which pieces you want to display, and I'll sell them for you. We can decide together what to sell your work for and I'll add my commission fee on top of that. How does that sound?"

I made a show of thinking about it. I pointed to the more colorful Aubrey portrait. "How much do you think I could get for that?"

Dandy Veers rubbed the back of his balding head and stared down at the painting thoughtfully. "I think it could easily bring between five and ten thousand. This kind of art is in high demand right now. And your talent is unquestionable."

I almost swallowed my tongue. "Are you fucking serious?" I laughed, hardly able to believe it.

Mr. Veers nodded. "I'm very serious. X—is that your real name?"

"No, my name is Maxx. Maxx Demelo," I told him.

"Okay then, Maxx, you've built quite a following. And street art is huge right now. There are major collectors out there wanting to be the first to discover the next big thing. And you could be the next big thing. I mean, to my eye, you already are."

Dandy Veers might have been a little quirky, but I liked him. And he was willing to take a huge chance on an unknown artist who had literally wandered in off the street. It was more than I could have hoped for.

"Sure. Yeah, let's do it," I said, nodding.

Mr. Veers grinned and held his hand out. I shook it. "Great! Let me go get my calendar and we can talk about scheduling a date."

chapter thirty-eight

aubrey

On the drive to Compulsion, the numbness wore off and the anger resurfaced. It felt good to be pissed rather than annihilated.

I waited in line at the old factory impatiently, barely aware of the people around me. When I got to the front, I was surprised by the lack of derision for my anticlub attire. The bouncer, a guy I didn't recognize, stamped my hand and waved me inside.

And here I was again. Looking for Maxx.

Compulsion had been our beginning. And it had proven our end as well. It was a sad full circle.

I pushed through the teeming crowd, craning my neck to look around. The place was heaving tonight, and I could barely walk two steps without colliding with someone.

There was a strange energy in the air. One that had me edgier than I already was. I made my way to the bar but didn't recognize the guy serving drinks. I waited my turn, and when the man wearing a tight leather halter top and bracelets up to his elbows came over to take my order, I shook my head.

"I'm looking for X!" I shouted over the music.

Leather halter guy frowned. "Who?"

"X!" I yelled in his ear.

The bartender shrugged. "I have no idea who that is. I'm new, though, so I don't know many of the regulars. Do you want anything or not?"

"No, thank you," I responded. I faced the dance floor and scoured the crowd, looking for Maxx. I had a sinking feeling I'd never be able to find him.

"You came!" April suddenly appeared beside me, her now brown hair plastered with sweat to the sides of her face. Her eyes were wide and sparkling.

"Yeah, I was just looking for someone," I answered dismissively.

"Oh yeah? Are you looking for Maxx?" It annoyed me that I was that obvious.

"Yeah, I am. Have you seen him?"

April shook her head, bouncing on her feet. "I haven't, no. But I could help you look."

"No, that's okay—" There was a loud commotion from the front of the building, and then a tidal wave of people started moving toward the exit.

"It's the cops!" I heard someone scream. And the club erupted into absolute and total chaos.

"Fuck! We need to get out of here *now*!" April shouted in my ear, grabbing hold of my hand and wrenching me forward.

I was shoved and pushed from all directions; everyone was in a state of panic as we all attempted to get outside.

"We need to hurry! They'll start using tear gas! I've seen it happen before," April yelled, throwing elbows as we tried to make our way across the room.

"Tear gas?" I gasped. *Oh my God!* Where was Maxx?

I tried to look around, scanning the faces, but it was absolute pandemonium. People were shouting, girls were screaming. I saw spotlights trained on the heaving, waving crowd.

"This way!" April yelled, pulling my arm toward the wall. We felt our way along the outer perimeter of the room. It was slow going, and in the darkness I could see police officers arresting people and pulling them outside.

Eventually, through pure luck, we located the fire exit.

"Come on, Aubrey! Hurry up!" April was starting to freak out.

"But Maxx might be in there!" I protested.

"Then he's fucked. Now come *on*!" she yelled, giving my arm a vicious pull, and then we were outside.

The insanity breaking loose inside could still be heard once we were out of the building.

"Oh my God!" I gasped, bracing my hands on my knees, trying to catch my breath.

"We can't stop! We've got to go!" April was pulling on me again. We ran along the outside of the building, steering clear of the police barricade that had been set up.

"What's going on?" I asked when we were finally able to stop. We had made our way back to the parking lot. In the craziness, we had gone unnoticed and were able to escape.

April was red in the face and breathing hard.

"It looks like a drug bust. Check it out," she said, pointing to the front of the club.

There were flashing lights everywhere. Police officers had swarmed the old factory, pulling partyers out of the club and handcuffing them. Others were being thrown to the ground. The din of the crowd was deafening.

A group of people joined us, others who had made their successful escape from inside. April's friends were among those who had gotten out in time.

"I heard someone say they were tipped off that there was a

huge drug deal going down tonight," a guy with purple hair said. Blood streaked down his cheek, and it looked as though he had an earring yanked out of his lobe.

Oh my fucking God!

Was Maxx in there? Was he a part of the drug deal gone bad? I left the group of people and moved forward.

"Aubrey, I wouldn't go down there!" April warned, but I ignored her. I walked to the police boundary and watched as people were thrown to the ground and arrested. I looked for Maxx in every face that was hauled out of the club and put into vans.

I recognized Marco, Maxx's friend, being led out by police. He was yelling and snarling, and I could see him fighting against the man who held him by the arms, leading him toward a patrol car.

If Maxx had been inside, there was only one way he'd be coming out. In handcuffs.

I knew then that I couldn't wait to see if Maxx was among those being pulled out of the club. I couldn't watch as the man I loved was carted away. I stumbled back, barely able to see through my tears.

"Hey! Aubrey!" I heard April yelling behind me. I stopped and turned to her.

"What's wrong?" she asked when she saw my face.

"Nothing. I'm fine. I've just got to go." I started walking toward my car. She called my name again, but I kept going. I had returned to the numbness. My heart felt like lead in my chest.

I made it to my car and got inside. I sat there for a while, the flashing police lights illuminating the interior of my car. I gripped the steering wheel, unable to turn the engine on. I had really thought this time would be different.

The saying goes, *Fool me once, shame on you. Fool me twice, shame on me.*

It was the goddamned truth.

I finally pulled away from the club. *I should go home. I'm ex-*

hausted. But instead I drove back to Maxx's apartment. My heartache seemed to always lead me there. I slowly walked up the steps and went inside, noting absently that I must have left the lights on when I had left.

I stared around the space, the numbness starting to fade.

Then came the fury. The anguish. The moment when my heart shattered into a million pieces. I screamed. And then I collapsed in a heap on the floor.

chapter thirty-nine

maxx

I couldn't wait to tell Aubrey about the gallery. I hoped she'd be proud of me.

I went to put my key into the lock of my apartment door and was surprised to find that it was already open. I went inside and saw that the lights were on even though I remembered turning them off before I had left to go to see Landon.

"Hello?" I called out, but no one answered. I walked back to my room and stood just inside the door. Nothing jumped out and caught my eye as being off, but I could tell something was different. Then I saw it. The pills I had only just stashed on the shelf earlier that day had been crushed on the floor.

I knew instantly what had happened. Aubrey had been here. For some reason she had gone through my stuff. Anger flared to life, an age-old response that I couldn't really control. How fucking dare she come in here and look around like I was a damn criminal! Who the hell did she think she was?

She was the woman I loved.

But clearly, she had come here and dug through my shit because she suspected something. She hadn't trusted me.

And that hurt like a knife to the heart.

I grabbed my phone and quickly dialed her number. It rang and rang, sending me to voice mail. *Fuck.* I had to find her. I had to explain.

I gripped my hair in my hands and berated myself for my idiocy. I should have flushed the stupid pills down the toilet as soon as Gash had given them to me. Why hadn't I gotten rid of them? Because I was a goddamned addict who needed my crutch.

I was staring at the white powder that had been my vice when I heard the front door open and then slam shut. And then I heard a scream, loud and painful. It was the most horrible sound I had ever heard.

I rushed into the living room and found Aubrey in a crumpled heap on the floor. I dropped to my knees by her side, terrified by the sight in front of me. "Aubrey!" I grabbed ahold of her shoulders and pulled her up. She was sobbing, her entire body shaking.

"Aubrey!" I yelled. She opened her eyes and looked up at me, her face paling as though she had seen a ghost.

"Maxx?"

"Who else would it be?" I asked, hardly able to hear her over the pounding of my heart.

"But I thought . . . I . . ." She was choking on her tears.

I got her up off the floor and practically carried her to the couch. I put my arms around her and held her while she noisily fell apart.

"What's wrong? What happened?" I asked her, crooning softly in her ear as I stroked her hair. Aubrey took a shuddering breath and finally stopped crying. She pulled back slightly, wiping her cheeks with the back of her hand.

"I found them," she said. It wasn't an accusation, just a simple statement. I didn't need to ask what she was referring to, because of course I knew.

"I saw," I replied.

"Where were you tonight?" she demanded, her eyes still wet with tears, but now lit with a fire that scared me a little.

"I told you, I was with Landon—"

"Don't give me that shit!" she seethed.

This was the moment. The moment I could tell her the truth. Tell her everything. Or I could be a fucking coward and hide the dark secrets inside me.

"Yeah, well, that wasn't my original plan, but I did end up over at my uncle's house," I began.

"What do you mean it wasn't your original plan?" She was angry. Now that she was over the tear fest, she looked ready to commit murder.

"If you found the drugs, you probably already have an idea."

Aubrey pulled out of my arms completely and moved away. "You were going to the club. I knew it, but I didn't want to believe it. But then I saw the painting—"

"Wait. What painting?" I interrupted.

Aubrey frowned. "The one on campus. The one for the club," she said, looking at me as though I had lost my mind.

"That wasn't me, Aubrey," I told her truthfully. I had no idea what she was talking about, but if there was a painting on a building somewhere for Compulsion, it wasn't my doing.

Aubrey didn't say anything. I grabbed her hand and held it, hoping she wouldn't pull it away. "You believe me, don't you?"

"I didn't know what to believe," she whispered, though she didn't take her hand away. Small miracles, I supposed.

"I came here. I found the drugs and I sort of lost it. So I went to the club to find you." Her voice was ragged and broken.

"You went to Compulsion? What in the hell, Aubrey!"

Aubrey's face flushed, and she gave me an indignant look.

"Yeah, well, given my discovery, I don't think you're in a position to give me shit about anything!"

Point taken.

"So I went there and there was a raid—"

"Wait! What? A police raid?" Marco had been right. The police *had* been watching the club.

I could have been there. I would have been caught in the middle of it. I needed to remember to thank my bastard uncle for inadvertently saving my hide.

"Police were pulling people out of the club in handcuffs. I saw your friend Marco get loaded into a patrol car."

"Fuck, really?" I ran my free hand through my hair. *Shit.*

"You thought I was there. That I had gotten arrested," I said, the reason for her meltdown making sense now.

Aubrey nodded, more tears slipping down her face. "Where were you tonight?" she asked again.

"Well, I wasn't selling, if that's what you were worried about," I tried.

"What else was I supposed to think, Maxx?"

"Okay, okay. I had been thinking about going back to the club, Aubrey. I won't lie to you about that. Gash made me an offer of quick money that was really tempting. I've been really struggling. You know that. I just wanted to be able to provide for our future."

Aubrey opened her mouth, and I knew she was getting angry again. "Let me finish, okay?" I begged, and after a moment, she nodded.

"It seemed like the easiest thing to do. It's what I knew. What I was good at. I could move some dope, score some cash, and be set. Gash said it would be a one-time thing, and I thought it seemed like the best choice." I took a deep breath and thought about how differently my night would have ended up had I decided to go.

"But then, this evening, I went to see Landon. And I had a run-in with David—"

"Your uncle?" she asked, and I nodded.

"Yeah. And he said some stuff that really made me think, and I realized I couldn't go through with it. That I would be putting myself right back in the very place I was a few months ago. And I couldn't do that to you. Or to Landon. And most of all, I couldn't do that to myself."

I carefully pulled Aubrey toward me, and she let me put my arm around her. I pressed her into my side, needing to feel her close.

"I came home and grabbed some of my artwork and then I went into the city. I found an art gallery and talked to the owner. He really liked my stuff, Aubrey. He's setting up a show for some of my pieces."

Aubrey's face, still flushed and swollen from her tears, brightened a little. "Really? That's great," she said genuinely, but then her face darkened. "You lied to me, Maxx," she said, her voice tight and angry.

I sighed. How could I expect her to forgive me for betraying her trust yet again? "I did lie to you. I deceived you. I kept things from you when I had promised I wouldn't. I'd understand if you wanted to walk out that door and never see me again."

Aubrey's eyes narrowed slightly. "Maybe I should, Maxx. Because I told you that I can't go down this path with you, not anymore. I can't be in a relationship with someone I can't trust."

I swallowed thickly, feeling tears prick my eyes. If Aubrey left me now, after everything, I wasn't sure I'd survive it. I had fought so hard to do this right, but in the end, here I was, fucking it up all over again.

"Aubrey, I'm a screwup. I'm a messed-up guy with a hell of a lot of baggage. It's going to take me time to figure out how to do this right. But I'm trying. I hope you can see that. And the only way I can become the man I want to be is if you're here, helping me."

Aubrey shook her head.

"I'm not using. Though every day is a struggle. I can't promise you that I won't mess up again. Because I probably will. A lot." I ran my fingers down the side of her face, stopping to cup my hand around the side of her neck.

She tensed slightly, her eyes focused on the second button of my shirt. "That's not exactly a ringing endorsement for me to stay," she said quietly.

"I wish I could make those promises. But I can't. I can only ask that you stick this out with me. Maybe it's selfish to ask that of you. But I truly think that we're better together than apart. I know that you bring out the best in me."

I ran my thumb across the heartbeat thudding under her skin. "*It made me better, loving you,*" I said softly.

Aubrey's lips quirked, and I knew she wanted to smile but wasn't about to let herself. "You and those damn quotes," she said, but without any venom.

"How about my own words then? Aubrey Duncan, I love you. I told you that I didn't want you to save me, but you have. Every single day you love me back you are saving me. And I will try like hell to make sure you never regret opening your heart to me. Because I was made to be yours. Just as you were made to be mine. I knew that the moment I laid eyes on you. And I feel it more strongly now than I ever have."

A tear fell down Aubrey's cheek, and she wiped it away furiously. "I need to be able to trust you, Maxx. I can't do this if I don't."

I lifted her chin so that she would look at me. "I will work every day for the rest of my life earning your trust. And I hope the day will come that your faith in me will be as easy as breathing. Because that life I dream of, the one I see in my head every night before I fall asleep, I will fight to the death to have it. I told you I wouldn't give up on you . . . on *us.* I just ask that you don't give up on me."

I had laid it all out there. I didn't know what else to do. It was all up to Aubrey now.

"I just . . . Maxx . . . I don't know." She got up, grabbed her keys, and headed toward the door. She paused for a moment, not looking at me, her head bowed.

Don't leave! I pleaded silently, feeling the walls closing in around me. Aubrey finally looked at me, her eyes wet. She was going to leave. This was it. I had ruined everything. For good this time. Then, surprisingly, she walked back across the room. She dropped down to her knees in front of where I still sat on the couch. She reached out, her hands almost touching mine . . . but not *quite.*

"I'm not walking away, Maxx. I'm not shutting the door on us. I just need to wrap my mind around everything that's happened tonight. You hurt me. *Again,*" she whispered, her voice broken.

I wanted to grab her and pull her close, never letting go. She said she wasn't walking away. But the look in her eyes had me doubting her words. I shook my head. "Don't leave me."

Finally, she bridged the physical distance. Her fingertips pressed into my cheek, branding me hers forever. There was a promise in her touch.

"You have to trust me, Maxx. Just like I have to trust you," she said, speaking to the unspoken fears in my mind.

Trust. We were always coming back to that basic, fundamental concept. Aubrey slowly got back to her feet, lingering for only a moment. And then she was gone, the door closing softly behind her.

I just sat there, the silence of her departure ringing in my ears. Aubrey was right. I had to trust her. I had to trust that she wouldn't obliterate me completely. I had to trust in both of us. It was the hardest thing I'd ever had to do.

epilogue

aubrey

two years later

I felt itchy beneath the hot polyester gown. Sweat trickled down from my hairline, and I readjusted the cap that sat precariously on my head. I looked out into the crowd, searching for the people I knew would be there.

My parents waved at me enthusiastically, and I waved back.

They were staying the weekend of my graduation and were planning to take me out to dinner after the ceremony to celebrate. It was hard to believe that there was a time when I had resented them so much that I couldn't bring myself to see or talk to them. Sure, things weren't perfect, but I was just happy to have them back in my life.

I tilted my head back and looked up at the sky. *I love you, sis,* I said silently to the girl who wasn't in the audience.

The wind picked up and whipped around me, giving me a brief respite from the overbearing heat, and I could imagine for a moment that it was a gift from Jayme. A message letting me know that she still loved me, too. It didn't hurt as much to think of Jayme anymore. The dull ache in my heart would never really go away, but every day I was healing.

I was feeling antsy and more than ready for the ceremony to get started. It felt like a long time coming, but I was finally here, graduating with a bachelor's in education. It had only taken me an extra two years to get there.

Two weeks ago I had accepted a position at the elementary school the next town over. I'd be starting in the fall with a group of twenty-two first graders. I was sort of terrified. But it was a good sort of terrified.

"Hey, Aubrey!" a familiar voice called out from the front of the crowd. I looked up to see Brooks, who stood with Renee, waving at me. I waved back, glad they were both there. I hadn't seen either of them in months. Renee had graduated on time two years ago. She had moved back home with her parents for a while until she had found a job. She eventually accepted a position as a paralegal for a big law firm. She had moved into her own place and claimed she was happy.

But sometimes I wondered.

Things with Iain had never really worked out, and she hadn't dated anyone seriously since then. I worried about my friend, but knew better than anyone that she had to go her own way and heal in her own time.

Brooks had gone on to graduate school in Maryland. I had honestly thought that once he had moved away, we would lose touch. Even though I had meant it when I had told him our friendship was the kind that would last a lifetime, I had doubts that he'd ever truly forgive me for going back to Maxx. I was delighted when only a few weeks after he had left he had called me, telling me to turn to channel ten. I did as I was instructed and discovered *Deuce Bigalow* playing. We watched it together, quoting the lines and laughing the whole time. It was almost as good as having him there beside me.

And even though we didn't talk as much as we used to, I knew that he'd always be in my life. I really was a lucky girl.

I lifted my hair off the back of my neck, fanning myself. I was sweltering under my cap and gown. The dress I was wearing underneath was soaked in sweat. I hoped Mom and Dad wouldn't mind coming back to the apartment with me so I could change.

There was a slight disturbance from behind me, then I felt cool fingers on the back of my neck.

"Hey," a voice breathed in my ear, and I shuddered, still as affected by him as I had ever been. I turned around to find Maxx. He had pushed two graduates aside and made room for himself on a chair just behind me. His blue eyes were sparkling as he looked at me.

"What are you doing? You can't be over here," I chastised, grinning back at him.

"It's only for a minute," Maxx said, not bothered that he was causing a bit of a scene.

He leaned over and took hold of my arm, then slipped something onto my wrist. I looked down to see the silver cuff bracelet Jayme had given me.

I gave him a questioning smile. "I thought Jayme should be represented on such an important day," he said, answering my silent question.

Shit. I was going to cry. And smear my makeup even worse than it already was.

"*Grow old along with me, the best is yet to be*," he murmured, leaning in to kiss me.

"Stop quoting Browning and go find my parents," I told him, though I was grinning broadly.

"I'll see you after," Maxx said, kissing me one more time.

I watched him slip through the crowd and make his way to the seat that Renee had saved for him. I remembered walking out of his apartment two years ago. I hadn't been sure I could move forward with Maxx, given his betrayal. I was unable to forgive him right away. My heart had been wounded all over again.

In the end, though, I had held true to my promise and hadn't walked away. Because he deserved better than that. We both did. We had fought too hard to not give it everything we had. And that included allowing myself to trust in the man who had already hurt me so much. The man who was trying to slay his demons for me. One vicious battle at a time.

But it hadn't been easy. Learning to trust Maxx didn't happen overnight. And there were days when I was still plagued with the doubts that had almost destroyed us before we had a chance to begin. But I had never been particularly fond of *easy*.

We had experienced some dark days on this path together. There were times he struggled with his dependence just as intensely as he had when he first stopped using. Even though he was relentless in his outpatient treatment, I knew that it would always be there. The addiction. It would be a part of him forever. It wasn't one of those things he'd ever truly heal from.

But somehow, he was making it work. We both were. Together.

And then, a month ago, Maxx had just gotten his latest commission from his art installation piece in New York City and had wanted to go out and celebrate. He had established himself as X, the mysterious street artist whose works were selling for astronomical prices.

He had taken me to the cinema in town. *The Doom Generation* was playing. He had arranged everything. And in the darkened theater where we had had our first date, he had slipped a diamond ring onto my finger and asked me to be his wife. Of course I had said yes. I had never been able to say no to Maxx.

After graduation I planned to move into his apartment in the city. And when Landon came home on holidays from his art school in Philadelphia, he would stay in the spare room. And we'd spend Christmas with my parents and have dinner parties with friends. And we'd have the life we'd always wanted.

The one Maxx dreamed of.

The dream we had both longed for.

Things weren't all sunshine and roses, and they never would be. We had to learn to accept the dark and ugly that would always be inside us. And when Maxx fell, I'd be behind him holding him up. And when I began to doubt, he'd be there reminding me of why I'd follow him anywhere. Because after all this time, I had learned that I could trust the man that I loved. I could trust in the love that had changed our lives.

And that was the only kind of happily ever after either of us needed.

Acknowledgments

It's time to thank the usual suspects.

To Ian and Gwyn: You are in every word and on every page. I love you.

To my parents, who always believed I could do anything, and to my grandparents, who gave me the tools to follow any road I wanted to take.

To Matt: You may be gone but will never be forgotten. You were my original cheerleader and biggest supporter. You've left a hole that will never be filled.

To my Bad Ass gals, Amy, Tonya, Claire, Stacey, Brittainy, and Kelsie: Your talent continues to awe and inspire me every single day. I'm so lucky to have you in my writing world.

To Kristy, the best PA and friend I could ever ask for: You keep me sane in complete insanity. What would I ever do without you?

To Michelle, agent extraordinaire: You are a superwoman! Seriously. You should buy stock in awesomeness.

To Elana and Alex, my amazing editors at Gallery: Your support and your belief in Maxx and Aubrey have made this all possible. Thank you for your endless patience and guidance!

To the fantastic people at Gallery who have supported these stories from the beginning: You have helped make this writer's dreams come true.

And most importantly, to my readers, to the bloggers, to the people who support me daily: This would mean nothing without you!